VEGENRAGE

Vegenrage

Demon Rising

Robert Spina

Library of Congress Control Number: 2017911694
ISBN: Hardcover   978-1-5434-3964-9
                 Softcover   978-1-5434-3965-6
                 eBook   978-1-5434-3966-3

Print information available on the last page.

Rev. date: 07/28/2017

To order additional copies of this book, contact:
Xlibris
1-888-795-4274
www.Xlibris.com
Orders@Xlibris.com
762887

Contents

CHAPTER 1

The Calm before the Storm

Vegenrage wraps his arms around Farrah and can't get enough of kissing her. He rolls her over as the bed of jewel they are lying in loses the form of Vegenrage's silhouette and hollows out. Vegenrage has kept his deep attraction for Farrah well under control until now, and he kisses her lips, her cheeks, her neck and wraps his legs around hers. He feels her hips, her breasts, and her stomach with his hands, rubbing all over her. He is very slow in his movements, feeling her with all of his body. Farrah has her eyes closed, and she is very relaxed, enjoying the moment. Vegenrage lifts his head and looks out of the carved-jewel bed. Looking at it from a horizontal view, you can see his head just break the surface of the bed, and he looks around his realm.

"What, Vegenrage? What is wrong?" asks Farrah.

Vegenrage looks at Farrah, saying, "Nothing is wrong, nothing."

"Then don't stop," says Farrah.

Vegenrage kisses Farrah more, and they both can feel passion heating each of them up. White lights start to emanate from their bodies like short, little lightning bolts, and the bed of jewel starts to melt like wax. They can feel themselves lowering as the bed is melting and shrinking. They don't stop kissing and feeling on each other as the bed melts away, and the Sapphirewell and the Octagemerwell reform. Vegenrage snaps his fingers, and the Sapphirewell teleports to Blythgrin, and the Octagemerwell teleports back to Oriapow. They are now rolling around on a metal floor, which is all that is left of what used to be Vegenrage's home. The fire pit and podium that were in the center of the metal floor are not there anymore. Vegenrage looks up and then lifts himself off Farrah and stands up. Vegenrage looks at Farrah lying on the metal floor.

"Can you feel it, Farrah? Can you feel it?" says Vegenrage.

Farrah points to Vegenrage's obvious excitement. "I want to feel that," she says.

Vegenrage smiles with a laugh, saying, "We are going to have sex. Come here, stand up."

"Don't you dare leave me hanging like this," says Farrah.

"Oh, don't you worry. I am going to make sure we are going to be real comfortable. Come on," says Vegenrage.

He bends down to her and holds out his hand. She grabs his hand, and he lifts her. He then levitates them off the circular metal floor and out onto the grass. Zevoncour has had Vegenrage's home leveled, and he has magically melted and cooled a floor of iron where he has conducted the demon-uprising ceremony.

"First things first—this metal is not of my making, and it does not belong here," says Vegenrage, looking to Farrah.

Vegenrage lifts his hands in the air and twirls them in circles. The entire metal floor lifts from the ground and raises into the air to about twenty feet, and then it begins to spin. Vegenrage then starts to twirl his right index finger like he is spinning a ring on it, and the metal spins faster and faster. It begins to melt from the outside edges, and molten pieces of the metal break off it and vanish. It spins faster and faster, and more and more of the metal breaks off and vanishes until it is all gone.

"Come on," says Vegenrage, grabbing Farrah's hand, and he walks her to where the center of the metal floor was. He stands facing her and looks up. He raises his hands from his hips to over his head with his fingers pointing up, and Farrah watches as the earth around them rises and forms over the top of them. Vegenrage's home has reformed itself, but the walls are bare.

All the books he has had are gone for good. The golden table in front of the room reforms itself with lots of comfortable big pillows before it. His dresser and mirror forms, and his clothes rack appears next to his dresser. Another dresser forms right next to his for Farrah. He points his hands to the top center of his home and pulls his hands down, and a big glass window forms in the ceiling. He then shakes his head, and the sky rolls around his realm, changing from the day sky to the night sky with soft, bright moonlight shining in through the window in the ceiling. He then points to the wall, and a big fireplace forms right into the wall, and a warming fire begins to burn, with all the smoke exiting the top of his home through a chimney. The floor is no longer concave; it is now level.

Vegenrage raises his hands from his hips in front of him to his shoulders, and a huge bed rises from the center of the floor. Vegenrage looks at Farrah, and she laughs, locking her hands together and holding her arms tight to her breasts with an excited and beautiful smile. He grabs her by the waist with both hands and picks her up, throwing her at the bed. She flies backward toward the bed in slow motion. She has the biggest smile on her face. She is a little startled but excitedly so, as she feels the excitement of an amusement park ride steal her stomach. Just before she lands on the bed, she falls back into real time and slams hard on the bed, but it is very soft and cushy, and she bounces a couple of times, laughing hard before coming to a stop, lying perfectly with her head on the pillow, looking at Vegenrage. He jumps in the air and flies at her in the same slow motion she has just been flying in and extends his arms out like he is doing a swan dive. His clothes rip from his body and magically appear on the clothes rack, and Farrah puts her hands on her cheeks with a huge smile, laughing as he flies toward her. He gets close to landing on her, and with a smile, he says, "You better be naked by the time I get there."

Farrah throws her arms out, and her clothes disappear and magically come out on the clothes rack. She smiles with her arms over her breasts and her legs bent to her left side as Vegenrage lands on her and scoops her in his arms as they bounce on the soft bed. He has set the bed in the perfect place so the moonlight shines down from the window in the ceiling, engulfing the bed in its soft silvery white glow. The light is dim, but they can see each other just fine, and he starts to kiss her. He slides his mouth down her neck, sucking real hard, and grabs her wrists, holding them to her sides as he lowers to her chest and kisses and sucks all over her. Farrah has a big smile, and she wraps her legs around his waist, driving her hips into his stomach as he continues to lower himself, kissing all over her stomach. He still has her wrists held tight to her sides, and she can't move her arms. He pulls her arms under her back and kisses very low on her hips. He then lets go of her arms and grabs her by the knees and spreads them, pushing her legs flush with the bed, and Farrah gets very excited. He spreads her legs as wide as he can without hurting her, just enough to where she is really stretching and feeling a burn down the inner lengths of her legs, and just when she thinks that is enough, he stretches her a little more, but he knows when to stop by the sound of her moans. This is the first time Farrah has been in an intimate situation, and her mind is in sync with her body.

In the past, when she was under charm, she had no control of her mind and no thoughts to go with what was happening to her body. The man or woman she was with was so fast, so quick to just jump her and have their way with her. These encounters usually ended very quickly, as Alisluxkana was very quickly there to take advantage of the occupied victim and end their life. Alisluxkana wanted Alluradaloni (Farrah) all for herself, so Alluradaloni was never allowed to experience what was really going on. Alisluxkana always ended the life of her victim before Alluradaloni ever had intercourse.

With Vegenrage, he is taking his time and exploring all of Farrah's body, and she loves the way her body feels with him. Then it happens: he starts to kiss her most sensitive regions, and she cannot believe what she feels. It hurts when he sucks real hard, but she wants more. He licks her and kisses her, and she trembles and shakes, waiting for the next feeling to shake her body. She doesn't even realize how loudly she is moaning, but he does. She squeezes her chest with her hands, and her groin, hips, and legs are on fire. He licks her harder and harder, faster and faster, and she feels excitement like never before. She is breathing very hard and fast, and her heart is racing. She doesn't know what to expect, but she can't wait, and then nothing—she feels nothing. She opens her mouth with an anxious inhale and looks down to see him, looking right at her, smiling.

"What are you doing? Why did you stop? Don't you tease me," says Farrah.

"You bet your ass I am going to tease you," says Vegenrage, laughing.

Farrah grabs his head and puts it right back where it has been, and he continues right where he has left off. And Farrah smiles, as the burning and the excitement come back. She can feel his tongue all over her, and her heart is racing in no time. This is something that Alisluxkana has done to her, but she can feel the passion in Vegenrage, as it warms her body, and her mind is connected to him with love.

She starts to breathe very fast, almost screaming, as she has never felt her insides feel like this. She feels like she wants to run, skip, and jump. Her insides are growing in a burning ball of fire, and she can't move. He is doing something to her she can't explain—something so fast, so soft—and she is breathing like she is running full speed, and it keeps getting more and more intense. She is moaning, and then she gasps over and over, as she feels something inside of her that has to get out. He grabs her inner thighs and pushes down on them and buries his face between her legs. She can't explain what he is doing, but it hurts real bad, and then she has one second of calm before her body explodes from her hips like unimaginable euphoria that spreads to her stomach, her chest, and then her mind. He doesn't stop, and she feels this smile that she cannot get rid of. She feels like she is sweating, like her body is on fire, and she is breathing crazy fast.

She can't believe as it is happening again, and she wants it so bad. She is waiting, and he unleashes her passion that comes to her again and again. She is trembling and shaking and thinks she is drowning him in her euphoria. She reaches down to him and pulls him by the head up to hers. He rubs his face all over her sweaty stomach, kissing her, and continues kissing on her chest, and she is smiling, very happily satisfied, but she wants more. He kisses on her neck, rubbing his left hand between her legs, keeping her so excited, and then she feels something she has never felt before.

She moans uncontrollably as she feels her body being spread apart by Vegenrage's body. He thrusts into her and then almost out of her. He thrusts into her again a little deeper, and she moans in sync with his movements. It hurts her so bad, but she still wants it. He moves fast and then slow, and Farrah is completely at his mercy. She has no thoughts, only feelings, and she is loving everything he is doing to her. After everything she has already felt, it is only feeling better and better. Her heart is racing stronger than before, and he is moving faster and faster in a steady rhythm that keeps her unconsciously moaning with his movements. Her excitement keeps growing as he continues to penetrate deeper and deeper into her body with his, and she can feel that feeling she has felt before when she has thought her head is going to pop.

She screams out loud when she feels his loins pound hers for the first time. Her hips ignite as he pounds on her very hard, and what she has felt before is just the beginning. She is gasping and moaning, as she very quickly climaxes, wrapping her arms around his back, trying to squeeze them together, but he rises to a push-up position and keeps pounding her loins until they are red-hot, and her whole body is now orgasmic. He drives deep into her and grinds slowly on her, and then he pumps her fast. Then he moves around, stretching her body with his. He has her feeling pain and euphoria, anticipation and excitement, and she has no idea what he is doing, but he is doing everything she has always wanted. He lowers to her and kisses her while he drives into her hips with his, and she wraps her arms around his back, holding his shoulders and their bodies close. She wraps her legs around his and holds him close to her, driving the heels of her feet into the back of his legs. He grinds slow and hard on her, and she can feel her excitement slowly grow as she feels him grow inside of her. She is so wet and so hot, but still when he moves inside of her, she can feel the friction, and she loves the feeling of his loins bumping against hers. He fills her with all of himself and grinds as hard as he can. He reaches his arms under her back and grabs her shoulders with his hands and holds her tight, crushing his loins into hers over and over, faster and stronger.

Farrah is whimpering in a combination of pain and pleasure; a great feeling she has never felt before consumes her body. She has nothing to grab hold of, so she digs her fingernails into his back, leaving long scratches on him, not knowing she is doing this. She can feel that feeling coming inside her again, only this time it is deep within her, and it feels like he is pushing right through her. The sound of his heavy breathing and moaning adds to her anticipation, and she feels him get bigger and wider in her, and her head is trying to remember to breathe. It is almost like she is trying to keep herself from passing out. He just keeps grinding on her, he keeps her body ready to explode over and over, and every time is better than the last. She feels her insides waiting for him, and she feels him explode inside of her. She climaxes through the sheer excitement of this moment, and the feeling does not go away. She feels him inside her twitching and pulsating, giving her all he has, and this is the greatest feeling she has ever felt in her life. He lies on her, breathing heavily, and she loves his breath on her neck. He moves up to kiss her, and she is crying.

"What . . . what is wrong?" asks Vegenrage.

She does not talk; she is breathing heavily, and a smile consumes her face.

"Are you OK? I didn't mean to hurt you," says Vegenrage.

She has tears falling from her eyes down the sides of her face, and she looks deep into Vegenrage's eyes as he lowers to kiss her. They are both sweaty, and their lips are moist and warm. She loves the feeling she feels right now and holds him tight to her body with her legs and arms. Vegenrage raises his head and wipes the tears from her face. "I hope those are tears of joy," he says.

She just looks deep into his eyes, motioning her head up and down. He starts to roll over, and she squeezes him tight, holding him right where he is. "Don't move. I just want to feel you right here, just like you are, for as long as I can," she says.

He smiles and lowers down to kiss her neck. She holds him tight, squeezing with her arms and legs, holding their bodies together, and she loves this feeling, like they are one. She loves the feeling of her heart beat slowing, and she can feel his too. She loves the feeling of his heart pumping his blood, which she can feel inside of her where they are still joined. She puts her hands on the sides of his face, and she pulls his lips to hers and kisses them. She can feel his pulse inside of her, and she squeezes his genitals with hers, feeling his strength inside of her as he twitches and moves within her. He returns the feeling with a throb, which sends waves through her body, and they lie there for an hour, feeling and kissing each other. Vegenrage starts to roll over, and Farrah squeezes him and sighs. "Umhum."

He laughs, saying, "Well, I am sorry. I have to go to the bathroom." He laughs and pulls her arms from around his back and lays them to her side. He tries to get up, but she still has her legs wrapped around his, and she is holding them together. "Farrah, I have to go pee."

She whimpers, "Ummm."

Vegenrage reaches his arms between her legs, pries them open, and pulls himself from her. She gets a jolt of chills as he exits her body. He sits on his knees, looking at her. "OK, I don't care. I am just going to say it. You are the most beautiful woman I have ever seen. You are absolutely stunning." He grabs her knees, runs his hands down her legs and up her sides, and squeezes her breasts. Farrah smiles, completely comfortable being naked with Vegenrage. He leans down and kisses her. "I will be right back," he says.

"You better come right back," says Farrah.

Vegenrage vanishes. He appears outside his home on the edge of his realm, looking off into space. It is a night sky, and there is a bright white moon and a lot of stars all around, which he looks at happily. He pees off the plane, and it floats down into the dark realm of space. Farrah appears right next to him.

"Must be you wanted to see me pee," says Vegenrage, looking at her.

"No, I have to pee too. Why didn't you use the bathroom in your home?" asks Farrah.

"You mean *our* home," says Vegenrage.

Farrah creates a magical chair that she can sit on, with her back facing space, and pees off the plane like Vegenrage did.

"OK, I will tell you something. I was afraid you would be out here trying to see if someone needed help, and then you were going to leave," says Farrah.

"And you thought I was going to leave without you?" replies Vegenrage.

Farrah looks at him embarrassed and finishes peeing. "I thought that a little," she says.

Vegenrage grabs her by the hand and pulls her to him. "Listen, I am never going to leave you. I am always going to be yours. Is that what you want?" he asks.

"Yes, that is what I want," she says.

"OK then, it is so. You and I are together now because I want you too," says Vegenrage, looking off into space, which is only visible from the outside edge of his realm. "You know, there are such great views on the earth."

"What are the views like on the earth?" asks Farrah.

"Well, if you are sitting on a warm beach overlooking the ocean when the sun comes up, it's beautiful. The night sky grows bright, and you can see as the sun starts to come up from below the horizon, and there are huge fluffy white clouds in the sky, and they are beautiful. The clouds may be hundreds or even thousands of miles from you, but they look like they are right there, and you can reach out and touch them, but you can't. All you can hear is the waves of the ocean rushing to the beach, and the salty wind is blowing into your body. It's great. There are so many other views too. You could be in the woods on a freezing night with lots of snow covering the ground, and the full moon brightens up the dark woods by shining on the snow-covered land, and it is beautiful. There is no sound, just the sound of your breath and your feet crunching through the snow. Even though it is dark, you can see the shadows left by all the trees from the moon, and it is beautiful. There are deserts and forests and mountains and rivers and so many things. I could never have seen them all in all of my life, but there is one view I don't think I could have ever seen from the earth."

"What view is that?" asks Farrah.

"This one," says Vegenrage, extending his arms out, presenting the view to Farrah, and they look out into the vast realm of space. There are whirlwinds of dots in white, blue, red, purple, and all the colors in between. For as far as they can see, there are all kinds of shapes and sizes in all kinds of colors, making this view astonishing. Everywhere they look, far and close, there are all kinds of marvelous shapes and colors.

"This is the most incredible view of anywhere I have ever been, and this is our home, our view, our realm. Come on, walk with me," says Vegenrage, grabbing her hand, and they walk in the beautiful moonlight totally naked, and the thick grass feels good under their feet. The warm, fresh air cools their still warm and sweaty bodies, and they walk hand in hand toward their home. When they look up, the sky is that of moon and stars. It is only from the outside rim of their realm that they can see into the depths of space and see its splendor.

"So are we going to go back and do that again?" says Farrah.

"Do what?" says Vegenrage, smiling.

"You know, that thing you did to me earlier," says Farrah.

"I don't know, you were crying," says Vegenrage, still smiling.

Farrah laughs, saying, "Yes, I was." She turns to Vegenrage and wraps her arms around his back, squeezing her chest into his. "You remember when we were walking from Mourbarria to Valvernva and you said you loved me?"

"Yeah," says Vegenrage.

"Well, I love you too. I want to be with you always," says Farrah, leaning back from Vegenrage, holding on to him with her arms, smiling and shaking her hair behind her, letting him support her weight. She pulls herself up to him, hugs him, and kisses on his neck, which is perfectly placed to match her height. Vegenrage picks her up in his arms, walks them back to their home, and lies her on the bed. Vegenrage inspects her entire body, kissing her, holding her, squeezing her, and loving her. Farrah loves the way he touches her and flips her around, examining her whole body like he is looking for flaws, but she knows there are none. He tickles her and kisses her, and she lets him do whatever he wants, and they spend hours wearing each other out in frenzied passion until they both fall asleep in each other's arms.

Farrah is the first to wake up, and the moonlight is still shining on the bed just like before. The warm silver-white light shines on the bed, and the rest of their home is like a dim shadow, but this is the perfect light for her tired body. The fire is still burning red-hot logs, with very little flame rolling over them.

Farrah can see Vegenrage sleeping by her, and his face is right there. She kisses him on the cheek and pulls back, smiling, waiting to see him wake up. She kisses him again, and he breathes in deeply, and she watches him wake.

"What are you doing?" says Vegenrage, turning his head and stretching out his body.

"I'm watching you wake up," says Farrah, rubbing her left leg over his, and she rubs her hand from his groin and up his stomach and chest to his neck. Then she rolls over and tries to sit up; she relaxes back to a lying position next to Vegenrage. "Oh, what did you do to me?"

"Everything," says Vegenrage, laughing.

Farrah tries to sit up. "Vegenrage, my hips are so sore. Oh, my stomach is so sore I can't even sit up." She laughs as she slowly sits up through the burning in her stomach. "Vegenrage, the outside of my hips are killing me." She stretches her legs out and rubs them.

Vegenrage sits up, laughing hard. "My stomach is killing me too. You know what that means?" says Vegenrage.

"What?" asks Farrah.

"That means whatever we did to each other we did it right," says Vegenrage, sitting up on the bed and standing up, turning to see Farrah. She is lying there, bending her legs to her chest, and spreading them. She massages and stretches the sore out of her body, and Vegenrage sees her looking at him with total seduction in her smile, and it works. He gets so excited that it's like he is at attention, and his arms are at his sides.

"Vegenrage, what are you thinking?" asks Farrah, who can't stop her laughing and big smile as he crawls on the bed and approaches her from between her legs. He crawls on all fours, kissing her hips, stomach, chest, and neck until they are face-to-face; and he enters her again. She gasps as she feels him much bigger than what he has been before. Her eyes close, and her heart and breathing race as he holds her hands above her head. Her sore legs and hips begin to burn as he strokes her with passion, and she forgets about all the soreness, as initial pain turns to smooth pleasure. The friction of his body thrusting in and out of hers sends her whole body into throbbing sensations.

All her previous feeling of soreness turns to heat, and she pulls her hands from his and puts them on his butt, trying to control his movements. She wants to feel everything and pushes on his butt when she wants him to go faster and holds him where she wants to feel him in her. She raises her bent knees along his sides as far as she can and then spreads her legs as wide as she is able to. She runs her arms over his back and under and over his arms, holding him by his neck and just moving in every way she can without even thinking about it.

Vegenrage just has her writhing with all kinds of
excitements, and she is twitching and squeezing him any way
she can. She loves the intensity she feels from Vegenrage when
he gets so hard and fast. She wants to take his power and feel
it all, but he is so strong. She opens her mouth wide and gulps
for air, squeezing him as tight as she can, bending her knees,
reaching as far up his sides as she is able to. He is so deep
inside of her, and she feels like she is going to pass out from
a combination of pain and pleasure all in one. It's amazing,
and she wants her body to explode at the same time his does,
and she knows he is going to. She tries to wait for him, but
she is taken with excitement, and her insides send shock waves
through her body, making her moan uncontrollably.

He keeps pounding on her, sending pleasurable bombs
that shoot from her hips up her body, and she is breathing so
hard that she is moaning so loud. She wants to rest now, but
he has her on a constant thrill ride, and it's like she is going
to explode for real. He drives deep into her, and she feels
him push as hard and deep inside of her as he can. She yells,
feeling him pound on her and grind on her long and hard,
short and fast over and over. She can feel him get more and
more intense. She can feel him get harder and faster, and the
excitement and anticipation makes her climax over and over,
and she loves it. It feels like he is going to drive his hips right
through hers, and she wraps him with her arms and legs,
squeezing with everything she has.

Mind-numbing intensity consumes Farrah as she feels
Vegenrage shoot inside her for real. Her body twitches and
trembles every time his does inside of her. She gasps with
every movement. She can feel Vegenrage slow, and she slides

her knees down from high on his sides. The heels of her feet are on the loins of his back above his butt, and she runs them down his butt and locks their legs, holding them together. She has her arms around his neck and holds him to her because she needs to rest, and she wants to just feel them both holding each other tight as their bodies, heartbeats, and breathing slow.

"Whew. You see, you're not sore anymore, are you?" says Vegenrage, lifting his head from her hold, laughing and smiling. He kisses her cheek and tries to get up, but she holds him tight to her. He lifts himself, but she holds him with her legs. "I have just what we need. Come on." Vegenrage pries her legs from around him.

"Slowly, slowly," says Farrah as her whole body trembles, feeling his form exit her. She watches as he gets up. "I am really sore now." Farrah's loins are burning and throbbing with every heartbeat, and she is really sore, but it was worth the pleasure. She rolls to the edge of the bed. "What are you doing?"

"I have exactly what we need. Come here," says Vegenrage.

Farrah gets up and almost falls. Her legs are burning on the outsides and on the insides. She has to regain the use of them by slowly walking around. She bends up and down a few times, saying, "Vegenrage, I am really sore."

"Well, I have just what you need then," says Vegenrage, motioning his hands while standing in between the bed and the fireplace. A divot sinks in the floor and fills with superhot water. "Come on, come here."

Farrah walks over to him and holds his hand. He guides her into the pool of hot water treated with salts and moisturizers that fizzes when their skin comes in contact with the water. They slowly step down the steps into the pool and move to the side, where they can sit comfortably and adjust to the very hot water. Farrah sits on his legs, laying her head on his shoulder. "Oh, Vegenrage, this feels so good," she says.

"I know, what did I say? This is perfect," he says.

"So this is our home? We can live here, and no one can come in because you can block them all, right?" says Farrah.

"Yup, I can. Well, I cannot stop entry entirely, but I will know if anyone enters Vollenbeln," says Vegenrage.

"Well, that is good because I need time to just be with you and rest for a while without fighting and killing. Now that Vemenomous is dead and the demons are gone and the dragons did not harm us, we can be together and not worry about everyone else. We can just be together now," says Farrah.

"Wait, what are you talking about? Vemenomous is dead? The demons are gone, and the dragons did not harm us? What are you talking about?" asks Vegenrage.

"You don't remember? Ah, that's right, you were under the charm of Zevoncour. Well, he lived, but all the other demons were killed by the dragons," says Farrah.

"What? When did all of this happen?" asks Vegenrage.

"It happened just before you and I—it happened right here in Vollenbeln. I don't know how, but the demons had you in the bed of jewel, and you were unconscious. Vemenomous charmed me and brought me here. The demons were trying to kill Mezzmaglinggla, and they were going to spill her blood on you and then—I don't want to talk about it. The dragons came and killed them all. Cormygle got away, but he protected his mother, Mezzmaglinggla, from the demons. The dragons were going to kill him, I think, but he got away. They killed all. But Zevoncour, Cormygle, and—oh yeah, Xanorax got away too. They got away, and then it was just me, and you were lying in the bed of jewel. The charm spell that Vemenomous had me under went away, and I was surrounded by the dragons. I was so scared, but it was amazing. I was ready to fight them and protect you, but Gwithen and Blethstole would not let the dragons harm us. They said you protected their young and that they would not let any harm come to you. Then all the dragons left, and it was just you and me, and this is how I want it to be, the way it should be," says Farrah. Farrah hugs Vegenrage and snuggles her head on his neck, but she can feel he is absent. She looks up at him and sees he is thinking about something.

"What, Vegenrage, what is it?" she asks.

"*The Probable Path*," says Vegenrage.

"What?" says Farrah.

"It is one of the books that Hornspire wrote. He talked about different scenarios that were going to play out. The way he saw things play out was that I would be killed by the demons, and you would fight Vemenomous to your death, and then Vemenomous would force Gwithen into mating with him, but she would not. Mezzmaglinggla and Gwithen would be killed, and a dragon named Quailrain would be forced to mate with Vemenomous, but this did not happen. He also had a scenario where the dragons would save you and me and—oh, Farrah, this is very bad," Vegenrage says, looking very seriously at Farrah.

"No, Vegenrage, don't say that," says Farrah.

"Farrah, this is very bad. You know what this is?" says Vegenrage.

"I don't want to know. I want to be right here with you," says Farrah.

"Farrah, this is the calm before the storm," says Vegenrage.

CHAPTER 2

Zevoncour Raises Maglical Hell

Zevoncour has appeared in his inner realm. He is the demon master king of the Maglical System, and his home—his inner realm—is in the planet of Strabalster. He has waited a long time to get the true book of knowledge, the *Wogenkeld*, and now that he has, it he can unlock a lot of evil secrets that have been hidden from him and all the inner realms until now. He walks down a corridor made through solid rock, and it turns red and glows as he walks by. The walls turn molten as he passes by, and molten rock flows down the walls and cools when he has gone. He walks into a large chamber where molten lava flows underneath a rock ledge that spans far out over a river of lava, and he extends his arms, relishing the heat as he walks to the end of the ledge.

A podium grows from the end of the rock ledge, and Zevoncour lays the book on it. He is now standing over a huge pool of lava flowing right into and underneath the rock wall. The entire room is completely surrounded in rock, with the only way in or out being the corridor he walked in from. He breathes in the toxic gases and exhales with a huge smile on his face.

The book starts to crack and change color. It turns a burned black color and is engulfed in flames. The pages start to turn slowly and then faster and faster until the end of the book is reached. The book slams shut, turning a dark lava red color.

"Yes, yes, *Wogenkeld*, you are in the inner realm in sole possession of me, Zevoncour, the demon master king of the Maglical System. I desire all knowledge of the inner realms. It is time for the release of all my demons to the outer realms and the connection of Maglical Hell with the inner realms. Work your magic, *Wogenkeld*. Bring forth the knowledge I ask for. I demand it," says Zevoncour out loud, cutting his left arm with a claw from his right hand, bleeding huge drops of blood on the *Wogenkeld*. He points his right hand to the lava far below, and a stream of lava flows magically up through the air and into his hand, which he pours on the *Wogenkeld*.

The *Wogenkeld* slowly flips through the pages, and as it does, words written in demon blood and lava script themselves on the pages and harden. The pages flip very slowly, forming words in demon writing, which no one on the surface can read, not even Vegenrage or Gwithen. The pages start to flip quicker, and the words are being written faster and faster. The book flips all the way to the end, and it is a very large book; it takes nearly thirty minutes to script all the words, and it slams shut when finished. The book starts to crackle and turns red-hot, with veins of bright red lava forming and flowing through its cover and binding. The book cools and hardens, and Zevoncour slams his right hand on the book and picks it up in both hands with a smile on his face, holding it to his chest.

"The outer realms have no idea the demons are about to take over, and I am their king, soon-to-be king of all the Maglical System," says Zevoncour out loud, laughing.

Zevoncour walks back to the way he entered and heads into another much larger cavern with lava flows racing along the bottom of it. All the souls are whipping around in here like hot rushes of air with a barely visible face, followed by a yellowish flash of light. There are rock ledges that form spiderweb walkways that crisscross the cavern high above the lava flows below. Zevoncour walks out to the center, holding the book tight to his chest, looking above him, smiling, and watching all the souls flying around.

"Ah, my babies, my souls, it is here in my hands. The *Wogenkeld*, the true book of knowledge, and the name of our true master, the name of the ruler of Maglical Hell, shall soon be revealed, and we all will make our way to the outer realms to do whatever we please. Ah ha ha ha ha ha ha ha! Demons of Strabalster, come, come to our greatest gathering and be a part of the raising of Maglical Hell."

Zevoncour calls to all his demons in a voice that is loud, piercing, and echoing throughout all the caverns in his inner realm. The demons race into the cavern from entrances all around the cavern walls. There are a little more than fifty demons all together here in Strabalster, and they come in all forms. Some of them have their original human form, and from that form, many have added all different kinds of hideous adaptations, giving them unique and deadly abilities. Some of the demons have formed like the creatures of the outer world they are from with predatory adaptations, and the deadly forms the demons have taken come in all different ways of causing death to the living. Some of the demons with the greatest imagination have formed into horrific monsters never seen by any other than the souls and demons of the inner realm.

Zevoncour looks around, laughing and smiling, saying, "My children, the time has come, the time to raise our true leader, and the time of the demons is coming to the Maglical System."

Zevoncour turns in a circle and glides his right hand waist-high with his palm down, and the rock ledges start to shift and change their form into straight ledges that run from caverns in the walls out to a center formation large enough for a stone podium to grow in front of Zevoncour, and he lays the book on it. The rock ledges almost form a solid floor, and all the ledges grow to a dugout in the cavern walls with a single demon standing in the entrance of each dugout.

Zevoncour looks around, saying, "And now, my children, I will read from the *Wogenkeld* and raise our ultimate power." There is a hush throughout the cavern. The souls stop flying around, and the demons stand motionless. Even the sound of the rushing lava comes to a halt, and silence fills the inner realm. Zevoncour puts his hands on the cover of the book, and bright, red-hot words form on the cover in the demon language. Across the center of the cover of the book, the word *Gowdelken* appears. Underneath it, a line forms across the entire cover. And under that, more words appear. Zevoncour reads the words. "*Gowdelken* raising Maglical Hell."

Zevoncour opens the book and flips through to the first page and begins to read. "The *Wogenkeld* is the true book of knowledge and, in the hands of a king, becomes the sought-after knowledge of that king. The *Wogenkeld* has become the *Gowdelken* in the hands of Zevoncour. It now shall bring forth Maglical Hell." Zevoncour reads from the book for twelve hours, and all the souls and demons stay motionless until he finishes. Listening to him read from the book is horrific. He is starting a war between the living and the dammed, where the demons of the inner realms are able to move to the outer realms.

There are some extremely disturbing events that are unfolding as he reads. The most notable is that now, for the first time, the leader of Maglical Hell has been named, and his power is now unleashed. Zevoncour reads, "The name of the almighty leader of Maglical Hell shall be unleashed when his name is spoken, and his name is Roartill." By speaking the name Roartill, Zevoncour has opened Maglical Hell, and the master of Maglical Hell has been unleashed. The book explains all kinds of things that can now happen, and it ends with the speaking of Roartill's name.

When Zevoncour finishes the book, the streaming lava beneath the rock ledges starts to swirl and becomes more fluid, looking more and more like blood. The liquid starts to rise as a head almost the entire size of the pool rises from the bloody liquid. The head has huge horns that grow up and curve inward, facing each other. The rock ledges crumble and fall, all except the one Zevoncour is standing on, and that ledge recedes back to the wall, with Zevoncour standing on it. The huge head rises above Zevoncour and looks down on him.

The head of Roartill speaks to Zevoncour. "Zevoncour, my master demon king, hand over the *Gowdelken* to me."

Zevoncour does, and Roartill takes the book from him, saying, "I shall keep this book in my hell with me, and it shall never be taken from my hands to be used against me and my demons. Zevoncour, you and only you shall have the power to unleash our demons to the surface, and all of you, the children souls of hell, shall one day become a demon. The souls of the dammed, take power into your own hands and overpower as many of your brother souls as you can because only the strong become demons here, and with Zevoncour's blessing, you can ascend to the outer realm, where you will live for eternity and do as you please. Remember, if you are killed by the living, your soul falls to Maglical Hell, where it is mine forever. Zevoncour, you are the demon master-king, and you shall rule the inner realms of all three worlds alone. You can travel to all of these inner realms and are free to choose whichever demons you want to take form on the outer realms. With the blessing of Zevoncour, any of you demons can take a well to hell to the outer realm. Now go cause chaos and havoc." Roartill laughs and sinks back into the bloody pool where he came from. The swirling blood thickens and forms back into lava and starts to flow as it has done before.

Zevoncour has unlocked many secrets on this night. He can now speak directly with Roartill; he can bless and send any demon he wants to the outer realm by way of a well to hell. The demons who travel to the outer realms do not have the use of magic, but they may have a spell or two inherent to them that they may use. The use of breath attacks is available to some of them also. Only Zevoncour can use an arsenal of magic on the outer realms with a few demon exceptions. The demons with special adaptation to their bodies will be able to use their adaptations with no problems, but they must be careful on the outer realms; they have no healing magic on there, and if they die, they will be the property of Roartill. They become flesh and bone on the outer realm, and many of them are used to being able to heal very quickly in the inner realm, where they gain strength from all the souls subservient to them. All this goes away on the outer realm. Zevoncour has healing magic for demons, and he is one of very few who do.

Zevoncour looks around at all his demons in the inner realm of Strabalster and wastes no time. "My demons, I bless you with the power of Roartill. Go as you please. You have the right to enter the outer realm," says Zevoncour as he raises his hands, and red lightning radiates from his entire body, extending in squiggly and twirling lines, flowing into each of the demons standing around the cavern. This goes on for a few moments, and the lightning stops.

"Now, my children, you have the ability to reach the outer realm at your pleasure, but remember, you are flesh and blood on the outer realm. I will go to Fargloin and Kronton and release our brothers from their inner realms as well. When I return, I will have a mission, a very dangerous mission, to undertake. Those of you who wish to wait and serve me directly will gain special graces from me. For those of you who cannot wait, go to the outer realm and bring your chaos with you," says Zevoncour, laughing as the souls begin to fly through the air, and the demons liven up with yells and screams. The loud sound of the flowing lava comes back, and Zevoncour disappears.

Zevoncour has great magic, and he is the only demon possessing all the demonic schools of magic. He travels dimensionally to the inner realms of Fargloin and Kronton, releases his demons there, and lets them know that he alone is now the demon master king of all three worlds. He lets the demons know of the great book, the *Gowdelken*, which is now in the hands of Roartill, and that Maglical Hell has been awakened. He blesses all of his demons and tells them all the same. For those who wish to serve under him, he has a great mission. Zevoncour leaves and goes back to his throne in Strabalster.

Back in his realm, Zevoncour walks down a corridor surrounded in solid black granite. He enters his throne room. It is a very simple small circular room carved out of solid black granite. There are small veins of molten lava flowing from under one side of the wall on the floor to the other side of the room, and the lava exits underneath the wall. He walks to the back of the room and sits in his chair, which is carved right into the granite, and when he sits, he sinks into the wall unseen unless looking at him from his front. He sits there for a while and then gets up, walking to the center of his chamber. "Roartill, I ask for your knowledge," says Zevoncour out loud. The room shakes a little, and Zevoncour maintains his stance. There is no physical presence, but Zevoncour can feel the spiritual presence of Roartill.

"What is it that my demon king wishes to know?" Roartill's voice is heard.

"My lord, I have blessed all of my demons so they can reach the outer realms as they please. I have asked those who wish to serve me directly to wait for me. I have a personal problem that I wish to eliminate. The demons who travel to the surface will find the animals and the races of man to be manageable for the most part, but the dragons will be a big problem, and they can kill the demons easily. The magic-using races of man will be a big problem as well. I do not fear the dragons so much because they are very small in numbers and should be easy to avoid. The races of man can fight well with their arrows and swords, but the magic-using races of man will be very difficult to deal with. They have powerful magic that can kill my demons quickly. The dragons have helped our cause greatly, killing a lot of the magic-using races of man, but there are still very powerful magic users among them. There are two in particular, Vegenrage and his mate. They are most certainly a powerful force against us, and I wish to deal with them personally. It was his blood that allowed for the demon uprising's beginning. The blood of Vegenrage is the main ingredient in forming and creating the demonian dragon, Vemenomous. Of course, Vemenomous has been killed, but he can rise again with the blood of Vegenrage or his mate. Once I have the blood of Vegenrage, we can give rise to Vemenomous, and the demonian-dragon-to-be shall be reborn and continue to eliminate the remaining dragons of the Maglical System. If Vemenomous is not to be reborn, then there is always the option of Cormygle or Mezzmaglinggla, who can still be transformed into the demonian dragon. By killing Vegenrage and his female, this will be a serious blow to the magic-using races of man, and we need to eliminate them quickly. I ask for the service of Practu, Zebkef, Zenondour, and Ulore to assist me in the elimination of these two very powerful magic users, and I will harvest the blood of both of them," says Zevoncour.

"You cannot have them. They are in my service now, and there they shall stay, like all who are in my service. I know of Vegenrage and his female. Vegenrage is not from the Maglical System. I was well aware of his presence here when he first arrived, and the dragons who had planned to kill him for a thousand years have failed. He is from another system, and his power has grown and still grows. He is the doorway to another world and a whole new race of man waiting to be exploited. I do not want you to kill him. I want you to bring him to me alive. This will be very difficult, and he may very well destroy you if you try to bring him to me, but bring him to me you will, and all your desires shall be granted. He has only one weakness, the girl. The girl has always been his undoing, and now his love for the girl is sealed. This will be his doom," says Roartill.

Zevoncour gasps, saying, "Do not say the L word, my lord."

"Use the girl. She has grown very strong, but her mind has a weakness. She has fallen under a charm for much of her life, and this is the only weak link in the two of them. You must use the girl to bring Vegenrage to me. Capture her by exploiting her weakness and always be on guard. They have great magic at their disposal at all times," says Roartill.

"What of the dragons, my lord? I was there, and the dragons had Vegenrage, and they did not kill him. Why did they not kill him and the girl?" asks Zevoncour.

"The dragons have allied themselves with the magic-using pair, and now they protect each other. The dragons are a dying race. Their numbers are so low now that they are near extinction. Cormygle was in our service, and he turned against us because of his mother, Mezzmaglinggla. You must have your demons attack and kill her. This will send Cormygle over the edge, and we can bring him back to our service. The dragons may kill Cormygle, but we do not want this. He has hate in his heart, pain and confusion in his mind but not enough to bring his soul to us. We want him alive. By killing his mother, he will have nothing, and then we can bring him back to us because we can restore his magnificent form and transform him into the demonian dragon if need be. He will desire this and fight the dragons for us once his mother has been killed," says Roartill.

"My lord, the dragons now huddle together. They protect each other. How can we get close to them? They will end us with their breath attacks and their magic," says Zevoncour.

"I only tell you what needs to be done. You must figure out how to accomplish it," says Roartill.

"My demons do not have the use of magic, my lord. This is a great disadvantage for us against the dragons and magic-using races of man. Can my demons gain magical knowledge to be used in the outer realms?" asks Zevoncour.

"No, they cannot. Only you are magical with few exceptions, but you are supreme in power. You must protect your demons and use your magic wisely. The demons have very limited magical knowledge, so use them accordingly to maximize their magic and breath attacks," says Roartill.

"Yes, my lord, and the girl, we must use her to get Vegenrage," says Zevoncour.

"Yes, and remember, Vegenrage and the girl will rush to help those in need. You can use this to your advantage against them. The races of man in need will call upon Vegenrage, and you can use this to serve you. I will grant you the knowledge of Practu, Zebkef, and Zenondour so you will know all the races of man on all three worlds," says Roartill.

Zevoncour starts to shake as Roartill infuses his mind with the knowledge of the other demons, and now he knows all they know. He knows the locations of the races of man, as well as the locations of the dragon lairs. He also gains a lot of personal knowledge of very specific individuals who will help him greatly in his quest to eliminate the most powerful of the Maglical System.

"Do not be afraid to use Xanorax. He is a powerful ally, and his magic is significant. He is our top lieutenant on the outer realms, and he will serve you faithfully. The first thing you should concentrate on is bringing Cormygle back to us. He will prove very helpful in your quest for power," says Roartill.

"What if he resists us?" asks Zevoncour.

"Then kill him. Your priorities are set. I care not how you proceed. The only important and useful thing for us is the capture of Vegenrage, and he must be brought to me alive. What happens other than that I care not. I will always have my souls coming to me, in addition to this new world. The world Vegenrage is from will be most interesting. I would love to confront the leader of their hell and bring him to his knees," says Roartill.

"My lord, I cannot bring the living to the inner realm. I do not have that power. How do I get Vegenrage and the girl to the inner realm?" asks Zevoncour.

"You must capture and subdue him and then call for me, and I will make it possible." Roartill laughs, and his laugh fades as does his presence.

Zevoncour makes his way to the main chamber, where most of the demons and souls are, and he calls for the demons who wish to serve with him. He is actually surprised to see that none of the demons have gone to the outer realm. "My children, wait here. I will be back with demons from the other two realms, and we will see how many of us are there," says Zevoncour. He then goes to the inner realm of Fargloin, and again, none of the demons have gone to the outer realm. All wish to serve with him. The same is true for Kronton.

Zevoncour brings all the demons to his home realm in Strabalster and takes all the demons to a special cavern where no souls are allowed. This is a great time for the souls because they can fight for dominance over one another without the demons interfering, and the souls battle on to create new demons. Zevoncour looks over his 250 mostly hideous and deformed demons with a smile on his face, saying, "My children, I am pleased to see you all here with me. We will take over the outer realm, and it is good you stick together for now because the dragons will be most difficult to defeat. The magic-using races of man can cause us death as well. We must be cunning in our methods. We must avoid the magically powerful living when possible and kill them when conditions are right, for right now, we have a priority. There is one very powerful magic user by the name of Vegenrage and a female by the name of Farrah. We need these two alive so we can bring them to our lord, Roartill. They can lead us to another world, a fresh new world, for us to plunder. I know where they live, and I can bring us there, but we must be careful not to kill them. They have great and powerful allies in the dragons. There is one dragon named Cormygle whom we may persuade to join us. He has one great weakness we must exploit, his mother. If we kill her, his hate can bring him to us as an ally. Fear the dragons because they are very powerful, but Cormygle lives alone and is no friend to the dragons. My sense tells me Cormygle has no friends at all, and we may get him to join us just by asking.

"Cengorge, I am sending you to the Carbonheight Hills on the planet Fargloin. Seek audience with Cormygle and ask him if he will come back to the demons. Tell him we hold no ill will toward him and that he is free to join us. He is most important as an ally to us in the fight against the dragons. If he will not join us, then we have to use other means to persuade him to join with us." Zevoncour approaches Cengorge and places his hand on his head. His eyes flutter, and he shakes as Zevoncour imbues him with special magic. "You need not fear Cormygle. If he decides to use magic on you or if he decides to strike you in any way, you will be transported back here with no harm caused to you. I am sending you to the inner realm of Fargloin. From there, take a well to hell to the surface and seek out Cormygle. Go now, my child."

"Yes, Master," says Cengorge, and he is teleported away.

"Now, my children, we wait to hear back from Cengorge, and soon we ascend to the outer realms," says Zevoncour, his laugh echoing throughout the caverns and chambers of the inner realm.

CHAPTER 3

Cormygle's Decision

Cengorge appears in the inner realm of Fargloin and looks up to see a well going straight to the surface. He can see the light of day quickly approaching as he flies up the tunnel toward the surface. He exits the tunnel and rises high in the air before falling to the dark carbon earth. He is on one of the hills in the Carbonheight Hills, where Cormygle makes his home. The well to hell closes up after he exits, and he looks around the dry black hills.

"Cormygle, I have come for you to bring you back into the service of demons. Zevoncour has sent me to offer you a place within his legion. Zevoncour recognizes that, with his help, you are the most perfect and lethal of all the dragons. He extends his hand to you, and it would be wise to accept his offer because soon he will be the ruler of all the inner and outer realms of the Maglical System," says Cengorge. He hears Cormygle laugh as his form rises from the carbon earth in monumental proportions as he has done in front of Gisewear.

Cormygle leans forward toward the miniature demon, growling and snarling at Cengorge, saying, "So if Zevoncour wants me back in his ranks, why would he send you to ask me?"

"I am Cengorge, lead lieutenant for Ulore, who was killed by the dragons. Now Zevoncour rules all the inner realms, and I am his servant. I do as my master wishes, and he wishes to have you back in his services, or you will be an enemy of his," says Cengorge.

"I am an enemy of the dragons and of the demons, and that is the way it should be. I have been an enemy to everyone my whole life, and that is just the way it is. That makes you an enemy as well," says Cormygle.

"I am not your enemy. I come as your friend to escort you to the inner realm. Once there you can join us as it was meant to be, and we will take over the outer realms of the Maglical System together," replies Cengorge.

"Everyone is my enemy. I was in service with the demons against the dragons, and that is when I realized that there was one dragon whom I could not kill, and Zevoncour only wants to kill everything and everyone. I cannot have this. I have made my choice, and now it is too late to side with dragon or demon, so I am on my own. Here in my homeland is where I am meant to be alone. I have created all this with my own magic, and no one and no demon shall ever come here and leave without my saying so," says Cormygle.

"Do not be a fool, Cormygle. Join with us," says Cengorge.

"You are no friend of mine, and hell is waiting for you," says Cormygle, leaning back, and he sends a carbon spear up from the ground, hitting Cengorge in the groin.

Cengorge has a protective force around him, and it stops the carbon spear from penetrating his body, but it sends him flying high in the air.

"Zevoncour, my master, teleport me back. Cormygle is attacking me. Teleport me back!" yells Cengorge.

Cormygle laughs, swinging his right wing and hitting Cengorge higher into the air. Cormygle laughs some more, saying, "Do you really think your demon king can protect you here? This is my land imbued with my magic. The magic of Zevoncour is powerless against my magic here in the Carbonheight Hills."

Cengorge falls to the ground, and the carbon is like fine sand that softens his impact. Cengorge stands up, saying, "You cannot harm me, dragon. My master has protected me from your magic and your attacks."

"You have no way out, Cengorge. You cannot create a well to hell here in the Carbonheight Hills. There is no escape for you. How long do you think that protective magic will last?" asks Cormygle, grabbing Cengorge with his swinging right paw. And of course, in his carbon form, Cormygle is perfect.

Cormygle slams Cengorge to the ground face-first, and a very sharp, pointed carbon shaft rises from the ground right in the center of Cengorge's chest. The protective magic is strong, and the shaft cannot penetrate past the magic to reach Cengorge. Cormygle pushes with great force, and Cengorge cannot free himself. Cormygle picks Cengorge up high in the air. In this form, Cormygle is solid black, even his eyes. He is nearly two hundred feet tall, which is very intimidating, and this is only him from his stomach up.

Cormygle looks at Cengorge and, with a sigh, says, "Let's see how this protective magic stands up against this." Cormygle grabs each of Cengorge's legs with his paws and rips Cengorge in half. He rips from the groin right up to the neck, and his head stays intact with the left side of his body; he is killed instantly. Cormygle laughs, half of Cengorge in each of his paws. The ground below forms into a bowl, and Cormygle puts the two halves of the demon together in his paws and wrings them like a towel, and the demon blood drips into the bowl. He continues to wring the body dry of fluid, and then he crumples and breaks the rest of the body into small pieces and drops them into the bowl. Cormygle then shrinks down to the true decrepit dragon that he is and eats and drinks the demon—flesh, blood, bone, and all. He looks up to the sky and speaks magical words in the dragon tongue.

"Fleesshhhmmboo cunsummme earthody constalay emcasshhton." Cormygle starts to laugh, though he is in great pain. His front deformed legs start to grow and form more correctly to his dragon form. His hind legs start to crack and lower to their correct position, and his back and front legs after a few minutes have transformed into anatomically correct dragon legs and paws. His wings have not changed at all, but Cormygle laughs, standing on his hind legs and reaching his front legs to the sky. "I have done it. The process has begun. Father, I have done it. My body has accepted the demon flesh. It works. I am going to be the demonian dragon. The transformation has begun. Father, I wish you were here," Cormygle says, looking straight up into the air. The ground around Cormygle starts to sink, like a great sinkhole is forming right where he stands. He lowers into the carbon earth and is buried in the black sand.

Cormygle walks down a tunnel dug out of the black earth and lit by a shimmering diamond light in the sandy walls, and he talks out loud to himself. "Father, you were right. The prophecy is true. I don't know why, but when the time came for me to kill Mother and put an end to the dragons, I could not do it. I would have been held high in the ranks of the demons. Vemenomous, along with Vegenrage, would have taken care of the few remaining dragons. Why was it so easy for me to kill you when you entered the Carbonheight Hills, and why was it so easy for me to kill Gisewear? When the time came for me to bring harm to Mother, I could not do it. I had to protect her. What is in these books that knows what we will do before we do the actions ourselves?"

Cormygle comes to a large lair with no visible entrance or exit, just the tunnel he was walking down. It is a large open cavern, very high and wide, with torches lit all around, giving plenty of light and causing small diamonds in the walls to shine brightly. All the diamonds in all the walls throughout the tunnel continue to lit up. The smoke from the torches rises and magically seeps into the ceiling and filters to the surface. The torches are stuck in the ground, sitting high on wooden posts and in the walls around the cavern. There is a waterfall that enters the lair and flows right out of the wall, falling down on the black carbon sand to the cavern floor and flowing across the floor, into the opposite wall, and into the earth. Cormygle walks up to the stream and takes a drink of the cold, pure water. The ground is soft like sand and is marked with his footprints wherever he walks. The walls seem to be the same soft sand, and Cormygle has used great magic in order for his lair to maintain its form. This is a very insipid lair with no adornments, but very cool magic on the torches allows the smoke to rise up and out through the ceiling.

The only forms in the room are statues of his two brothers, whom he killed young in their life. He also has a statue of Griyile, his father, whom he killed here in the Carbonheight Hills, and a statue of Gisewear. Cormygle walks up to the statue of his father, which is in its true form and color. Griyile is much larger than Cormygle and has a beautiful orange color with yellow along his stomach and lower neck, which forms a yellow ring just above his shoulders. He has red spots all over his body, imitating fireballs, and he is a beautiful dragon. He is on his hind legs, with his tail supporting his weight. His right paw is stretched out like he is going to strike, and his left paw is close to his chest like he was in motion when he was immortalized as a statue. His mouth is open like he was roaring, and he has two horns, which come straight out from just below his jaw for two feet, and then they turn back toward his body. His horns then arch around and forward, giving them just a little more width than his head, and they are very sharp. Then the horns veer toward his mouth but below it and parallel, ending just a little bit in front of his mouth. These horns are very similar to those of Blethstole. Griyile has been a fantastic dragon, and his life has been cut short before he has ever had a chance to rise and give challenge for the dominant dragon position.

Cormygle looks at his father, reflecting on how his life has progressed and how he has gotten to where he is now. Cormygle talks to the statue of his father. "My hatred for the dragons always had the best of me, Father, but it made me strong. It kept me alive against the dragons who tormented and hated me. You were my first real test, and by killing you, I gained the magical strength that I needed to carry this decrepit body. You came to me wanting to talk, but I thought it was all a plan by you and the dragons to rid the Maglical System of me. I remember you saying that I was to be the next form of great and superior dragon, the demonian dragon. I remember you saying I would save Mother from demons and feast on their flesh and that my body would transform into the perfect dragon. I thought you were diverting my attention away from you so you could make a quick and lethal end to my miserable life. I remember you saying there was a book that spoke of this, and you believed it would come true. I remember you presenting the book, and I used your distraction to kill you. As I look back, I wish now I had listened, but, Father, you live on. You live through me. Now let's have a look at this book and see what it has to say."

Cormygle speaks some magical words in dragon tongue. "Coommss livv shwaakeenn beff ortthh fallssownn bakein." The statue of Griyile starts to move, and the two front paws reach into his chest and pull it apart. A book falls out onto the ground, and the statue forms back the way it was. Cormygle picks the five-foot-tall-by-four-foot-wide book, looks at the cover, and reads it out loud. "*The Demonian Dragon: Vemenomous, Mezzmaglinggla, Cormygle.*" Cormygle walks over to the wall of his lair and sits down; he opens the book and begins to read it for the first time.

Blethstole and the dragons who have been on Vlanthis and helped eliminate the demons so they may not get Vegenrage and Farrah have made their way back to Blethstole's lair. Now all the remaining dragons are here.

Quailrain brought her young dragons here before all the dragons went to Vlanthis. Gwithen teleported her young, the youngest of all the dragons here, and Gairdennow swore to guard them with his life. The third dragon feast has brought about change in the dragons' way of life and in a superfast way. The dragons, after the second dragon feast, suffered losses of life to the races of man for the first time, and this was very concerning to the dragons but not enough for them to change their thinking and way of life.

Now after the third dragon feast, they have suffered such catastrophic losses to their numbers that they have to change. The reality now is that it may be too late for them to survive as a species. There are three draglets, and the majority of surviving dragons are very young and all male. The adult female dragons are only three, and the surviving dominant dragons number only five. This is the lowest number of dragons present in the Maglical System ever, and now they are the most fragile species, even more so than the Glaborian dwarves. The dragons now know they have to protect their young and make sure they become adults. Not only do they need to produce female offspring and grow their numbers but this also takes centuries for dragons to do.

Blethstole walks around, looking at all the dragons, who just fit into his lair and surround him. The walls of his lair are still covered in the molten gold that clings to the walls, so there is a golden hue surrounding all the dragons. Blethstole speaks up for all to hear. "The dragon way of life is not changing. It has changed, and we now have to stick together and protect each other. We have to watch our young and make sure they grow to adulthood. We cannot live as solitary individuals anymore. We have to band together and live in wide well-protected lairs. Gannream, you have a very nice, big, and spacious lair in the Mountain Creek Hillyards, which is well suited for this. My lair here is well protected, and of course, Gwithen has the best lair for us to live in," says Blethstole.

Pryenthious snarls, showing his teeth, and confronts Blethstole. "We would not have to live in fear that the humans would hunt us down if you had taken out Vlianth and the female when we had them. My lair is unknown to all the races of man, and there is complete safety for me there. The same is true for Gairdennow and Dribrillianth. We planned throughout the entire dragon feast to kill Vemenomous, Vlianth, and the female. Vemenomous is no more, and we had the prophetical human in our hands. Why did you let them live?"

Gwithen responds to Pryenthious. "We let Vlianth live because he had many paths in which he could follow. One path was to kill Vemenomous and the dragons. One path was to be killed himself, and his flesh and blood would bring in the reign of a new dominant dragon who would have killed all of us. There was one other path Vlianth could have followed, and this is the path he chose. He chose to protect and save dragons. My young draglets were facing certain death, and Vlianth showed up and saved them from Zevoncour and his minions. Vlianth gave me his word that if I or my young were in danger, he would be there to help, and he did so by almost giving his life to protect me and my young. I in turn returned the favor by cloaking the descent of the dragons into Vlanthis, where we killed the demons and saved Vlianth and the female. We now have a great ally in Vlianth. We need to be cautious because he is caught in the middle, and I know you see this. If we continue to feed on the races of man, he will be torn. He will be forced to take sides, and there is no question he is capable of killing any of us. I can tell you this: Vlianth will not hunt us, with the one exception being if we hunt his kind. We are small in numbers now, and there are plenty of beasts on the worlds for us to hunt. We need to leave the races of man alone, or they will unite and hunt us down. We need to leave the races of man alone because they have another threat to keep them occupied, and this threat to the races of man will leave us time to replenish our numbers, which we need to do now, or we will not survive as a species."

"And what threat is that, Mother?" Dribrillianth asks.

Blethstole turns to Dribrillianth and looks over the dragons, saying, "Gannream, Pryenthious, Dribrillianth, Mezzmaglinggla, Gwithen, and I were all just in Vlanthis. Do you all not remember that the demons were there? I know you do because you feasted on their flesh, but Zevoncour escaped, and the demons will make their way to the outer realms of the Maglical System. This means they will hunt the races of man. They will hopefully leave the dragons alone, but Cormygle escaped as well, so he may fall back into the ranks of the demons. Cormygle may hunt the dragons. This is what we must prepare for and be ready to defend against."

"That Cormygle—I say we hunt him down and kill him right now," says Pryenthious.

"Pryenthious, we have hunted enough for now. We cannot afford to lose any more dragon life. Any attack, any threat to us will be met with the strength and might of all the remaining dragons," Blethstole says as he looks over the surviving dragons, hoping they will understand and see the changing wisdom of Blethstole, who is one of the fiercest dominant dragons to have ever reigned over the Maglical System.

Gwithen changes the subject, saying, "We cannot stay in my lair. It is most certainly the most ideal place for all of us to live, but the demons have been there. They will find it easy to climb their way back into my lair, and this will be a great place for them to ambush us. I think we need to split into three groups. Dribrillianth has a perfect lair for a handful of dragons to reside in. Same goes for Gairdennow and Pryenthious. Your three lairs are perfect. These lairs are not known by the races of man, and our only threat will be Cormygle."

Mezzmaglinggla enters the conversation, saying, "The demons have taken Razcour from me. Vlianth took Emzwer from me, but there is a difference. The demons called Razcour with the intention of killing him and me. Vlianth killed Emzwer, protecting his female. It was us dragons who captured Vlianth, and the female came to his rescue. Then when we captured the female, it was Vlianth who came to her rescue. We should learn from these two. Gwithen and Blethstole are right. We need to help and protect each other. If the demons come for us, we need to fight in force together and feast on their flesh. As far as Cormygle goes, there is good in him. I know it. I watched him grow and fight the torment caused him by us dragons, always beating him, always shunning him, and never including him as a dragon. He took that pain and did what he had to do to be great. You all saw in Vlanthis that when ordered to attack me, he openly refused the demons. I will not go so far to say he will ally himself with the dragons, but I do not think he will be a threat to us anymore. I am certain he will not harm me."

Gwithen walks up to Mezzmaglinggla, comforts her, and then tells her what she does not want to hear. "Mezzmaglinggla, do not be fooled by Cormygle. He is your offspring, along with Rungrunger, Jarclause, Reegaallia, and Megalla. But none of you be fooled by Cormygle. He has spent his whole adult life studying demonology and killing dragons when he can. Cormygle is still torn, and he protected the only one who ever protected him, and that is you, Mezzmaglinggla. But hear me, all of you. If faced by Cormygle, remember he has killed all dragons who have faced him in his adult life. Hatred has consumed his heart, and he is no ally to the dragons. All of you, listen to me good. Do not face Cormygle. If you see him, leave immediately," says Gwithen.

Pryenthious cannot control his disgust and speaks out. "Even if that sniveling coward were to come begging on his knees, I would rip his head off and serve it to the flies."

"I agree with Pryenthious in this case. Cormygle has made his choice. He killed Gisewear, who approached him to bring him back into the dragon society, but no, that abomination took Gisewear and killed him. There is no pity and no forgiveness in me for this scoundrel. I will kill him on sight," Dribrillianth says.

Blethstole speaks in a commanding voice. "Enough of Cormygle. He has made his choice, and he is an enemy of the dragons. Mezzmaglinggla, you are the only dragon who may reason with Cormygle, but none of the rest of us will make any attempt at this. Now let's stop this bickering. Enough of looking back. We are where we are, and now we move forward. We gather now as a completely united species, and we take to three lairs, like Gwithen said. Our females are all fertile, and we need to grow our numbers. If anyone does not agree with this plan for our future, then speak now. Otherwise, let us dragons get to the business of replenishing our species and looking forward and surviving." No one speaks, and there is a silent moment of understanding and acknowledgment that this is how the dragons will proceed from this point on to the foreseeable future.

Zevoncour is standing in the great cavern in the inner realm of Strabalster. He is standing on the rock ledge over the running molten lava far beneath him. His eyes are closed, and all the souls are flying around, echoing their chilling sounds. The demons are standing in the tunnels that lead from the large cavern to their respective lairs in the rock. The souls are flying and making all kinds of noise, but the demons and Zevoncour are motionless, just waiting, and then Zevoncour opens his eyes. He raises his head with a grumbling deep voice, saying, "My demons, wait here for my return."

Zevoncour yells, "Roartill!" He vanishes and appears in a room where the wall in front of him is the face of Roartill.

"Zevoncour, your calls and cries are already becoming most tiresome. What is it you seek now?" asks Roartill.

"My lord, Cormygle has killed my top lieutenant, Cengorge. He is no ally to the demons," says Zevoncour.

"Zevoncour, listen to me. Do not call me for help anymore, or I will find a new demon master king of the Maglical System, one who will lead and not come sniveling to me for help. I will give you some knowledge, and from this, you get things done or else. First of all, Cormygle will come to the demons. That is because Cormygle may be the true demonian dragon, and he will kill more demons. Do not let this bother you. In fact, give your strongest demons to Cormygle. This will only make him stronger, and in the end, after he has fully become the first and true demonian dragon, he will seek you out and be your strongest ally against the living.

"Second of all, you must bring darkness to the worlds of the Maglical System in order to give your demons the edge in all conflicts. Figure out how to block the sun and kill the worlds. This will make you and your demons invincible. Take your most valued demons and have them take over the bodies of the Helven. This will give your demons an elven form, masking them from the races of men.

"Last of all, give your demons something they can sink their teeth into. Give them the flesh of dwarves. The dwarves of Glaboria hide in the sanctuary of Symbollia. They are all here, grouped together, waiting for the return of their king. There is no better time to act than now. Send all your demons to Symbollia. Have them rise from the earth to the bottom of the mountain, where the dwarves wait, and slaughter them. The race of dwarves is all there, waiting to be erased from the Maglical System." Roartill's hand rises from the molten floor, grabs Zevoncour by the neck, and squeezes until Zevoncour cannot breathe. "Now go, Zevoncour, and do not return until you have captured Vegenrage and the female," says Roartill, throwing Zevoncour, who vanishes, appearing back in his inner realm of Strabalster.

CHAPTER 4

Slaughter in Symbollia

Zevoncour stands on the rock ledge looking to all the demons standing motionless in the tunnels leading away from the cavern. "It is time, my demon children—time to feast on the flesh of dwarves. We go to the inner realm of Fargloin, and from there, we rise into the mountain—the mountain known as Symbollia, where all the dwarves hide. Here, the dwarves feel safe from all the land predators of the outer realms, and they are, but they have no idea the demons are coming from beneath them. We will rise, and we shall feast on the flesh of dwarves. We will grow strong, and the dwarves will fall from the Maglical System as the first victims of the demons."

The demons start to liven up. They snarl and show their very sharp predatory teeth and flex their muscles. Zevoncour points his hands at each demon at a time, and they teleport to the inner realm of Fargloin. Zevoncour does this very quickly, and a few minutes later, after he has inspected the entire cavern and made sure all the demons have been teleported, he himself vanished to the inner realm of Fargloin.

Zevoncour appears in the center of all the demons. They are in a large cavern, all huddled on a huge mass of rock, and

Zevoncour raises his hands in the air, laughing and chanting magical words. The earth above them starts to crumble and roll down the walls. The rock beneath them starts to rise, and the demons are raised through the earth.

The dwarves in Symbollia have waited patiently for the return of their king, but many of the dwarves have returned to mining in the mountains. Many of the dwarves have gone to see what has become of Glaboria, their great mountain city, which has been destroyed. The leaders of the Dagi have all gone with Glimtron, but there are a dozen very young Dagi who have been studying the dwarven magical arts, and they have all gone to the Dagi Bluffs. The Dagi Bluffs are on the mountain right behind the Glaborian Mountains and has been spared from destruction in the dragons' last attack.

The Dagi have created a magnificent magical bridge that takes the Dagi back and forth from Glaboria to the Dagi Bluffs. The bridge looks like blue glass with long legs that reach the mountain floor from arches underneath the top portion of the bridge. There are times when the clouds pass by the walkway, and it is a beautiful sight. Sometimes the rains create beautiful rainbows that arch over the bridge. The Dagi use magic when on the bridge, and they are carried across very quickly, like being on an escalator.

The Dagi Bluffs themselves are magical. The bridge stretches to the peak of Dugunstor, which is the mountain the Dagi Bluffs are on. The bridge has eight legs that span from the end of the bridge to both sides and middle of the Dugunstor mountaintop. There are three legs on each side of the bridge and two that lead right to the center top of the Dagi Bluffs. The legs on the sides all lead to a tunnel that goes into the mountain. The top of the mountain has been carved through the use of dwarven magic, and here, on top of the world, they meditate for long periods.

Farther down on the mountain, there are great shelves that have been carved into the side of the mountain, and this is where the dwarves practice sparring with their magic. They practice raising elementals here and the use of offensive magic. The dwarves have used their best craftsmen to help carve and polish this place alongside the Dagi, who have used great magic to move huge masses of rock. There are tunnels beautifully created that traverse the top half of the mountain, and the Dagi can reach any part of the Dagi Bluffs from these tunnels. There is a teleportation platform here in the Dagi Bluffs, from where the Dagi can reach any part of the Glaborian mountain range. The Dagi have platforms all throughout the mountains, making travel for them far quicker than for anyone else.

The young Dagi here are not nearly as powerful as those who have gone with Glimtron, but they are good magic users, and they already sense that the Sapphirewell has been used in a very unusual way. Without this magical jewel, they cannot summon elementals, but they still have very good healing, defensive, and offensive magic. The Dagi meditate and work on their magic. The miners continue to mine for the riches of the mountains, and most of the dwarves wait in Symbollia for the return of their king, Glimtron.

The dwarves always have hunting parties in the mountains for the Kimeek, which is a form of deer that live in great numbers on the mountains. They can walk on the vertical walls of the mountains and feed on the grasses and plants that grow there. The dwarves have large openings all around the mountains, and they grow plants here purposely to trap the deer. Other dwarves head out to the Sand Marshes of Smyle, where they can hunt the Tamaleel, which is a very large form of deer living in the marshes. They also collect potatoes, carrots, and celery, which grow naturally in the sand marshes.

The dwarves are in a state of flux now that Glaboria has been destroyed and their king, along with their best warriors and magic users, has gone to fight the dragons. They are starting to get their mind-set back and are ready to begin rebuilding. They pray for the safe return of their king and friends but have no idea that doom is traveling for them right now. The dwarves in the main gathering area of Symbollia are enjoying this temporary respite until their king returns, and then it's back to the work of rebuilding. They are eating and drinking and engaging in conversation when the walls start to shake, and the rocks around the room start to crack and fall, which is very unusual. The dwarves are silenced as they all look around. Earthquakes are nonexistent here, but the walls start to crack, and large rocks fall from the ceiling and walls. The dwarves protect themselves from the falling debris as horror escapes from the walls.

The demons burst out of the walls and fall onto the unsuspecting dwarves. The walls are bursting large rocks onto the dwarves, followed by demons, and panic strikes all. The dwarves here include all the women and mostly children, and the demons descend on them, ripping, tearing, and biting any who get in their path. The demons begin to feed immediately. The male dwarves present use chairs, knives, and forks to stab and fight the demons, but the demons are too strong. The demons feed, only stopping to fend off attacking dwarves. he scene is instant chaos, and Zevoncour rises from the floor in an explosion of rock rising high in the air. He is laughing and pointing his hands to the exits, blocking them with magical barriers so no one can escape.

A few dwarves have magnificent Foarsbleem swords, battle axes, and bows. They start hacking and shooting at the demons, causing very serious injury to them and killing some. The dwarves attack the demons in groups of three with devastating blows from their axes and lethal strikes from their swords, sending demons to Maglical Hell, never to return. Foarsbleem arrows soar, and demons are mortally wounded by their incredible accuracy.

Zevoncour watches the bloody massacre as his children feast on the dwarves, and he shoots the dwarves fighting back with black claws from his fingers. The dwarves struck by Zevoncour's claws can do nothing. Once the claw penetrates their flesh, it starts to rot, and the black grows through the body of the dwarves, rotting their flesh and killing them in minutes. The dwarves with weapons are not short on courage and bravery, and they fight with incredible rage and hostility. They are killing way more demons than Zevoncour had expected, so he drops to the ground and walks right at the fighting dwarves. The claws that Zevoncour has shot from his fingers have grown back, and now they grow to four feet in length. He swipes his claws at the dwarves and leaves deep slicing wounds in them, sending the deadly rot through their bodies. The dwarves with bows fire at Zevoncour, and he is struck many times with lethal Foarsbleem arrows. Zevoncour faces the direction where the arrows have come from, and before he can send lethal magic at them, he is struck above the right buttocks with a battle ax, sinking deep into his flesh, and a sword is driven right through his left thigh. Zevoncour sinks into the earth before he takes any more damage, and the demons start to focus on all the fighting dwarves.

The Dagi became aware through their magical sense that Symbollia is in great danger, and they have all teleported to Symbollia. Zevoncour has magically blocked all the exits and entrances, but the Dagi have the ability to teleport into Symbollia by way of a teleportation pad. They have these pads all throughout the mountains, and there is one in Symbollia in the main hall, where all the dwarves being attacked are. The Dagi arrive to see horror and gore like they have never imagined. All the demons, by now, have tasted and consumed the flesh of dwarves, which is very important. This gives them much needed strength to survive and be strong on the outer realms. The Dagi all use magic missile spells, which are very effective against the demons. The magic missiles strike the demons and explode demon flesh and blood all over. They are killing the demons easily, and the demons dig their way back into the earth.

The Dagi head to the floor, and seeing all the dwarves who are half-eaten and dead makes it hard for them to concentrate on healing. It takes them a few minutes to compose themselves, and they help those who can be helped. Most of the dwarves are in a panic, running around, trying to find friends and family. A lot of them are crying, having found those close to them already dead, but there are many who are trying to stay calm and be ready for the next round of battle. The Dagi split up into three groups. The first group of four work together, helping heal those who have not been wounded too badly so they can help in the fight. Those who need immediate attention get it, and many deaths are prevented by the combined magic of the Dagi. The second group of Dagi is moving rubble and large stones out of the way with telekinetic magic while helping those who have been trapped by the debris. The third group of Dagi is working with those dwarves who have axes, swords, and bows, and they are preparing for any more attacks. They are being as aware as they can, paying attention to the ground, ceiling, and walls for any more intrusions by the demons. The dwarves fought fiercely, and they are very tough.

The demons lost many, and once they see one of their kind die, they know that is it—no more soul, no more nothing—so they scamper, run, and hide. But they have now tasted the warm flesh of the living, and it is not long until the hunger and the craving for more flesh take over the fear, and the demons will regain their full confidence. That is already happening.

Some of the dwarves are fleeing through the tunnels, but they are called back, warned that in the tunnels they will be easily picked off by the demons. The Dagi do not have the power of the Sapphirewell, so they have no summoning magic in the mountains. Most of the dwarves stay in the great hall, where they use all the tables to make barricades and form a huge circle in the middle of the room from which they can defend themselves. There are fires around, which have been kicked or knocked over, and there are red-hot logs burning and smoldering here and there. But this room is huge, and the dwarves have used their magic to make a network of very small tunnels that reach the outside of the mountain. The way they have constructed the ventilation tunnels is workmanship of the most wonderful kind. There is a constant flow of fresh air in and through the great hall in Symbollia and most of all the mountains here. All the smoke from the smoldering fires is blown out of the great hall in Symbollia, and fresh air is always a constant.

The Dagi have not wasted time; they are running dwarves as fast as they can to the teleportation pad and getting as many dwarves to safety in the Dagi Bluffs as they can. They are very quick in doing this, but something bad is happening. The dwarves are starting to get very hot. They are starting to sweat and wipe their brow a lot. "What is happening?" asks Brimetor as he wipes his brow. "It is getting really hot in here. I don't like this. It never gets this hot."

"I know. I am getting a bad feeling," says Tillbon, one of the Dagi. Tillbon looks to the floor and feels it with his hand. He looks up, yelling to his Dagi brethren, "Hurry, we have to get everyone out of here now. Hurry!" Tillbon stands up. "Everyone, to the teleportation pad now!" There are way too many dwarves here to get them all out at once. There are hundreds of dwarves, and only a few can teleport at a time, that is, with the help of a Dagi.

The floor starts to get so hot that is starts to melt. The dwarves start searching for higher ground. The wooden tables and everything made out of wood touching the floor starts to burn. The great ventilation in this case is a kind of curse because there is great oxygen flow, and all the wood starts to burn fast. The dwarves are screaming and yelling because there is not enough high ground for them all to get to, and more and more of the floor is becoming a molten lava pool. Many of the dwarves are caught in the lava, and it is so hot that their bodies start to burn.

Demons erupt from the lava and sink back in it with captured dwarves, who die very quickly from being submersed in molten lava. The demons can now consume the dwarves in the lava with no worries about attacking dwarves. Those dwarves who have made it to higher ground watch in horror as their kin are pulled into the lava and die. As the dwarves burn, the demons rise out of the lava and start to consume the dead and dying. Those on higher ground with bows launch arrows into the demons, but the demons sink into the lava before they get hit.

The Dagi are getting as many of the dwarves out of Symbollia as they can, but now the lava is starting to rise, and it is rising faster and faster. Soon the teleportation pad will be under lava, and the Dagi will not be able to get any more dwarves out. The dwarves have no choice but to try to exit through the tunnels. This is, as they feared, a deadly trap. The demons have blocked all the tunnels a quarter of a mile away from Symbollia, and here the dwarves are trapped. The demons can move through the earth and pick dwarves and take them back into the ground, where the dwarves are disoriented and quickly killed and consumed. The lava is rising into the tunnels as well, and this is a double disaster for the dwarves.

Many of the dwarves fight bravely until it is all over; the slaughter in Symbollia is complete. The dwarves have suffered a 90 percent loss to their race. They are now not endangered as a race but gone. There are not enough of them left to replenish their race. The demons sought to eliminate the dwarves all together, and they have pretty much succeeded at this. This is not the only goal of Zevoncour though.

The Glaborian Mountains are the largest mountain range on all of Fargloin. Zevoncour is following the wishes of his master, Roartill, by raising lava into the mountains so he can fill the skies with volcanic ash. He has hundreds of mountains here, and he can fill all of them with molten lava, and eruptions from all these mountains will cover the planet in a blanket of ash, killing all the life that depends on sunlight. This will start a chain reaction that is most pleasant for the demons but very bad for everything else.

The Dagi have rescued almost three hundred of the dwarves from Symbollia, and they are all resting on the Dagi Bluffs. There is only confusion and fear here. The Dagi know they cannot return to Symbollia; they know the teleportation pad has been destroyed. The Dagi here work hard together trying to summon the other Dagi with their king through telepathy. The other dwarves who have been rescued sit around quiet and fearful of another attack, but they are alert. The dwarves are on a high peak on Dugunstor, which has been carved flat with a large ring of seats around the perimeter of the platform. This is large enough for most of the dwarves to sit on. The Dagi are all concentrated in the center of the platform, trying to reach their king and the eldest Dagi.

The dwarves sitting are starting to notice rumbling and eruptions. They stand, and tears fall down their faces as the great mountain of Glaboria starts to fall in front of them. The front portion of the mountain explodes in an inferno, followed by rivers of lava and billowing smoke that rises seemingly a mile high. The horror does not end, as all the dwarves now watch as Symbollia, Myrenthia, and Dugunstor—the mountain they are on—now follow the same explosive path. The Dagi work fast, teleporting all the dwarves to the Sand Marshes of Smyle. They get everyone out just in time as Dugunstor explodes, losing the top half of the mountain, and the Dagi Bluffs are gone forever. The less than three hundred Glaborian dwarves now watch as dozens of mountains are billowing toxic smoke into the air. The dwarves do not know what to say. They just stand and watch as one mountain after another falls and becomes a billowing tower of toxic smoke.

All the dwarves, including Glimtron, Logantrance, and Oriapow, have made their way to the Sephla Theater. This is the large amphitheater carved out of the earth by the elves halfway between the courtyard and the Great Erken. Ulegwahn has called another meeting of all the elves. He starts out by saying how saddened he is by the loss of life to the elves and the dwarves who have come to help the elves in defense of their home. "It has been three days now, and the third dragon feast is at an end. The Erkensharie has been spared for the most part this time, but there has still been great loss of life because of Vemenomous and the dragons like Dribrillianth and Gairdennow, who ravished the Erkensharie just before the dragon feast. There is still work that needs to be done in rebuilding the main gate that was destroyed by Vemenomous. Not only that but we should be vigilant to any further attack from the minions of the Ilkergire or a possible dragon attack."

Ulegwahn calls Oriapow to the stage with him and makes an announcement to the audience. "I want to share with you all that this Vemenomous is so powerful"—no one here knows that Vemenomous has been killed—"and that he stole the Octagemerwell while all of us were here. Still, our champion Oriapow chased him down and got the Octagemerwell back for us." The crowd of elves cheers and claps.

Oriapow smiles and waves, saying, "It was with the help of Vegenrage that I was able to retrieve the precious jewel. We must still be vigilant because evil will most likely come for the jewel again, and we have to be on guard. Vemenomous is so powerful that no one should attempt to confront him. If Vemenomous comes for the jewel, he is so powerful that he will kill anyone in his way. I will defend the Octagemerwell with my life, and anyone who decides to defend the jewel with me against Vemenomous will do so at the risk of their life." There are still plenty of elves who openly volunteer to defend the Octagemerwell with Oriapow.

Shastenbree yells out, "What of Vegenrage and Farrah? Does anyone know what has become of them or where they are?"

"Yeah, we have to go to Vollenbeln to see what has happened to Vegenrage!" shout out some of the dwarves.

Other dwarves shout out, "Farrah too!"

"Everybody, everybody." Logantrance commands attention, waving his arms in the air. "I can tell you this: Vegenrage and Farrah are still alive. I know they are. I can still feel Farrah's presence. If either had perished, I would have known, but you are right. We should go and see what has happened to the two of them. Vegenrage has grown very powerful, and his realm has been blocked from all travel and all telekinetic thought. It takes very powerful magic to make this happen. I feel he will show himself when he has had some greatly needed rest," says Logantrance.

Whenshade and some of the others who have been in Vollenbeln and witnessed the demons and those who have lost their lives there look at Logantrance with curious eyes. Logantrance just glances back and nods so not to alarm any of those who are not fully aware that Zevoncour has risen to the outer realms with other demons.

Logantrance notices Trybill, Grenlew, and Blythgrin moving to the side of the theater. Glimtron and the surviving dwarves follow them. Logantrance and Oriapow, along with the other magic users, start to feel a great magical surge flowing through them. This is not a good surge, and those gifted in magic know a great loss has just happened. The Dagi know instantly that the Dagi Bluffs have been lost, and quickly everyone notices the great concern shown by the dwarves. Logantrance approaches Blythgrin, saying, "Blythgrin, what is it? What has happened?"

Blythgrin responds, "Logantrance, the bluffs, they are gone. That is not all. Glaboria, it . . . it . . . it's gone."

"What do you mean it is gone?" asks Logantrance.

Blythgrin looks up to Logantrance, saying, "Our people and our mountains, they are gone."

Glimtron and the other dwarves huddle around, asking, "What do you mean it's gone? It can't be gone. What about all our kin?" asks Glimtron.

Blythgrin pulls the Sapphirewell from his bag of holding, which has been teleported to him by Vegenrage. He looks to

Trybill and Grenlew, and they all concur. "The remaining Dagi are still alive, but as far as the Glaborian dwarves are concerned, the sense is that most of them have lost their lives," says Blythgrin.

Logantrance looks to Glimtron and then to Oriapow, who is up near Ulegwahn at the front of the amphitheater. Oriapow and Logantrance are starting to get the sensation that warns them of great evil. They can sense the demonology at work here. Oriapow whispers to Ulegwahn, who replies, "Oriapow, I have seen the images in my head. The Octagemerwell informs me. It gives me knowledge, and I am aware now that demons have ascended to the outer realm, our realm." Then he calls Logantrance and the dwarves of Glaboria to the front. They all approach and stand in front of all the Erkensharie elves.

Ulegwahn speaks. "Everyone, I cannot believe this. First, Cloakenstrike breaks into the Great Erken and kills our king. Then the third dragon feast brings dragons, the minions of the Ilkergire, and this Vemenomous to our gat. And now to my understanding, for the first time ever on Fargloin, demons have made their way to the surface. It would appear that great demonology has raised the molten hell of our planet and consumed the Glaborian mountain range." Ulegwahn looks to Glimtron and reaches out in a gesture of friendship. "Our friends, the Glaborian dwarves have come to aid us in the protection of our homeland. I grant permission to anyone who wishes to help the dwarves in any way they need." Ulegwahn looks to Glimtron again, saying, "Glimtron, you have my services in any way you need."

Glimtron looks to Ulegwahn with great thanks in his eyes. He looks to Oriapow, Logantrance, and the crowd of elves in the amphitheater, unsure of what to say. He has not grasped completely what has happened and will not until he sees what has happened to his homeland. The same is true for everyone here except for the magic users, who sense the great loss of life and heritage, which is gone forever. "It was an honor to serve and fight with the elves of the Erkensharie, but it is time we go home now and see what has happened," says Glimtron.

Blythgrin and the Dagi consult each other, and Blythgrin addresses Glimtron, saying, "Glimtron, there is nothing we can do there. What is done is done. The mountains are gone."

This enrages Glimtron, and he says sternly with the sense of fear that a lot of his kin have died and that he may never see them again. "Then we must get to our home now immediately. There has to be something we can do to help our kin. They cannot all be gone. They just can't be all gone," says Glimtron.

Blythgrin replies, "Glimtron, remember the Dark Bush has overgrown a lot of the Long Forest. We cannot pass without very strong magic. We said we would help the elves find the Changenoir responsible for this scourge and destroy him so the Long Forest could heal. We know this Changenoir lives in the Changenoir Vanuary. What are we to do, Glimtron? Do we find the Changenoir and reverse the Dark Bush, or do we dare try to pass the Dark Bush to go back to a home that is not there anymore?"

Glimtron looks around, agonizing in confusion. The strong sense of honor and fighting for a friend weighs heavy on his left side, and the fear of losing his homeland, which is already gone, is weighing on his right side. Glimtron looks to Logantrance, Oriapow, Ulegwahn, and his dwarven friends with the utmost confusion. No one has ever seen Glimtron like this. For the first time, Glimtron feels overwhelming fear and is consumed by the unknown. Tears fill his eyes, and he says, "I don't know! I don't know what to do! I have lost all of my people! I don't know what to do!" All of Glimtron's family members are there, and this has been a very trying time for everyone. All have been stressed, and most everyone here, elves and dwarves alike, have lost loved ones. The elves have a lot of rebuilding to do at the front gate, and they will have to search and find the Changenoir responsible for spreading the Dark Bush in the Long Forest.

Glimtron regains his stern personality after long talks and a good meal with friends. "I am sorry for my small breakdown," says Glimtron, and he continues to talk with everyone's attention. "I have come to a decision. I will return home. Even if our home has been destroyed, I must go and see what has happened. I have to go see if there is anyone needing my help. Logantrance, Oriapow, I ask for your assistance. Will you help us to our home? I have to see firsthand what has happened in Glaboria. I will go with my brothers here. We must go and see firsthand what has happened."

All the dwarves nod in agreement. Ulegwahn, Oriapow, and Logantrance all understand. Logantrance says he will take Glimtron through a dimension door. The Dagi will bring the rest of the dwarven party. Oriapow cannot leave the Great Erken, but Whenshade says he will help with the travel to the Glaborian Mountains. Crayeulle, Shastenbree,

Thambrable, and Cellertrill all wish to travel with the dwarves and lend any assistance that may be needed. The party does a lot of figuring and works out the details so the magic users are able to take through the dimension door everyone to the Sand Marshes of Smyle. The dwarves say their goodbyes, and everyone watches as the party of dwarves, Logantrance, and those elves helping leave by magical means.

The elves of the Erkensharie begin the work of rebuilding the main gate in the courtyard, which has been destroyed by Vemenomous. King Ulegwahn heads back to the Great Erken with Oriapow and the surviving leaders to discuss how to move forward and deal with Interford (the Changenoir), the suspected culprit in spreading the Dark Bush throughout the Long Forest.

CHAPTER 5

Basters's Secret

King Basters is sitting in his throne room. He is all alone and just thinking to himself. He looks around, feeling the gold in the chair he is sitting on. He picks the solid gold scepter that rests along the right side of the chair and looks at this one piece of gold masterfully carved by Ugorian master crafts elves and imbued by the magic of Shenlylith. Through this scepter, Basters can focus great magical power. He can direct lightning bolts. He can shrink specific objects, or he can shoot laser fire. The things he can do with this scepter (the king's scepter) are limitless. He sits on his throne, pulls the snow gold trinket from his chest with his left hand, and rests it on his palm, just looking at it. He stands up and heads out of his throne room. He walks through the palace to the courtyard and calls for everyone to hear. "Elves of Ugoria, my first magical act will be to bring back those who have been banished." Basters raises the king's scepter in his right hand and holds the snow gold trinket high in his left hand. "I call upon Shenlylith. I call for Shenlylith because we need her to correct a wrong that has been done."

The elves start to peek from over the walls. They come from around the sides of the palace and from the woods. They all listen and watch to what Basters is doing.

Basters calls out, "Shenlylith, I call for you to appear and correct a wrong."

Shenlylith grows very large from the snow gold trinket in Basters's left hand for everyone to see. Shenlylith looks to her king and says, "My king calls for me. What is it my king would ask of me?"

"Shenlylith, the bow elves of Ugoria launched arrows at me in defense of their kingdom and were banished to Shenlylith's Prison as a result. I ask as king of Ugoria and the protected of Shenlylith herself. I ask that the magic of Shenlylith return the bow elves of Ugoria to their homes. Return the elves to their homes and families," says king Basters.

Shenlylith replies, "It shall be done."

Shenlylith raises her enormous fluffy snow-white wings and turns them, facing a large space in the courtyard. She brings her wings together, curling them in a ball on the ground, and opens her wings, exposing all that have been sent into the Krasbeil Mountains, otherwise known as Shenlylith's Prison. Shenlylith shrinks back down into the snow gold trinket, and Basters puts it back around his neck.

The elves look around very happily, surprised to be back in Ugoria and even more surprised to see that the Ugorian Palace has been rebuilt and that Basters is now the king of Ugoria. Friends and family rush to the rescued elves, and Basters is making a lot of new friends with the elves.

Basters calls for Verlyle. "Verlyle, where are you?"

Verlyle shows himself and bows to one knee as a show of respect to the new king. "My king calls for me."

"Verlyle, please stand and take me to Willithcar. We have some healing to do."

"What kind of healing do you mean, my king?" asks Verlyle.

"Take me to Willithcar, and you will see," says Basters.

"OK, follow me," says Verlyle, and he turns and heads into the palace.

Basters follows, and they end up in a room where Willithcar is being tended to by a very attractive elven woman, who is bandaging his arms. Willithcar is sitting with his arms facing up, and both arms have been cut off just below the elbow by the Lavumptom sword, which is still at his side, of the then-Bastrenboar.

Willithcar gets noticeably excited, and Basters steps back, raising his arms in the air, saying, "It is OK, Willithcar. I am here to heal your arms for you. Just give me one moment."

Basters holds up his king's scepter and recites some magical words. Right before the eyes of Verlyle, Willithcar, and Abraveln (the nurse helping Willithcar), his arms start to grow and reform to their natural state. This is very powerful magic, and Basters uses a lot of his energy to make this happen. This news spreads quickly and becomes well-known by all, and Basters is gaining a lot of respect with the elves.

Basters has to go to his chambers and rest because the healing has used all of his energy. Basters's personal chambers are very luxurious. His room is very large, and he has a large bed with a beautiful canopy covering it. The wood is finished in dark brown and has great carving all throughout it. The beam to the left of the front headboard that goes up has a cylinder attached to it, and Basters's king's scepter fits perfectly in here. He has a very large dresser, with a very large mirror on top, but very few clothes to put in it. This is definitely a king's bedroom with a bath off to the side. Basters goes to bed, and he never takes the snow gold trinket off his person. This is protection for him all the time, even when he sleeps, and Basters will easily sleep the night through.

Basters wakes before the sun rises and gets out of bed. He has slept very well and feels great. He gets up, walks to the dresser, and looks in the mirror. He looks around his new room and finds a brown leather hide that is lying over the back of a chair next to his dresser. He has requested this hide a few days ago, and it is ready for his use now. He puts on his favorite black leather pants and uses his magic to craft the leather hide into a well-fitting vest. It stitches in Xs right up the front and leaves his arms bare. It is a semi-shiny dark brown leather clothing, and it looks good with his leather pants. He also makes two armbands that fit nicely around his arms from his wrists to his elbows. Basters gets his bag of holding, which he has hung from the side of his mirror on his dresser the night before, and puts his scepter in it.

Just as Cloakenstrike has told Basters long ago, the snow gold trinket will increase his magic significantly, and powerful magic is now at the fingertips of Basters. The addition of Delvor, the bag of holding he got from King Trialani, comes complete with a trove, a valuable item, and a wealth of magical knowledge that Basters now controls. Basters is a force to be respected. He still has his Lavumptom sword and a whole arsenal of magical power at his disposal now.

The very interesting thing here is how the snow gold trinket, powered by Shenlylith, works. Once a king has taken the throne by means of force, which has been the way in Ugoria since Shenlylith has been entombed in the snow gold trinket, that king then inherits the snow gold trinket, and the magical entity of Shenlylith works to soften, calm, and relax the new king. She imbues the new king with tenderness and serenity but do not let that fool any would-be adversary to the kingship. The defense of the king's life and the kingdom of Ugoria and its elven kind is met with abrupt and decisive authority.

Basters goes to the main eating hall, where there are already a lot of elves eating breakfast. Basters has done well to not make any enemies and befriending those he has spoken with so far. He still does not have any elves who report to him directly. He has given the elves free rein to live as they will, and when matters arise that involve the defense or the use of great wealth, then Basters will have to be informed, and he will give his opinion in full discussion with those elves present. Basters will have the final decision, but no major decisions or conflicts have come about yet. Basters sits alone and eats alone. The elves find him more down-to-earth than they have expected, and so far, he has represented himself very capable and able for a human.

Basters finishes his breakfast and announces to those in the dining hall that he will be leaving Ugoria for the morning and will be returning this afternoon. The elves pay him very little attention, but Basters has made his absence known and heads back to his quarters. Once there, he puts the snow gold trinket in his bag of holding, and he walks through a dimension door.

He walks into his old home, where he was king of the humanors. He waves his hands, and the fireplace roars with a flames and settles to a nice burning fire. Basters looks around, feeling like it was so long ago that he has ruled here. In fact, it has only been less than a year since most of the humanors have been wiped clean from Hunoria by the elves. The area has been leveled, and all the structures have been burned. The only remaining structure is Basters's (or Bastrenboar's) home. This has been well camouflaged by Bastrenboar's magic with the help of Cloakenstrike, so the elves never know it is there. His home is actually underground, and very few ever make entry here. Bastrenboar and Cloakenstrike are the only two to ever come here, and it is by magical means.

Basters walks down past the fireplace and up the rise to his solid black coral chair, and he sits in it. He smiles, remembering how much he enjoyed this place. The humanors have always done whatever he wants, and he has studied and learned so much magic here. There are books lining the walls, and some very good ones teach and instruct on the use of magic, but they are still elementary compared to what Logantrance, Cloakenstrike, and Vegenrage have or had in their libraries.

Basters reaches his fingers on both hands under the armrest on each side of his chair and pushes a button on each simultaneously. To his right, on the wall is a panel that slides to the right, exposing a single shelf, and on it rests a book. This book is very valuable, and Basters smiles as he gets up, walks to the book, and puts his right hand on it. This is no small book; it is five feet tall by four feet wide, and the shelf is deep enough in the wall to easily accommodate its size. Basters smiles, saying out loud to himself, "Now I can make this book more manageable, and finally I can read it."

Basters closes his eyes, concentrating and chanting, "Ohh div iinn nnaatt hhhhaaatttion smallen shre bilder recleem warii delo colate griften." The book starts to shrink down to a size that is much more manageable for a man to read. The book is fairly thin, but it grows thicker as Basters picks it from the shelf. He turns around and puts it on the podium behind him. He reads the cover out loud, which is written in dragon language: *Divination: Demon, Dragon, Elf, or Man.* Basters flips to the first page, excited like a child opening a present on Christmas. He cannot wait to read and see what secrets await him in this very secretive book.

Before he reads even one word, the fire in the center of his room blazes very high and settles like a rush of wind has hit it. Basters slams the book shut, saying, "Show yourself, Cloakenstrike. I know you are here."

Cloakenstrike walks in from the air like a watery silhouette until he is visible on the opposite side of the room, which Basters is on. "I knew you had the book. The whole time, I knew you had it. All those years I spent looking for the book *Divination*, and you had it all the time. So clever of you, Basters," says Cloakenstrike.

"Yes, I had it the whole time," says Basters.

"I did not give you nearly enough credit. I had no idea your knowledge was so well hidden. I have to ask though. How did you even know about the book in the first place, and how did you find it and keep it hidden from me all this time?" asks Cloakenstrike.

"I had told you the story of Somgla, or at least some of it, after you had saved me and my army from Arglon, well, after you had prevented us from becoming pigs and we became the humanor. Anyway, you would be surprised to know even elves will tell all if they think it will save their lives. I never told anyone this, but Somgla and I were lovers. I thought we were in love. I was half-right. I was in love, but Somgla was not an innocent woman at all. She had many affairs with human men for hundreds of years before she even met me. After we had been lovers for a long time, I caught her seducing an officer in my army, and I confronted her. We began to argue and shout at each other. She had broken my heart, and I was mad as hell. I pushed her and pushed her until she spilled her guts, telling me how I was just another in a long line of human men who, Somgla said, were easy to seduce and even easier to persuade. She used her beauty to seduce men and bounced from one man to another. She said human men were so much more fun than elven men because human men would try so hard to please her, and she loved many different human men in her life. I could not bear to hear this. I raped her in rage, and afterward, many of my men heard us arguing, fighting. And before I knew what was happening, I threw her to my men, allowing them to have their way with her.

"Somgla begged me to let her go, but I was in a rage, and she told me she would tell me the greatest secret if I would just let her go. She produced the book *The Ugorian Stand*, which I could not read because it was written in dragon language. She told me this book was written by the great dragon Hornspire himself, and if I would not harm her anymore, she would tell me where she had another book, which would be the most powerful book ever read. She told me this book called *Divination: Demon, Dragon, Elf, or Man* would explain the future to the person who read it first. I have to say Somgla had a way about her beauty that was so captivating. She was so seductive, so sexy, so beautiful, but I was going to get even with her for breaking my heart. I told her I would not harm her anymore, and I did not lie. After she told me where the book was, I let my men have her, and I left. I kept my word. I did not harm her anymore, but I swear I did not think my men would kill her. She was so defensive. She fought so hard and ended up hurting a lot of my men, and in turn, they beat her back. And ultimately, before I got back, she had died. I had three men executed the next day, and right after that, the next thing we all know we were changing into pigs. That is when you stepped in and prevented myself and my entire army from becoming pigs.

"Somgla had told me how Arglon was in love with her, but she told me her heart belonged to me. I begged Arglon to spare my men and take out his vengeance on me, but he would not listen and began changing all two thousand of us. I know Trialani was there somewhere, but I never saw him. For all I know, Somgla was playing us all just to get her simple pleasures. I never thought to ask you how you came to be there at that particular moment when Arglon had cast his spell on us and left us all to become pigs. Then when you were reading *The Ugorian Stand* to Fraborn and me, it hit me when you read the passage referring to the changing of the Lycoreal army from warrior to pig. I remember you telling me a long time ago that you had read parts of another book. I think you said it was called *The Rising of Vemenomous*, and in this book was written where and when my army and I were being transformed. I knew that is how you knew the exact time and place to save us. I never questioned why. I only sought your knowledge and leadership, and you never let me down.

"It was two hundred years before I even went to look for the book that Somgla had told me about, and sure enough, it was buried right where she said it would be. I still could not read it, so I hid it here in my Hunorian throne room. I wanted to see if I ever would gain the snow gold trinket and its magical power and knowledge, which you had always told me about, and now we are here. And yes, I can finally read dragon language. I can even speak dragon tongue," says Bastes.

Cloakenstrike interrupts, "Wow, I must say, I had no idea. I am very surprised I never felt the book here. I am even more surprised about Somgla. I mean, it was well-known that Somgla was a free spirit and that she was not shy at all about having many relationships. In fact, her father, King Jardilith, went to battle many times for his daughter. Jardilith loved Somgla very much, and he backed her all the way. Jardilith told everyone that his daughter was a philanderer. She was not someone to be held to one relationship, and Jardilith understood this about his daughter. It was Trialani who ultimately disgraced Jardilith and challenged him to battle, where Trialani actually killed him. Trialani disgraced Jardilith so badly that Jardilith accepted the challenge and put the snow gold trinket aside for the winner to hold. Trialani was victorious, and this was only months before Somgla had been killed herself. I have known you for eight hundred years and never knew you had an affair with Somgla. You see, you never really know someone, do you?"

"So where do we go from here? I have always found a great sense of pride and security in our relationship. I must say, I was quite surprised when you accepted to take the lead of the magical order in Ugoria. You always have been a traveler, a loner. I always loved the way you sought out adventure and power. The one thing I never knew about you is your end game. I mean, what is it that you want out of life? I would not be surprised if this book here is next on your list of treasures," says Basters.

"Yes, you are right, Basters. I have searched hundreds of years for this book and all the books written by Hornspire. I am really amazed you have it, and I must say, I was always drawn to your strict nature. No matter what, every time I came to see you, you were practicing, you were studying, you were always doing what I had asked you to do. I never saw this in anyone ever. Not only did I see this in you but I also saw it in the entire race of humanor. As you grew in number, your whole race was so focused that you were all in such great sync with one another. I have to admit. I thought you were going to become someday the dominant race, dominant over all except the dragons. I thought the humanors were going to be greater than the dwarves, humans, and elves, but it was not to be. I must admit to you I did not read all of *The Ugorian Stand* to you and Fraborn. There were parts that I left out, but now we are here, and we have to decide how we are going to proceed from this point on," says Cloakenstrike.

"What parts of *The Ugorian Stand* did you leave out?" asks Basters.

"Well, the book says that Hornspire did track down Somgla not to hurt her but to give her two books. The first book was *The Ugorian Stand*, which will find its way to the king of Ugoria. I intervened, and you gave the book to me, so it never made it to him. However, now you are the king of Ugoria, and you know much of the book. So in part, it did make its way to you, the king of Ugoria. *The Ugorian Stand* also says that the king of Ugoria will lead the great magic user to the book *Divination*. I never understood this part of the book until now. I guess you were always meant to bring me to the book, and here we are. I tell you what, Basters. I have always liked you, and I do not want to war with you. I would much rather we continue our prosperous and cooperative friendship. I have always told you that your magic would grow tenfold with the snow gold trinket in your possession. You say you can read dragon tongue now, so why don't you read *Divination: Demon, Dragon, Elf, or Man* and let me listen? After all, we have been allies for eight hundred years now, and it has worked well for both of us," says Cloakenstrike.

"You have no need to think of me as anything less than a friend. I have always admired your independence and your lack of fear of the unknown. I still think of you as my teacher and always will. I just want to read this book for myself. Are you ready to listen to what it has to offer?" asks Basters.

"Yes, I am very curious to what is in the book. Please read it out loud," says Cloakenstrike, who stays to the other side of the room while Basters reads the book aloud. Basters reads a lot that has already come to pass—a lot about the dragons and their losses to Vemenomous, the loss of the last of the humanor in the cave to Hornspire, the death of Trialani, and the human with pig blood to become king of Ugoria and return to human form. This part really grips Basters and Cloakenstrike:

The leader of the Lycoreal army was almost turned to pig, along with his army, but they were saved midtransformation by a powerful magic user. The leader with pig blood beheaded me [Hornspire] with a magnificent sword, but I was reborn, thanks to my wings of rebirth. I was to be killed again by the magic user, who traveled with the half-man-half-pig, and this used the last of my wings of rebirth. I knew it was soon after this that an event I could not defend against was going to happen. The bright light was to be my end. There was no way for me to defend against my third death, so I had to plan a way to be reborn yet again, and there was no better way to be brought back from the dead than by those who had killed me twice—Cloakenstrike and Bastrenboar, who is now Basters.

These two are now in the throne room of Bastrenboar. The once-thriving humanor are now almost extinct. They do not know yet, but the demon uprising has begun. The planet of Fargloin is the first targeted by the demons. Already, the Glaborian dwarves have mostly been eliminated, and their mountains now serve as a melting pot spewing hundreds of millions of tons of molten ash into the air, slowly blocking out all the sunlight, killing the world of Fargloin. The end of the third dragon feast is here, and it has nearly made humanor, dwarf, and dragon extinct, making the rise of demons and the demonian dragon inevitable. The demons will target Strabalster next, and their location is the Krasbeil Mountains. The demons will try to rise molten lava into the mountains and erupt them just like on Fargloin, but Basters, now king of Ugoria and the holder of the snow gold trinket, will attack the demons. And when the demons attack back, Shenlylith will appear and send the demons from under the mountains to the top of the mountains, where they may never escape.

Basters pauses from reading and looks up to Cloakenstrike, saying, "I can't believe how accurate this is, all except the part about you and me bringing Hornspire back from the dead. I mean, this is a dragon who is dead, and he wrote this book when? I can't believe I am reading this. Is this how you felt when you read *The Ugorian Stand* for the first time?" .

"Yeah, pretty much," says Cloakenstrike. "Read on, Basters, read on."

Basters continues to read from the book, and it ends midway through. The second half of the book is bare pages with no writing on them. "Well, that is all it says. The only thing that has not happened, at least not yet, is the part about the demons attacking the Krasbeil Mountains. What do you suppose Hornspire meant that you and I will help him come back from the dead? We took care of his remains, remember? How can he come back from the dead?" asks Basters.

"I do not know. That is a very good question, but remember, the last time we saw Hornspire, he wanted your head," says Cloakenstrike.

"Oh yeah, I remember. It was you who got Fraborn and myself out of there just in the nick of time, but it was that other being who scared the crap out of us all, remember? That thing Vemenomous, who flew from the sky in blinding light and attacked Hornspire. Anyway, Fraborn, he is alone in Ugoria. We had better get back, but I am concerned. Hornspire wrote you and I will bring him back from the dead, but how? Well, my old friend, we have fought elves, and now we rule them. We have fought dragons, we have survived Shenlylith's Prison, we have fought Clawbominals and Charumpaboons, and still we live. We have even faced down Vemenomous. How bad can some demons be?" says Basters.

"I am sure we will find out, old friend. I am sure we will find out," says Cloakenstrike.

"Come on, let us go back to Ugoria. I get the feeling something will happen soon," says Basters. He puts the book in his bag of holding, and he walks through a dimension door. Cloakenstrike walks through a dimension door of his own, and they both arrive back in Ugoria.

The first thing Basters does when he gets back is get the snow gold trinket from his bag of holding and place it around his neck. Cloakenstrike says to Basters, "You know, Basters, I have to be honest with you. There are very good magic-using elves here, but I am not too interested in being their magical master. I was curious to see what kind of magic was going on here, and it is very good, but I am more of a free spirit. If you want to keep the book *Divination*, then you keep it, but I must be going soon. Basters, you have been my loyal student for eight hundred years, and I have seen you hold the snow gold trinket and become the human being you were before I ever knew you. There is little I can teach you now. You have to learn on your own now, and there are very few who can rival you magically. I consider you and Fraborn to be my only friends, and if you should every need of me, you will know how to reach me. Should demons ever threaten your borders, I will be here, and we will thwart them like all adversaries we have encountered in the past. I must be going, old friend, but I will never be far."

Basters has been waiting for this. He knows Cloakenstrike very well, and he is not at all surprised to hear him say this and go. Basters simply says, "Farewell, old friend. Until we meet again." Cloakenstrike walks through a dimension door, and he is gone. Basters walks around the palace and is pleasantly greeted by the elves and makes small talk with them. It is a good feeling for Basters knowing that he has been accepted, and it pleases him to see and witness how comfortable the Ugorian society is to him.

He walks until he finds Fraborn on a practice field with a regiment of warrior elves, and they are practicing their skills and swordplay in formation. The entire regiment, including Fraborn, bows to one knee in respect to the arrival of Basters. Basters addresses them, and they all stand at attention. "You are a fine-looking regiment. You are formidable, and if ever tested, you will make all of Ugoria proud. Continue your training," says Basters, and he turns to walk away.

"My king Basters," calls Fraborn.

"Yes, Fraborn," says Basters.

"Basters, the night jewel on your Lavumptom sword, I have never seen it white before," says Fraborn. Basters looks to his sword and the night jewel, which sets on the bottom of the handle of his sword, which when sheathed like now is facing up. Just as Fraborn has said, it is pure white like the glow of a well-lit moon on a very dark night.

Basters looks up, very concerned, saying, "Fraborn, gather all the warriors and call all bow elves and horse riders to the palace. We may very well be needing all our defenses." He turns and walks through a dimension door.

CHAPTER 6

Swallgrace, Ledgehorn, and Morlinvow

Going back in time over a millennium, Logantrance sits up in his bed. He is fast asleep, and a strong magical calling wakes him from his sleep. He rubs his eyes, and again, a calling enters his mind. He recognizes the call of his teacher, Swallgrace. It has been just a few short months ago that Logantrance is called to the planet Kronton, where he has witnessed Swallgrace battling Cloakenstrike. This is the first time Logantrance has ever seen Cloakenstrike, and it has taken them both to defeat and drive away this new and powerful adversary. Logantrance and Swallgrace stay with Ledgehorn for a week after this encounter, mostly to help ease the tension all the people of Breezzele are under. Cloakenstrike has killed over a dozen people, and it is all just to steal the book *The Beasts of Kronton*, which he does not get.

This is still a few hundred years before the second dragon feast, but there are rumors going around, and all the strongest and wisest magic users are hearing about books that tell about the future. Rumor has it that the elves have these books, making them very hard to acquire if you are human.

Cloakenstrike has heard these rumors, and he is seeking out all the most powerful of magical books that he can find. He has tried to steal *The Beasts of Kronton*, written by Ledgehorn, and failed. Now he is after the book *Tougher Skin*, written by Morlinvow.

Morlinvow is considered one of the wisest and most knowledgeable human magic users on all of Kronton, along with Ledgehorn. Ledgehorn lives in Breezzele on the eastern edge of the Elbutan Forest, and this is hundreds of miles southwest of the Quiltneck Wild Lands, where Morlinvow lives. The humans on the planet Kronton are starting to come into their own now, and magic users are on the rise. Morlinvow is the leading magic user for the Kawarum Kingdom, and his apprentice Inglelapse is a good-spirited young fellow with a great personality. Morlinvow has heard what happened in Breezzele a few months ago, and he has even been by to see Ledgehorn, and they talked about the attack made by Cloakenstrike. Ledgehorn has warned Morlinvow of this new adversary and that Cloakenstrike might attack in Kawarum.

The book *Tougher Skin* has become very popular, and the great magic users have come by to learn from Morlinvow. Sure enough, a few months after the attack in Breezzele, Cloakenstrike makes an attack in Kawarum. He is after the book *Tougher Skin*, and Morlinvow is waiting for him. Cloakenstrike is still a very young magic user at this time, but his magic is growing at an exceptional rate, and he makes the mistake of scouting the Kawarum Kingdom for too long.

The Kawarum people have lots of wooden houses built in the southern region of the Quiltneck Wild Lands. This is still a very wild region with a lot of very dangerous predators, but the people here have built very sturdy homes, and they are very close to one another. The humans here are just now beginning to expand their population, and they number almost one thousand. They have a small army with regiments of archers, horse riders, and swordsmen. Of course, Morlinvow has fairly powerful magic, and he is training four apprentices, and Inglelapse is his favorite. The woods here in the Quiltneck Wild Lands are fairly thick, but where the Kawarum Kingdom is, the woods have been cleared out by the people and built upon.

The king and his family live in the largest home, which is in the center of all the other homes, which have been built in a circle growing outward from the king's home. There are nearly four hundred homes now, and they span out for tens of miles away from the king's home. This gives the most protection from the predators of the woods to the king and his family. The homes farthest out obviously have the least protection, and there are families and people who still fall prey to the large land predators that still exist in Quiltneck Wild Lands during this time.

Morlinvow has a most unique homestead. It is almost like a barn. It is a very large home with a high roof, two floors, and a cellar. The cellar is where Morlinvow keeps all his most valuable artifacts, books, and magical items, and the first floor is where he teaches his apprentices and meditates. The second floor is where he lives.

It is late at night, and everyone is home sleeping. Morlinvow is in his home, meditating, and Cloakenstrike is wandering around Kawarum using his concealing magic and looking for the home of Morlinvow. It just so happens that Morlinvow picks up on the presence of Cloakenstrike, and the first thing he does is send telepathy to Ledgehorn and Swallgrace. Ledgehorn is already very old, and so is Morlinvow. These two magic users are very powerful in knowledge and applicable magic, but they do not have youth with them anymore.

Cloakenstrike has learned after his encounter with Ledgehorn that he has to be swift and decisive, and this time he is. When Morlinvow sends telepathy, Cloakenstrike picks up on this magical energy and teleports right to the source. Morlinvow is very surprised to see Cloakenstrike appear right in his home, and he rings a magical bell that calls all his apprentices to his home, and only the apprentices can hear this. Inglelapse is first to get there, but he is already too late. He enters the home of Morlinvow to see he has been killed. Inglelapse rushes to Morlinvow and starts to cast the best healing magic he can, but it is not working. The other apprentices show up and help Inglelapse, but Cloakenstrike has taken no chances this time. Not only has he killed Morlinvow but he also has cast heal block on the body of Morlinvow, which means no healing magic will work on him. The apprentices are all working on Morlinvow when Cloakenstrike comes up from the cellar, and he has the book *Tougher Skin* in his hands.

"Hey, who are you, and why do you have that book? You killed our teacher," yells Inglelapse, and he charges Cloakenstrike. Cloakenstrike waves his hand at Inglelapse, and he flies across the room. Bristan, one of the apprentices, shoots a lightning bolt at Cloakenstrike, and it reflects back at him, killing him instantly.

Cloakenstrike laughs. "Come on, would either one of you two like to take a shot at me?" he says, walking at the two apprentices who are still trying to help Morlinvow. Trymegil and Grothen say nothing and watch as Cloakenstrike raises his hands, and he still has the book in his left hand.

Cloakenstrike is about to cast a spell on them when Inglelapse throws a magical punch, hitting him in the side of the head, knocking him over. "Take that," yells Inglelapse. He actually punched Cloakenstrike, but there was a magical little barrier like a shield over his arm and hand. Cloakenstrike gets up quickly and thrusts both hands and arms in the direction of Inglelapse, who is thrown right through the wall into the woods outside.

Cloakenstrike turns just as Trymegil comes across his face with a right hook, knocking him to the ground. Cloakenstrike stands up quickly and clinches his left hand in front of Trymegil, which puts a magical stranglehold on him and raises him off the ground. "That is the second time I have been punched in a very short time. I will have to get better defenses to take care of this," says Cloakenstrike as he twists his left hand to the right, snapping Trymegil's head to the left, breaking his neck. Cloakenstrike motions his left hand and arm toward the hole in the wall where Inglelapse has flown, and Trymegil's body flies through it.

Cloakenstrike looks at Grothen, who has just cast fire on him. Cloakenstrike's cloak of reflection works in this case, reflecting the fire back on Grothen, who goes up in a blaze. Cloakenstrike kicks the air in front of him, and Grothen flies through the wall, still on fire.

Cloakenstrike turns to the wall where Inglelapse has flown and looks into the dark night, walking out of Morlinvow's magical homestead, when an invisible magical rope snatches the book out of his hand and pulls the book away from him. His initial instinct is to run after the book, but very quickly, it is out of sight into the dark woods. He does take a quick step, following the book, and then he slows, looking down with a smile on his face, saying, "Inglelapse, the young apprentice. I know your name is Inglelapse because I heard the other boys calling you by your name. Of course, the other boys are dead now. I like you, Inglelapse. You seem to have a little more spirit than the other boys had. I tell you what, you give me the book, and I will let you live, or else I will hunt you. What shall it be, Inglelapse?"

Cloakenstrike has his attention drawn to the air as he hears something. He hears the unmistakable roar of a dragon and then crashing, like a bulldozer driving through houses. The crashing and the rumbling are getting closer and closer to Cloakenstrike. He is no longer paying attention to Inglelapse, who has escaped, and now the cries and screams of people are being heard through the woods. Cloakenstrike looks up in the night sky to see the silhouette of a huge dragon swooping down toward his location. The dragon's silhouette disappears in the trees, and Cloakenstrike hears a great thrashing in the not-too-far-off woods, like a tornado is sweeping through. The cries and screams of all the people stop, and there is the abrupt sound of silence.

Cloakenstrike, for some reason, stays where he is. He does not flee; he can hear the footsteps of the great dragon approaching him, but he does not run, and he does not travel dimensionally. He waits and watches as the dragon walks through the trees toward him. The dragon is twenty feet tall walking on all fours. His head is high, and he has very large horns protruding from his joints on all four legs. He has horns jutting out from his shoulders and from the base of his head, forming a very protective barrier. He has horns along his tail, and his skin looks like it is made out of grayish-colored granite.

Cloakenstrike watches as this magnificent dragon walks through the trees, pushing them to the side with his girth and great weight. The moons of Kronton shine silvery white, and Cloakenstrike can see very well as the great horned dragon towers over him and directs his breath of Groinike at the homestead of Morlinvow. The home and all its contents are destroyed, shredded to bits by the tons of granite shards that explode from the mouth of the dragon and grind the house to nothing in seconds. This is the most awesome power Cloakenstrike has ever seen. The rush of air and the energy given off by the blast of the breath attack knock Cloakenstrike over. The dragon stops his breath attack and looks at Cloakenstrike, who sits up.

"You are Cloakenstrike. You are becoming a feared and great magic user among the races of man. Not yet but soon you will be recognized as one of the best magic users and one to be feared by all. I am Hornspire, the teller of the future. I am not here to harm you. I am here to arm you. I am going to arm you with knowledge of the future. I know you were here to steal the book *Tougher Skin*, written by Morlinvow, whom you have just killed. Don't worry about that book, just like the book *The Beasts of Kronton*, which you failed to get but no matter. I have the books you want to get. You want the books that will tell you the future. Your future has power in it. Your future is to rule by means of force and strength, but there is one who will challenge you. There is one who is more powerful than you, and in order for you to defeat him, you will have to study long and hard. You will have to master the ways of magic. You will need the most powerful books ever written. It is good that you have sought these books here but not the end of the world, if you do not acquire them. I am going to give you knowledge of the future because I need you. You will see my death twice, and I will need you to bring me back from the dead a third time because I am going to tell you some things now that will come to pass, and you will desire my help when the time comes.

"There will be a man from another universe, and he will be called Vlianth in dragon tongue and Vegenrage to the races of man. A thousand years from now, you will have mastered all magic, and there will be no equal to you until the time of Vegenrage comes. You will make your one true friend on the eve of a princess's death. A leader and his army will be changing into pigs from an elven magic user, but you will save them, creating the humanors. The man will give you a book called *The Ugorian Stand*, written in dragon language. You will collect many books between now and then, but this book will remind you of this encounter. It will confirm your only friend and the new race that will follow you until they have been mostly eliminated by me. You will search for the joining book called *Divination: Demon, Dragon, Elf, or Man*, which you will find after the man whom you prevented from becoming a pig is helped back to human form by you. You will not own the second book, but you will hear its contents read to you, and you will again be reminded of the great horned dragon. The book will not be finished until my return from the dead. For now, take these items and enjoy their benefits." Hornspire extends his right wing, and the necklace of intensity, the helmet of missile deflection, and a bag of holding named Getcher fall to Cloakenstrike's feet.

"You are now a magic-using human who has just grown in presence, so be mindful of your whereabouts, and remember trust no one except the man with pig blood. Everyone else will be out to get you, but it is you who will be doing the getting," says Hornspire, looking around, and he is tall enough to look over the trees. "They are coming for you now. It is time you leave now, and remember the elven princes will draw you, and that is when the time of Cloakenstrike becomes known and feared by all. Go now, and I will be seeing you just after the third dragon feast. Go now."

Cloakenstrike does not say a word; he walks through a dimension door and is gone. Hornspire can hear that the people of Kawarum have gathered and are coming his way. Hornspire has destroyed many homes and killed a lot of people already, and they have strengthened courage, thanks to Swallgrace, Ledgehorn, and Logantrance, who have come because Morlinvow has summoned them just before he has been murdered.

The people of Kawarum have gathered archers, and they have special arrows tipped with Smithgan, which is a metal created magically by Morlinvow, that can penetrate dragon skin. Morlinvow's book, *Tougher Skin*, has all kinds of new armors and magically enhanced metals that can be made and used to penetrate different armors, as well as dragon skin. This book details the magic Morlinvow has used and his magical wording to create the most protective armor of the time. He also describes the magically enhanced metals that can be used to pierce the armors of the world today. This is a very important book and one that a warfare strategist will do most anything for. Cloakenstrike has had this book in his hands, but at the last moment, Inglelapse has snagged it from him. And now Inglelapse has returned to the people of Kawarum, who are currently almost to Hornspire, who sits at the home of Morlinvow, which has been destroyed right to the ground.

"Swallgrace," yells Inglelapse as he approaches his people, following the magic users. It is very dark and late at night, but some of the people have torches, allowing everyone to see fairly well as they walk through the woods. "Swallgrace, you can't go there. Morlinvow has been killed. So has Bristan, Trymegil, and Grothen. There is a dragon there and a magic user, one I have never seen before. The magic user tried to steal the book *Tougher Skin*. I was able to get it from him at the last moment. Here, Swallgrace, I give this book to you because Morlinvow would have wanted you to have it." Inglelapse hands the book to Swallgrace, who takes the book and puts it in Behaggen.

"Thank you, Inglelapse. I will take good care of this book. Now let us see about this magic user and dragon and find out why they have made such terrible actions on Morlinvow and the people of Kawarum," says Swallgrace.

"Swallgrace, you cannot go there. There is nothing left of Morlinvow's home. The dragon used his breath attack and destroyed everything. Morlinvow's home is gone. His library is gone. So is all of his magical items, and even Morlinvow himself has been disintegrated. Why would anyone do this? Why would a dragon show up here right after some magic user, and why would they just cause death and destruction? Is this the way of magic and its use? This is not what I was thought by Morlinvow, and this is not what he stood for. Why would anyone just kill him?" says Inglelapse, who starts to breathe harder, and tears fall from his eyes.

"There now, my boy, you are right. This is not what Morlinvow stood for, and we are going to see that justice is done. We are going to make the wrong right," says Ledgehorn.

"I don't want any part in this. This whole night is wrong, and I don't want any of it," says Inglelapse, who gives no one else a chance to say anything before he runs off and is never seen by Swallgrace or Ledgehorn ever again. Logantrance has never known Inglelapse, and this is his only encounter with him, and of course, it is very brief.

"Inglelapse, Inglelapse," yells Swallgrace, who has his attention drawn away by the people of Kawarum, who are moving in the direction of Morlinvow's home. It is dark, but the moon shines bright on this night. The people see Hornspire, who is sitting on the remains of Morlinvow's home.

Hornspire can sense the people coming toward him, and he speaks for them to hear. "Ah yes, the people of Kawarum. You have come to avenge your dearest magic user. How touching of you all. And I see you have come prepared with your little bows and arrows. Wait a minute, do I sense the presence of magic? Is that you Swallgrace and Ledgehorn, the greatest of human magic users? Well, not for long. I sense a third magic user. Now this one is someone of interest. This one will amount to some very important things in the future, but for now, you all are just ants in my little game, so are we having fun yet?" says Hornspire with a sinister grin, chuckling and laughing at the humans who are taking position in the trees around him.

"Ready, aim, release!" yells Criven, leader of the archers. Fourteen arrows fly from the trees and make painful contact, piercing Hornspire's very tough skin, which for the first time ever is penetrated by human weapons. Hornspire makes a terrific roar, sending all the animals of the nearby forest running or flying away in the night.

"What is this?" yells Hornspire as he takes a deep breath and unleashes his breath of Groinike in an arch along the tree line where the human archers are.

Swallgrace steps forth and stabs his staff into the ground, saying, "Crom don blegile antobwarben bloenkecked verflection." A greenish blue belt of magical light rises up and outward from the staff, covering the tree line where all the men are. The breath attack of Hornspire is reflected up into the air, and the granite shards fall far away into the forest.

Hornspire laughs. "Nicely done, magic user. So you do have some skill in the art of magic," says Hornspire.

"Release!" yells Criven, and another round of arrows painfully spur Hornspire into more action.

Hornspire raises his head straight with another powerful roar and looks into the tree line. "OK, you puny humans, dare tangle with a dragon. Well, let's see how you like this," says Hornspire, who starts to flap his wings very powerfully, sending enormous gusts of wind at the tree line.

Swallgrace is sent flying into the trees, and most of the men are thrown back a few yards. The wind is very strong, and the men fight it by holding on to trees and whatever they can hold that is not blown away. Hornspire is laughing like he is having the time of his life, just playing with the humans.

Ledgehorn is hiding behind a very wide tree, and he chants, "Owillith magnith umothen knatten fongondra probob seebobin iscus flygegin." Ledgehorn begins to turn into a dragon gnat.

This monstrous gnat is four feet tall with long, thin legs that are twice as long as its body with incredibly strong and hard barbs at the ends of the feet. It is very well armored and has a fortified proboscis able to penetrate the toughest of dragon skin. It has four wings on its back, allowing it great mobility when in flight. The dragon gnat takes flight around Hornspire and lands on his back right between his wings. This is the perfect location because any dragon cannot bite the gnat or swat it with his wings here. This is the location where the gnat can sink its proboscis and get a very nourishing drink of dragon blood. The gnat does have to be very weary of the dragon tail, which sometimes has a dagger or some sort of hammering device at the end, which can reach the gnat. The initial insertion of the proboscis into the dragon is very painful, but this subsides quickly because the dragon gnat releases an anesthetic around the wound of the dragon.

The gnat sinks its blood-drinking proboscis into the back of Hornspire, and he roars loudly into the sky, flapping his wings, ready to take flight. Swallgrace notices this and releases a magical lasso, catching Hornspire off guard and right around his mouth, so he cannot speak any magical spells or cast his breath attack. Swallgrace shoots the end of the lasso into the ground, pulling Hornspire to the ground by his head. Hornspire plants his feet and lifts his head with all his might, but the rope is pulling him to the ground. The archers charge from the woods and release their arrows at will, sending painful waves all throughout Hornspire's body.

Hornspire starts to rage, thrusting his head back and forth, violently realizing that he is being bested by humans. He turns his body, swinging his tail just above the ground, taking out a half dozen men and trees before Swallgrace casts a spell of force. Hornspire's tail rises and misses the rest of the men. Hornspire has his back to Swallgrace and the men now, and he drops his head to the ground and raises it as fast as he can with all his might, breaking the magical rope cast by Swallgrace. Hornspire flaps his wings and jumps into the air, taking flight.

Ledgehorn has taken a large drink of dragon blood, releases his proboscis from Hornspire, and flies back toward the men. He makes the mistake of taking his eyes off Hornspire, who turns and swoops right at him. Swallgrace yells to Ledgehorn to look out for the dragon, and Ledgehorn turns to see Hornspire at the last moment, but it is too late. Hornspire releases a dozen javelins from his right wing, which he swings at Ledgehorn, who is still in the dragon gnat form. Ledgehorn is able to dodge most of the javelins, all except one, which hits him right through the chest. He falls to the ground, changing back into his human form. Four of the men on the ground are hit by the javelins thrown by Hornspire as well, and these are all lethal hits, killing all of them.

One of the archers releases an arrow, and it strikes Hornspire right under his right wing, and a very large book falls from a harness under Hornspire's wing. Hornspire hurries for the book and focuses completely on its retrieval. Logantrance takes advantage of this, casting a lightning bolt spell, hitting Hornspire just in front of his right wing and knocking him from the sky. Hornspire falls, badly wounded. He is burned, electrocuted, and dazed, falling to the trees on the other side of Morlinvow's home. Swallgrace has run to the aid of Ledgehorn, who is dying.

Logantrance runs to the book and scoops it into Quintis, his bag of holding. Hornspire stands stumbling and regaining his composure. He sees that Logantrance has taken his book and charges at him. Arrows fly through the air, striking Hornspire in the head, and he is taking serious damage. He takes flight, yelling, "You wait, Logantrance. The next time we meet, you will not have Swallgrace, Ledgehorn, and all these archers to protect you. Your protégé will not be there to protect you either. You wait, Logantrance. Come the demon uprising, we will meet again, and my book will be returned to me. I warn you, magic user, if you so much as open my book, your doom will be sealed." Hornspire is hit with more arrows, and he seriously needs to go heal himself. He takes to the skies and flies out of sight into the night.

Logantrance runs to Swallgrace, who is working on Ledgehorn. Swallgrace is casting powerful magic on Ledgehorn, and he has become strong enough to move around, and soon he will go back to his home in Breezzele.

The archers and the people of Kawarum tend to those who have lost their lives, and the magic users help for the next two days. Inglelapse is never heard from, and no one knows where he has gone. A memorial is made and placed right on the spot where Morlinvow's home has been. All of Morlinvow's books, magical items, and precious objects have been lost on the night Cloakenstrike and Hornspire have attacked, and this is a day never to be forgotten in Kawarum.

The Kawarum people are victims of the second dragon feast, and they are hunted to extinction by the dragons. There are some survivors, but all the humans in the Quiltneck Wild Lands are displaced and moved to Breezzele, Shaspar, Noireen, Valvernva, or Mourbarria. The people who does not leave have fallen prey to a fearsome, evil new human adversary named Xanorax. After the second dragon feast, Xanorax quickly gains a name for himself, terrorizing population centers around the planet Kronton. Swallgrace and Logantrance gets Ledgehorn back to his home in Breezzele, but he is already very old, and he soon perishes.

The books that Logantrance has helped protect and keep safe with their creators have made their way to his personal library after the death of Swallgrace. The book that Logantrance has stolen from Hornspire is given to his master, Swallgrace. Logantrance has told Swallgrace what Hornspire has said when he has taken the book. Swallgrace says the dragon is just trying to prevent him from reading it.

Swallgrace reads the cover of the book, which says *The Sleeping Dragon*. Swallgrace cannot resist, and he reads the book and begins to teach Logantrance how to read the language of dragons. Swallgrace learns of the evil that was

taking over Kronton, as well as how he, Behaggen, and
Logantrance can steal the magic of the white mare and create
a world that can exist in a bottle. Logantrance cannot stop his
master from carrying out his desire to seek adventure and try
to thwart the forces of evil. It seems like only a week since the
horrible destruction in Quiltneck, and already, Swallgrace is
off to subdue the most elusive witch of all time, Alluradaloni.

CHAPTER 7

Glimtron Returns to Glaboria

Logantrance is shaken by Whenshade, and he is startled from his dream. "Logantrance, you are having a bad dream. Wake up, Logantrance," says Whenshade.

Logantrance looks up and sits up, leaning against a tree, and the warm breeze blowing from the Smildren Sea is hitting him right in the face, blowing his long grayish silver hair to his back. "What is it? How long did I sleep?" asks Logantrance.

"It is nearly midday. You were sleeping, and just recently, you started to shake and say things like the demon uprising. You must have been having a bad dream, so I woke you up," says Whenshade.

"Yes, it was a bad dream. Have Glimtron and the dwarves come back yet?" asks Logantrance.

"No, they have not come back yet. They are still in the mountains, but I don't know how or why. There is obviously no way anyone can be alive in there," says Whenshade, and they both look to the Glaborian Mountains. Every one of them, for as far as the eye can see, is billowing huge plumes of toxic ash from their tops.

"I will be with the others. If you need me, I will be right here. OK, Logantrance?" says Whenshade as he walks over to the elves who have traveled to the Sand Marshes of Smyle. The elves are sitting around a fire, waiting for the dwarves to return from the mountains.

Logantrance has been sleeping on a blanket, and he has another blanket covering him. He has a pillow between his head and the tree as he looks to the mountains, saying out loud to himself, "Don't ever underestimate dwarves. They can survive in places where no others can."

Logantrance puts his middle finger between his eyes, rubbing the bridge of his nose up and down. He cups his right-hand fingers over his right eye and rubs the side of his face up and down like he has a headache.

"The book . . . the book, what happened to the book? *The Sleeping Dragon.* What happened to the book? Hornspire, the dragon Hornspire. It was never Cloakenstrike. It was Hornspire who set up and had my teacher Swallgrace killed. It was the dragon. The dragon had set us all up from the beginning."

A long time ago, Logantrance was in his home, Richterblen, and Swallgrace had come to see him there. Ledgehorn had just died mostly from old age, and Swallgrace had come to tell Logantrance how the forces of evil were heavily outweighing the forces of good. Swallgrace was going to change this by first seeking out the seductress Alluradaloni, but if he were to fail, he had a secondary plan where Logantrance was going to have to put the white mare to sleep, thus taking her magic from her and using it to put the world of Kronton in a bottle. Logantrance could not change his master's mind no matter what he did or said, and ultimately, he went along with the plan Swallgrace had put in motion.

Logantrance is called from his memory as Whenshade calls for him. "Logantrance, Logantrance, come quick! We have found some survivors. We have found some of the Glaborian dwarves who are here in the sand marshes," yells Whenshade, getting the attention of Logantrance. Logantrance shakes his head, looking to the elves sitting around a fire.

Logantrance puts his blankets and pillow in his bag of holding and walks over to the elves.

"What? What is it you say, Whenshade? You have found some survivors?" says Logantrance.

"Yes, Crayeulle and I have found the presence of the dwarves. Come, sense for yourself," says Whenshade.

Logantrance sits next to the elves, and they all concentrate.

"Yes, yes, I can sense them, and they are not too far from us. They are heading south toward us. Let me try to reach them telepathically," says Logantrance as he concentrates. "I have them. I have contacted them." Logantrance takes a moment in silence, concentrating. "The Dagi have survived, and they have saved some of the dwarves. They are going to bring them here by way of teleportation. Make way. Stand clear. I will guide them here."

Everyone stands clear, and one of the Dagi appears from a dimension door with five of the dwarves with him.

"Logantrance, it is you. Oh, thank the heavens," says Brandelbig.

"Yes, Brandelbig, it is me, and I am with some elves from the Erkensharie," says Logantrance.

"Good, good. Wait here, the Dagi and I will bring the others," says Brandelbig. The surviving dwarves make their way to the elves and Logantrance, and it is very disturbing and sad to see that less than three hundred of the Glaborian dwarves have survived what has happened in Symbollia. Some of the dwarves are familiar with Logantrance and the elves, but most are not. Most of the surviving dwarves have never even been to the Erkensharie.

"Brandelbig, what has happened in the Glaborian Mountains? How is it that all of them seem to have erupted at the same time? I know of no magic that can make this happen," asks Logantrance.

"Logantrance, this is no magic from the outer realm. It is demons and demonology. The demons from the inner realm have made their way to the surface. I never thought this could be possible. I always thought that demons were not even real, but they are," says Brandelbig.

"Demons? Demons, you say. So it is so. The demon uprising has begun," says Logantrance out loud but to himself as he looks to the mountains.

"The demon uprising? Is this something you know about, Logantrance?" asks Brandelbig.

"It is not something that I know about but something that was said to me a long time ago, and recently, I had a dream that brought this back to my attention. I fear very bad things are coming for all of us in the Maglical System. Brandelbig, can you and the Dagi here find Glimtron and the dwarves who are with him? Some Dagi are with Glimtron as well. They cannot get into the mountains, right?" says Logantrance.

"Well, they may be able to get into the mountains, but it depends on just how much of the mountains are actually full of lava. Oh no, if Glimtron and his party make it into the mountains, the demons will surely be waiting for them, and they will be ambushed," says Brandelbig.

"Well, hurry. You must find them and get them back to us. Take all the Dagi here and see if you can find them," says Logantrance. Brandelbig wastes no time and gathers all the Dagi, and they walk through a dimension door to find their king.

Whenshade walks up to Logantrance, asking him, "Do you think they will find Glimtron and the dwarves in time?"

"Let's hope so, Whenshade. Let's hope so," says Logantrance.

Brandelbig and the Dagi have walked out of their dimension door. They are a mile from the first mountain, and this is Glaboria. The whole front of the mountain has been blown out, and lava is flowing from midway up the mountain. This is as close as the Dagi can get to the mountain. The lava is flowing like a small river down the front of the mountain and to the east right toward the Smildren Sea. All the other mountains are flowing lava rivers as well. This sight sinks the hearts of the Dagi, and they know their homes are gone.

"Come on, gather yourselves. Let us concentrate together and find our king," says Brandelbig, grasping the hands of his kin on either side of himself. All the Dagi hold hands, and they all start to concentrate, calling for their leaders. They are calling for Blythgrin, Trybill, and Grenlew.

Brandelbig opens his eyes, saying, "I can't believe it. How did they get there?"

"I don't know. More importantly, how are we going to get them out of there?" says Tomsworth.

"You guys know the demons had to have put them there. We have to get them out of there now. It has to be a trap. We have to break through the mind barrier," says Rillsons.

"Wait, all of you, wait. This is a trap, and we all know it is. Our king and his party have been captured, and the only reason the demons have not descended on them is because they are waiting for just this scenario to play out. They are waiting for us to come in and try to rescue our king," says Brandelbig.

"Well, I am not going to sit here and do nothing. I am going with guns blazing and try to rescue my king. If I fail, then I fail, but I will try," says Rillsons.

"I know, Rillsons, I know, but we must be smart. We must have at least some sort of plan. Let us at least have hope for the safe return of us all, and that means we have to fight. We have to fight demons, and none of us are familiar with demonology. None of us have studied the school of angel blessing, which is the best magic to use against demons," says Brandelbig.

"We have to hit and run, so to speak. We have to get in there and show our king the way out. Blythgrin surely has the Sapphirewell. They have to be trapped, and for some reason, their magic is useless. We need to get in there and be able to get out the way we got in," says Rillsons.

"Are you serious, Rillsons? Do you really think that we can do what Blythgrin, Trybill, and Grenlew cannot? I am going to call for Logantrance and Whenshade. You all stay alert and be watchful that the demons are not on to us already, OK?"

says Brandelbig, and he calls telepathically for Logantrance and Whenshade. His message is heard, and Logantrance and Whenshade show up with all of the Erkensharie's elves, and this is an uplifting sight for the Dagi.

"Logantrance, you all have come," says Brandelbig, who happily gives Logantrance a hug around his legs.

"Yes, Brandelbig, we have located your king as well, and this is very bad. You all know Glimtron and the dwarves with him are being used as bait. The demons allowed them into the mountain, and then once inside, the demons cut off all entrances and exits with lava flows. Blythgrin is using the Sapphirewell with the combined strength of Trybill and Grenlew to great effect, holding off the demons, but they cannot escape the lava cage they are in, nor can they use teleport or dimension magic to get out," says Logantrance, looking to the skies.

"Logantrance, what are you looking for up there? Demons come from below us," says Brandelbig, pointing to the ground.

"Yes, this is so, but we have more to be mindful of. Everyone, be watchful of the earth and the skies as well. I have a bad feeling dragons are about," says Logantrance.

"Dragons, you say. You think dragons are about? The dragon feast has just ended. The dragons will leave the humans alone for a thousand years now, won't they?" asks Whenshade.

"I don't know! I have a bad feeling the dragons have known about our current situation for a thousand years now, and they have planned well to rip the magic-using races of man from the Maglical System. That includes elves, humans, and dwarves," says Logantrance, looking to each of the races as he speaks. All the magic users can sense a powerful sensation, and they are stunned to see Farrah walk out of air through her dimension door.

"Why, Farrah. Oh, my child, it is so good to see you again," says Logantrance as he walks up to Farrah with arms wide, giving her a hug.

"Logantrance, it is so good to see you again," says Farrah, returning the hug, and they both are smiling big. Farrah is not familiar with any of the dwarves here, but she is with the elves, who all greet her with smiles and hugs.

"Farrah, you have grown incredibly in magical power. I mean, I could feel you before you were even visible. You had better have Logantrance teach you how to conceal your power because it is very noticeable," says Whenshade after hugging Farrah.

"Thank you, Whenshade. I will do that," says Farrah.

"Farrah, where is Vegenrage?" asks Logantrance.

"He said he needed to check on something. I know he can't be far. We were both coming here. He said he may be a minute behind me," says Farrah. Just then, Vegenrage walks from his dimension door spell, and he is wearing all black. He has black leather pants and a black T-shirt on with black sneaker boots, and he looks at everyone, very concerned.

"Everyone, please listen to me. The demons have captured Glimtron and his party. They are waiting for a rescue attempt so they can spring their trap and get more of us. We cannot fall for it. We have to throw a little surprise at the demons and fight fire with water. Logantrance, I know you are well versed in angel blessing, and that magic will come in handy very soon. Crayeulle and Whenshade, get ready your angel lights magic because this is extremely potent against the demons. I am going to bring the demons to us. We stand a much better chance against them out here in the open than we do in the lava-filled mountains, where they gain much strength from the earth. Anyone who is not ready or wishes not to fight the demons, speak now because they mean to kill Glimtron, all the dwarves with him, and all of us. I say if it's a fight the demons want, then a fight we will give them but out here, not in the earth. It will take all my strength, and I will need all of you to protect me, but I can get Glimtron and his party out here. Is everyone ready for the demons?" asks Vegenrage. The dwarves spread out as do the elves and Logantrance. Farrah stands a few feet from Vegenrage.

"Vegenrage, I am Brandelbig. What is the plan? What are we to do?"

"I am going to teleport Glimtron and the dwarves here. I have located their presence, and I have the strength to bring all eighteen of them back, but first, there are some allies that have survived the demon uprising here in Glaboria. Everyone, get ready for some friends of the dwarves to help us. Everyone, stand back," says Vegenrage as he steps back to the stream with a twenty-yard-wide waterfall and raises his hands in the air, bringing them together in front of himself with his eyes closed. Four stone giants appear in the middle of the onlooking dwarves and elves. They are Fillsmrend, Osworns, Cremnole, and Nordiath. They look around at everyone around them and at Vegenrage. Fillsmrend walks up to Vegenrage.

"Vegenrage, Glimtron has told us about you, and your magic got us out of the lava trap?" says Fillsmrend. Vegenrage nods.

"We are all that has survived of our kind?" says Fillsmrend. Vegenrage nods.

"Thank you," Fillsmrend says and looks to the dwarves. "Would you guys like some help clobbering demons?" All the stone giants have huge clubs, and they are smacking their opposite hand with them. They all have huge crossbows slung over their backs as well. All the dwarves nod in unison.

"Wait, there is more. There are golems who have survived the eruptions and lava flows as well. I will bring them here," says Vegenrage. The stone giants step back with the others, completely towering over them all with their ten-foot-high stature. Vegenrage brings his hands from above his head to his front, and fourteen golems appear where the stone giants just have been. The golems look to Vegenrage, slightly bowing their froglike very large heads, showing respect and knowledge that they know it was Vegenrage who has rescued them from the lava traps that would have eventually killed them. Golems look very much like the Tronglebire, but the golems have telepathy and limited magic to go along with their acid venom, which they can ignite at will.

The golems were actually copied from when Ubwickesdon and Interford created the Tronglebire and let them loose in the Ilkergire. Dwarven Dagi from long ago ran into some Tronglebire who ventured into the Long Forest and, through magical means, changed them to be able to communicate with the dwarves. They became golems and moved to the mountains, where they have created a home for themselves and served as guardians of the mountains, now destroyed and erupting.

The dwarves, stone giants, and golems have all just lost their homes, and they are not exactly close to one another, but they are allies, and all of them live in and protect the mountains, which have just been invaded and destroyed by the demons. They all are eager and ready to fight the demons to whatever end.

"OK, that is all who have survived except for Glimtron and his party. Everyone, get ready. I am going to try to bring them here now. There is very strong magic holding them where they are, but I should be able to bring them here. Everyone, be ready. There will most likely be a lot of demons following them here. Is everyone ready?" asks Vegenrage. Everyone looks around, weapons in hand, and they nod yes.

Vegenrage closes his eyes and raises his hands above his head, bringing them down in front of him slowly. He is grimacing, and everyone can tell he is concentrating hard when, out of the ground, in front of Vegenrage, flames shoot very fast and hard, grabbing him around the throat. The flames take the form of an arm, with the shoulder flush to the ground. A powerful bicep up to the elbow emerges and then the forearm and the hand, which has a tight grip around Vegenrage's throat. The flaming arm is trying to pull Vegenrage into the ground. He is fighting the force and casting repulsion spells from both hands, looking like red and yellow lightning bolts shooting into the ground. His neck is being burned, and his knees are bending as he fights to not be pulled into the ground. The repulsion spells he is casting is reversed on him, wrapping around his wrists, and now his own magic is acting like ropes pulling him into the ground by his hands and arms. He is being suffocated by the burning hand that has a hold of him.

Farrah runs in, slashing with two drawn swords of Quadrapierce. They have a stunning effect on the flaming arm. When Farrah slashes at the flaming arm and hits it with her blades, they cut the arm, and huge flames burst from the wounds like flamethrowers and put the arm out, and it disappears. Vegenrage falls to his knees, gasping for air and holding his hands just off his neck, which is badly burned and obviously causing him a lot of pain.

Before Farrah can bend down to help Vegenrage, a huge thud hits the ground in between both of them, and the entire party except for Vegenrage is thrown into the air away from him, like they were attached to large bungee cords, yanking them away. Vegenrage takes a deep breath and clenches his fists, grimacing greatly and standing up as the burn to his neck heals, and he recomposes himself. He opens his eyes, looking at the decrepit Cormygle, who forms standing right in front of him. "So you are back in the services of the demons, huh, Cormygle? Why have they not given you your perfect form?" says Vegenrage.

"Wrong, Vlianth. I am here in the services of myself. My perfect form is coming, and it will not be something borrowed. It will not be something that can be taken away. It will be real. It will be *me*." Cormygle yells as he says the last word and throws something at Vegenrage, which hits him in the stomach and cuts deep into his flesh. Vegenrage clutches his stomach with his left hand and falls to the ground, bending at the waist and bringing his knees to his chest like he is in great pain. He rolls to his side and onto his back, moaning as pain takes over, and he rolls back to his side, lying motionless on the rock ground, just feet from the stream behind him and about thirty yards back from the waterfall.

"Yes, it hurts, doesn't it, Vegenrage?" says Cormygle, laughing and pulling a book from under his tiny deformed wing on his back. His wings and his front legs are much smaller than they should be. They look very weak, and they are. His hind legs are actually normal, and his head is too, but that is all that is normal about Cormygle. He is still hunched forward, and he has to use magic to bring the book out in front of him so he can read from it. He turns away from Vegenrage and roars surprisingly loud, and this causes another expulsion spell, giving him a few more minutes before anyone from the party with Vegenrage will approach him.

Cormygle turns, and the book opens in front of him. A very large golden necklace, with a tooth hanging from it and a small capsule of blood attached to the thick end of the tooth, falls from the book and hovers just under it. Cormygle reads from the book *The Demonian Dragon: Vemenomous, Mezzmaglinggla, Cormygle.* "With the blood tooth, the dragon shall rise from this decrepit deathly image." The necklace with the tooth starts to move toward Vegenrage. "The necklace of rebirth shall bring forth the new dragon in the image of his true form, only much more stunningly powerful than before, more the dragon he imagined himself to be. The image he desires for himself shall become his true form." The necklace moves faster and faster, flies out into the water, and falls into the stream. "The dragon shall rise, brought back from the bones of former perfection, now dead and waiting to be alive."

The necklace is falling deeper into the water, and it falls right on the head of Hornspire, who is lying at the bottom of the stream. Hornspire's head and tail is intact, but his body has been eaten, all except for the bones. The necklace goes over his head like a necklace should. "And now I call for the power in me and all the magical power held by the book *The Demonian Dragon: Vemenomous, Mezzmaglinggla, Cormygle.* I call upon the power of my soul. Rise this dragon. Rise this dragon anew and make me what I am supposed to be."

Cormygle finishes reading, and the book in front of him starts to wiggle in the air. He starts to get noticeably excited, thinking greatness is coming his way. The book starts to flap, and the pages flip back and forth, and the book flies into the stream, immediately followed by the rising of Hornspire out of the water. He pounds his paws on the rock edge on either side of Vegenrage, who is still lying motionless on the rocks, unable to move. Cormygle cannot believe his eyes, which widen to the size of huge saucers.

Hornspire rises, with the water running off his splendid new color and form. He is now the color of bronze and brown with granite gray sparkles throughout his rough, rock-textured dragon scales. He is immaculate. He is powerful and strong, the epitome of youth and strength. His eyes are a wonderful combination of green and brown, and he still has horns protruding out of his body, but now he looks much more elegant, and he just looks so much more dangerous and attractive. He has a fan along the top half of his head just behind his eyebrows, which can lie flush with the back of his head and neck. He can raise the thick, bony fan, which has four horns protruding, giving him a great weapon and protection for his head. He looks all the part of a dominant dragon.

Hornspire laughs. "Cormygle, you have done well, just as I knew you would a millennium ago. You have brought me back right on cue. The real interesting part happens right about now," says Hornspire. Cormygle starts to shake and loses his balance, as the ground he is on starts to quake. He looks to the left of him as the ground shakes and explodes debris all over. He looks away to protect his eyes as Zevoncour rises from the ground right next to him.

Zevoncour is humongous, about fourteen feet tall in his perfect form, with his huge smile and that unmistakable horn running up and over his head and then down his back. He towers over Cormygle with that never-ending smile and his bright white teeth shining against the deep, rich red color of his body. "So here you are. You were given greatness by me, and you turned your back on me. You betrayed me after I made you what you wanted to be," says Zevoncour, who runs his right hand perpendicular to the ground around him. "Rise Splamdor. Rise with the shard hammer."

The ground starts to shake, and Cormygle inches backward away from Zevoncour, keeping his eyes on him but lowering his head. Splamdor rises from the earth, and he looks like a fat ogre with a head that is very thick. He has very broad shoulders and arms with a mean snarl about his mouth and face. He rises to his full height of eight feet, and he looks very sturdy and solid. His head, shoulders, and arms are hunched forward, and his arms just hang in front of him. He faces Zevoncour, raising his right arm, which is holding a very large weapon. This weapon looks like a piece of wood that has been carved by hand with a pointed hilt, which can be a dangerous stabbing weapon. The other end is a T hammer to one side and a pointed spike at the other side. The whole weapon is a deep, dark red, almost black in color, and it is made out of a quartzlike material. It is not glass, and it is not rock but some sort of combination of the two.

Zevoncour takes the weapon from Splamdor in his left hand and raises it in the air, laughing. He lowers his hand, facing the magical weapon at Cormygle. "You tried to prevent me from having the *Wogenkeld*. You tried to stop Vemenomous from becoming the demonian dragon. You thought you were going to be the demonian dragon, but that is not going to happen. With this the shard hammer, I will break Vegenrage. I will crush the life out of him, thus birthing Vemenomous, the true demonian dragon, and Vemenomous shall maintain all the ability that Vegenrage had, while the shard hammer will steal all the knowledge and memory of Vegenrage, pleasing my master. I will have the dead body of Vegenrage, but the shard hammer will send his soul to the inner realm, where my master can retrieve it," says Zevoncour, laughing.

"You cannot birth Vemenomous. He is dead. He was destroyed completely. I saw it," says Cormygle.

"Yes, we all saw it, Cormygle, but the seed of Vemenomous is in Vegenrage. Once again, thanks to you. You just immobilized Vegenrage with the flesh, blood, and bone of Vemenomous, and from the glass staff of the demon uprising was made the shard hammer, which has the blood of Vemenomous still in it. When the shard hammer draws blood from Vegenrage, Vemenomous shall be reborn intact and unchanged from before. You are afraid of me, Cormygle, but you should not be. I am not going to hurt you, but I will take great joy in watching Vemenomous eat your flesh," says Zevoncour, laughing and turning toward Vegenrage. Zevoncour is startled and takes a step back, noticing for the first time Hornspire, who is still standing over Vegenrage.

"Dragon," yells Zevoncour, holding out his left hand and the shard hammer in front of Splamdor as an act of protection, preventing him from approaching the dragon. "What is it you want, dragon? You want war? We shall give it to you."

"No, no, relax, demon. I am not here to war with you. I am here to watch you splatter the skull and brains of Vlianth all over the rocks here below me. Here, I will step back for you," says Hornspire as he wades back deeper into the stream, with the beautiful waterfall at his back.

"Why would you want to watch me kill Vegenrage, dragon? This will bring forth Vemenomous, and he will eat your flesh, which I will enjoy watching very much, but why would you want this?" asks Zevoncour.

"Vemenomous will kill most all the dragons but not me. The dragons have turned against me, and Vemenomous will take care of them for me, but do not kid yourself, demon. Vemenomous is no match for me, the great horned dragon of foresight," says Hornspire. Zevoncour walks toward Vegenrage as Hornspire backs away.

"With this shard hammer, I shall end Vegenrage and bring forth Vemenomous. We shall see if Vemenomous is no match for you, great horned dragon," says Zevoncour as he raises the shard hammer over his head and straddles Vegenrage, ready to crush his head with the magical weapon.

Zevoncour gets ready to swing the great weapon from behind his back over his head when Farrah appears right in front of him, hovering in the air. She has her hands and arms over her head with one of Quadrapierce, ready to strike. Farrah swings both arms and sword right at the head of Zevoncour. Zevoncour moves his left arm to block the strike, still holding the shard hammer with his right hand. Farrah swings her sword as hard as she can, and it hits Zevoncour in the middle of his forearm. He is so large and his muscular arm is so thick that the attack does not completely sever his arm, but Quadrapierce has sunk more than halfway through it, with the blade stuck in his bone. Zevoncour yells in pain, which he loves, and he starts to laugh. "The female here to save her savior!" The sword is still stuck in his arm.

"No! Not the female with a tainted mind!" yells Hornspire, who runs toward Vegenrage.

Logantrance appears, standing on the rock's feet from the head of Vegenrage. He swings his left hand and arm over his head, and his right arm comes from around his side. He swings both arms and his body toward Hornspire, who is running through the water right at Vegenrage. "Ellen assten inngten ommten imgorten rineldon!" yells Logantrance, and bluish gray clouds appear from his hands and fly at Hornspire, hitting him dead center at his chest.

Ssspppuuufff. The first repulsion hits Hornspire, stopping his forward momentum and raising him off his front two legs. Sssppuuufff. The second repulsion hits him, raising him out of the water. Sssppuuufff. The third repulsion hits him in the belly, sending him back through the air. And the fourth hits him—ssspppuuufff—sending him flying back into the waterfall on the other side of the very large stream.

Logantrance bends down and grabs Vegenrage by the right shoulder, and the two of them vanish. Splamdor reaches to grab Farrah by her feet because she is hovering high in the air, and he can just reach her feet. But before he gets to her, Glimtron appears by his right leg and swings Glimtronian as hard as he can, and this severs the right leg of Splamdor, who falls to his right side, clutching his stub, which is gushing blood. The rest of Glimtron's party appear all around the two demons, along with the Dagi. Those who have been expulsed by Cormygle's magic start to appear as well.

The ground starts to shake, and demons start to rise. Everyone on the ground is more concerned with keeping their balance than anything else, and this lasts for a few minutes. This works to Farrah's advantage since she is hovering, and she fights, rocking her sword back and forth, working it out of the arm of Zevoncour. Zevoncour is moving back and forth with the moving ground, and his right arm is up and down and all over with his movements, but when Farrah releases her sword from his arm, she pulls her arms back to strike again. Zevoncour is swinging the shard hammer at Farrah. Thanks to Cleapell, Farrah sees the attack and can easily evade its path. She moves to the right, ready to strike Zevoncour, when a demon on the ground in her back reaches her with his long tail. It wraps around her neck, immobilizing her. She cannot evade the next attack of Zevoncour, and the shard hammer hits her in the stomach with its pointed T end. Zevoncour yanks the weapon from her stomach, ripping blood and flesh from her, and she falls to the ground, bleeding badly from the wound that has been left on her. He stands high above Farrah, motioning the demon who had caught her to move away its tail. Zevoncour looks up with that big white smile against his bloodred body, laughing.

"You are not what I am looking for, little girl, but ah!" Zevoncour sighs loudly, smiling and looking into the air, happy with himself. "You are not what I am looking for but, ah yes, a means to an end. It is all the same, and the more pain and the more destruction, the more misery I can cause and, ah, the better. Come, my children, let us go home. Come, my children, let the races of man try to salvage their world," says Zevoncour as he sinks into the earth. "Come, children, let us go now." Zevoncour looks to Farrah, who is watching him sink into the earth. "Bring him to me, tainted mind. Bring him to me. You have no choice. You have no free will. You have no mind of your own. Bring him to me, tainted mind. You are ours." Zevoncour laughs as he sinks into the earth with the demons who have just surfaced.

CHAPTER 8

The Trap

Just before leaving the Erkensharie with Logantrance and a handful of the Erkensharie elves, traveling to the Glaborian Mountains, Glimtron addresses all the elves present at the Sephla Theater. Glimtron walks to the front, and he steps up a three-tier stairs so that everyone can see him as he addresses the congregation. "My friends, the Erkensharie elves, so much has changed. So much destruction has happened so fast and touched us all. My dear friend, King Estine, your king, was taken from you all by an evil magic-using man. The dragons have attacked the Erkensharie, and the beasts of the Ilkergire have ascended. The Long Forest has been overrun with Dark Bush, and many of us have lost loved ones. I set out with thirty-five of my best dwarves to show my brotherhood my loyalty and my deep respect for all of you as soon as I heard what had happened to King Estine in the Great Erken. We all have been touched by evil. I lost seventeen of my closest and dearest friends in Altrar, Nomberry Pass, Vollenbeln, and here in the Erkensharie, fighting alongside the greatest friends the dwarves could ever have, the Erkensharie elves. My brethren did not die in vain. They died fighting alongside our brothers who have and will do the same for us.

"It has come to my attention that the Glaborian Mountains have been lost. What could have done this? I must go see for myself. I thank all the elves for their hospitality, and I wish you all safe and successful days to come. Some of your brothers will travel with us back to Glaboria to see what has happened. I give King Ulegwahn and you all my deepest thanks. Farewell. Until we see each other again," says Glimtron, who gets thunderous applause from the elves as he shakes Ulegwahn's hands and leaves the stage.

Glimtron gathers all the dwarves who have survived the journey from Glaboria to where they are now in the Erkensharie. A lot of elves approach Glimtron and all the dwarves, thanking them for traveling to the Erkensharie to help the elves protect their homeland during the third dragon feast. Best wishes, food, and personal items made especially for the dwarves are given to Glimtron and his party.

After an hour of goodbyes, Logantrance, the Dagi, and the elves traveling with them make their way through dimension doors. And the party of nineteen dwarves, Logantrance, and five Erkensharie elves make their way to the Nomberry Pass just before the Long Forest. Once there, Glimtron asks Blythgrin to inspect the pass, which is still blocked, to see what he can find out. Blythgrin and the Dagi go to the pass and use the Sapphirewell to scan the forest, and they are quickly back to Glimtron and the others with the terrible news.

"The forest is dying. The Dark Bush is everywhere, and just as Logantrance told us the last time we were here, it will not go away until the caster of the evil spell has been killed," says Blythgrin.

Glimtron looks to Logantrance, saying, "This is terrible, and we will find who is responsible for this, but right now, we need to get to Glaboria."

"You are right, Glimtron. We need to gather together all of us," says Logantrance.

They all get together, and the Dagi, along with Logantrance and the elven magic users, all work together to fly the party over the forest. They get to the other side of the forest very quickly, and Glimtron and the dwarves make a point of stopping by the memorial where Ukker and Londwer have been killed by the Meglasterns and the Changenoir. They pay their respects to their good friends whose journey have ended here on the outskirts of the Long Forest.

From this point, the party walk through dimension doors to the Ruin of Altrar, where again the dwarves pay tribute to those who have lost their lives to the dragons and Salcendreeps, who attacked them here. Debbrier, Carboul, Cingelin, Breemkin, Leersee, Dodgker, Glurtain, Kreil, Siller, Drypes, and Alitch all have lost their lives here in the ruin of Altrar. The dwarves say many words remembering their slain friends here, and the elves pay their respects as well. Fimble and Eebil look at each other, and they both draw their Foarsbleem swords, which they inherited when Reger and Dormins have been killed by Cormygle's lightning bolt spell in Vollenbeln. Silgeqwee and Fimble draw their swords, and all four dwarves hold their Fireod Four swords high above their head in unity and silence to the friends they have lost on this journey. The party stays here for about an hour, and then they walk through dimension door spells to the Sand Marshes of Smyle.

It is nighttime now, and the party walks out on a high dune of sand. The sand marshes are so odd. There is a high dune of sand that runs all the way to the Smildren Sea, and then there is a lowland where the shallow forest grows and another high dune of sand on the other side. This phenomenon goes on for hundreds of miles all the way to the base of the Glaborian Mountains. The dwarves are immediately dumbfounded staring at their homeland, which is casting shadows of red from all the lava that is flowing from the base of the mountains. All the forest that is run over by the lava on its way to the sea is a blazing fire, adding to the reddish yellow sky. Everyone can see that the sky around the mountains have already been filled with the toxic ash that is spewing from the mountaintops, and by tomorrow, the skies will have sunlight blocked maybe as far as the end of the Sand Marshes of Smyle.

"I could not have believed this unless I saw it with my own eyes," says Glimtron.

"What ungodly magic could have caused or made this?" asks Crayeulle.

"It was not magic. It was the power of hell unleashed on the outer realms. This was done by Maglical Hell and its ruler," says Logantrance.

"So he or it is not just a fantasy. He really exists. The leader of Maglical Hell really exists, and he plans to unleash all of hell here on the outer realms in the Maglical System," says Whenshade.

"Well, we will have to do something about that. Blythgrin, Grenlew, is any of our transport platforms still functional? Is there any of our kin still alive?" asks Glimtron.

"Yes, there are many platforms still in operation," says Blythgrin after he pulls the Sapphirewell from his bag of holding and concentrates for a moment.

"Logantrance, Whenshade, Crayeulle, Shastenbree, Thambrable, and Cellertrill, I thank you all so much for coming here with us. But from this point, I ask you to please give me and my dwarven brothers a night to inspect our home. If all is lost in there, I beg you to please let myself and my brothers here see what has happened and mourn in our own way. I ask you to please wait here till morning for us to return," says Glimtron. Logantrance and the elves all respectfully nod in agreement with Glimtron. The Dagi speak among themselves.

Grenlew approaches Logantrance. "Come, we know just the place for you to rest until we get back. There is a place right by a beautiful stream where I and a lot of the dwarves take our children to camp and play," says Grenlew, and all the dwarves smile and nod, knowing exactly the place Grenlew is talking about. The party walk through dimension doors created by the Dagi, and they all appear next to a beautiful wide stream with a small but fantastic waterfall in the background. Again, the entire party can look up and see the mountains spewing toxic ash and the red glow of the lava that is flowing from the mountains all the way to the sea.

"I ask you all to wait here while I and my party inspect our home. If we need your help, the Dagi will call for you telepathically," says Glimtron. All the elves and Logantrance shake hands with the dwarves and say goodbye for the night. They all plan to be reunited by tomorrow. The dwarves walk through dimension doors, and Logantrance and the elves make a fire and get comfortable on this beautiful location by the slowly flowing stream. The mountains are continuously erupting, and toxic ash is spewing. Red-hot lava is flowing from the mountains, but the night is beautiful. The red glow from the lava and the ash blowing into the night sky is terrible, but here many miles away just sitting by the stream and watching the mountains through the trees, there seems to be great beauty in the scenery. The breeze is light and has the right warmth. Logantrance curls up on a blanket next to a big tree, and very quickly, he is fast asleep, while the elves are resting and talking by the fire.

The dwarves exit the dimension door, and they are just a few miles from the first mountain of Glaboria. They can see that the top front half of the mountain has erupted, and lava flows like a slow-moving river from it to the east toward the sea. All the mountains they can see are releasing more lava than they ever thought is possible.

"How are we going to get in? There is no way we can enter by foot. Blythgrin, you said there are teleportation pads still operational. Which ones can we still use?" asks Glimtron.

Blythgrin pulls the Sapphirewell from his bag of holding. He concentrates for a while and looks up to Glimtron. "We can still enter Glaboria, the Glimwill Mines." Blythgrin looks to Glimtron, who interrupts him.

"Stop. We are going into Glaboria. I must see my throne room, the armory, the treasury, and my chambers, if they are still intact," says Glimtron. Blythgrin will take seven of the dwarves into Glaboria with him, and Grenlew and Trybill will each take six with them. They all enter into a dimension door and arrive inside of Glaboria on a teleportation pad, which is just behind the armory.

All the teleportation pads throughout the Glaborian Mountains are secret and known only by the Dagi and the king with a few exceptions, like the one in the great hall in Symbollia, which has already been, destroyed. The teleportation pad here in Glaboria behind the armory is one of the more secure, and it is strategically located so that the dwarves have quick access to weapons, healing products, and food. Glimtron is the only dwarf here who is really familiar with this section of the Glaborian Mountain. There are fantastic Foarsbleem weapons here, and the dwarves quickly are amazed and excited to see all the armor and weapons from which they can choose. Not only that but there is a lot of very good food here as well, and the dwarves begin to fill their bellies with salted pork and bread and drink the delicious mead made only here in Glaboria from the honey of the bees that inhabit the mountain cliffs.

"Anyone here who does not have a Foarsbleem weapon and anyone here who wishes to upgrade their armor, take anything here you like. No one else will be needing these weapons and armor," says Glimtron as he chews on salted pork and chugs a mug of warm mead.

Olgerp, Miker, Twaln, Belse, and Nelster have been very quiet on this journey; and for the most part, once in the Erkensharie, they have stayed in and around the courtyard with the elves, helping them protect it from intruders. They are a tight group of five, and they are always in competition with one another to see who the best Glaborian archer is. Glimtron trusts them with his life, and they have all been to the Erkensharie with Glimtron before. All five of them have personalized, powerful, and accurate bows, but it is always a good thing to have a sharp and deadly Foarsbleem sword at your side. All five of them find exquisite swords and strap them to their sides. Ahnkle and Churcher find beautiful two-sided battle axes, and they strap them to their backs in much the same way Glimtron carries Glimtronian.

The dwarves browse the weapons and eat, but Eebil is obviously distracted and cannot wait any longer; he leaves the armory in a hurry. "Eebil, Eebil, wait, where are you going?" says Krimzill, following Eebil, and all the dwarves quickly follow behind.

Fimble runs and catches Eebil from behind, turning him and saying, "Eebil, where are you going?"

"I have to find her. I have to find Regalamda. I know she is alive. I know she is," says Eebil with tears forming in his eyes. Eebil turns and heads out of the armory.

"Wait, wait, Eebil. We will all go together," yells Silgeqwee as all the dwarves follow Eebil.

Blythgrin stops to look into the Sapphirewell, which starts to shine a deep blue. "Guys," yells Blythgrin. The Dagi look and walk over to Blythgrin as all the other dwarves follow Eebil, who is now running to find his lost wife.

Blythgrin looks up from the Sapphirewell at Grenlew and Trybill, yelling, "Glimtron, it's a trap. The demons are here. The demons are here." It is too late. The trap has been sprung. All the dwarves—except Blythgrin, Grenlew and Trybill—have exited the armory, and there is a ledge that runs along the wall of a humongous cylinder-shaped opening that runs from deep in the mountain to the outside hundreds of yards up. The bottom of the cylinder is full of lava, and toxic ash is billowing upward and out of the mountain, yet there is still breathable air for the dwarves. The ledge all the dwarves are running on falls like a shelf that has been unlatched, and all the dwarves are falling toward the lava-filled bottom and certain death.

Solmbus grabs hold of Ahnkle and Churcher, chanting a teleport spell, and he is able to teleport the three of them by the Dagi next to the Sapphirewell. The rest of the dwarves are falling through the rising ash, and just before they are incinerated by the lava, three air elementals appear and scoop up the dwarves in their large arms and hands and float them back to the ledge that is still intact in front of the armory. The dwarves are set down by the Dagi, and the air elementals fade backward and disappear. The rescued dwarves can see the Sapphirewell is shining a bright blue hue.

"Thank you, Blythgrin. That was close," says Glimtron.

"We are in trouble. The demons are here, and this is all a trap. The mountain has been blessed with demonology, and we cannot use teleportation magic to get out or travel within the mountain. The strength of our magic is fading. That is why the elementals disappeared. We were allowed in, but there is no way out. We have to walk our way out. The bottom half of the mountain is filled with lava, and the only way out is up." Blythgrin looks up, saying, "The elementals, maybe we can band our strength together and have the elementals fly us out."

The lava in the bottom of the cylinder starts to bubble and rise, and from the lava rises a huge form of Zevoncour from his head down to his waist. The lava goes up the cylinder until Zevoncour is looking at the dwarves. "Now, now, little race of man. We have no intention of hurting you," says Zevoncour.

All the archers draw their Foarsbleem bows, and Blythgrin stops them, raising his arms. "Do not fire. Your arrows will have no effect. Do not waste your arrows," says Blythgrin. The dwarves all lower their bows.

"Let me refrain. I meant to say I have no intention of hurting you myself. My children, on the other hand—well, let's just say you will be tasty dwarf kebabs for them to snack on." Zevoncour laughs. "Actually, you are safe for the time being because you are a very important part of this nice little trap. This trap is so exquisite. I have set this all up to have you, Glimtron, and all the surviving Glaborian dwarves come home right here. I have set it all up so you can come on in, but you cannot leave. You see, it is Vegenrage and the female whom he loves whom we want, and they will be coming for you because he cannot let the dwarves go extinct. You know what? There may even be a dragon or two who will come to save you. Yes, it is true. The dragons may come to save you, but enough of this small talk. Rise, my children, rise," says Zevoncour as he raises his arms and swirls in the cylinder.

The walls start to crumble, and large shards of earth and stone fall, splattering molten lava all over. Demons sprout from the walls and cling, waiting for the OK from Zevoncour to pounce on the dwarves and make meals out of them. Zevoncour laughs, saying, "Crikelringe bor unkle dim excavalusuave intrns capsulblation!"

The floor and walls around the dwarves start to crumble and shake. The dwarves are shaken to the ground. The walls fall out, and the ceiling rises. The dwarves are tumbling and rolling with all the large rocks and boulders, which is very dangerous because they can easily be crushed and torn up by the heavy, sharp rocks. The lava starts to rise in the cylinder, and it flows into the room where the dwarves are. The floor rises in the middle.

Blythgrin is chanting, holding on to the Sapphirewell. An earth elemental rises, scooping all the dwarves in its arms and holds the dwarves above the rolling debris on the floor. The floor forms a bowl that is higher than the swirling lava, which forms a very wide moat around the dwarves. Zevoncour reaches his long arm into the room from the cylinder and grabs the elemental by its head, and he crushes it. The earth elemental disappears.

The demons flood into the room, forming a wall of evil predators just waiting for their master to give the word so they can feast on the flesh of dwarves. Zevoncour laughs, chanting more demon magic, and the lava around the dwarves rises from the moat straight up to the ceiling. There is no escape for the dwarves. They cannot teleport or use dimensional magic, so the only escape is through the lava, which will kill them instantly. They are trapped, and the lava is lined with demons just waiting to spring on the dwarves.

Blythgrin, Grenlew, Trybill, Solmbus, and Greeter are in a circle, drawing as much strength from the Sapphirewell as they can, and the rest of the dwarves have formed a protective circle around them. The dwarves have been shielded from casting teleport or dimensional travel, but they have other magic still at their disposal.

Zevoncour becomes noticeably distracted, and he pulls back into the cylinder. He looks up to the top of the volcano, saying, "My children, the time has come. My children, stay here and wait. The time is near. Get ready to feast on the flesh of dwarves. Get ready and wait here for my return. It is time to spring the second half of the trap. Be ready, my children. The human may make his way here, so be ready." Zevoncour falls into the lava, and he is gone, moving through the earth and rising right next to Cormygle and the stream where Vegenrage lies immobilized.

The dwarves still in the trap stand around the Dagi with swords and bows drawn, ready to protect the Dagi should the demons attack. The Dagi concentrate on their magic, working out what is most effective for them in this situation. Fortunately for the Dagi, the absence of Zevoncour means the magical power of evil around them is much weaker now, and already they can feel their magical strength grow. They still cannot travel dimensionally or teleport because Zevoncour has them trapped in a magical cage of molten lava, but the Dagi are working on this barrier. The Dagi are in their home, Glaboria, and they are not far from the Glimwill Mines, where the Sapphirewell has been found. The jewel of sapphire and the magical strength of the Dagi will not be denied. Slowly but surely, the Dagi get stronger, and the Sapphirewell gives them the strength to teleport out of the mountain. They appear to see Farrah battling Zevoncour.

While the trap has been set for the dwarves, Cormygle battles with Vegenrage. Hornspire has been reborn from the dead for the third time, and Zevoncour has risen from the earth beside Cormygle.

Basters is in his throne room in Hunoria, where he has ruled as Bastrenboar. Basters is reading to Cloakenstrike from the book *Divination: Demon, Dragon, Elf, or Man*. Basters has finished reading what is written in the book, and they both go back to Ugoria, where Cloakenstrike has said his farewells to Basters, and they have parted as friends. Cloakenstrike has gone back to his home in the high cliffs on the Briganyare Sea. Cloakenstrike has admitted to Basters that when he has read *The Ugorian Stand* to Basters and Fraborn, he has left out parts of the book, and he has reminded himself of these parts by admitting this to Basters. He has hurried to his home so he can study the book again because he remembers something that is really pissing him off. This time he worries not that there may be a trap for him, and he walks into his home from a dimension door.

Cloakenstrike waves his hand, and a fire roars from the logs in the four-foot-high fireplace in the middle of his cave, which has remarkable ventilation; the smoke naturally flows up and out. He sits on his bed and pulls *The Ugorian Stand* from his bag of holding and finds the part he have not read to Fraborn and Bastrenboar. "Ah, here is the part I am looking for," Cloakenstrike says to himself out loud, and he begins to read.

The human magic user will save the two half bloods from my breath attack, and the half-blood leader will attack me with a deadly sword that multiplies. The magic user will hit me with a lightning bolt and then the bright light. I cannot see what happens after the bright light. I can see no scenario where I survive the bright light. I know my flesh is consumed by Vemenomous, and I cannot be reborn because the magic user and the half blood teleport my remains to Fargloin. The stream with the half-mile-wide waterfall is 160 miles south of Glaboria and 20 miles west of the Smildren Sea. Here, they will deposit my remains into the stream. The magic user will find a tooth stuck in my rib, and he will extract this tooth magically. He will then magically encapsulate blood and flesh from my tail to the tooth. He will cast this into the Carbonheight Hills, where the black carbon sand will prevent the rebirth of Hornspire, the great horned dragon. Should my remains be destroyed or should my tooth, blood, and flesh not be cast into the Carbonheight Hills, I will be reborn for the third time by the dragon cast out using demonology. Cormygle, the cast-out dragon, will use my tooth, blood, and flesh to enhance his personal being. Without them, he will have me reborn in exchange for his perfected personal form.

Cloakenstrike slams the book shut, saying out loud, "He set us up. The dragon set us up from the beginning." At that very moment, when he has finished that sentence, he feels the rebirth of Hornspire. The presence of Hornspire is well-known to Cloakenstrike. Even Basters, who is on the world of Strabalster, knows the dragon has been reborn. Cloakenstrike does not like to be bested. He does not like to be used without his personal authority. He loves the challenge of battling, stealing, fighting, and conquering. He is going after Hornspire, and he wastes no time.

Cloakenstrike walks through a dimension door, and he appears right next to Farrah, who is lying on the ground, clutching her bleeding stomach. Right next to Cloakenstrike appears Fraborn and Basters, who walk from a dimension door made by Basters.

"Where is the dragon?" yells Cloakenstrike.

"There. There he is, Cloakenstrike, by the waterfall," yells Fraborn, pointing to Hornspire. The dragon is standing in the water after just being hit with four energy blasts from Logantrance, who has teleported away with Vegenrage before Cloakenstrike, Basters, and Fraborn have gotten there.

"Cloakenstrike, I will avenge the death of Shandorn!" yells Whenshade and Crayeulle.

Cloakenstrike ignores the Erkensharie elves and flies right at Hornspire, throwing magnificent balls of molten lava at him one after the other. This is meant as a distraction to keep Hornspire paying attention to the molten balls of fire that, if ignored, will do serious damage.

"You used me, dragon. You set us up so that you could be reborn. You set us up so you could be the demonian dragon. Well, you may have come back a third time, dragon, but you will not come back a fourth time," says Cloakenstrike, stopping in midair and swinging both arms at Hornspire, releasing a magnificent lightning bolt spells from both hands that meet into one supercharged bolt and head right for Hornspire. Hornspire simply catches each molten lava ball thrown at him with his front paws, and the magic dissipates.

He diverts the lightning bolt spell into the woods on the other side of the stream, reflecting it with his paw.

"You just figured it out, magic user. Well, not bad, but you are too late. What is done is done, and I am here. There is no stopping me, especially by a human. Your time is coming, magic user. Your time is coming," says Hornspire with a laugh as he flaps his wings hard and rises in the air with the water running off his beautiful new color and form. Hornspire flies into a dimension door, and he is gone.

"Can this be? We are going to be saved from that dragon for a second time by—are you kidding me?—Cloakenstrike," says Glimtron, looking to Blythgrin.

Basters bends down to Farrah, seeing she is in great pain and wounded very badly. He puts his hands over her wounds and starts to cast healing magic, and Farrah starts to feel stronger. She starts to heal herself with her own magic, and very quickly, she is feeling better. Basters helps Farrah to her feet, and she asks, "Thank you, stranger. Who are you?" She looks at Basters with a very curious look, like she wants to say something, but she just can't get it out.

"I am Basters, king of Ugoria," says Basters, and he watches as Crayeulle and Whenshade fly right at Cloakenstrike, but Cloakenstrike vanishes. The elves make their way back to the shore where Basters has just helped Farrah as do all the elves and dwarves.

Farrah looks at Basters with a very confused look on her face, saying, "You seem very familiar to me, but I have never seen you before. Have we met before?"

"No, my lady, we have never met before. If we had, I would have never forgotten you," Basters says to Farrah, taking notice of all the attention he is getting from elves and dwarves.

Whenshade notices the snow gold trinket around the neck of Basters, and he and all the elves bow to one knee. "My king, why is the king of Ugoria not in his palace? Why is the king of Ugoria on Fargloin and with no escort? How is it that the king of Ugoria is not elven?" asks Whenshade.

"These are all good questions—questions that should be asked by our brothers here on Fargloin. I am here because I sensed the rise of Hornspire, and I have come to destroy the dragon who foresees the future and gives the dragons of the Maglical System a constant advantage over the races of man. I have missed my opportunity, and now I must return to my palace. You are all welcome to visit Ugoria anytime you wish. I would love the opportunity to speak with you all some more. I must be going now," says Basters as he turns and walks through a dimension door.

The elves are stunned to see a human wearing the snow gold trinket, but this is a clear sign that Basters is the king of Ugoria. Farrah is staring straight ahead, daydreaming, and she sees Bastrenboar calling her his queen when they have been in Vollenbeln. "Farrah, Ms. Farrah," says Eebil, tugging on Farrah's shorts. Farrah snaps back to her senses and smiles, looking at Eebil.

He is quickly pushed out of the way by Krimzill, who smiles and looks at her, saying, "Are you OK, Ms. Farrah? You look like you have seen a ghost."

"Yes, I am fine. Glimtron, do you remember when we were in Vollenbeln and Hornspire was beheaded by Bastrenboar?" asks Farrah.

"Yes, I remember that," says Glimtron.

"Who was with Bastrenboar?" asks Farrah.

"Why, it was Cloakenstrike," says Glimtron, stroking his beard, staring off across the stream. "What are you getting at, Farrah?"

"Basters, the king of Ugoria—he is Bastrenboar, the humanor. I don't know what this means, if anything at all, but it is very odd to see these two characters here now and Hornspire too. We need to get to Vegenrage," says Farrah.

"Do you know where Logantrance has taken Vegenrage?" asks Whenshade.

"Yes, Logantrance has taken Vegenrage to his home, Vollenbeln. I can feel it now. Vegenrage is in a lot of trouble. I can feel it. I can sense the evil growing in Vegenrage as it did once before," says Farrah.

"No, Farrah, not again," says Glimtron.

"Yes, again. Whenshade and the elves, Glimtron and the dwarves, do you all know how to get to Vollenbeln?" asks Farrah.

"Yes," says everyone in unison.

"Then, Blythgrin, have the Sapphirewell ready because we have to get to Vollenbeln immediately. Vegenrage needs our help," says Farrah, and she walks through a dimension door.

Crayeulle looks to Whenshade, saying, "Farrah just walked through a dimension door of her own. She is becoming very powerful. I can sense that her presence is very strong and getting stronger all the time."

"I know, Crayeulle, I feel it too. Come on, let's all get to Vollenbeln. We need to help Vegenrage," says Whenshade. All the dwarves and elves walk through dimension doors cast by the magic users.

CHAPTER 9

Hornspire's Return

Hornspire exits his dimension door, and he is flying up the tallest mountain in the Swapoon mountain range. This mountain is called Talpilmouth, and no race of man has ever climbed to its highest peak. It is very cold here, and ice covers the mountain walls. The top of the mountain reaches so high that clouds cannot pass, and to the west is the Ackelson Desert, where no moisture reaches the land. Gairdennow has his lair on this mountain, and it is a good four hundred feet below its peak. From here, the great eyes of a dragon can watch the Gwippen uprising and the Swapoon floodlands, and Gairdennow never goes hungry for too long without spotting a meal. Now, of course, there are seven dragons here, but still, there is plenty of food, and all the dragons are able to hunt for themselves.

Hornspire is flying right for Gairdennow's lair, and this is a very interesting situation. All the dragons have sensed the death of Hornspire twice, confusing them greatly. Hornspire is not an enemy of any of the dragons per se; however, Blethstole and Vergraughtu have entombed Hornspire in Blethstole's lair over a thousand years ago. Hornspire knows that only

Blethstole and Vergraughtu (Vemenomous) are aware of what happened to him in Blethstole's lair so long ago, and Hornspire has known it is going to happen anyway, thanks to his foresight.

Hornspire flies through the snowy clouds that butt up against the mountain. This is a very cold place, and the wind whistles loud as it passes over the frozen mountain face. There are always snow flurries swirling in the foggy and icy air. Now Hornspire returns to spread his predictions again. He lands on a large ledge with a huge opening for a dragon lair. The ledge extends out to about twenty feet, and then it reaches the mountain face that rises straight in the air. The entrance is large enough for a dragon twice the normal size to easily walk into, and Hornspire walks in snorting through his nostrils, making his entrance heard before he is seen. The entrance slopes downward and bends to the left and then opens to a large cavernous room that has been sculpted and crafted by the magic of Gairdennow, and it is immaculate. The floor is made from crushed stones right from the walls, which make a fine sand for dragons to lie on. The walls are roughly textured, not smooth by man's standards but smooth for dragons. The room is huge.

Mezzmaglinggla, Gannream, and their four offspring lie in this room. Mezzmaglinggla and Gannream have been paired for over 1,500 years, and Rungrunger, Jarclause, Reegaallia, and Megalla are all their offspring, making all the dragons here except Gairdennow's Mountain Creek dragons. Gairdennow lies further back in the cavern where he has a very large mound of gold, jewels, artifacts, and magical items he is resting on. The Mountain Creek dragons have a large bounty in their lair, but even though the dragons are changing their ways and they are united and working to protect one another, they still do not break the unspoken rule. Dragons will never bring their treasure to another dragon's lair. A dragon will never steal the treasure of another dragon. This amounts to war with no exception.

All the dragons watch as Hornspire enters the cavern, and they all notice the new color and form that he presents. The dragons are lying down, and they do not get startled; they calmly raise their heads, and like nothing out of the ordinary is happening, they watch as Hornspire enters the lair. They certainly notice the remarkable new form and color of Hornspire; at least the older dragons do. Gairdennow walks down from his bed of gold onto the sandy stone floor and walks up to greet Hornspire.

"I thought you had been killed. As a matter of fact, I thought you had been killed twice. I guess you can't kill someone who can see the future," says Gairdennow.

"Well, you can try," says Hornspire.

"I would have thought you, of all the dragons, would have been there to stop the deaths of so many dragons. We have suffered greatly, and now we must band together, or all the dragons may be gone soon," says Gairdennow.

"I tried to warn you all. I tried to tell you all. I tried to prevent all of this from happening, but the dragons, including you, Gairdennow, and you, Gannream, would not listen to me. You would not read the writings I presented to you, and now here we are. Maybe now you will listen to me. I have much worse news for you now that we are in this predicament, and if you do not listen to me now, all may be lost," says Hornspire. The Mountain Creek dragons all move closer to Hornspire and rest near him, paying attention to his every word. Even Gairdennow folds his legs and settles to the ground like a 2,400-pound cat sitting down and tucking its legs under itself, getting comfortable. Hornspire now has all seven dragons sitting in a half circle around him, calmly listening to what he has to say. Hornspire freezes for a moment in awe because he cannot believe he has such an interested group, and they are all dragons. They are calm, they are quiet, and they are all united together.

"Go ahead and tell us what you see, Hornspire. We have no reason to not listen to you. We are less than thirty dragons now. If you want to help preserve the dragons, then do so," says Gairdennow.

"I can tell you all. We have to unite all of us—and fast. We have to unite, and we have to kill Vegenrage. Vegenrage, like before, is the host that will birth Vemenomous again," says Hornspire.

"Wait a minute. Vemenomous is dead. I watched Blethstole tear him apart and dissolve his remains. There is no way Vemenomous is coming back from that," says Gannream.

"Yeah, the same goes for Zenondour and Ulore. We were all there in Vlanthis, the home of Vlianth, and witnessed the death of the demons and Vemenomous, not to mention the death of my son, Razcour," says Mezzmaglinggla.

"This is true. This did happen, but Cormygle had two teeth, and both were planted by me. One tooth was from Vemenomous, and one tooth was from me. Both teeth had blood and flesh from myself and Vemenomous. I saw that Vemenomous would kill me, and I was able to plan ahead and create a way for myself to be reborn. I knew Vemenomous would lose a tooth in the battle with me. The tooth was left in my rib for the human magic user Cloakenstrike to find, and he was tricked by me to discard this tooth in the Carbonheight Hills, where Cormygle would find it and use it to immobilize Vegenrage. This tooth had the blood and flesh of Vemenomous in it, and again, Vegenrage's body has been invaded by the demon seed of Vemenomous, who we all know was Vergraughtu. I had one of my teeth teleported into a book held by Cormygle. I tricked Cormygle into thinking the tooth would make him the first demonian dragon, but instead, it was used to have me reborn by Cormygle's own magic. The tooth left by Vemenomous was used by Cormygle to immobilize Vegenrage, and Vegenrage was supposed to have been killed. I would have killed Vemenomous as well, eliminating the threat to all the dragons by Vemenomous and Vlianth, but this did not play out. Vegenrage was supposed to have been killed by the demon Zevoncour, but Vegenrage's love—Farrah, the female with a tainted mind—saved him and thwarted the demons. I saw the death of Vegenrage, but this did not happen. This means that Vemenomous will rise again from Vegenrage at some point, and all the dragons are still in great danger of being hunted by Vemenomous. I have been with the dead for a long time now, and all my visions are no longer valid since Vegenrage was not killed. This means I have caught up to my visions," says Hornspire.

"What does it mean you have caught up to your visions?" asks Gairdennow.

"That means I have no visions of the future that are valid. They will all change. However, I do still have great insight into future events. It will take time, and new visions will come to me, but I do not know how long it will take before it does. Vegenrage did not die, and all my visions counted on this pivotal moment in time," says Hornspire.

"So what you are saying is that, right now, you are just like the rest of us, meaning you don't know the future?" asks Gannream.

"Well, kind of. I do have insights from my visions even though they are all going to change now. I can tell you that, in all my previous visions, the demons kill Mezzmaglinggla. I have seen her killed three different ways, but again, this was all after the death of Vegenrage. Vegenrage did not die, but it is fair to assume that the demons still want Mezzmaglinggla dead," says Hornspire.

"Well, that is good to hear," says Mezzmaglinggla sarcastically. "Why do they want me dead?"

"I can only see visions of the future. I do not have all the answers to why things happen. I just see what happens. Sometimes I see different scenarios play out, but if a certain vision that I have does not play out, like Vegenrage being killed, then all visions after that are subject to change, and my visions will start showing me new scenarios of the future. Sometimes my visions will come in a few weeks. Sometimes it is a few months. For now, we dragons have to protect one another. We cannot just sit and hide. The demons are actively trying to kill the worlds of the Maglical System—Fargloin, Strabalster, and Kronton in that order. I still believe this is certain. They are doing this by erupting all the volcanoes on each planet, releasing volcanic ash into the atmosphere. Eventually, this will block out all the sunlight, killing the worlds. We cannot let this happen. This will give the demons too much power, and they will eliminate us all if this is allowed to happen. We have to unite all the dragons, and we have to stop the demons before they kill the worlds. They want us dead. That is for sure. They want the demonian dragons, who will serve the demons and watch the skies for them. We have to kill Vegenrage because he harbors Vemenomous inside of him right now, and if Vemenomous rises, he will hunt and kill the dragons like he did before," says Hornspire.

"I tell you what, Hornspire. I have no problem going after the demons. I have no problem going after Vegenrage, even the female with the tainted mind, but the fact is we have lost. Look around you, Hornspire. There are eight dragons right here, and we represent one-third of all the remaining dragons alive in the Maglical System. We have lost. You want to go out in a blaze of glory, I really don't care, but right now, I am going to rest for a while. You go and get Blethstole. You go and get Gwithen, and if they are with you, ready to fight, then I am with you, ready to fight. Right now, I am right here, and I am going to rest for a while," says Gairdennow as he rises and walks over to his golden bed and lies down. The other dragons get up and move back to their respective resting places against the wall, which is very comfortable for them.

Hornspire looks at the retreating dragons, grumbling and saying, "All right, I will go get Blethstole and Gwithen. They will know what I say has to be done. I will go see Pryenthious. He will surely be more eager to save the dragons than you are. I will be back with the other dragons."

"Oh, Hornspire. Blethstole and Gwithen have said that Vegenrage and the female saved their draglets from the demons. Gwithen and Blethstole both protected the humans from us. It would seem that Blethstole, Gwithen, and the humans are allies," says Mezzmaglinggla.

Hornspire turns and exits the lair. He takes to the wing and soars through the cold air just below the clouds, and he knows Blethstole will be a tricky dragon to go and see. He has no problem seeing any of the dragons except for Blethstole because he does not know what Blethstole will do. This is the first time in Hornspire's life where he has no idea how the future will turn out, and this is a frustrating feeling for him. Hornspire decides to face Blethstole last, and he heads to the world of Fargloin, where he can sense a large dragon presence at the lair of Pryenthious.

Hornspire exits his dimension door over the world of Fargloin near the Glaborian Mountains, which spew their toxic ash. He exits here on purpose because he wants to witness the erupting mountains firsthand, and he is saddened to see this happening to the world of Fargloin. Hornspire knows a handful of dragons are in the lair of Pryenthious, and he flies through his dimension door. He exits above the Hiltorian remains, heading toward the Brunst Rock Plateau, home of Pryenthious.

Hornspire soars high into the air, ascending with the gradient of the rock that rises like a pyramid. The Brunst Rock Plateau rises some 1,200 feet and has many ledges all the way up its gradual incline, overlooking the Bankle Lake to the south. There are many types of birds and mammals that have nests, boroughs, and lairs here. The whole Brunst Rock Plateau is a combination of rock and earth, making it a perfect natural habitat for a lot of different animals.

Pryenthious has commandeered the top of the plateau, where his lair is, large and spacious on the inside and the outside. The top of the plateau is like the lid to a pot. The top is made from very hard stone that has been smoothed by hundreds of years of erosion. There is a wide square of earth around the entrance to Pryenthious's lair, and this is the perfect place to lie and watch all the lands around the plateau.

Pryenthious is here with six of the younger dragons just reaching adulthood, and this is not to the liking of Pryenthious, but he concedes and allows the dragons to stay with him. The younger dragons can tell Pryenthious is very confident and not worried about any threat, and they all sit around the outside of the entrance to Pryenthious's lair, giving him his privacy. They all just watch the surrounding areas while they lie and relax, and then they hear Pryenthious exiting from inside. He is snorting, and he stands proud, looking into the distance. The other dragons sense it too but much later than Pryenthious does. They all look, and here comes Hornspire, flying through the air toward them. Hornspire soars around and lands.

"I thought you had died twice," says Wisekee.

"Actually, I died three times, kind of, and I think that is enough," says Hornspire.

"Yes, that is enough," says Pryenthious, walking toward Hornspire. "You look different, Hornspire. Your color is different, and I must say you look stronger."

"Maybe now you believe that I can see into the future, Pryenthious? Maybe now you will listen to my warnings," says Hornspire.

"What warnings? I say you are already too late. The dragons are less than twenty-five now. We are an endangered species," says Pryenthious.

"We are indeed, but Vegenrage has been stung and implanted with the demon seed of Vemenomous, and if we do not destroy him now, then Vemenomous will rise again and continue to devour the last of the dragons."

"Vegenrage," yells Pryenthious. "We had him. We had him and the female. Gwithen and Blethstole said they had allied themselves with the two humans. They said the humans are friends." Pryenthious snorts and walks around, looking at the ground. All the younger dragons give way as he walks and thinks. All the dragons, even Hornspire, stay silent and wait for Pryenthious to speak. "What do you see, Hornspire? What will happen if we leave Vegenrage alone, and what will happen if we move to destroy him?"

"I have been with the dead for too long, and my visions have been nullified," says Hornspire.

"What do you mean nullified?" asks Pryenthious.

"I saw the death of Vegenrage, but that vision did not come true. Since Vegenrage did not die, I have no visions at this point that are accurate. I know that Vegenrage has the demon seed in him, and if we do not kill him, Vemenomous will rise again, and we dragons cannot have this. This will be the end of us, and Vemenomous will begin the demonian dragon reign. I can tell you that the demons have risen, and they mean to rule the Maglical System with the demonian dragons at their side. Together, they mean to exterminate our species of dragon," says Hornspire.

"I am no friend to the humans, but Blethstole and Gwithen say Vegenrage is their ally. We dragons must stick together now. There is no way around this. Our numbers are too low. We will all go to Blethstole, and you tell him what you have told us. We need to see what he and Gwithen say," says Pryenthious.

This is not what Hornspire wants to hear, but if Pryenthious and the other dragons go, he will feel a little more comfortable. Hornspire is very capable, but still he does not have the killer instinct that Blethstole has. He has no way of knowing how Blethstole will react to seeing him after all that has happened. Hornspire feels a little better that he will be with seven dragons, including Pryenthious, to go see Blethstole, but he does not even know where the remaining dragons are. He just follows Pryenthious and ends up on the planet Kronton, and soon enough, he can sense that the remaining dragons are in Dribrillianth's lair.

They are flying over the Terrashian Grasslands toward the Swoolfig Forest. The grasslands get wetter and sandier as the forest begins. There is forest all around, but there is a phenomenon here for a five-hundred-mile circle—the forest is all petrified. Around the petrified forest is the Swoolfig Forest, still alive, well, and mature. For some reason, the forest inside and on the Blimith seashore has been petrified, and here is where Dribrillianth has his lair. The forest that is petrified is on very wet, sandy land, and the forest surrounding the petrified woods is much more normal and stable. Dribrillianth's lair is not on the water's edge as you might think. His lair is right in the middle of the forest, where the petrified forest meets the natural and still alive

Swoolfig Forest. This is where Dribrillianth makes his home, and the land his lair is in is petrified as well. The entrance to Dribrillianth's lair goes underground.

Pryenthious and the other dragons land and approach the lair. Hornspire takes the lead, snorting loudly, announcing his intention to enter the lair. Hornspire leads the way, and the other dragons follow. This is a most spectacular entrance. There are petrified trees, very large ones, that have grown together across, and they are almost twenty feet in diameter. The trees have been carved out, and the entrance goes in to about six feet, and then it slants down into the ground, which is petrified as well. The entire outside of the lair has been magically imbued with diamond skin and spider touch. This combination of spells means that nothing can penetrate the shell surrounding Dribrillianth's lair, and if anything or anyone tries, Dribrillianth will know it with no exception. He will also know if anything walks, crawls, or moves in any way on the ground, in, or around his lair.

Hornspire walks down the slanted entrance for about five yards, which leads right into a cathedral-sized room that looks like it has been glazed in honey sand. There is a warm feeling the sandy golden blond color gives off, and of course, the golden plunder of Dribrillianth is astounding, adding to the warm golden ambiance. Dribrillianth is lying on his bed of gold, and Quailrain is off to the side, lying on a bed of sticks and foliage, which is perfect for her and Gwithen's young, who sleep close to her. Elbonic and Krigeblore are lying to the other side of the room, and Dribrillianth stands and walks down from his bed of gold. "I am surprised to see you, Hornspire. You have a new form. You had the wings of rebirth, but you must have exhausted their power," says Dribrillianth.

"Yes, I did. I have come to face Blethstole and warn him and all the dragons that we must act. We cannot sit around and wait. Vegenrage has been immobilized, and the demon seed of Vemenomous is in him again. Vemenomous will rise again, and we cannot let this happen. The demons will destroy the worlds of the Maglical System, and we cannot let this happen," says Hornspire.

"Yes, we know, Hornspire. Gwithen and Blethstole have gone to see Vegenrage, and if Vemenomous rises, they will be waiting for him. Gwithen and Blethstole protected the humans from us dragons, saying they are our allies. Vegenrage saved Gwithen's young, and Gwithen returned the favor, but you should know this. Have your visions failed you?" asks Dribrillianth as he walks between Hornspire and Quailrain, blocking Hornspire from the young. All the dragons walk around Hornspire, and he gets a very uneasy feeling.

Gairdennow and the Mountain Creek dragons walk into the lair. They are followed by Pryenthious and all the dragons who have been in his lair, and now all the dragons are here except for Gwithen and Blethstole. Hornspire is surrounded, and should the dragons take lethal action on him, even in his exquisite form, he will be way overpowered and outmatched. Hornspire takes a very submissive stance, lowering his head.

"It is true. I have lost my visions. I was brought back a third time, and although this time I was brought back by rebirth, I also included magical genesis, which has strengthened my physique and enhanced my magical prowess, but I may have lost my ability to see the future. I had tricked the races of man and Cormygle to use my flesh, blood, and bone to bring me back a third time. This same magic was used to immobilize Vegenrage and implant him with the demon seed of Vemenomous, but Vegenrage was supposed to die, exterminating Vemenomous for good. I know the dragons have united, and I am still a dragon. I am still here to see our species dominate the Maglical System. I do not want to watch the rise of the demonian dragon. My visions are no longer accurate, but I know the demons intend to rule the Maglical System with the demonian dragons, and they intend to kill us all. I can tell you for sure if Vemenomous should rise, he will be the greatest threat to the dragons. We cannot let Vemenomous rise. We must kill Vegenrage."

"Enough," says Dribrillianth in a stern voice. He snorts loudly. "Mezzmaglinggla, Gannream, you stay here with the Mountain Creek dragons and protect Quailrain and the young. Elbonic and Krigeblore, you stay here as well. Hornspire, you and the rest of us will travel to see what Gwithen and Blethstole have to say about this. My sense tells me they are in Vlanthis, and Vegenrage must be there as well. Let us go and see if Vemenomous is to rise."

The dragons all exit the lair into the petrified forest and head through dimension doors to Vlanthis.

CHAPTER 10

The Clash in Vlanthis

Logantrance has arrived in Vollenbeln with Vegenrage, who is unconscious. The tooth from Vemenomous has entered Vegenrage's stomach and dissolved, acting like a powerful anesthetic, preventing Vegenrage from waking. The blood, flesh, and bone of Vemenomous is flowing through Vegenrage's veins, and just like before, Vemenomous is growing inside of him, waiting to birth by erupting from his body, killing him in the process. Logantrance knows exactly what is happening; he knows and has felt the demon seed. Blethstole has implanted Logantrance with a demon seed, and Vegenrage has saved Logantrance before it has birthed naturally. Logantrance does not know how to save Vegenrage, but he knows how to slow the process and give Vegenrage time, which is what he is doing now.

Vollenbeln is lit by soft white moonlight, and the sky is full of stars. It is very beautiful, just the way it has been when Vegenrage and Farrah have left it after loving each other for days. Logantrance wastes no time and runs onto the mound of earth covering Vegenrage's home after lying him on the soft grassy earth. The ceiling window looking into Vegenrage's home is far off to the side and does not interfere with what Logantrance is doing.

Logantrance pulls two large golden staffs from Quintis and stabs them into the ground on either side of Vegenrage. Logantrance starts to chant a spell. "Kaioppiolla seekont tennss hion inchiieenn vioeessee!"

White lights, like thin squiggly lightning bolts, grow from the amber jewels at the top of both staffs. They grow slowly and down toward Vegenrage, but they do not touch him. The lines of white light race back and forth, creating a man-sized protective dome of magic all around Vegenrage.

Logantrance sits off to the side of Vegenrage, looking up into the night sky, and then rests his head in his hands. "Oh, what am I going to do? I do not know how to remove the demon seed like Vegenrage did for me. Well, I cannot just sit here. I have to try something," says Logantrance out loud, and he stands up. He pulls the staffs from the ground and puts them back in his bag of holding, and the protective shield around Vegenrage disappears. "This is the home of Vegenrage, and surely his strength here is unmatched. Forgive me, Vegenrage. The only thing I know to do is to try to magically excise the demon seed from your body."

Logantrance raises his hands toward the moon in the sky and chants, "Encar gangalia encar rezipincor under tressel encarincor." He walks to Vegenrage's feet, pulling one of the golden staffs from his bag of holding, and points the amber jewel at the end of the staff at Vegenrage's chest, chanting, "A bouved reinleave akeemsten remooel." Logantrance raises the staff in the air quickly, and Vegenrage's shirt rips from his body. Logantrance points the staff at Vegenrage's chest.

"I am sorry, Vegenrage, but this is all I know to do. *Cutringe ornalippen deoffsgringe.*"

After Logantrance finishes his chant, he touches the end of the amber jewel on Vegenrage's chest just below his throat and runs the jewel down to his belly button. This makes an incision that cuts through Vegenrage's ribs, but Logantrance is not prepared for Vemenomous, who is already forming, and he bursts from Vegenrage's chest.

Long black fingernails puncture out from within Vegenrage's rib cage. Vemenomous's hands grab hold of Vegenrage's ribs and forces them outward until they are flush with the ground. Logantrance hears the bones of Vegenrage crack and break as Vemenomous rises his head out from Vegenrage's chest cavity. All of Vegenrage's chest innards are draped atop Vemenomous's head, and they all fall to the side and back into his chest cavity after Vemenomous quickly rises to his hips from within Vegenrage. Vemenomous is soaked in Vegenrage's blood, and it splatters Logantrance, who yells, "No, you spawn of hell! Go back to the hell you come from."

Logantrance swings his staff like a baseball bat and strikes Vemenomous right across the face. Vemenomous is slammed to the right. His head now has a permanent indentation of the amber jewel on the left side of his snout, and a tooth has been knocked out by Logantrance's strike. Logantrance swings again from over his head, coming down with his staff like he is chopping wood, and Vemenomous blocks the swing with his left forearm. The swing is powerful, and the loud crack and the V shape of Vemenomous's left forearm are proof of how powerful this strike is. Even Vemenomous is not impervious to pain, and he screams out loud, thrusting his right arm and fist at Logantrance, hitting him with a force spell that sends Logantrance flying back through the air. Vemenomous snaps his left hand and wrist like he is shaking water off it, and his forearm snaps into its correct and healed form.

Vemenomous digs his claws into the earth next to Vegenrage's mutilated body and pulls his lower body from within Vegenrage's opened chest. It's amazing to watch, as Vemenomous is more than twice the size of Vegenrage, yet still he births from his chest. Vemenomous rises to his feet, feeling the left side of his snout where Logantrance has left a permanent scar and an empty tooth socket. Vemenomous turns to see the innards of Vegenrage start to move and form back to their original size and position. His ribs start to fold back and close, fusing back to their correct shape.

"What is this magic? You are not going to come back for a second time, magic user," says Vemenomous, and he raises his arms and points his fingers at the body of Vegenrage. He is hit with a lightning bolt that is shot from the end of Logantrance's staff. Vemenomous is knocked off his feet and shot some fifteen feet back through the night air, sizzling and smoking. The lightning bolt hit him right on the chest under his left arm, and the full intensity of the spell is reverberating through Vemenomous's body. His skin glistens with the light of lightning that shoots at incredible speed throughout his skin for a minute, nearly roasting him. Vemenomous lands hard and is immobilized for over a minute, as the spell is very powerful and has almost killed him.

Logantrance runs as fast as he can to Vegenrage, who appears to have healed from this second rising of Vemenomous from his body. Logantrance grasps Vegenrage's left forearm, and his band of life becomes visible. Logantrance can see the golden *I* disappear from the band.

"Wake up, Vegenrage, wake up. Come on, boy, wake up," says Logantrance, gently slapping the side of Vegenrage's face. Logantrance can see that Vemenomous is dazed but getting up and stumbling around, still smoking.

"Vegenrage, wake up. Come on, Vegenrage, get up. We have to move," says Logantrance, but Vegenrage still does not move.

Vemenomous shakes his head and looks at Logantrance. "This time I will finish you off, Logantrance, along with all the magic-using races of man. This time I will finish you, as well as the dragons. Now the demons and demonian dragons will rule the Maglical System," says Vemenomous as he starts to walk toward Logantrance.

Logantrance stands between Vegenrage and the approaching Vemenomous when Farrah appears in the air, hovering just in front of Logantrance.

She yells, "Dragon-slaying hands!" Farrah points both hands at Vemenomous, and a magnificent bright yellow and orange light shoots from her hands.

Vemenomous quickly responds with his breath attack, and the two spells negate each other as they collide. Both spells dissipate in a bright light where they meet, and after a minute, they both stop the spell and breath attack.

"My queen, why fight me? You are going to be mine. It is only a matter of time. And why fight me when you can and will have all you want? Anything, you name it. It will be yours, my queen," says Vemenomous.

"I will never be your queen. I will never be owned ever again. I will have free will from now on. You are nothing more than a shadow—a shadow of the man I love, a shadow whose strength and power is stolen from his master. Vegenrage is your master, and you are no match for him," says Farrah.

"We will see about that," says Vemenomous.

"Yes, we will," says Farrah, and she lowers herself magically to the ground, standing next to Vegenrage, who is now fully aware, awake, and standing with a dead serious look on his face, looking at Vemenomous.

Vegenrage raises his hands to his shoulders and slowly starts to swirl them in circles. Blue streaks brighten the air behind his hands. He brings his hands down, holds them parallel to the ground straight out from his shoulders, and swings them back up, clapping once above his head. The night sky and moon swing under the horizon of Vollenbeln, and the sun and bright sky rises. Instantly, it is daytime. Vegenrage starts to walk toward Vemenomous, dead serious, and Vemenomous starts to laugh. "I love it. This is great. Rise, my master, rise," says Vemenomous.

Vegenrage looks down to the left and to the right and starts to move back toward Farrah and Logantrance. The ground shakes a little, and Zevoncour rises from the earth to the left of Vemenomous. Zevoncour pulls his legs up from the earth and stomps on the ground with loud thuds, laughing. Vemenomous has constantly been growing from birthing from Vegenrage and is now fifteen feet tall, and Zevoncour is about twelve feet tall.

"This time we have a little surprise for you that you were not ready for, magic user," says Zevoncour, who points his hands at Farrah.

She screams in pain as blood and red fire shoots out from her stomach where she has been struck by the shard hammer. She falls to her back, screaming, and Vegenrage has to move to her side because flames are shooting from her stomach. Vemenomous and Zevoncour are laughing and watch as Vegenrage puts his hands over the flames and contains them like he is holding an invisible bowl that extinguishes the fire as he gets closer and closer to her stomach. Vegenrage keeps moving closer and closer until his hands are flat on her abdomen. He concentrates with his eyes closed. Farrah has seemingly gone, unconscious from the pain.

"Now, Vemenomous, go and get her while they are occupied!" yells Zevoncour.

"Yes, Master," says Vemenomous, who heads toward the humans.

"Not so fast," says Logantrance, who walks toward Vemenomous with his golden staff in hand. The Dagi, Glimtron, his party, and the Erkensharie elves all walk through dimension doors behind Logantrance, who looks around smiling with renewed confidence. Vemenomous looks at Zevoncour behind him and then at the races of men.

"Let's see how you like this, humans," says Vemenomous, raising his right fist in the air.

Before he punches the ground with it, Logantrance yells, "Komblianth kamph com blanchard!" and he thrusts his staff at Vemenomous, hitting him dead center on his stomach with an expulsion spell, sending Vemenomous flying back.

Zevoncour ducks just in time to avoid being hit by Vemenomous. He walks at Logantrance. "My turn, magic user," says Zevoncour. His black fingernails start to grow. He is still twelve feet tall, so he is an intimidating and large presence to deal with. He shoots his fingernails of rot, and Logantrance shows no sign of backing down as he walks right at Zevoncour, swinging his staff with lightning-quick reflexes, swatting the deadly fingernails to the ground until they all disappear.

The air opens up above Logantrance, and a bright white light momentarily disorients everyone as Gwithen flies through a dimension door and lands just in front of Zevoncour. She stands on her hind legs and spreads her wings wide, shining and gleaming a crayon-white light that blinds Zevoncour even in the daylight. Zevoncour has to cover his eyes with his arm because Gwithen is naturally the white color of angel blessing, and she can shine this natural toxin to demons and the like at will, like she is doing now. By opening and spreading her wings, her white color is invisible to human eyes; but to evil, it is like looking directly into the sun. His skin will start to burn if he is not shielded from her magnified color soon as well. Zevoncour covers his head with his arms, blinded by Gwithen, yelling, "Get her off of me, Vemenomous. Do something."

"You have bigger worries than my blinding light, demon," says Gwithen. The air to the left of Zevoncour opens up, and Blethstole flies out from a dimension door. With his jaws wide open, he snatches Zevoncour right in the midsection of his body. Zevoncour is massive in size, but Blethstole turns his head to the left and sinks his teeth deep into the ribs and back of Zevoncour, lifting him and violently slamming him to the ground, driving his head and shoulders right into the earth.

Vemenomous flies up and over Blethstole, casting twelve magical javelins that fly one after the other right on target and lancing Blethstole four times across his back. One of the javelins tacks his left wing to his back. Blethstole roars in pain, looking up at Vemenomous as he flies high and out of reach. Zevoncour pulls free from the earth and rests lying on the ground. Gwithen takes to the wing and heads for Vemenomous. Blethstole chants in dragon tongue, expelling the magical javelins from his back. He rests, magically heals, himself, and breathes very hard because he is still in a lot of pain.

Blethstole is startled as Vegenrage walks up to his left side and puts his right hand on Blethstole's neck, just above his left shoulder. Blethstole tilts his head to the left and looks at Vegenrage with serious eyes, and everyone in Vollenbeln stops what they are doing to watch this. Vegenrage looks back at Blethstole with very serious eyes and puts both his hands on Blethstole's scales. Vegenrage closes his eyes and rests his head against Blethstole's side, listening to him breathe. Blethstole, who absolutely dwarfs Vegenrage, starts to breathe calmly and begins to shine. His scales are magically being scrubbed clean, and he looks stronger and more aerodynamic, and his horns that have been taken by Farrah begin to grow back to their original size and form. Everyone and everything stops and watches as Vegenrage steps back from Blethstole with that same serious look in his eyes. Blethstole looks back very seriously. Blethstole nods very slowly. It is like the two of them are talking without saying a word.

Vegenrage turns toward Zevoncour, who stands up. Vegenrage darts into the sky fifteen feet above Zevoncour. From his fingers and thumbs shoot ropes the width of his fingers and thumbs with hooks on the ends of them. They shoot away from Vegenrage and then arch with incredible speed and hook deep into Zevoncour's flesh. Vegenrage swings his hands and arms over his head to Zevoncour with incredible speed and force in an arch and then slams him brutally into the ground.

"How did you like that? Huh, demon? How do you like the outer realms now? Let's see how you like this," says Vegenrage, who swings Zevoncour the same way right back to where he has been, only this time rock spikes thrust up from the earth, making a bed of spikes intended to impale Zevoncour many times. Zevoncour is slammed onto the bed of spikes, and his body is shredded and punctured all over. Vegenrage slams Zevoncour over his head one more time, and his legs and arms break off. Flesh and blood are thrown through the air from the great force Vegenrage is using. Zevoncour's body slams into the ground and breaks apart in many different pieces. The ropes and hooks are reeled back into Vegenrage's hands, and he looks at the bloody clumps of flesh and bone. Zevoncour's head is mutilated and full of stab holes, and there is a barely distinguishable mouth.

Zevoncour still manages to laugh. "I like you, Vegenrage. I like you a lot, but it will not be that easy to get rid of me. I am going to hate having to kill you, Vegenrage. I won't have to kill you if you come and serve me." His body starts to dissolve, and all his remains go up in smoke.

Vegenrage looks to the air and sees that Vemenomous is hovering, flapping his wings just hard enough to keep him where he is, and he has been watching as Vegenrage bonded with Blethstole and defeated Zevoncour so it seems. The same is true for Gwithen, and they both are watching as Vegenrage lowers to the ground. Everyone else is watching too. With a snap of Vegenrage's right arm at Vemenomous, his arm turns into a rope the width of his arm. A barbed spear at the end flies very fast and strikes Vemenomous right in the stomach, and Vegenrage grabs the rope with his left hand and turns his body, falling to his right knee. He pulls his left hand as hard as he can to the ground in front of him. Vemenomous flies by Gwithen very fast and slams into the ground just before hitting Vegenrage, crashing deep into the earth and nearly breaking his neck. He lands on his stomach, and his arms are buried in the earth under his chest. Vegenrage stands and turns to face Vemenomous, who smiles and laughs and gets up from the earth, towering over Vegenrage.

"What are you going to do now, magic man? You are the only thing that stands between me and my queen. You know you cannot stop it. She will be mine. Puny, little man, you think you can stop me? I think I will do this the old-fashioned way," says Vemenomous, who swings his right arm over his head, making a fist with which to crush Vegenrage's head.

Vegenrage has not moved a muscle. He stands with a dead serious look on his face, just watching Vemenomous. Vegenrage does not say a word or make a move until the last moment. He raises his open right hand over his head, catching Vemenomous's arm with a magical hand just before it hits him. Vemenomous kicks Vegenrage, and he goes flying over Logantrance, the elves, and the dwarves, who have been asked by Vegenrage to watch Farrah while he takes care of Vemenomous. Vegenrage lands hard fifteen feet behind his friends, who are protecting the unconscious Farrah. Vemenomous laughs and walks toward Farrah, and the dwarven archers let their Foarsbleem arrows fly. The elven magic users cast magic missiles, lightning bolts, and flaming arrows. All the arrows and spells make their mark. Vemenomous is able to heal very quickly from these arrows and magic, and the wounds heal right in front of everyone as Vemenomous continues to walk toward them.

Blethstole has been patiently standing off to the side, and now he confidently walks over, cutting off Vemenomous before he reaches the races of men. All the elves, the dwarves, and even Logantrance have never seen anything like this ever before. Blethstole walks between Vemenomous and the races of men and puts his back to the latter, clearly protecting them. Gwithen glides over and lands behind Blethstole, and again, the races of man are speechless. Gwithen walks over toward the men, and they are perplexed. They don't know whether to be scared or not; regardless, they are all shaking. Gwithen walks over, and she towers over the men. They are shaking and nervous but in awe at the pure magnificence and beauty they are witnessing.

Gwithen looks at Logantrance, who is on his knees, protecting Farrah. Gwithen sniffs the air and looks right at him. "The man who puts dragons to sleep, the man who steals the magical strength of dragons, the man who cares enough to protect his kind, the man who does not kill when not warranted. I am proud to have shared magic with you,

Logantrance," says Gwithen, walking to the right side of Farrah, and the men to that side of her give way and walk over behind Logantrance. None of the men can take their eyes off Gwithen, and they just hope they will live to tell this story.

Gwithen looks at Farrah lying unconscious on the ground, and her eyes noticeably grow teary. "Poor girl," Gwithen says, looking up and turning her head toward Vegenrage, who is getting up from his sudden impact with the ground and flies up and over Gwithen and the men, landing by Blethstole.

Gwithen looks at Logantrance. "Come on, Quintis. Come here, boy. Come on, Quintis, come here," says Gwithen, looking at Quintis. Logantrance looks at his bag of holding in disbelief as it unties itself from his waist and floats up to Gwithen, who sits on her hind legs and holds Quintis with her front paws.

"Come on, boy, wake up. Come on, boy," says Gwithen. Quintis has two eyes that pop open and a mouth with a long tongue that starts to lick Gwithen all over her face, and she laughs and smiles like she is remembering a long-lost pet. The men and dwarves look at one another with speechless faces, and they continue to watch as Gwithen plays with Quintis.

"OK, boy. Yes, boy, I miss you too," says Gwithen as the long tongue of Quintis licks her all over her face, and she laughs like it tickles. "Go on. Go back to Logantrance now and take good care of him, OK?" Quintis floats back down to the waist of Logantrance.

"Logantrance, Quintis holds the book *The Sleeping Dragon*. It was this book that was used to give Swallgrace and yourself the knowledge to use my magic and harness its strength while I slept. I had known you were going to put

Kronton in a bottle and put me to sleep for a very long time. Hornspire had told me of this. When you first gained this book from Hornspire, you put it in Quintis, and Quintis held the real true book within him. You and Swallgrace and Vegenrage all read the exact same words of the book, but the book passed to Vegenrage and, destroyed with all the other books in his library, was a replica," says Gwithen.

"You knew?" says Logantrance.

"Of course, I knew. You did not think I would just let you walk into my lair, my home, and put me to sleep for a thousand years, did you?" says Gwithen. Logantrance grins and shrugs with a long look on his face. "You have made me proud, Logantrance. You did not use this power for your own use. You used this power in the manner in which you were supposed to. You are an honorable being, Logantrance, and I consider us friends. You brought equilibrium to the Maglical System. The dragons all knew of Vlianth long before man knew Vegenrage, but man grew so strong so fast. Man has always been poised to take over the Maglical System, and the dragons fear this. Right now, Blethstole faces the challenge that will determine if he is to live with man as his friend or if he is to die believing he is the heart of the Maglical System. No matter what happens here, Quintis will give you a book at some point in the future, a book that is now forming from the two books written by Hornspire in your bag of holding, my friend, from long, long ago. When Quintis gives you this book, read it and follow its instructions."

Gwithen looks to Vegenrage, standing by Blethstole. Logantrance and the races of man all look to Vegenrage and Blethstole. Vemenomous is twenty feet from the two of them, staring them down. Vegenrage puts his right hand on Blethstole again and looks up. Vegenrage steps to the side and is now facing Blethstole head-on. Vegenrage raises both his hands and puts them on Blethstole. His arms are extended all the way and just reach Blethstole's scales. Blethstole looks up as his eyes tear up and drop large droplets that shine and glimmer in the sunlight before hitting the ground. Vegenrage can feel Blethstole's heartbeat and he can hear him breathe. Blethstole's right wing starts to grow back, and he starts to flap them both. Vegenrage steps back, looking at Blethstole, and then he turns, stepping to the left beside Blethstole, and starts to stare at Vemenomous, who so far is just watching what is taking place. Blethstole is looking up, and tears are swelling slowly but constantly in his eyes and falling like huge water balloons splashing into the Vollenbeln grass. Blethstole tilts his head toward Vegenrage and looks down with his left eye and sees that Vegenrage is not paying him any attention. Vegenrage is concentrating on Vemenomous. Blethstole looks back up and sniffles. He looks back down at Vegenrage.

"I was afraid Vlianth was coming to destroy all the dragons. I was wrong. I was afraid Vlianth would be stronger than the dragons, and I was right. My fears were misplaced, but now I am straight. Vlianth has come to be the equalizer. You are the heart of the Maglical System. I had always believed I would be that strength, but it is not to be. It was us dragons who made you kill, and it was us dragons who brought about the demon uprising. It was us dragons who knew of your coming and stole from you without your knowledge. Now it is all on you to fix what we started, what we continue, and what we force on you," says Blethstole, who looks at Vemenomous. Blethstole looks at Vegenrage, who is still focused on Vemenomous, and turns to walk away. He takes a few steps and looks back at Vegenrage. "If you ever need a steed or anything like that, the honor would be mine." Blethstole walks back toward the races of men and Gwithen, who is smiling.

Logantrance looks up to Gwithen, and all the men do as well. Logantrance asks her, "What just happened?"

"Blethstole conceded to Vegenrage. You have all just witnessed man become the dominant species of the Maglical System," says Gwithen.

CHAPTER 11

Vemenomous Rises in Vlanthis Again

Vegenrage focuses on Vemenomous with a calm seriousness. Vemenomous has remained motionless, just watching as Blethstole heads behind Vegenrage toward Gwithen and the men. Vemenomous still has his flat head with very big glassy brown eyes. He has very pronounced ridges over his eyes and long round sharp teeth like those of an alligator. He has a very humanoid neck, arms, chest, and abdomen that are all chiseled and very muscular. He has very long black claws at the end of his lengthy fingers. His yellow belly, chest, and neck give way to flame-red-colored skin reminiscent of reptilian hide. His tail is long, and his wings extend above his head and are just a little wider than his shoulders, but when he spreads them, they are much wider and very muscular. He is definitely intimidating with his fifteen-foot-high stance and his calm, confident demeanor.

"Vemenomous, you were Vergraughtu, known as the Violet Violator. You took the writings of Hornspire, and you manipulated them to carve out your desired future. You became one with the staff of barrier breath. You were in my presence, and you were in my dreams, but I gave you, staff of barrier breath, to Farrah. I suppose you were really mad when I made that move, weren't you?" says Vegenrage.

"What are the chances you would give me away just before I had all your power? I was so close. You are of a rare and uniquely strong constitution, Vegenrage, and you were to be mine. You gave me away, and I had to find another way to get into your blood. You are smart. I did not think you would figure it out," says Vemenomous.

"It took me a while, but I understand the staff was planted on me so you could steal my essences and combine it with yours. You were slowly making a link to my mind, gaining control over my images and thoughts as you have done with Farrah. My very significant contribution—and what a significant one it is—is the ability to cast magic without speaking any words. I suppose you can do that now that you have my blood in you, dragon and human magic combined with demonology. And of course, you plan on stealing the Octagemerwell and the Sapphirewell, adding elven and dwarven magic to your essence. You want it all, don't you, Vemenomous, the almighty himself? I have not figured out how you fell into the services of the demons, but no matter, we all know they will exact a toll from you, and that is never a good thing," says Vegenrage.

"I want it all. I want to do whatever I want because I am physically the strongest. I want to be magically the strongest, and I want to do what I want to do whenever I want to do it, and I am getting a little tired of talking with you, Vegenrage. I think it is time for us to settle some things," says Vemenomous.

"Yes, I think it is time," says Vegenrage.

Vemenomous slams his hands together and pulls them apart, and the ground opens up and spreads, heading for Vegenrage. Vegenrage claps his hands shut, and the ground shuts. A spike shoots up from the ground right in front of Vemenomous, and instead of stabbing or lancing him, a ball appears at the end and hits Vemenomous in the stomach, sending him flying high and back through the air. Vemenomous lands on his belly, and a huge divot flies out behind him. Vegenrage flies into the air and swings his right arm and hand at Vemenomous, swinging a magical blade of sharpness, which hits dead center on Vemenomous's back. The blade of sharpness stops dead like a sword hitting a solid brick of steel. Vemenomous stands up, laughing.

"You are going to have to do better than that, human," says Vemenomous, extending his wings and taking flight high in the air.

He breathes his combined breath attack, and Vegenrage cannot avoid it. Vegenrage puts his arms in front of his face, forming an X, and curls up into a ball. He starts to fly backward from the energy of Vemenomous's breath attack, and he disappears like he traveled through a dimension door. Vemenomous looks around for a while, confused. He sniffs the air and looks around. Slowly, he glides in circles down to the ground and looks the sky over. He looks at the races of man and the two dragons blocking him from Farrah. He is still a good twenty yards away from them, but he knows Vegenrage is just playing with him; at least he thinks his attack has not killed Vegenrage.

"Come on out. I know you are here. Come on out, coward. Face me!" yells Vemenomous, looking around the sky and plane of Vollenbeln.

There is one thing for sure: Vemenomous cannot sense Vegenrage, and he never will. The cloak of concealment is definitely one of the most valuable magical items Vegenrage has ever acquired. Vemenomous looks at the two dragons standing between him and the elves and dwarves, and behind them, Logantrance is kneeling beside Farrah. Vemenomous walks toward Blethstole and Gwithen.

"Blethstole, you knew this day was coming. You did not really think you were going to be the true demonian dragon. You did not think it was going to be you to rule supreme over the Maglical System side by side with the demons for the next one thousand years and sire the entire demonian dragon population. No, it is and always is going to be me," says Vemenomous. On the next step he takes, Vegenrage appears above Vemenomous's back, and he is flying down at an incredible speed. He hits Vemenomous in the back and drives Vemenomous into the ground. This happens so fast that even the dragons are startled and surprised at the speed and violence. Vegenrage has just used his body to hammer Vemenomous into the ground. Earth and grass is flung over everyone, and before they look up, Vegenrage has stood up on Vemenomous's back.

Vegenrage reaches his arms and hands toward Vemenomous's hands, and angel ropes fly from Vegenrage's hands and lasso Vemenomous's. The ropes loop many times around Vemenomous's wrists, and they are wrapped around Vegenrage's wrists and held by his hands. Vemenomous raises his head from under the earth, and Vegenrage steps on his head with his left foot, driving his head back into the ground. Vegenrage then pulls up as hard as he can with his arms and lifts Vemenomous's arms back and toward him. Vegenrage is grimacing and yelling like he is straining with all his might, pulling Vemenomous's arms all the way back like there is no further back they can go. Vegenrage reaches down on the ropes like he is shortening the slack and pulls with a yell, driving his foot into the back of Vemenomous's neck. Vegenrage is yelling with his eyes closed, looking blindly into the sky. Vemenomous's muffled screams are heard from under the earth. His wings are flapping up and down, but they have no effect. Vegenrage steps back and now stands between Vemenomous's wings. One can hear the muscles, sinews, ligaments, and bones cracking and giving way in Vemenomous's shoulders to the incredible force being applied by Vegenrage. Vegenrage gives another yell, and Vemenomous's arms are ripped from his shoulders.

Vegenrage falls back and quickly stands up. The arms of Vemenomous are pulled by the ropes to Vegenrage's hands, and he catches them by the wrists. Vemenomous cannot lift himself out of the earth, but he can roll over using his wings. He rolls out of the divot onto the earth, and Vegenrage is waiting for him. He jumps on Vemenomous's chest and starts to beat him in the head with Vemenomous's own arms. Vegenrage beats him silly with crushing blows over and over until Vemenomous's arms have been broken and ripped. Vemenomous himself is a bloody mess, being cut all over his face by his own claws. His head has cuts and bruises all over. Vegenrage takes advantage of the fact that Vemenomous is disoriented and dazed, and he uses a blade of sharpness to cut off both of Vemenomous's legs. Vegenrage then ties both arms and legs together with the angel rope and lays them on the ground. Vemenomous now is just a torso, head, and wings, but Vegenrage lifts him by his head using a magical hand and slices off Vemenomous's wings with a blade of sharpness. He then ties the wings with more angel rope and lays them beside the arms and legs.

Vemenomous starts to laugh. With his face bloodied and his arms, legs, and wings cut off, he laughs with blood trickling from every corner of his body like he is winning this battle. "What are you waiting for, Vegenrage? Kill me. That is what you want, right? So do it. Kill me. End this right now. Kill me here and now and be done with it," says Vemenomous. Vegenrage grabs Vemenomous by the neck with a magical hand, lifts him in the air above his head, and looks at the mangled beast as he bleeds.

"Logantrance, what is he doing?" asks Crayeulle.

"Yeah, I have to admit this is a little over the top, even for Vegenrage," says Glimtron.

"Logantrance, what is he doing?" asks Blythgrin.

Logantrance stands up, confused about what Vegenrage is doing just like the others are. "I do not know what he is doing. I do not understand myself," says Logantrance.

Gwithen is standing off to the side of the men, and she responds, "Vegenrage cannot kill Vemenomous."

"What? What do you mean? Why not?" asks Logantrance.

"Vegenrage cannot kill Vemenomous because, if he does, Vemenomous will rise from within Farrah. Vegenrage cannot kill Vemenomous, but he can contain him," says Gwithen.

"What do you mean? How can Vemenomous rise from Farrah?" asks Logantrance.

"The time Farrah was here in Vlanthis under Vemenomous's mind control, he infected her blood with his DNA. Look at her neck," says Gwithen.

Logantrance looks at Farrah's neck, and he can see the puncture marks on it and her back where Vemenomous had punctured her with his long sharp fingernails. "Vemenomous did this?" asks Logantrance.

"Yes, Farrah was and is very susceptible to mind control because of the witch Alisluxkana, who had charmed Farrah all of her life. Vemenomous took advantage of this, knowing she would be a great magic user because she is the love of Vegenrage. Farrah is now with child, Vegenrage's child. Vemenomous can now exploit this fact. If Vemenomous is to die, the baby growing in Farrah will be devoured by Vemenomous because Vemenomous planted a demon seed in Vegenrage and in Farrah before they mated. Farrah was struck by the shard hammer, which had Vemenomous's blood in it, and it was imbued with demonology. The baby growing in Farrah is Vegenrage's, but Vemenomous's DNA is present, and the death of Vemenomous here will culminate in his presence growing in Farrah. Farrah has one life left from her band of life, but the baby will be consumed by the demon seed of Vemenomous if Vegenrage kills him here and now. The baby will die, and Vemenomous will rise from Farrah just as he did from Vegenrage. This will be more than Farrah can fight against, and she will be swayed into becoming Vemenomous's queen. Of course, she will still have to consume the blood and flesh of Vlianth to become a viable mate for Vemenomous, but all the ingredients have been put into place by the forces of evil to have Farrah transform and become the demonian dragon queen. Now we watch. Now we see how Vegenrage handles this situation. Not even I know how, but I do know it has to be Vegenrage who somehow sends Vemenomous to hell or permanent purgatory," says Gwithen.

"If Vegenrage cannot contain Vemenomous, I will," says Blethstole.

"Yes, well, let us hope Vegenrage somehow puts an end to Vemenomous right now," says Gwithen.

Vemenomous is very weak from trauma and blood loss, and he looks at Vegenrage with his bloodied face. "So you figured it out, didn't you? I mean, you figured out that you cannot kill me. You are smart, human. You have been a very difficult adversary to deal with. You know you cannot contain me. These angel ropes will not hold me forever, and when they wear out, I will be back. I will be back for my queen. You may win now, but I will win in the long run, magic man. I will be there when you are not looking, I will be there when you are not ready, I will be there," says Vemenomous. Vegenrage says nothing and has his left hand pointed at Vemenomous's arms, legs, and wings, which are tied with angel ropes and lying on the ground. Vegenrage's right arm is pointed at Vemenomous's torso, which is still hovering about six feet in the air. Vegenrage starts to swirl his left arm clockwise, and a golden dust starts to form and circle around Vemenomous's limbs, which start to levitate into the air. Vemenomous starts to laugh. "Well, I guess it's about that time."

Vegenrage looks up into the air very seriously and looks back to Gwithen and Blethstole, yelling, "Dragons."

Dribrillianth exits his dimension door and lands by Gwithen and Blethstole, and he is followed by Pryenthious, Gairdennow, Limbrone, Icerock, Oninblind, Wisekee, Bonaro, Moredown, and Hornspire. All the dwarves, elves, and even Logantrance are trembling in fear, not knowing if they should even draw their weapons or not. They all hold their fear in check and form around Farrah, protecting her no matter what happens. One thing is for sure: this is by far the most amazing thing any of them have ever seen in their lives. The dragons are massive. Their scales are glistening in the sunshine. Their muscles are rippling, and their breath is heard through their nostrils. They shake their heads, and the waves of air flowing from their huge bodies are enough to send chills through the bodies of the men. The dragons take notice of the men and pay them little attention.

Dribrillianth starts to address Blethstole when Hornspire yells from the air. "Blethstole, you have your horns, and your wing is back as well. So be it." Hornspire flies up and circles very fast toward Vegenrage. Hornspire flies right at Vegenrage and unleashes his breath of Groinike. Vegenrage uses telekinesis to move the torso of Vemenomous to his limbs on the ground, and he stands in front of the live remains, shielding the two of them from Hornspire's breath attack. Vegenrage turns his head down toward the left side of his body because the noise is deafening, and although his magic is shielding him and Vemenomous from the actual damage of the attack, it is still an instinctual action. The shards of rock are deflected around Vegenrage's magical shield of force, but it is a very scary place to be. The rock shards are devastating the earth all around, and dirt grass and debris are flying off

Vollenbeln into space. Hornspire flies faster and faster right at Vegenrage and finally stops his breath attack. Vegenrage looks up to see Hornspire almost on top of him, swinging his tail like a golf club, hitting Vegenrage with tons of force, and sending him flying out into space. Hornspire immediately attacks Vemenomous with his breath attack and kills him instantly, leaving very little of him. Vemenomous is nothing but pulp when Hornspire finishes his attack.

"No!" yells Gwithen.

"Hornspire, you cowardly, squirming lizard of a dragon," yells Blethstole, who is running, jumping, and flying with both of his wings spread wide and strong, attacking Hornspire. Hornspire turns his body away from Blethstole and swings his tail with its massive club and horns at the end, slamming perfectly into the side of Blethstole's head, sending him flying into the ground ten feet to the right. Hornspire's horny tail has left a large hole in the left side of Blethstole's head.

Gwithen flies to Blethstole's aid, yelling, "Blethstole." He is critically wounded and dying. Gwithen begins to heal him magically.

"That is right, heal him, Gwithen. We still need him," says Hornspire, landing on the ground and walking toward Gwithen, still talking. "I have waited over a thousand years for this moment, Blethstole. I have to admit I did not know what scenario was going to play out, but now I do. Unfortunately, this is the one where Vegenrage lives. You will have to wait, Blethstole, but be ready. I will be waiting for you, old friend." Hornspire now stands over Blethstole, who is lying on his right side, and Gwithen is magically healing him.

Blethstole has not thought Hornspire has it in him and has been not at all ready for the lethal strike by Hornspire. He lies dying, but Gwithen is there to bring him back and mend the terrible wound to his head. Blethstole comes to, groggy and sluggish as he looks up to see Hornspire in his brownish bronze sheen and his confident new strut and swagger. Hornspire jumps in the air and flies toward a dimension door. Blethstole gets up, regaining his full awareness, and watches Hornspire fly away.

"Our time is coming, Blethstole. For now, you all watch as Vemenomous gets one step closer to being the first true demonian dragon. Watch as Farrah gets one step closer to being the demonian dragon queen. All of you, watch helpless as there is nothing you can do. What is done is done," says Hornspire as he flies through his dimension door, and he is gone.

Dribrillianth looks around, very confused. "I do not trust him. I am going home to make sure the young and females are OK," says Dribrillianth who does not hesitate at all; he flaps his wings powerfully and is gone through a dimension door.

"Me too," says Pryenthious, and he too flies through a dimension door. Vegenrage flies back to Logantrance and kneels down beside Farrah, who is still unconscious. Vegenrage pays no attention to the fact that there are dragons, dwarves, and elves all standing around, and they are all quiet and focused on Vegenrage. He puts his hands on Farrah's cheeks and concentrates. Farrah gasps with a deep breath and opens her eyes. Her eyes are hazelnut brown except the center of her eyes, which look like cat eyes with that standing-up black oval. Her eyes are mimicking Vemenomous's eyes. Farrah has the look of great fear in her face. She breathes very heavily, and tears fall from her eyes.

"Vegenrage, he is in me. He is in me, Vegenrage. I can feel him. This is what he has wanted all the time. His blood is mated with mine now. Vegenrage, he has killed our child. I can—ah!" Farrah gasps and screams, closing her eyes and grabbing the bottom part of her shirt (Cleapell) and lifting it to the bottom of her breasts. Farrah screams, looking at her stomach. "Vegenrage, Vegenrage!" Farrah yells as her eyes open very wide, and she watches her belly grow, like a child is growing inside of her. "Vegenrage, what are we going to do? Vegenrage . . . wh—" Farrah falls silent and unconscious as Vegenrage puts his hand on her forehead and gently lays her head back on the ground.

Vegenrage looks over his shoulder, looking like he is very distraught, and speaks to everyone with definite anger in his voice. "You should all leave now," says Vegenrage, and then he looks up and points his hands to the ground. He is on his knees, and there is an upside-down V from his head to his hands, which are only feet from the ground. Vegenrage starts to shake, and red lightning shoots from his hands into the ground, and a red glow moves around his realm as the sun falls and the sky darkens.

"What is he doing?" asks Glimtron, looking to Logantrance.

"I am not sure, Glimtron, but I think we had better take Vegenrage very seriously, and we should all leave now," says Logantrance.

"He is releasing his protective magic. He is calling the demons, all of them," says Blethstole to Gwithen.

"He is saving Farrah. That is what he is doing. Come on, we have to go. We have to go now," says Gwithen, and she takes flight and heads through a dimension door. All the dragons follow, but the men stay and watch, captivated by Vegenrage.

Farrah awakens, and she looks to her stomach as the weather instantly changes, becoming very windy. The men start to get a little anxious, as the trees grow very fast way off to the other side of Vollenbeln, leaves begin to whip around like it is fall, and the wind keeps getting stronger. The sky fills with clouds, lightning starts to flash, and thunder roars. The sky becomes a deep ocean blue with fantastic streaks of pure white lightning shooting through it. Rain starts to fall very hard, and Logantrance says to all the men, "We had better not stick around any longer. We need to go now." They do not procrastinate any longer, and the men all walk through dimension doors.

Farrah calls to Vegenrage, as they are both pelted with huge raindrops and soaked to the bone already. Vegenrage is still concentrating with his eyes closed and his arms forming an upside-down V up to his head. "Vegenrage, you are not going to let me die, right? You are here. We are still going to be together, right? Vegenrage, I'm scared. I need you, Vegenrage," says Farrah.

Vegenrage again has red lightning shooting from his hands into the ground, and it stops. He opens his eyes with water pelting him and being blown off by the heavy winds. "This is not going to be fun, Farrah, but it is necessary. You are going to be fine. You are no good to them alone. I am no good to them alone. They need both of us. Tell me you trust me," says Vegenrage.

"I trust you, Vegenrage," says Farrah.

"Tell me you believe in me. Tell me you believe in us," says Vegenrage.

"I believe in you, Vegenrage. I believe in us," says Farrah, gasping, and her eyes are continuously closing from the rain falling on her. Vegenrage leans down and kisses Farrah. He sits back up on his knees. Farrah's hands are still holding her shirt just below her breasts, and her belly is exposed. It looks like she is at full term, ready to give birth to a baby. Vegenrage runs his right index finger across her belly, and it splits from her left side to her right side, and blood washes away, flowing with the rain.

Farrah screams, "Vegenrage, what are you doing?" This exposes the demon seed of Vemenomous that is not fully formed yet but is almost a miniature replica of the fifteen-foot beast. Vegenrage reaches into the belly of Farrah and grabs the demon seed, and it bites him over and over, making bone-chilling hisses and screams. He gets a hold of it by the neck and squeezes hard, pulling it from Farrah's belly. The powerful rain washes the blood away surprisingly fast, and Farrah's belly heals as Vegenrage runs his free hand over it.

The demon seed is two feet tall and is still forming, becoming a small Vemenomous. It is scratching and clawing and biting and drawing lots of blood from Vegenrage, but he ignores the pain; he ignores the screams from the small beast and focuses on healing Farrah with his free hand. Farrah's eyes flutter up and down, and she falls, unconscious. Vegenrage stands, grasping the miniature Vemenomous with his left hand around its neck, and he faces his right palm at it.

Lightning shoots from the thunder clouds above and heads right for Vegenrage's head. The lightning breaks apart just before it hits him and splinters into five lines. They enter him down his right shoulder and arm, and another five lines enter him down his left. The lightning looks like a blanket that enters Vegenrage from his shoulders down to his arms, and this lasts for about ten seconds. The lightning flows through Vegenrage's body and out of his right palm in smaller lightning streaks and into the small Vemenomous, who is not killed but put in a trance of some sort and falls limp.

When the lightning stops flowing from the sky and into Vegenrage, the rain stops. The deep ocean blue and rainy atmosphere starts to change. Vegenrage lays the seemingly dead Vemenomous on the ground and stands looking at his realm. "So the evil I was brought here to face was more than Xanorax. It was not the dragons. It was the demons who were always going to make their way to the outer realms. You knew this, didn't you, Behaggen? The dragons knew this too. Did the races of man know this as well?" says Vegenrage out loud.

Behaggen unties himself from the waist of Vegenrage and floats into the air, with his eyes popping into view and his mouth, the opening in the top of the bag, answering Vegenrage. "It is true the dragons always knew that the demons were always going to make their way to the surface someday. The dragons always thought it was them who are to be the strongest. They did not want interference from the races of man. They did not want to believe that Vlianth would come and steal all the power and be chosen to be the bright light of good, the champion of the heavenly light, even though the dragons had Hornspire, who had seen and written about you, the man who would save the Maglical System from evil. Swallgrace was always thought to be this man, but he failed in his quest. He never held the staff of barrier breath. That was to be you. You are the true Vlianth. You are Vegenrage, the magic user. You are Vegenrage, the dragon reclaimed. And now you are Vegenrage, the demon rising. You have grown supreme in your power here in Vollenbeln, and they cannot hurt you here, but they can take Farrah, and they can hurt you on the worlds in the Maglical System. From here on out, no prophecy has been told regarding your future. No power other than yours can stop the demons, and only you can save Farrah from their evil grip and plans. You have opened the door, and now you must face the demon rising," says Behaggen, and he falls back to Vegenrage's waist and ties himself back into place.

Vegenrage tilts his head to the right and up toward the sky and watches as all the clouds in the sky darken and the deep ocean blue color turns to a dark gray color. The rain has stopped, but the wind still whips. The clouds do not flow across the sky; instead, they overturn like they are being spun. Off to the other side of Vollenbeln where all the trees have just grown very fast, they are still growing leaves incredibly quick, and the leaves keep blowing off the branches and through the air.

Vegenrage is startled and takes a step back, as his home, which is pretty much the center of the plane, erupts and explodes upward. The earth grows upward like a volcano is growing into the air. It grows up and explodes like a volcano would. Instead of running out from the volcano and along the earth, lava flies straight up and into the sky, evaporating the clouds and turning the sky into a dark cloud of molten lava quickly covering the sky. The atmosphere becomes dark red. If not for the glow of the lava, everything will be dark.

Vegenrage hears a scream coming from something that is obviously very big. Erupting from the volcano is Roartill. He explodes from the volcano and is just as wide as the volcano itself. He rises to his waist, and the volcano that has just been in the center of Vollenbeln is now the hips, torso, chest, arms, shoulders, neck, and head of Roartill. He towers one hundred feet in the air, and Vegenrage leans down to protect himself and Farrah with a force barrier, which deflects a lot of rock and lava thrown at them when Roartill exploded from the earth.

Roartill is massive, and he can take any form he wishes. This form has a rounded, oblong torso rippled with muscle and a pitted-looking rubbery dark grayish red reptilian skin. He has shades of red throughout his belly and under his arms, which are extremely muscular with deadly long black claws. His neck has muscle running from his shoulders up along his neck, supporting his very wide round head.

Vegenrage faces the overwhelmingly large figure, takes a jump step, and kicks the seemingly dead Vemenomous like it is a soccer ball. "Here, take your little imp and keep him in the inner realm. The next time we run into each other will be the last. So what is the name you go by?" asks Vegenrage. Vemenomous flies at Roartill, who opens his right hand, shooting incinerating red lightning into Vemenomous, which burns him to ash before he gets to his hand.

"That is right, Vegenrage. The next time you see Vemenomous, he will extinguish your life. He will bring you to my domain, where your powers will be severely handicapped, like mine are now here in your domain. You will succumb to my will, and the female will be the demonian dragon queen. Vemenomous will rule the Maglical System, and the female will be his queen. My demons will rule the land and waters, and the demonian dragons will rule the air. You can try, but you cannot stop it. Here in Vollenbeln, you are safe from my control, but you are not safe on the worlds of the Maglical System. You will not be able to save the girl with a tainted mind, and she will bring you to me, and this will be the time of your end. I have come to your call, Vegenrage, and I expect you will come when I call. I am Roartill, ruler of Maglical Hell, and your divinity shall never come to pass. I will see to that," says Roartill.

Vegenrage levitates up in the air, looking up, and the ash clouds spread apart in a perfect circle as he rises in the air. Golden light shines down on Vegenrage. He hovers motionless in the air and looks at Roartill, facing both his arms at him. "I am starting to feel and know why I have come. I know what my final destiny is, but it is still far off. You will never have power over me, Roartill. You stay in your realm because, if you venture to the outer realms, you will face certain destruction. The power I have here in Vollenbeln only grows, and my power on the surface of the worlds of the Maglical System is still greater than yours. Take your demons and stay in your realm or be destroyed," says Vegenrage, and he faces both his arms and hands at Roartill. "If you ever doubt that my power is absolute, then here is something for you to think about as you send your demons to their destruction because I will hunt them. I will destroy them unless they stay to the inner realm."

The golden light from the clouds shines down on Vegenrage and then flows from his arms in a funnel shape, which hits and engulfs Roartill in golden light that starts to burn and melt his flesh. Roartill yells in pain and looks up, laughing as his flesh melts. He looks at Vegenrage, relishing the pain as his body melts. Roartill starts to shrink, yelling, screaming, laughing, and pausing. "Vegenrage, you are not the savior. You are not what you think you are. The blood of my being will grow, and Vemenomous will rule supreme. You wait, Vegenrage. You wait," says Roartill, shrinking and falling into the volcano, which also shrinks.

All the rock and earth that exploded up and out starts to pull back into the ground from which it has come. The sky drops lava in a river that flows right back into the volcano, and this goes on for a few minutes. The clouds follow as well until they are all gone, and the sky is sunny and beautiful. The trees on the far side of Vollenbeln grow back to a mature size, and the leaves grow back and are full grown, beautiful, and rustling in the slight warm breeze. The earth pulls back, Vegenrage's home is reformed, and everything looks like it did before.

Vegenrage kneels down beside Farrah and puts his hand on her cheek. "Farrah. Hey, Farrah, come on, baby, wake up," says Vegenrage, and he slides her shirt up a little and can see that there is no scar left from where he extracted Vemenomous. He rests his right palm on Farrah's stomach, closes his eyes, and concentrates. Farrah opens her eyes, and they are her beautiful hazelnut-brown-colored eyes, which match so perfectly with her platinum blond hair. Farrah looks at Vegenrage and can see he is concentrating. She puts her left hand on his right hand, which is on her stomach, and Vegenrage looks at her.

"We lost our baby. Vemenomous took our baby with him," says Farrah.

"I know," says Vegenrage.

"We will never have peace. We will never be able to settle down. Destruction and chaos is all they know and all they want. Vemenomous has now birthed from you and I. He has both of our blood in him, and he has the blood of Roartill in him as well. I don't know how I know that, but I do. I don't know if we can kill him, destroy him, and get rid of him, but I will give my life trying because if we do not get rid of him, he will cause death and destruction forever," says Farrah. She sits up and hugs Vegenrage, who holds her quietly.

CHAPTER 12

Shenlylith Calls Basters

Zevoncour is leading his demon army up from the Strabalster inner realm. He is leading them into the Krasbeil Mountains, where they plan on erupting all the mountains. Like in Fargloin, the plan is to have all the mountains erupting ash into the atmosphere, eventually blocking out all the sunlight. They plan on starting here and then moving on to the Swapoon mountain range. They want to start in Krasbeil because they know Gairdennow lives in the Swapoon Mountains, and the demons want to avoid him as long as possible.

The demons have no knowledge of Shenlylith and her past, and fortunately for Zevoncour, he hesitates and halts. All the demons are below him, following like they are all tied to him by a rope. Zevoncour uses great magic to melt the rock as they ascend to the outer realm, and all his demons are pulled up as he rises in the world's crust. There is great pressure in the inner realm, and as Zevoncour rises and melts his way through the rock, the molten inner core rises behind them faster and faster as they get closer to the surface.

Zevoncour stops and says he is being called by his master, Roartill. He leads his demons underneath the mountains and leaves them to rise into individual mountains with the lava. The demons anxiously do so. Lava is being forced up into the mountains from all the pressure below. Zevoncour heads back down into the depths of the world, and his demons rise. Demons do not have a lot of magic, and most of them have no magic on the outer realm, but there is inherent magic that all demons have; for example, all demons have lava flow. This is magic that allows demons to melt their form and become one with lava, flowing with or through the lava and returning to their demon form at any time. There is magic that all demons are immune to, like death magic, and they are all fire-resistant. Demons are also immune to spells of rot, corrosion, and decay. They also have immunities that may come into play; for example, the Dark Bush has no ill effect on demons, so they can easily travel through forests overgrown with the deadly Dark Bush.

The lava has reached the base of the mountains, and the demons have the ability to steer the lava through the rocky crust of Strabalster. The demons start to separate and lead the lava into separate mountains. They know the dwarves have been in Symbollia, and they all have attacked there, but here in Krasbeil, they just want to erupt the mountains and start the deadly flow of lava and ash into the atmosphere, eventually blocking out the sunlight.

The demons have no idea what is waiting for them. They have no idea that the Krasbeil Mountains are home to Shenlylith. The races of man know this is Shenlylith's Prison, but the demons do not. Zevoncour has been imbued with a whole lot of knowledge from the fallen demon master kings by Roartill, but he still does not know everything. Demons, obviously, are impervious to heat and fire, but cold is their second biggest weakness behind angel blessing magic, and both of these schools of magic are Shenlylith's strengths.

The demons spread and head toward a mountain of their own. They are very excited because the possibility of fresh, live meat awaits them. It does not have to be man; any animal is fine and greatly anticipated by the demons. There is a small bubble of space between the molten lava flowing from the core of the world and the solid rock melting and giving way to the rising lava. The demons use their lava flow ability and ride the leading edge of the lava. They are in their demon form from the hips up to their head, and the rest of their body is a part of the lava, which allows them to ride the front edge of lava like a wave. The lava flows in the direction the demons face. This is how the demons can direct the lava into separate mountains.

Once the lava enters the bottom half of the mountains, all the demons quickly realize and feel the shake, the tremble that quivers in their spines. Even though they are demons, they still feel fear, they still feel pain on the outer realm, and they sure know something is not right, but this does not stop them. The demons still rise into the mountains on huge flows of lava. Out of the solid rock comes what the demons have never thought possible. Shenlylith's wings appear in the small bubble between rock and lava, and the demons, one at a time, are engulfed and disappear, teleported to a single location outside and high up in the Krasbeil mountain range. This is exceptionally draining to the demons. They appear on a ledge somewhere atop the mountains, and the cold immobilizes them very quickly. The demons have one saving grace here. They very quickly are frozen solid. This does not kill the demons; it simply freezes them, but they can still be brought back. Zevoncour has sent fifty of his demons into the Krasbeil Mountains, and it takes Shenlylith only thirty minutes to teleport all the demons to the mountaintop ledges and less than two hours for them to be frozen into ice demon statues.

Unfortunately, the damage has been done. The molten lava has made a passageway from the core of Strabalster to the Krasbeil Mountains. It is only a matter of time before the pressure and the lava find their way out of the mountains. Shenlylith tries to hold back the lava with her magic, but she cannot, and before the day is out, the lava erupts from many of the mountains, starting a chain reaction. And by the next day, almost one hundred mountains here are flowing lava, and the air is filling with toxic ash at a catastrophic rate. This is destroying the mountains and, with it, Shenlylith's magical power.

Shenlylith is losing her strength, and this sends magical reverberations that are felt by those who are very strong magically, and of course, Basters feels this, and he has been waiting for just this feeling to overcome him—the calling of Shenlylith, which he has read about. Like Cloakenstrike, who has not shared all he has read from the book *The Ugorian Stand* with Bastrenboar and Fraborn, Basters has done the same, not sharing all he has read about with Cloakenstrike from the book *Divination: Demon, Dragon, Elf, or Man*. He knew from his readings that Shenlylith will be calling for him and that this will start the end of his kingship in Ugoria.

It is very early, and Basters is woken by a dream. He sits up in his bed and looks around. "I was waiting for this, but I did not think it would come so soon," Basters says out loud as he gets out of bed and dresses himself. He sends a telepathic message to Cloakenstrike and gets no answer. He then goes to the dining area and has one of the elves fetch Fraborn for him while he eats some breakfast. Fraborn shows up shortly and sits down to have some breakfast with his king. Right on cue, Cloakenstrike walks from a dimensional door and sits with his two longtime companions.

Basters is eating heartily, and Fraborn and Cloakenstrike get plates of their own and start to eat. Basters and Cloakenstrike have had many meals together over the past hundreds of years, as well as many adventures. This breakfast is very unusual. They are very quiet and do not talk at all, eating heartily like it is their last breakfast together. It is a very quiet and somber breakfast for these three adventurers, who all know something is up. Fraborn has only adventured with Basters and Cloakenstrike since the day he has been adorned with armor and his Lavumptom sword from Cloakenstrike, but he has always been the loyal soldier and known when to stay quiet, like now. The three of them finish breakfast, and their plates are taken away by servants. A short silence is broken by Cloakenstrike. Even though Basters is now king and even though he has insight, it has always been Cloakenstrike to start and lead conversations for these three, and this still holds true on this quiet morning.

"I have felt the disturbance in Krasbeil. A great magic has been awoken and diminished. I have felt the presence of good replaced with that of evil. A great magical shift is happening.

I think it is time we make a trek back into that frozen land in order to save our king, Basters," says Cloakenstrike.

"What are you talking about? You can't mean the mountains where we lost Rothglon. Why would we want to go back there?" says Fraborn, looking at Basters.

"Ever since I first held the snow gold trinket and was transformed back into my human form, I knew that I was supposed to give it back. I knew that I was supposed to bring Ugoria its true king. I did not know it would be so soon, but Shenlylith has called for me. I am going to the Krasbeil Mountains, and I ask that the two of you come with me. I believe the final pages of the book *Divination: Demon, Dragon, Elf, or Man* will be written, and I believe somehow this will bring the true king of Ugoria to the throne. If you two do not want to come, I understand, but our adventure continues. And if I am to lead you, Cloakenstrike, the great magic user, to something great, I believe this is it. What do you two say? Do you want to travel with me? We leave now," says Basters.

Fraborn stands up and draws his Lavumptom sword, saying, "I will follow my king and my friend."

"Let us not waste any more time. We follow the king of Ugoria, and I bet some of the elves may wish to travel with us as well," says Cloakenstrike. He remembers his encounter with Hornspire a very long time ago and Hornspire telling him the book *Divination: Demon, Dragon, Elf, or Man* will be finished when Hornspire is resurrected.

"Well, I do not want to waste any time, and the curiosity is killing me. I want to get to Krasbeil and see if the book *Divination: Demon, Dragon, Elf, or Man* is somehow magically written in, plus Shenlylith has called for me. I can feel her calling. I am going now. Who is coming with me?" says Basters.

"I am," says Fraborn.

"I am as well," says Cloakenstrike.

"Come follow me," says Basters, who makes his way to the courtyard and announces he is traveling to the Krasbeil Mountains. The elves present listen and watch as Basters walks through a dimension door, followed by Cloakenstrike and Fraborn.

Hornspire has made his home very secretly and been able to keep his lair hidden from all the dragons except for Gwithen, who knows it is at the northeasternmost edge of the Krasbeil Mountains. His lair is actually at the base of the last mountain called Ventcallis Mountain. This is the start of one of very few frozen places on all three worlds in the Maglical System. The Frozen Thundrase is the land from the Krasbeil Mountains north and east to the Briganyare Sea. It is true that Hornspire has fully expected Vegenrage will die to the hands of Zevoncour near the Smildren Sea, and since this has not happened, all of Hornspire's visions are now inaccurate. However, he still has great insight as to events; and for things that are going to happen, he just does not know exactly what the outcome will be.

Hornspire has planned for over a thousand years to not be the ruler or the dominant being like Vergraughtu or Blethstole, but instead, what Hornspire has used his fantastic foresight ability for is the preservation of his personal being and his personal success. Hornspire has manipulated his writings and placed them in the hands of chosen races of man and dragons to lead them into situations that Hornspire has seen and been waiting for. Now one may think this will all work out just great for Hornspire, but still there are so many variations and so many different things that can happen; it is still very difficult to make events in the future happen exactly the way they are planned. Hornspire has done exceptionally well to bring about events the way he has planned. Vergraughtu has taken the writings of Hornspire and changed them as well, so there is so much going on here. But Hornspire is the prophetical master, and he has just felt what he has been waiting over a thousand years for—the shake in the Krasbeil Mountains, the diminishing of Shenlylith's power.

Hornspire knows exactly what this means. His visions are going to be different now, but he knows that soon Basters, Cloakenstrike, Vegenrage, and Farrah will be here in the Krasbeil Mountains. Hornspire has seen himself kill Cloakenstrike, but that has depended on the death of Vegenrage, which does not happen. The very last vision Hornspire has had is the vision in Krasbeil, where Shenlylith has become visible, and four magic users, including Vegenrage, are with her. Hornspire has never seen the outcome to this scenario. This scenario is to happen if Vegenrage has survived the encounter with Zevoncour at Hornspire's resurrection. Hornspire remembers in other visions this is where he has killed Cloakenstrike and takes back the magical items he has given to him, but there is a new future to play out, and Hornspire does not know its outcome.

Vegenrage and Farrah are sleeping in their bed in their home in Vollenbeln when Farrah sits up and rubs her face. She looks over to Vegenrage, who is still sleeping, and rubs his back, waking him. "Vegenrage, do you feel it? Do you know what that is? I feel some sort of magic. I feel it hitting me like waves of warm air blowing over me," says Farrah.

"Yes, I feel it. There is a great disturbance in Strabalster. This is a very powerful magic that is shifting. This is Shenlylith, the ancient snow elf. She is calling for her master. Her master is the king of Ugoria. I can feel he is traveling to her, and he has company. It is Cloakenstrike. They are going to the Krasbeil Mountains. I can feel the presence of great evil. The demons are making their way to the surface on Strabalster, and Shenlylith has captured them. She has stranded them in Shenlylith's Prison. This is good. The demons have no defense against the cold here. They will be immobilized and imprisoned here," says Vegenrage.

"Vegenrage, how do I feel this? I have never felt this before," says Farrah.

"You are becoming very powerful. Your magical being is starting to grow, and you are becoming an independent force. This means you have achieved magical prowess. The Maglical System is full of magic, and it is a shifting force. Magic flows toward the strongest pull like water flows down the easiest pathway. If a magical energy feels your presence, it will flow toward you and strengthen you. You have to be very conscious of this because other magical beings will be able to sense you and track you. We need to find you a magical cloak to conceal your magical presence, like the one I have," says Vegenrage.

"Well, what about this magical sense I feel? Does this mean I should go to it, or should I avoid it?" asks Farrah.

"This is something you have to concentrate on. You have to know the source of the magic you are feeling and make sure it is what you think it is. Just because you feel magic and you think you know who or what it is does not mean that it is not masked or cloaked to mislead you. This is something you will get good at. You remember when we were in Glaboria right after the dragons had destroyed it and I went down to the ground to investigate a weapon that I sensed?" says Vegenrage.

"Yes, I remember, and the Mountain Creek dragons rose from the ground and captured you," says Farrah.

"Exactly! The dragons masked their presence and heightened the presence of the battle ax, which caught my attention. I was concentrating on the past of the weapon and its owner, and the dragons rose and captured me. This is how deceit is used in magic to trick others," says Vegenrage.

"So what about the magical power in Strabalster? Should we investigate this?" asks Farrah.

"Yes, I think we should, but we should bring friends of our own with us in this instance. I think we should go to the Erkensharie, get Logantrance, and consult with the elves," says Vegenrage.

Farrah gets up from their bed, and the moonlight is shining down from the window in the roof of their home. Vegenrage watches, smiling because Farrah is so beautiful and so naked. He watches as she walks to her dresser and uses her magic to brush her hair. The moonlight is dim, and the shadows line the home in gray. Two logs burn in the fireplace, nothing more than red-hot coals burning with little flame and light. Farrah can see in the mirror on her dresser that Vegenrage, still lying on the bed, is watching her, and she smiles as, magically, her long hair is perfectly pulled back by a barrette and hangs down the length of her back. She magically opens her dresser drawers, and Cleapell floats out and covers her while she just waves her arms through the air and smiles at Vegenrage in her mirror. Vegenrage gets up, walks behind her, and hugs her from the back, kissing her shoulder and neck. Farrah smiles, feeling his warmth. She turns and watches as Vegenrage magically clothes himself in his favorite leather pants and snug black T-shirt. They both accessorize with their bags of holding and Farrah with Quadrapierce.

"Wait, before we go, I have one little thing to do," says Farrah, kissing Vegenrage and smiling.

"OK, I think we are ready now. Hey, one thing I am curious about, do you think you can communicate with Logantrance telepathically? Try to see if you can contact him. You have been learning magic at such a fast rate that I think you may be able to contact Logantrance and tell him we are coming," says Vegenrage.

"OK, I will try," says Farrah.

Logantrance has gone to the Erkensharie with the dwarves and elves who were in Vollenbeln, and here Glimtron has gathered with Ulegwahn and the high-class elves to discuss what is to happen with the surviving dwarves of Glaboria. Ulegwahn has provided sanctuary for the dwarves in the Erkensharie, but it is only temporary. All the dwarves and elves agree that all the races of man must unite to fight against the demons and push them back to the inner realm, where they belong. The dragons are an interesting topic. It is not understood what is happening with the dragons and the races of man, but it will appear that, at least for the time being until the demons have been driven from the outer realm, the dragons have united with the races of man.

Vegenrage and Farrah are a topic of concern as well because they are two of the strongest forces for the races of man. Ulegwahn has shown great interest and wants to lead a small band of warriors and magic users back to Vollenbeln to help Vegenrage and Farrah. In reality, he wants to help Farrah and see her, but he keeps this thought to himself. Logantrance has decided against this request, and so have those who have seen the look on Vegenrage's face when he has asked them all to leave. Great and powerful magic is happening, and for now, they all wait to hear from Vegenrage and Farrah. It has been a few days now.

Logantrance is getting ready to go to back to Richterblen when he gets telepathy from Farrah. He immediately calls Oriapow and asks that they talk with Ulegwahn and Glimtron. "Oriapow, I have some great news that Ulegwahn will be excited to hear. I have been contacted by Farrah. She and Vegenrage are fine, and they want to come here. They are coming to the courtyard, and they will be here soon."

"I will inform Ulegwahn. You go to the courtyard and wait for them with the others," says Oriapow.

Logantrance goes to the courtyard and gathers the dwarves and elves, and they wait for the arrival of Vegenrage and Farrah. They do not have to wait long as Vegenrage and Farrah arrive from their dimension door and are greeted by Glimtron and the dwarves. The magic-using elves, Oriapow and Ulegwahn, show up as well. There are smiles and handshakes and all kinds of questions, and of course, Farrah is surrounded by the dwarves, showering her with shy affection, which she loves so much.

Ulegwahn announces that they all shall feast in the courtyard, and soon there are tables and food for all in the Erkensharie midmorning. Ulegwahn has shown a more-than-obvious interest in Farrah in the past, and he continues his somewhat misplaced courtesy as he directs Farrah to a table to be seated right next to him. The dwarves are a little disappointed with this. Vegenrage is engaged in conversation with Logantrance, Whenshade, Crayeulle, Blythgrin, Trybill and Oriapow.

"Vegenrage, how did you make it out with Farrah? I could sense the demons were coming to Vollenbeln, and I could sense that Vemenomous had implanted a demon seed in Farrah. I know there is only one way that the demons could make their way to Vollenbeln, and that is if you had allowed it. I am very curious to know what happened there. Did you defeat Vemenomous once and for all?" Logantrance asks Vegenrage, and all the others listen contently.

"It is true, Logantrance. Vemenomous invaded Farrah, planting a demon seed in her, and I was able to extract him before he reached maturity, but still, Farrah and I lost our baby. She seems to be managing well. Vemenomous has the blood of Roartill in him, along with mine and Farrah's. Vemenomous is now under the wing of Roartill. We will see him again, and he is still after Farrah. The demons have invaded the outer realms, and they intend to erupt all the mountains on all the worlds, blocking out the light, increasing their power significantly. I am not sure how we will defeat them, but Farrah and I have felt they have made their presence in Strabalster. They are trying to erupt the Krasbeil Mountains. I have felt great magical power here and sought your guidance. I have felt the great snow elf Shenlylith. I thought we should help her if we can. Not only that but I have felt the convergence of more magic coming to meet with Shenlylith as well. It is Cloakenstrike and Bastrenboar, but Bastrenboar has changed. Something is different about him. His magic is much more powerful now, and I feel he is connected to Shenlylith. I wanted to see if the elves here in the Erkensharie had insight into this unusual situation," says Vegenrage.

"Yes, I have felt it as well, Vegenrage. Let us go and meet with Ulegwahn and see what the elder class of magic users here know," says Logantrance.

They all quickly notice Ulegwahn has Farrah sitting close to him and that he is talking very close to her. "Ulegwahn, it is good to see you," says Vegenrage, and Ulegwahn ignores him.

Farrah gets up, smiling. "Thank you." She moves over to Vegenrage, standing behind him and holding him. "Ulegwahn is creeping me out," she whispers into Vegenrage's ear.

"Sit, everyone, sit. Let us eat," says Ulegwahn. Vegenrage sits right next to Ulegwahn, where Farrah just has been, and she sits next to Vegenrage. Logantrance, Oriapow, Whenshade, Crayeulle, Blythgrin, and Trybill all sit at the table.

Vegenrage begins the discussion about what he has felt and sensed in Krasbeil. He asks if anyone knows about

Bastrenboar. He can sense great tension between him and Ulegwahn, sitting right next to him, which makes him a little uncomfortable. Fortunately, Oriapow takes over the conversation and explains why there is a connection between Shenlylith and Bastrenboar (Basters). Farrah adds that she knows that Bastrenboar has been changed to human form and is now Basters. Whenshade knows the story of the Lycoreal humans who have been changed into humanors eight hundred years ago and that Bastrenboar is Basters, who now has been changed back into his human form. This must mean that he has become the king of Ugoria and that he is protected by Shenlylith. The demon rising in the Krasbeil Mountains is why Basters and Cloakenstrike are going to Shenlylith's Prison. If the mountains are destroyed, this will kill Shenlylith and end the power of the snow gold trinket.

"This is a great dilemma. I do believe we should go and help protect Shenlylith, but it is her sworn oath to protect the king of Ugoria, and if this is Basters, he and Cloakenstrike may not take so kindly to us. They may try to have us imprisoned, never to leave. The snow gold trinket is the second most powerful elven magical item. I think we should take the Octagemerwell to protect Shenlylith from demons, but Basters and Cloakenstrike will surely try to steal it from us," says Oriapow.

"You mean that man we saw in the sand marshes was Bastrenboar? Basters is or was Bastrenboar? You mean Cloakenstrike and Bastrenboar saved us twice now from that dragon, Hornspire? This is crazy. Those two villains make no sense at all," says Blythgrin.

"Well, no matter, I do not want any of you going to Strabalster. I especially do not want the Octagemerwell leaving the Erkensharie. I will tell you all something else. This dragon, Hornspire, has written prophecy about Vegenrage, but his prophecy has all been planned from the start. He has manipulated his writing to bring him to his end, and that end is not what he has written. His writings are designed to lead us all into traps. His writings are designed to keep us all under control of the dragons," says Ulegwahn.

"All the same, Vegenrage has done right by all the races of man. And if he leads us to Strabalster, I will be there to help him in the fight against the demons, Cloakenstrike, and Bastrenboar or Basters or whatever name he goes by," says Logantrance.

"Hold on. Everyone, hold on one second. Ulegwahn is right. Hornspire has manipulated his writings from the start to craft and mold the outcome he has planned for a very long time. The one big thing is that I was not brought here to protect the races of man from the dragons, which is what Hornspire wanted everyone, including the dragons, to believe. I was brought here to unite the races of man with the dragons, and if this does not happen, then dragons will be replaced by the demonian dragons, and the races of man will become extinct. I do not know what Hornspire had envisioned for his personal end, but I know I need to unite our two species so that we, together, can fight against the demon uprising that is now taking place here on Fargloin and Strabalster and will find its way to Kronton as well. I will go to Krasbeil because the demons must be stopped before they get too strong. We have to face them head-on. The one huge disadvantage the demons have is that they do not have numbers on their side. They can be killed on the outer realm, and if killed here, they cannot come back ever. The damage in Glaboria has been done. From now on, wherever the demons show themselves, we must face them and destroy them, or else they will win. This is a war against Maglical evil, a war that has begun, and those who sit around and think the demons will leave them alone will die. I am going to the Krasbeil Mountains because this is where the demons are, and they will be at a disadvantage in the cold. This is why I was brought here. I go to destroy the demons. Cloakenstrike, the magic user who all by himself entered the Great Erken and killed King Estine and Shandorn, plus many other elves of the Erkensharie, will be there as well, and we will have the upper hand on him for a change. This magic user and Bastrenboar, who is now Basters, have surprised me on more than one occasion, and for the first time, I get to surprise them. I will go to Krasbeil, and any who want to take the fight to the demons before they bring the fight here to your doorstep, the time is now. Let the demon uprising meet its end now," says Vegenrage.

There is a pause, and Glimtron stands. "Vegenrage, I am with you. The demons have destroyed my home and killed most of my people. I will go wherever they are, and my ax will sever their evil bodies until they are gone forever," says Glimtron. The dwarves present stand and unite behind their king, and all know the dwarves are unified in following their king and ready to fight the demons.

"I will go," says Crayeulle.

"Me too," says Whenshade.

"Let the demons taste my Foarsbleem arrows," says Shastenbree.

"Mine too," says Thambrable.

"My sword, Swooping Death, will slash the demons into many pieces," says Cellertrill.

"I feel it is upon us to take the initiative, like Vegenrage says, and take the fight to the demons. I believe the dragons will be by our side, and I for one think the dragons will show up to see the elimination of the demons after all the demons wish to destroy all dragons and replace them with the demonian dragons. I will be traveling to Strabalster as well," says Oriapow. This statement draws a hush from all the elves except for Ulegwahn.

"I cannot have the protector of the Great Erken leaving his post to go battle demons. This is unacceptable. Oriapow, you must stay here and protect the Great Erken with your life, if need be. You have sworn to this, and I will not allow your leaving," says Ulegwahn.

"I believe I have to go in order to save the Great Erken. We can stop the demons on Strabalster. They have already destroyed Glaboria, and now they work on the mountains on Strabalster. We have to stop them. Then we have to work on mending the mountains here on Fargloin. If the demons are allowed to erupt all the mountains on all the planets, they will become too powerful for us to fight against. Vegenrage is right. We have to fight them now. If we wait until the light is blocked from the sky, it will be too late. The demons do not dare attack us while we are strong. They wait until they have the advantage, and that is darkness. We have to take the fight to them wherever they show themselves. I will go with Vegenrage, Glimtron, and the others," says Oriapow. Ulegwahn storms off toward the Great Erken and vanishes. "It is settled. I am with you, and we have no time to waste."

"You know it is going to be very cold there. We must dress very warm, and the air will be thin. Cloakenstrike and Bastrenboar have eluded and bested us in every encounter. Are you sure this is a good idea?" asks Logantrance.

"Dress warm and get ready because it is time we start playing offense instead of defense. The demons will surely try to rescue their imprisoned demon brethren. Shenlylith will surely have to defend her king, Basters, and Cloakenstrike will surely be looking for any kind of magical gain he can. I don't know what will happen, but I know this time we will be the instigators, and we will be the ones with bad intentions. I am tired of playing around. Let us see who and what makes their presence dominate in Krasbeil. Are you all ready?" says Vegenrage, and he grabs Farrah by the hand and walks through a dimension door.

"Oh, I hate when he gets that serious look," says Logantrance, looking to Oriapow and Glimtron.

"Oh yeah, it is time to go and get some," says Glimtron.

"Let's go. Everyone, let's go," says Oriapow, swinging his right arm over his head and walking through a dimension door, followed by ten of his elven brethren. Glimtron and the dwarves follow the Dagi, and soon all have left the courtyard in Erkensharie and are high in the freezing Krasbeil Mountains.

CHAPTER 13

The Krasbeil Plan

Vegenrage walks out onto a frigid ledge. Farrah walks out right behind him, quickly gets her leather armor from Parnapp, and dresses herself. Vegenrage pulls a surprise from Behaggen that Farrah never knows he has. He pulls out a magical shirt that covers his body in a magical skin that becomes invisible and protects his body from cold. "Well, that is nice. Do you have one of those for me?" asks Farrah.

"As a matter of fact, I do," says Vegenrage as he pulls another shirt from Behaggen and gives it to Farrah.

She puts her leather away and wears the shirt. This looks very amazing.

The others, who are still dressed in warm-weather clothes, walk out of their dimension doors next to Vegenrage and Farrah. The dwarves are all clothed in very heavy, thick, warm clothing. The elves have a green trench-coat type of clothes. It is very beautiful, looking like a thin stretchy material covered in feathers, but it is a full-body coat that fits them very snugly from their neck down to their arms, chest, and abdomen. The coat buttons right down the front, and it splits at their crotch and then wraps their legs down to their matching green boots. The legs of these body coats are held by one button at the bottom of the legs, which when unsnapped allows the clothing to be unwrapped and removed very easily. This is a very thin flexible material, called Insulermal, with designs of feathers, but it keeps the elves warm in the coldest of temperatures.

"Ah, you have made good use of my master's magical items. Very good, Vegenrage," says Logantrance, who wears a more traditional, very warm looking thick white fur coat with a thick tuft of fur that surrounds his face. He wears fur leggings, which keep him warm, along with fur boots.

Vegenrage has his arms stretched above his head, and he is concentrating. Everyone has to yell to talk because it is very windy. "What is Vegenrage doing, and aren't they freezing?" asks Shastenbree.

"He is protecting our presence. He is shielding us from Cloakenstrike and Basters. They are on the mountain across from us," says Logantrance.

Vegenrage finishes his concentration, lowering his arms and turning to answer Shastenbree. "Yes, Farrah and I wear Colness. These were gifts from Swallgrace from Morlinvow a long time ago. They will protect us from the cold. Oriapow, can you communicate with Shenlylith? She is Ugorian, but she is still elven, and though very distant, the Ugorian elves and the Erkensharie elves are related," Vegenrage says.

"I can already feel that she is communicating with Basters. She is aware of our presence. You could not shield us from her. I do not think she has told Basters we are here. I can try to communicate with her, but I think the magic users with her will know if I do," says Oriapow, so he does not try to communicate telepathically with Shenlylith.

"Vegenrage, why are we here? I mean, did we come here just to fight with Cloakenstrike and Basters? We all hate them, and they will pay for attacking the Erkensharie, killing our king, and stealing the Octagemerwell, but did we really want to come to the mountains to fight with them?" asks Crayeulle.

"This is a very important and pivotal time for all of us. It took me a long time to realize that Hornspire was conspiring all the time he was writing his books of the future. All the books he wrote were designed to maintain the dominance of the dragons over the Maglical System. Hornspire always knew the demons would rise, and he had set plans in motion to keep him alive and prosperous." Vegenrage is shouting so everyone can hear him. He waves his hands in the air and encapsulates the entire party in a shell of magical force, keeping the wind out so they do not have to shout to talk with one another, and this also protects them from the very strong and cold wind. "There, that is better," he says when he finishes casting the magical force. "As I was saying, I have four of the books written by Hornspire, and I have read others. His prophecies end here in the Krasbeil Mountains, and I am not present in his writings, which leads me to believe he did not think I would survive this long. These books—*The Dragon Catastrophe*; *The Probable Path*; *The Sleeping Dragon*, which Logantrance has, but I have read it; *The Valvernva Uniting*; and *The Ilkergire Ascent*—all make reference that Hornspire will kill Cloakenstrike here in Krasbeil. Also, he mentions that the dragons and demons will do battle here in Krasbeil.

There is a wild card here today, and that is us. The fact that I am still alive and I am here with dwarves, elves, men, and women means that we can shape and form the future to a more peaceful one, a future without the murderous ways of certain magic-using men. Hornspire refers to two men, Cloakenstrike and Basters, who will both be killed in the days to come, and Shenlylith aids the dragons in destroying all the demons, ending their uprising. But again, his writings do not take us into account unless he planned this all along."

"Well, I did not come all this way to sit up on this mountain. Let's form a strategy and attack them. Let us exact vengeance for King Estine, who was slain by Cloakenstrike," says Glimtron.

"Well, that would throw a monkey wrench into everything. That may even take the demons out of the equation for a while, and I don't know about the dragons. They could be watching right now, but I do not think they will attack us. That just would not fit. I agree with Glimtron, but Shenlylith will not allow her king to be hurt. I will have to draw Shenlylith away, and then you all will have Cloakenstrike and Basters to contend with. Are you ready for that?" asks Vegenrage, and the elves quickly reply yes.

"Vegenrage, what are you going to do?" asks Logantrance.

Vegenrage reaches into Behaggen and pulls out a book. "It just so happens I have this. This was in my library, and before all my books were taken, I saved some of them." Vegenrage shows the book to Logantrance.

"*The Shenlylith Truth*. Vegenrage, my boy," says Logantrance with a smile on his face.

"That is right, Logantrance. I felt this book, along with others, was of great importance, and I packed it away in Behaggen."

Farrah looks at the book, *The Shenlylith Truth*. "So what is so great about this book?" she asks.

"This book was written by Shandorn, who was killed by Cloakenstrike not too long ago. Anyway, this book tells the whole story about how Shenlylith came to be the great snow elf and why this here is Shenlylith's Prison. There is something very important in this book that may help us in this instance," says Vegenrage, opening the book, and he flips through the pages until he finds the page he is looking for. He faces the open book to everyone. "This here is a picture of Shenlylith's sister, Crystara."

"Well, how does that help us?" asks Farrah.

"Actually, Farrah, you can help us all," says Vegenrage.

"Me?" says Farrah, pointing to her chest.

"Yes, you see, anyone who intends harm to the king of Ugoria is met with the wings of Shenlylith, sending them here. There is a big difference between being sent here by her wings and teleporting here like we did. We can leave here with our magic. However, if sent here by Shenlylith, then all travel magic is distorted and will not work properly. The only escape from here if sent here by Shenlylith is by walking, and if you look around, you can see walking out of here is very dangerous and nearly impossible. In fact, Cloakenstrike, Bastrenboar, and Fraborn are the only three ever to escape her prison. We can attack them, and when Shenlylith appears, we have only a few seconds to give her pause. Farrah, can you shift your form? Can you take the shape of Shenlylith's sister, Crystara?

If you can and if you can give Shenlylith pause when she appears to send away her king's attackers, I can appear behind her and teleport the two of us away. I can keep her away long enough for the rest of you to capture Cloakenstrike, Basters, and Fraborn. Then we can take them back to the Erkensharie, where they can stand trial for their crimes. Well, what do you think? Can you do it?" asks Vegenrage.

Farrah smiles and looks at Vegenrage, snapping her fingers, and in a second, her appearance is that of Crystara. She is very beautiful with long brown hair in ponytails that hang down to either side of her breasts. She has deep brown eyes and stands only four and a half feet tall with pointed but attractive ears. Farrah snaps her fingers, and she is back to her normal appearance. "You mean like that?" says Farrah.

"Yup, just like that," says Vegenrage.

"Well, do you have a plan, Vegenrage?" says Glimtron.

"I do," he says.

For the first time since Shenlylith has been consumed by the snow gold trinket, she has summoned her king, who happens to be Basters. She has called for her king to come to the Snow Gold Summit. This is a magical place of beauty and mystery, and a surreal sense of spacious enlightenment consumes those who set foot here twenty-two thousand feet above sea level. The clouds circle the mountain for five hundred feet below the Snow Gold Summit and stop where the summit begins. This place is surrounded by mountains on all sides, but if anyone were anywhere below this mountain, they would not be able to see the summit because the clouds would block the view. The mountains here have not been named because only those sent by Shenlylith have ever been here, and they have all died here except for Basters, Cloakenstrike, and Fraborn.

Basters knows magically where to travel, thanks to Shenlylith, and he forms a dimension door where Cloakenstrike and Fraborn can follow him through. They appear on the Snow Gold Summit and are immediately consumed with awe. This is a very magical place. The mountain is very wide, and the summit they are on seems to have been carved with a knife the size of Ugoria itself. The mountain has been sanded smooth so it seemingly runs all the way to the back side of the mountain, which is left alone and grows up hundreds of more feet into the sky. When looking at the mountain from above, the grain of the rock looks like the circles on a butterfly in gray and black colors.

Basters walks to the edge of the mountain and looks into the clouds that ring the mountain, and there is a fantastic phenomenon that happens here. He can see the clouds, and after he looks at them for a few seconds, he can see through them to the surrounding mountains, and it is beautiful. Another phenomenon is that there is no wind here, and it has a very comfortable temperature, so they do not have to wear winter clothing. Another amazing thing about the Snow Gold Summit is that the air is easily breathable by the men. Cloakenstrike is amazed. "I never knew this place existed."

"This is the most fantastic thing I have ever seen. This is way better than the last time we were here in these mountains. I wish Rothglon were here to see this with us," says Fraborn, who is looking off the side of the mountain with Basters. Cloakenstrike walks beside his companions and looks into the mountains. The three of them are startled and look to the center of the summit to see that Shenlylith has taken her true form, and she has a demon dropped on the floor. Shenlylith is absolutely beautiful, and all three men are speechless as Shenlylith kicks the demon and slides him on the floor. The demon is not dead, but he is seemingly unconscious.

"I called for my king, no one else," says Shenlylith.

"That is OK. These two men are Cloakenstrike and Fraborn, my companions of hundreds of years, and we go everywhere together. We know everything about one another, and there is nothing you can tell me that you cannot tell them," says Basters.

"Yes, my king," says Shenlylith, bowing her head slightly. "Demons have attacked the Krasbeil Mountains from underneath, rising lava into them, and this will destroy the mountains, turning them into spewing geysers of molten lava and toxic ash. This will destroy my home. This will consume my power. I have sent all the demons who have attacked my home into different mountains here in my prison, and like this demon here, they are all immobilized by the cold. They are not dead, but they are rendered motionless by the cold. I have used much of my power to halt the flow of lava any higher into the mountains for now, but the pressure will eventually overcome my magic. It is only a matter of time, and when the mountains erupt, I will die with my home. Basters, this time was always going to happen, you were always going to be the king of Ugoria, and you have the book *Divination: Demon, Dragon, Elf, or Man*. This demon here is your calling. This demon here will finish the book with its blood. The book *Divination: Demon, Dragon, Elf, or Man* has been waiting for a thousand years to be finished. Place the book on the demon, and the final pages will be written,"

Basters looks to Cloakenstrike and reaches into his bag of holding. He pulls out the book, which he has read to Cloakenstrike in his throne room in Hunoria. He walks up to the demon, who looks like a curled-up, hairless rodent that is a little bigger than a dog. The demon is bloodred, and Basters lays the book on the demon. Shenlylith's wings grow from her back, and lightning shoots from the tips of her wings and hands into the demon, who shakes and it cries out in pain as he shrinks and shrivels. The pages of the book start to flip, and when it gets to the bare pages, words begin to appear in demon blood. The writing is in demon, but no one knows that yet, and the demon continues to shrink. His blood is pulled through his skin and enters the book. This goes on for a while until the demon has completely vanished and the book has flipped through all the pages, writing words in demon blood. When finished, the book lies on the ground, close where the demon has been.

Shenlylith lowers her arms, her wings shrink back in, and she looks very exhausted and is breathing heavily. "It has been done, my king. You now have the answers you have been seeking, and you have the answers that will preserve myself and the snow gold trinket. The demons can be sent back to the inner realm, never to reach the outer realm ever again," says Shenlylith.

Basters walks up to the book and bends down. Vegenrage appears on his knees in front of the book and grabs it, startling Basters. Vegenrage stands and grabs Basters around the neck with his right hand, holding the book in his left hand.

Shenlylith's wings grow from her back, and Farrah appears to the right of Shenlylith, floating in the air as the exact replica of Crystara. Farrah yells, "Shenlylith." Shenlylith looks to see her sister, and this gives her pause. Perfectly executing the plan, Vegenrage releases Basters and takes three running steps to Shenlylith; and when his right hand reaches her, they both disappear. Blythgrin, Trybill, Grenlew, Solmbus, and Greeter appear off to the side on the summit; and they are in a circle, concentrating, with the Sapphirewell in the center of them.

Cloakenstrike has been completely focused on Vegenrage, and as soon as Vegenrage and Shenlylith disappear, the Dagi appear and cast the reflected-detain spell. This looks very cool. From the Sapphirewell shines deep blue light that shines at a forty-five degree angle above Cloakenstrike's head; and like there was a mirror in the sky, light is reflected right on Cloakenstrike, and he is caught. He cannot move at all. The Dagi have caught for the first time ever the magic user Cloakenstrike, who cannot escape.

Fraborn draws his Lavumptom sword, and Basters takes a step back beside his longtime companion Fraborn. Shastenbree and Thambrable appear to the left and Rifter, Olgerp, Miker, Twaln, Belse, and Nelster to the right of Basters and Fraborn with their Foarsbleem bows drawn on them. Whenshade, Crayeulle, and Oriapow appear in front of Basters and Fraborn, and all three of them cast in unison timespell. This spell slows time by ten times on Fraborn and Basters, but time feels the same to them. Behind the Erkensharie magic users appear Cellertrill, Glimtron, Silgeqwee, Krimzill, Fimble, Eebil, Ahnkle, and Churcher. Logantrance appears behind Fraborn and Basters and is just about to put his hands on their backs when—roar!—an incredibly long and loud roar is heard throughout the summit. Everyone looks around, not knowing where the roar has come from.

Farrah is still floating about eight feet in the air, seemingly safe from all danger, but there is a problem that no one has thought about. When Vegenrage and Farrah both put on Colness to protect them from the cold, this magic has taken precedence over all other magic, meaning that although Farrah is wearing Cleapell she does not receive the magical protection from it, and this miscalculation on the part of Vegenrage will prove fatal as Hornspire appears from a dimension door right at her back and swings his tail at her. His tail has three four-foot-long spikes, and Farrah cannot evade the attack. One of the spikes goes right through her back and stakes her to the tail of Hornspire, who laughs as everyone watches him raise Farrah to his front paws, grabs her head and shoulders with one paw, and seizes her legs with the other paw. Elves, dwarves, and Logantrance are all crying "no" as they watch Hornspire twist and pull Farrah in half. A deafening silence sweeps the summit as Farrah dies and Hornspire falls to the ground, landing on his hind legs. He is not far from the stunned and motionless races of man with half of Farrah in each of his front paws.

"This is the second time I have had to eliminate this female. Now the demons have one less chance, one less option in creating their demonian dragons. This time she will not return. This time I shall see my future and the future of the dragons to our rightful and dominant end," says Hornspire as he throws Farrah's two halves over the side of the mountain, and Farrah falls out of sight. "Now for the second treasure,

I have come for Cloakenstrike. And yes, he is completely immobilized by the dwarves, just as I knew he would be. All thanks to you, Basters. You have fallen right into my plan, reading the book exactly as I intended so that Cloakenstrike would follow you here and the two of you thinking you were going to read the final pages of my book *Divination* when in fact you have lead Cloakenstrike to his end. Time to settle up, magic man. Time to return my treasure to its rightful owner."

Hornspire charges at Cloakenstrike. Hornspire is near the center of the summit, and the races of man are still a good fifteen yards from him. All the elven and dwarven archers draw and let loose their Foarsbleem arrows. Hornspire waves his right paw in an upside-down U, and all the arrows stop and fall to the ground. He roared with laughter, which turns to fright as he looks in the air above him and raises his paws like he is going to block something.

Out of a dimension door appears Blethstole, flying very fast, and he lands right on Hornspire. The two dragons roll violently to the other side of the summit, hitting the upward growth of the mountain, coming to a crashing stop. Glimtron and the dwarves dash out of the way before being crushed by the huge rolling bodies of the dragons. Blethstole stands first, swiping his right paw at the head and face of Hornspire, slashing four deep wounds right across the left side of his face.

"Hornspire, you think you will rule the dragons? You think you will take me from my dominant position? You think you will bring down Vlianth and destroy his love?" Blethstole swipes at Hornspire's face every time Hornspire looks up, and now Hornspire has many very deep gashes, bleeding badly on the left side of his face. Hornspire extends the horns on the back of his head and swings his neck and head to the left as hard as he can, impaling Blethstole in the left shoulder. Three of the horns stick deep into Blethstole's flesh, causing great pain, and he roars loudly, looking straight up in the sky. Hornspire calculated wrong, as Blethstole, who now—thanks to Vegenrage—has his complete form, uses his four horns in their most lethal attack.

Gwithen falls from a dimension door far to the right of the races of men and far behind Blethstole, and she lands just in time to see Blethstole roaring into the sky with Hornspire's horns in his shoulder. She says to herself out loud but quietly, "No, Blethstole, no," and she watches as Blethstole lowers the snout of his head and drives it into Hornspire, just above and behind his left shoulder. Blethstole's four horns enter Hornspire's flesh and sink deep, surrounding Hornspire's heart. Hornspire roars in pain and fear.

"Don't do it, Blethstole. Don't do it. I have done everything to preserve the dominant reign of the dragons and to ensure the demons and demonian dragons do not destroy us."

"Ffrrss aammmeee blowthnin ccrrruuusssshhh!" says Blethstole, and incinerating fire and heat shoots from his mouth like a drill bit, cooking, searing, burning, and incinerating Hornspire's flesh and heart in a circle all the way through his body. Everyone watches as Hornspire dies in a few short minutes, and Blethstole stands firm and motionless after stomping his left forefoot on Hornspire's head until he knows he is dead for sure.

Gwithen sways her head back and forth slowly, heartbroken to see Blethstole kill Hornspire. Hornspire has been Gwithen's greatest love intellectually, and he has given her many children, who have all been killed; nevertheless, she does not fault Blethstole, and she almost knows this day will come. She slowly walks toward Blethstole, looking over the races of man, until she spots Logantrance. "Where is the female? Where is Farrah?" asks Gwithen.

"Hornspire has killed her and thrown her broken body over the side of the mountain," says Logantrance.

"I must hurry. I must get to her before the demons do. Where did Hornspire throw her?" asks Gwithen. Logantrance points in the direction that Hornspire has thrown the two halves of Farrah's body.

Gwithen looks over the races of men, saying, "Do not be alarmed by Blethstole. He has not come here to harm any of you. Blethstole and I are indebted to Vegenrage for saving our young, and we consider him an ally. We dragons now realize that the races of man and the dragons will have to unite, or the demons will take over and kill us all."

"Gwithen, hurry, go and save Farrah," says Blethstole.

"Yes," says Gwithen, and she flaps her wings powerfully, rising above the men, and flies over and down the mountain. A lot of them in the party have seen these two dragons before, but still this is an amazing sight to see, and the races of men are suspended in awe and beauty while watching this magnificent white dragon fly over them and down the mountain out of sight. This unfortunately distracts the magic users, whose magic slips a little, and this gives Basters one second, which is all he needs to counter the timespell cast on him. Basters has just enough time to cast the haste spell on him and Fraborn, which speeds their movements up just enough to where Basters can run to Cloakenstrike, followed by Fraborn, and then Basters in turn teleports the three of them away. The races of men quickly turn their attention to Blethstole, who kicks Hornspire a few times, and the corpse just flops. Blethstole turns to the men, grumbling in a very deep dragon tone. He walks toward them, and the men get very antsy.

"Do not worry. I am not here to hurt you. Gwithen and I were able to figure that Hornspire would possibly be here, and his intentions were to kill Vlianth. It took us dragons a long time to figure out what Hornspire was up to. He used his visions to fool all of us dragons and the races of man. We now realize Vlianth, or Vegenrage in human tongue, was brought here to unite the races of man with the dragons so that we could fight against the demons. The demons are trying to get Vlianth because he has great power that they seek and a knowledge that the demons desperately want. They will try to use Farrah to get to Vlianth, and Hornspire knew this. That is why he sent Farrah to where the demons are at the base of the mountain. The summit we are on is a very magical place, and the demons cannot gain form here, but they can lower in the mountains. Gwithen has gone to save Farrah, and I will go to help her. You should all go to your homes because Vlianth and Shenlylith have some issues to resolve, and when Shenlylith returns, you do not want to be here, as she will imprison you. Vlianth will make his way back to you, and Farrah—well, I will be honest. I do not know her fate. If we can, Gwithen and I will return her to you," says Blethstole, and he flaps his wings hard, jumps, and flies over the heads of the men and over the side of the mountain until out of sight.

The races of man take the advice of the dragons and head to their homes. Well, the elves and dwarves go back to the Erkensharie, but Logantrance goes back to Richterblen.

CHAPTER 14

Hornspire's Legacy

The instant Vegenrage touches Shenlylith, they are both teleported to Vollenbeln, where he is magically at his most powerful. They appear on the mound covering Vegenrage's home, and he steps back with the book *Divination: Demon, Dragon, Elf, or Man* in his left hand. "I have brought you here so that my friends would have time to capture Cloakenstrike, Fraborn, and Basters and take them back to stand trial for the murders and mayhem they have caused to so many. Basters somehow is now king of Ugoria, but he is not elven. This should not be. He committed murders as man, and he and his army were being changed into pigs when Cloakenstrike stepped in and thwarted this magic, changing them into the race of humanor. Now Basters is in human form again and king of Ugoria. I know you are sworn to protect the king always, but in this instance, you have to allow your good judgment to take precedence and let him to pay for the crimes he has committed against the Erkensharie elves. With the loss of the king of Ugoria, you will have to wait and see who will take kingship. I will see that all the possessions of the king will be returned to Ugoria and that the new king shall be in possession of the snow gold trinket and Delvor, the king of Ugoria's bag of holding," says Vegenrage.

"You have taken me from my home, the only place where I can hold my form unless in the presence of my king. I am here, and my form is still intact. You are not my king. I must protect my king," says Shenlylith.

She raises her arms toward the moonlit sky and draws lightning from the heavens, which shoot to her eight squiggly white streaks. Vegenrage steps back, admiring the fantastic white and diamond glitter of light that emanates from Shenlylith's glowing body. They enter her fingertips, and pure white wings with sparkles of diamond grow from her back as she smiles, illuminating the surroundings, looking at Vegenrage.

"You are very magically inclined, Vegenrage, and your home is a great source of power for you. I can feel you are becoming a paramount force of the Maglical System, and your magical strength is independent of all other magic. This is why I can hold my form here in your home. Someday I hope we may communicate with each other, but for now, my obligation is to protect my king. Use the book in your hands to protect the Maglical System from the demons. The dragon prophet will die very soon, but many of his writings have yet to be discovered. Some of his writings are still in the hands of enemies, and the demons will exploit this to destroy you and steal knowledge that only you possess," says Shenlylith as she slowly floats into the air and vanishes.

"Wait, wait, I have so many questions. Wait!" says Vegenrage, but Shenlylith has vanished.

Vegenrage falls to his knees like he has been hit in the back with a bat. "Farrah!" he yells.

Farrah is falling down the side of the mountain after being thrown by Hornspire. Her halves bounce and tumble down the mountain face, becoming torn and ripped by the sharp rocks. A laugh is heard, and Farrah's halves fall toward each other and join where she has been torn apart. She is still falling, her bones are breaking, and drops of blood are splattered alongside the mountain as she falls, bouncing off narrow ledges and outgrowths of the mountain. She is still alive, and she feels her head crashing against the rocks and her bones breaking. She feels her skin and flesh tearing and being sliced by the sharp rocks she falls against. Fear reaches new bounds for Farrah as she feels her fingers breaking and hears the bones in her body snap as her arms and legs are folded from crashing on the ledges of the mountain. Her sight goes black as her face smashes against the rocks, and her teeth, nose, and eyes are crushed and destroyed. She finally comes to a crashing halt after rolling and tumbling. She lies on a ledge, still some eight hundred feet from the bottom of the mountain; and her body is mangled, torn, splintered, and broken.

The laugh gets louder as Farrah tries to opens her eyes. She cries in pain, and her heart sinks, knowing that her body is ripped and deformed and that most of her bones are broken or fractured. Her legs start to straighten out as do her arms. She feels her ribs pop out to their correct form and shape, along with her skull. She slowly can move, and she is able to pull her left arm out from under her back. Her bones pop and snap back into place, and her skin starts to heal. The scar around her waist where her severed body has come back together starts to heal, and her skin regains its perfect color and softness. The scars all about her body start to heal, and she can sit up now. She is no longer protected by Colness because, when Hornspire has staked her and torn her in two, its magic has been destroyed and is now gone forever.

Farrah looks at her ring finger, and she sees the band of life become visible for a few seconds until it vanishes, having used up the last of its magic to save her for the last time. She hears the laugh, and the rock she is lying on forms a giant hand that grabs her around the waist. The rock around her rises, and the form of Zevoncour goes up from her left in the same size as she is. He kneels, putting his knees on Farrah's shoulders, holding her securely to the ground. Zevoncour laughs, lowering his face. He has a brilliant smile with teeth so white that they don't even look real. He grabs Farrah's arms with his large hands and holds her to the ground, moving his knees down by her legs, straddling her. Zevoncour runs his nose up the side of Farrah's face, smelling her. He moves his nose from her shoulder up to her ear and then raises his face in the air with a grand smile. Farrah cannot move, and when she tries to, Zevoncour puts more pressure on her arms and shoulders with the weight of his body, causing a lot of pain.

"What do you want, demon? If you want to kill me, then what are you waiting for?" says Farrah, who is buying time to gain her strength and unleash her now significantly strong magic.

"Yes, I feel your strength. You have grown very strong in such a short period. Remarkable! I can see why the chosen one is so attracted to you. You gain your magical strength from Vegenrage, the source of magic without the spoken word. It could not have been scripted any better. The dragon prophet dies, the prophet who told us all how to prepare for the future. Oh wait, the future is now." Zevoncour says in between laughs, running his very long black talons across Farrah's face, causing her unstoppable fear. "The dragon thought you and Vegenrage would not survive these days, but it is the prophet himself who has fallen, and now the time of the demons is here. Soon the dragons will fall, and the demonian dragons will spread the rule of demons to the skies. The Maglical System will soon be ours, and then we move to another solar system because Vegenrage will lead us there, and you will lead us to him," he says, laughing and looking at Farrah, lowering his brilliant red face close to hers.

"I will hunt you, demon. I will help Vegenrage destroy you and send you to the inner realm, where you belong," says Farrah.

"I think not," says Zevoncour, running his right talons down the face of Farrah and placing his thumb under her right ear, his pinky under her left ear, and his index finger under her chin. He puts just a little pressure on them, enough to pierce her skin, and little drops of blood become visible from the punctures. "The female with a tainted mind was always the undoing of Vegenrage. He will never let go of you, like so many others whom you have brought to their deaths, like so many others who once have gazed upon you and could not look away while their lives were stolen and their hearts ripped out. Vegenrage has loved you and will never let you go. Remember." Zevoncour's talons are digging deeper into Farrah's throat.

Farrah cannot stop the images, the memories that she has suppressed. She can see herself in the home Alisluxkana has created for her. She sees Brygil, the human warrior, with his Greenmail armor, who has actually made it into Alluradaloni's home. And once he has seen her, she has smiled and lowered her already revealing tube top, giving Brygil such pause that Alisluxkana has walked up behind him and stabbed him through with Cocoddlebrew. She sees the great Ugorian magic user Lieheam, who also has made it to her lair, and she has pretended to have a broken leg, sitting on the rocks in front of the pool in her home. She still has had the tiny tube top barely covering her beauty and her perfectly fitting underwear just covering her privates because the tiny skirt did not in her sitting position on the rocks. As Lieheam holds her left leg to mend it for her, again, Alisluxkana is there behind him, grabbing his head with both of her hands and draining his magic and life force. Farrah sees many images of men and women whom she has seduced with her beauty, and when they are not aware, Alisluxkana has killed them and stolen their life and possessions. Farrah has been doing so well to hide and forget about the evil she is a part of, and even though she has always been under the mind control of Alisluxkana, this is still a decay that eats away at her well-being. Farrah sees image after image of people being killed, and she can take no more, screaming out.

She wakes from her dream, shivering and freezing cold, lying on the rock outgrowth of the mountain, and Gwithen is there above her. Gwithen has landed on the rocky outgrowth, digging the huge strong talons on her hind paws in the mountainside, grabbing the ledge with her front left paw, and resting her right paw on the ledge to the left of Farrah. "Farrah, it is all right now. We have come to take you out of here," says Gwithen.

Farrah can hear the flapping of Blethstole's wings as he swoops to the ledge and slows his descent with his enormous strong wings, which are now fully functional. Blethstole lands on the vertical wall to the left of Gwithen and Farrah, looking down on them. "Is she OK? Is Farrah unharmed?" asks Blethstole.

"She seems to be fine, just a little shook-up. Come, Farrah, get on my back. We are here to take you to safety," says Gwithen. Farrah gets up, squeezing her chest with her arms because she is freezing. She gets her leather armor from Parnapp and puts it on. She is still freezing, but this gives her good protection from the cold. Gwithen lowers her neck for Farrah to climb on and sit at the base of her neck at her shoulders. Farrah looks at Blethstole, and he slowly nods down, showing his approval.

Blethstole looks around, very concerned, saying, "Hurry, Farrah, get on Gwithen. I sense demons are not far, and we have to get you out of here."

Farrah walks up to the neck of Gwithen, who extends scales on her neck, forming a sort of ladder that Farrah can step on. Farrah can't help but stop halfway up the neck of Gwithen to just gaze at the size, the power, and the beauty of this white dragon. She looks from Gwithen's head down her neck to her shoulders, belly, hind legs, and tail. She rubs her right hand along the smooth scales that form an airtight

armor, which Gwithen has the ability to extend out of her
body one at a time if she desires, like she is doing so Farrah
can walk up her neck. Farrah studies the way Gwithen's wings
fold and lie flat on her back when not in use. She feels and
sees the widening and narrowing of Gwithen's neck as she
breaths in and out.

"Hurry, Farrah. We cannot stay here. We have to go
now," says Blethstole. Farrah climbs up and sits at the base of
Gwithen's neck. Blethstole pushes off the vertical wall of the
mountain, and he falls, extending his wings and gliding away
from the mountain, just soaring through the air. Farrah gasps
as Gwithen pushes off the mountain. Farrah feels like she is
going to throw up as Gwithen falls faster and faster until her
wings spread wide and Gwithen levels out and soars still far
behind Blethstole but on the same path that he is traveling
on. Farrah's fear and upset stomach vanish as Gwithen levels
out, and these feelings are replaced with exhilaration and
excitement. Farrah cannot hold back the ear-to-ear smile on
her face as the wind blows her hair back, and she watches the
ground far below pass as they fly over. She can see clouds
below them, and she can hear the slow flapping sounds that
Gwithen's wings make as she flies through the air. Farrah
holds on to two scales with her hands and rests her feet on
two scales that Gwithen has extended. Farrah forgets about
everything that has recently happened, consumed with sheer
happiness.

It gets even better as Farrah rides Gwithen through a
dimension door created by Gwithen. They reappear over the
Mirrimya Mountains, and it is nighttime. Farrah still has
the biggest smile on her face, riding Gwithen, as she glides

downward toward the mountain. There is a very long, wide thick dark gray cloud below them, and Gwithen does not fly right down through it; she glides along the top of the cloud, and then when it ends, Gwithen lowers her head and dives right at the mountains. Farrah feels like her stomach is going to rise in her throat, and for a few seconds, she is very scared. Then she puts on that smile again, and exhilaration consumes her soul as she leans forward face-first into the wind and rides Gwithen right down to the mountains. Gwithen glides and soars, widening her wings, using the strength in her wings to slow their descent, and she heads right for the mountain. Farrah is so excited that she has no time to be scared as Gwithen swoops up along the mountain face and lands on the ledge that leads down a hole into Blethstole's lair.

"These are new days in the Maglical System. There has only been one human ever to make his way into this lair and live to talk about it, well, on his own accord," says Gwithen as she heads down the round hole into Blethstole's pitch-black lair. Farrah can feel her stomach rise in her throat, and then she feels them land. "That one human is Vegenrage. Logantrance was captured by Blethstole and brought here, and he was rescued by dwarves, but other than that, no other humans have ever been here and lived to talk about it. You, Farrah, are going to be the first human ever to be brought her on purpose peacefully, and you will bring other humans here to unite the humans with dragons." Gwithen spreads her wings wide, and torches around the lair light with fire, illuminating the gold-covered walls. "Hornspire had told me about this day over a thousand years ago, the day I would carry the female with a tainted mind to Blethstole's lair. Hornspire always knew I loved Blethstole. Hornspire thought it would be him to lead the dragons against the demons, and if not, he knew it would be Blethstole to bear witness to the uniting of the races of man with the dragons here in his lair."

"Why do I always hear myself referred to as the female with a tainted mind?" asks Farrah.

"You have been cursed since shortly after your birth. Your mind has been stolen and controlled. Vegenrage released you and shared the power of absorption with you, which means you grow magically. You may even already be able to cast magic without the use of words. You are the one he loves. You are the one who brings balance to Vlianth, the magic user. That is what Hornspire used to tell me," says Gwithen.

Farrah hears flaps and is completely overwhelmed to see many of the dragons fly into the lair, led by Blethstole. He is followed by the two surviving female dragons and all the dominant dragons. Gairdennow has the draglets magically protected under his right wing, and he releases the small draglets into Gwithen's care. "I see you have brought Farrah here. Vegenrage should be close behind," says Blethstole.

"Yes, he will be here soon," says Gwithen.

"How do you all know Vegenrage will be coming here?" asks Farrah.

"Hornspire has told me of the future long ago. He could see many futures depending on how events were to play out. He had told me of the demon uprising, and when the demons had made their way to the planet of Strabalster, there was the possibility of Hornspire being killed on the Snow Gold Summit. If he were to die there, he had told me that this would start a chain reaction, and a race for the final books of prophecy would begin. The demons have entered or tried to enter the Krasbeil Mountains. Hornspire's lair is there. Upon the death of Hornspire, this will release the first of the final ten books he has written on the future of the Maglical System. It will rise in his lair, and the demons will actively seek this book. Hornspire had told me that we need the help of Vegenrage and Farrah to find his lair and the first book before the demons find it. This book is important because it tells of the demons' attack strategy in the upcoming days, and also, it tells of the defenses of the races of man on Fargloin and Strabalster. Most importantly, it tells how to reach the second book of prophecy. Only Vegenrage and Farrah can embark on the search for Hornspire's lair because Farrah has been touched by demon flesh and"—Gwithen looks at Farrah with a sadness growing in her face—"Farrah, you have been wounded by a demon weapon. You have been infected with demon blood. You can sense the demons. You can use your dragon-slaying hands against the demons just as you do against the dragons, and this is a devastating power that no dragon or demon can defend against. Only Vemenomous can block this magic. You have the power to destroy us all. But, Farrah, your mind is tainted. It has been under the control of others for most all of your life, and only Vegenrage has freed you from this control. The demons will use this taint on your mind to try to control you. Hornspire has told me that you will be Vegenrage's greatest love and companion for all of his life, or you will be his downfall. You must never give in to the visions, the torment, and the pain that the demons will inflict on your mind. You have to learn to free your mind like Vegenrage did for you and never let the images that will come to you cloud your judgment. The only good that has come from the taint of demon on you is that you have learned the power of absorption from Vegenrage, and he has a book that he gained on the Snow Gold Summit. This book, *Divination: Demon, Dragon, Elf, or Man* was not completed until it touched demon flesh, which was the catalyst needed in order for the book to finish its writings. The writing is in demon language, and only you can read this. This tells the way to Hornspire's lair and the first of his ten last books of prophecy," says Gwithen.

Blethstole raises his head and looks around, sniffing deeply into the air, saying, "He is here. Show yourself. I know you are here. No harm will come to you and Farrah. We are allies now, and we all have a common enemy in the demons. You are welcome here, Vlianth."

Vegenrage becomes visible, sitting up on the ledge where he has first watched Blethstole when he has had the staff of barrier breath so long ago. Vegenrage jumps into the air, slowly floats down, and stands by Farrah's side. "Vegenrage," says Farrah, who gives him a very strong hug, and Vegenrage returns it. They break from their hug and look up around at all the beautiful, magnificent dragons around them.

"Vegenrage, you have the book *Divination: Demon, Dragon, Elf, or Man*. You just received it in the Snow Gold Summit. This book had its final pages written in demon language, and only Farrah can read it. It tells how and where to find the final books of prophecy written by Hornspire," says Gwithen.

Vegenrage pulls the book from Behaggen and flips through the pages until he gets past the words written in dragon language to the words written in demon language. He faces the book to Farrah and asks her, "Can you read this, Farrah?"

Farrah takes the book and looks at it. "I don't know how, but I can read it even though it is written in demon language," she says.

"You have the power of absorption. This is the power I shared with you back in our home. This means you have been touched by demons," says Vegenrage, looking at Gwithen and Blethstole.

"Vegenrage, you and Farrah must go and find the lair of Hornspire. This is where you and the dragons must part ways for now. It is your destiny to go and find the final books of prophecy. It has always been you two who were needed here in the Maglical System to stop the demon uprising. We dragons will be here, and if you should need our help, you just call for us, and we will be there to help you. Our numbers are so low that our fate as a species is almost set. You two must go back to the Krasbeil Mountains. You must find Hornspire's lair and start the end of the demon uprising. Hornspire had told me a thousand years ago that if he were to die on the Snow Gold Summit, his legacy would be the final ten books of prophecy. He also told me the dragons would be almost gone as a species, and it would be you, Vegenrage, who was brought here to stop the demon uprising with the help of your true love, Farrah, the girl of tainted mind," says Gwithen.

"What will you do? Will you just go into hiding?" asks Farrah.

"We will be unseen, but we will not be hiding. We will be watching, and we will be the eyes and ears of the Maglical

System for a very long time to come. If you should need us, we will be there to help you," says Blethstole.

"Fargloin has already been attacked by the demons, and they have started spewing their toxins into the atmosphere there, helping them gain strength and power from the darkness. Soon they will unleash their demon hoards on the ground and try overtaking the planet. This is my home planet, and I will go and try to protect it," says Pryenthious as he takes a few steps and flies into the air, exiting the lair.

"The demons try to do the same on Strabalster, my home planet. I will protect my planet like Pryenthious protects his. I will be there should you two need my help," says Gairdennow to Farrah and Vegenrage as he lifts off the ground and exits the lair.

Farrah reads from the book while the dragons talk and some of them leave. She tells Vegenrage that they need to go back to the Krasbeil Mountains and find Hornspire's lair according to the book she is reading out loud. "They need to go to the farthest mountain to the northeast that borders the Frozen Thundrase. Here, they will find Hornspire's lair, and here they will find the first book of Hornspire's last ten written books. This one is called *The Demon Swell*. Hornspire has set many traps that need to be sprung in a specific order, or his book will not be released from the magical hold securing the book. It also says that Vegenrage, with the help of the now-female magical master—" She pauses after reading this to look up at everyone and sees Vegenrage and the dragons looking at her. She smiles and says, "Am I a magical master?"

There is silence, and Farrah continues reading from the book. She looks to find her place, moving her finger through the lines of demon words on the page. "Ah, here it is. Vegenrage, with the help of the now-female magical master, will gain the book from its magical tomb. The king of Ugoria, with his magical leader and his warrior leader, will be diverted away by the demons and saved by the guardian of the mountains, Shenlylith." Farrah looks up with her finger pressed in the book, saving her spot. Vegenrage walks up to Farrah and gently closes the book and presses it against her chest. Farrah hugs the book, and Vegenrage steps back.

"Farrah, you have done it. You have learned magic and become a master. You have to now believe in yourself. You have to use your magic as an extension of yourself, an extension of your feelings and thoughts. It will flow through you, and you will be what you have always dreamed you will be. Close your eyes, hold the book, and do what I taught you in Vollenbeln. Feel the book, see the words, absorb the knowledge of the book," says Vegenrage.

Farrah closes her eyes, with the book clutched tight to her chest. Vegenrage looks to Gwithen and Blethstole, and the dragons look back at Vegenrage. There is a definite look of concern on all three of their faces as they realize Farrah is becoming one of the most powerful magical beings in the Maglical System. Farrah smiles with her eyes closed, clutching the book tightly. "Vegenrage, I am doing it. I can see the words. I can understand them and read them without opening the book. Vegenrage, I can do it," she says. She opens her eyes and gives Vegenrage a big hug with a huge smile on her face. "Here, here is the book," and she hands the book to Vegenrage.

"No, no, you keep it. I still cannot read the demon language. Only you can read it. It would be a good skill to have, and you can share this language with me," says Vegenrage. Farrah puts her right hand on Vegenrage's cheek and closes her eyes. He closes his eyes and lifts his head like he is looking up. A few moments go by, and Farrah pulls her hand back, opening her eyes, and Vegenrage opens his.

"I did it, Vegenrage. I transferred magical knowledge, just like you have done with me. I can't believe it, Vegenrage. I am becoming magical. I am feeling like I belong with you." Farrah hugs Vegenrage and hands him the book *Divination: Demon, Dragon, Elf, or Man*.

"Farrah, you hold on to this book. Put it in Parnapp, OK? You were the first to read this book, and you are its owner, OK? Oh, wait a second," says Vegenrage as he puts his right hand on the book and closes his eyes, absorbing its knowledge, and then gives it back to Farrah.

"OK," says Farrah as she puts the book in her bag of holding.

Vegenrage looks to Blethstole, saying, "What will the dragons do now?"

"You and Farrah have very dangerous days ahead of you. This has always been your destiny. The dragons were trials for you, and you have survived us. You are the Maglical System's leading force against the demons. You must face the demons, and should you ever need our help, we will be here for you. The dragons are on the brink. We need to increase our numbers if we have any chance for survival as a species. We will be out of sight unless confronted. All our wishes go with you, Vegenrage, the magic user," says Blethstole.

"Vegenrage, we have to go now. We have to get to the book in Hornspire's lair. I have absorbed the book, and I know where to bring us by way of dimension door. We have to put a stop to the demon uprising on Strabalster," says Farrah.

"We have to go now. The dragons cannot die out as a species, and I will always do what I can to make sure of your survival," says Vegenrage as he follows Farrah through a dimension door.

"We should have warned Vegenrage about the danger he faces with Farrah," says Blethstole.

"He knows. He knows as well as we do, and I still have hope. I have faith that Vegenrage can save her from the evil taint that will corrupt her mind," says Gwithen.

CHAPTER 15

Hornspire's Lair

Basters is able to teleport himself, Cloakenstrike, and Fraborn away from the danger they have been in, but his magic does not take him back to Ugoria as he has intended. Instead, the three of them have been teleported to a magical palace under the Krasbeil Mountains. The walls are all solid rock, and the ceiling is very high, over thirty feet, and there is a huge waterfall at the far end of the cavern, about six feet wide, dumping a constant stream of water into a beautiful deep blue pool of pure water. The water flows out of the pool and down the center of the cavern, exiting under the wall on the other end of the cavern. All the rock around the pool has been eroded smooth, and there are natural steps leading into the pool of surprisingly warm water. To the left of the pool is a beautiful throne made out of solid white gold, and there are wings that extend from the back of the chair, imitating the wings of Shenlylith.

The three of them start walking toward the pool and the throne. The floor is smooth like it has been eroded from hundreds of years of flowing water, with ridges and ripples throughout the stone, and the flowing water makes a slow-moving stream that flows through the room. The three of them can easily hop over it because it is only a few feet wide. They can see statues of three men against the left wall, and they move closer to investigate. "Who are they?" asks Fraborn.

"These are the kings of Ugoria who have been protected by Shenlylith. The last statue here is Trialani. The middle statue is King Jardilith, who was slain in a contest with Trialani. And the first statue is King Kwaytith, who was slain by Jardilith. King Kwaytith was the king of Ugoria when Shenlylith was consumed by the snow gold trinket and the first king of Ugoria to be under her protection. It was his wife, Queen Sharome, who had the snow gold trinket, made by the high magic users of that time," says Basters.

"These statues look absolutely lifelike and real," says Cloakenstrike, touching the statue of Trialani.

They hear a sound behind them, and they all look as a rock next to the water exiting the room starts to move and look very fuzzy. A form moves out of the wall, and right before their eyes develops a boar-sized demon changing to a bloodred color. This demon is very solid and thick, and he charges right at the three of them. Fraborn draws his Lavumptom sword and fearlessly takes a step toward the charging demon. The demon has a hunched back, and his head is very low, just above the ground, but he has very long and sharp horns that grow out from the sides of his head and then veer forward, becoming very deadly weapons. And he is charging right at Fraborn.

Fraborn drops to his knees, yelling, "Come on!" And the demon charges right at him.

Fraborn points his sword right at the charging demon, and the sword enters the demon's skull right between the eyes like a hot knife through butter all the way to the hilt. The demon falls over to the side, dead.

Fraborn stands up and pulls his sword out, saying, "Wow, I hope all demons are this stupid."

The three of them start to move backward toward the throne as they watch the entire back wall starting to become fuzzy, and before they know it, demon after demon starts to pop out of the wall. All the demons here are the same kind of charging boar, solid red in color, and all of them have very long sharp, lethal horns, which are their primary weapons.

"Ah, this is going to be a little more difficult," says Fraborn, looking at over a dozen charging demons all of the same form.

Shenlylith grows from the snow gold trinket, and her wings grow wide and scoop up all the demons, sending them to her prison high above them in the mountains. "I remember you reading this in the book stolen by Vegenrage. This is where we send all the demons to Shenlylith's Prison," says Cloakenstrike to Basters.

Shenlylith appears in front of the three, and she bows, saying, "My king, I have brought you here because I have grave news. The demons are growing in numbers, and they are trying to rise lava into the mountains here. This will destroy my home. In turn, this will destroy my power, ending my life and the power of the snow gold trinket. You have to learn of the demon power and how to destroy it. You can accomplish this by getting the books written by Hornspire. I know of these books because Hornspire's lair is here in the Krasbeil Mountains. He has hidden the first of his books here, and this will lead to the other books. These books tell of the demon uprising and their power and strategy in overrunning the Maglical System. These books will be very important in defeating the demons and sending them to the inner realm for good."

"This must be the book you are supposed to lead me to, Basters. It was not the book *Divination* at all. That is why Vegenrage got that book," says Cloakenstrike.

"No, that is not it at all. The writing in the book *Divination* said that Basters would lead the great magic user to that book, *Divination: Demon, Dragon, Elf, or Man*, and that magic user was Vegenrage, not you, Cloakenstrike. There is so many ways to interpret these books, and the correct interpretation is always the hardest. Vegenrage has already started his search for the book in Hornspire's lair, but you must get it first, or my home, my life, and the snow gold trinket could be lost for good. If you hold the book, we can use it to stop the demon uprising here in the mountains. You must get the book and bring it back here and fast. If the demons rise the lava into the mountains and they erupt, then my power and the power of the snow gold trinket will be lost. I can teleport you all there. Are you ready?" says Shenlylith.

Basters looks to Cloakenstrike, saying, "Did you feel the passing of a great magical power? It was a dragon. Was it Hornspire?" asks Basters.

"I believe it was," says Cloakenstrike.

"Shenlylith, is Hornspire dead?" asks Basters, and Shenlylith nods yes. "Well, this will certainly make entering his lair a little less stressful. We are ready."

Shenlylith waves her hands, and the three of them are teleported into the lair of Hornspire. They are on a rock floor that slopes down to a stream of water. It is dimly lit, and the ceiling is only about six feet high. The rippling water shines dim, dancing lights across the pitted ceiling and walls. The three of them can see that Shenlylith has teleported them just inside the entrance of Hornspire's lair. They can see outside, and it is snowy and obviously cold, but it is warm in Hornspire's lair. Basters says, "Follow me," as he walks deeper into the lair.

"Basters, hold on a second," says Cloakenstrike as he stops and concentrates with his eyes closed. "Basters, our magic is significantly reduced in here. For example, we have no flight or teleport magic in here. I suggest you adorn yourself with defensive armor from your bag of holding just in case. Fraborn is still wearing Fyshria, which is fantastic chain mail armor, great protection against all weapons, and it is fireproof."

Basters pulls his boots of speed and a most magnificent piece of clothing from Delver, the belt of speed. This golden belt, stitched with green elven lace along the middle, works in unison with his boots of speed. At the snap of a finger, Basters can move at twenty times the normal speed. This is fantastic, but he has to be careful. Wearing the two of these items at the same time takes a great toll on the wearer. This ages him at an accelerated rate. Provided he does not wear these longer than a day, he will be fine; but if he wears them longer than that without removing them, he will start to age at a noticeable rate.

Cloakenstrike pulls a different treasure from Getcher. First, he puts on his cloak of reflection, and then he pulls the staff of Coldstrike from his bag of holding. This is an awesome magical item and exquisite in its craftsmanship and beauty. It is made out of solid blapphire, a deep, dark ocean-blue gem that is mined and can be found only in the Glimwill Mines. It then is passed on to the Erkensharie elves, who have made this fantastic magical weapon. It has been in the possession of Cloakenstrike for a very long time now, and this is a fantastic weapon. Any living being stuck by the end of this staff, which is very sharp, begins to freeze until the entire body is frozen solid. This is an especially devastating weapon against demons. The drawback is that it is six feet long and bulky. It is deep blue yet almost see-through, with winding leather for gripping, where Cloakenstrike holds the long staff.

The three of them are ready to adventure as they have in the past, only this time Basters takes the lead. "Come on this way," says Basters as he heads into the lair of Hornspire. Fraborn and Cloakenstrike follow, and Cloakenstrike has to walk with his staff horizontal to the floor because it is so long. The small cavern, just high enough for them to walk down, turns to the right, so they cannot see too far ahead of them, and they venture deeper into the lair, which starts to slant downward and continues to veer to the right. The water, which is melted snow from outside, flows faster as the gradient of the passage starts to slant downward, and it now hugs the left wall as it follows the passage. The light starts to fade as they veer more and more to the right and walk deeper into the lair.

Basters reaches into Delver, saying, "I have just the thing for this situation," and he pulls a long black leather trench coat from his bag of holding. This goes very well with his black leather pants and his newly acquired elven shirt made of Shaylatin, a soft green material that is very stretchy and comfortable. He puts on the trench coat, which extends down just past his knees, and leaves the front of it unbuttoned. The shoulders have exaggerated pads on them, and a soft white light shines from them, acting like headlights that give warm light in a full circle around Basters.

"Very nice," says Cloakenstrike. They walk on, and the passage starts to straighten out, but the downward slant remains. The light shines for about ten feet, and then all they see is complete darkness. They keep walking, and just as Basters starts to see the passage widen and open into what must be Hornspire's lair, he sees Hornspire appear, standing at the entrance to his lair. Hornspire lowers his head and peers into the passage, giving pause to Basters.

"Cloakenstrike, I do not feel a presence at all," says Basters.

"It is not real. It is an image of Hornspire. This image cannot cast magic or cause physical harm. We must have triggered this image by walking into his lair," says Cloakenstrike.

Hornspire's image backs up, saying, "Come on in. I have been expecting you." They walk into the lair, and Hornspire steps back, looking up. Basters looks up to see a portion of the rock ceiling just above them slide up and sideways, exposing a thick ice that acts like the ceiling, but this allows light to enter and illuminate the lair, which becomes visible. Their jaws drop as Hornspire backs and starts to flap his wings as more and more of his lair becomes visible. The water flows from the passage in a small stream that runs right through the center of the floor, and it courses right off the ledge that

Hornspire has walked back off. He is now flapping his wings, backing farther and higher into his lair, which is lighting up.

Basters, Fraborn, and Cloakenstrike walk to the end of the ledge and look down at the splendor that is Hornspire's home. The light slowly reveals the twenty-foot drop of water and the pool that forms. The pool is about ten feet wide in a circle, and the water flows from both sides of the pool along the wall and around the circular floor to either side, and two smaller pools form. The water must be draining through the rock walls and floor on both sides of the lair. They can see across the entire lair now, which must be thirty feet back, and the ceiling must be at least fifty feet high. They can see at the back of the lair the enormous pile of treasure that Hornspire has accumulated, and it is ten feet high and twenty feet wide. "Look at all that treasure," says Fraborn.

Hornspire laughs. "Yes, it is impressive, isn't it? But you are here for the book, not the treasure. Before you three dare to figure out how to get to the treasure, let me show you what you are really here for."

Hornspire flaps his wings stronger (with no sound) and rises higher to the ceiling in his lair. He looks straight up and breathes what appears to be fire on a huge stalactite hanging from the center of the ceiling. The stalactite shakes, wobbles, and falls from the ceiling, impacting with the floor and driving into it until it is flush with the floor. The three watch, and nothing happens. Hornspire breathes fire on the ceiling where the stalactite has just fallen from, and the ceiling starts to crumble. Rubble falls until an ice ceiling appears, shining a laserlike focused white light on the fallen stalactite. The stalactite starts to spin faster and faster, digging and sinking into the ground until it is gone, leaving a four-foot-wide hole. Up from the hole rises a pure gold podium with beautiful etching on all four sides with black inlay, and it is so magnificent that the entire lair becomes golden from the shine. The focused light from the ceiling is reflecting the golden hue.

The eyes of Basters, Fraborn, and Cloakenstrike widen as the smooth top of the podium cracks right down the middle, and the two sides lift like someone was opening it. A book rises from within, and the top flaps of the podium close, with the book gently falling and resting on top. The book is fairly thick and seems to have been written for man and not the four-foot-high-by-four-foot-wide book written for dragons. Its cover is solid gold with black coral and red ruby inlay all throughout it, making the front, back, and binding very valuable.

"Look at that book. We must have it. Cloakenstrike, how are we going to get down there?" asks Basters.

"Ah, ah, ah! Let me give you some advice," says Hornspire, moving toward the three of them, and they back up as Hornspire flies over to the ledge and stands on its edge. "Before you attempt to get the book or my treasure, be warned. You are not of the strongest power here, and you will not get either my book or the treasure. Shenlylith has warned you of the demon uprising here in Krasbeil, and since you see this image, it means I have passed, and so shall the keeper of the mountain prison. There is nothing you can do to save the power of the snow gold trinket. You have the power to name the new king of Ugoria. Return to your short-lived home in Ugoria and name Limbixtil the next king of Ugoria or meet your fate. This is my gift to the human, the humanor, and the human again who became king of the elves. Do yourself the favor of listening to me now, and you will grow old and tell your story many times. Do not listen to me and die a fate worse than the king you stole the kingship from." Hornspire flies back into the air, looking down toward the book.

Basters, Fraborn, and Cloakenstrike walk to the ledge and look down as Farrah walks out of her dimension door, followed by Vegenrage. "Vegenrage," yells Cloakenstrike, who faces his hands together, and lightning shoots back and forth between his hands. And then he faces his palms toward Vegenrage and shoots very powerful lightning at him. Vegenrage looks up and blocks the lightning with his hands, and it is deflected into Hornspire's massive treasure trove, melting gold and silver and setting extremely valuable books and scrolls on fire. The podium starts to sink into the ground, and Farrah thrusts her right hand at Fraborn, who is sent flying high and back into the wall behind him, falling face-first and is very slow to get up.

"Vegenrage, the book, that must be the book we are here to get," says Farrah, who steps toward the book, which they are very close to.

"No, Farrah, do not touch it. Don't touch the book. It is a trap," yells Vegenrage.

Basters reaches his right arm behind his back like he is throwing a baseball, and a huge fireball forms in his palm. He throws a fireball the size of a beach ball right at Vegenrage. Farrah steps in front of Vegenrage and punches the fireball as it gets to her. One second before her fist makes contact with the fireball, it moves in slow motion, and there is a very small gap between Farrah's fist and the fireball. The fireball starts to freeze and break into cubes and shards, which fall to the ground.

Vegenrage is standing behind Farrah, watching, and he throws a lightning spear at Basters. Basters is just fast enough to avoid the lethal spell and turns to the side as the spear of electrical energy just grazes his trench coat, slicing and melting a line in it just below his nipples. The magical spear flies up into the stone ceiling, breaking and exploding lots of rock debris, which falls on Fraborn, knocking him unconscious.

"Farrah, don't cast any magic on Cloakenstrike. He is wearing a cloak of reflection," says Vegenrage.

"I know, but what do we do about the book? It is almost sunk back into the ground. We have to get it," says Farrah.

"Come here. I know what to do." Vegenrage grabs Farrah by the hand, and they walk to the back wall. He throws a magical rope, which lassos the book, and he yanks the book, which flies to him, and he puts it in Behaggen.

"No," yells Cloakenstrike.

"Damn you, Vegenrage. I will get that book. I will get them all," yells Basters. The podium has fallen into the ground, and the entire lair starts to shake. Basters and Cloakenstrike turn to see falling rocks completely sealing the entrance they walked in from. They each grab Fraborn by the shoulders and pull him away from the wall. Vegenrage and Farrah are trying to maintain their balance as the floor shakes and huge rocks start to fall from the ceiling and walls. The floor starts to split, and lava starts to seep into the lair.

"Vegenrage, I cannot teleport. I have no travel magic. How do we get out of here?" shouts Farrah. They both watch as the ledge starts to crack and crumble. Basters, Cloakenstrike, and Fraborn fall from the ledge and are covered by rocks and boulders.

"Are they dead? Do you think that killed them?" asks Farrah.

"I think they are still alive," says Vegenrage, holding her hand, and they weave and dodge falling rocks and boulders from the ceiling. They keep falling and getting back up because the floor is shaking like an earthquake.

"Oh, I don't like this," says Vegenrage, feeling like he is going to throw up. The shaking stops. The falling rocks stop, and Farrah and Vegenrage finally get a moment's rest. Vegenrage falls to his knees, and then he lies on the ground, rolling to his back.

"What is wrong, Vegenrage? Are you OK?" asks Farrah.

"I don't feel good. I feel like I am going to throw up," says Vegenrage. The floor starts to crack and rise. Farrah turns to see the head of a Doliath rise from the floor, opening its humongous mouth and roaring.

"Vegenrage, get up. Get up, Vegenrage," says Farrah, bending down and helping Vegenrage to his feet. The Doliath rises, pounding its front feet on the ground and lifting its massive body into the lair. Huge rocks and rubble fall from its massive form, and there is not much room left as it turns to face Vegenrage and Farrah. As if this was not bad enough, three Liecrawlers run up from the hole left by the Doliath. Lava is starting to slowly overtake the room, the red glow of molten lava is turning the lair red, and the heat is starting to be felt.

Rocks and boulders fly up from the other side of the room, gaining everyone's attention. Cloakenstrike stands, raising his hands and freeing himself, Basters, and Fraborn from their short-lived rock prison. Fraborn is gaining consciousness just in time to see a Liecrawler charge at them. It jumps in the air, heading right for Fraborn because it can sense he is wounded, but Cloakenstrike thrusts his staff of Coldstrike into it, and everyone watches as the Liecrawler is slowly turned into a frozen replica of itself. Cloakenstrike drops it on the ground, shattering the Liecrawler and freeing his staff.

One of the other Liecrawlers runs and jumps at Farrah. She easily dodges to the side, draws Quadrapierce from her left forearm, and cuts the Liecrawler in half while it is still in midair. The third Liecrawler wants no part of this and runs back into the hole, which fills with lava and starts to overrun the lair, but it is rising very slowly.

Vegenrage can see the Doliath is beginning its breath attack, and he moves in front of Farrah, telling her to hold on to him. The Doliath lets loose its inferno breath, which Vegenrage blocks with his magical force. This breath attack is so intense and powerful that it flows around the lair, and Cloakenstrike protects Basters and Fraborn with a magical force of his own. The entire lair is quickly engulfed in the inferno breath of the Doliath, and nothing can be seen or heard except flame and fire. The Doliath stops its breath attack, and Vegenrage thrusts his right arm at the hole in the ceiling made by Hornspire when he has breathed his imaginary fire on it. This shoots a magical rope that has a hook on the end, and it shatters the ice covering the hole. The hook on the end of the rope flies out the hole and sticks firmly on the ice. Vegenrage is pulled up and out of the lair while Farrah has her arms around his chest, and her hands are holding on to his shoulders. Farrah rides Vegenrage on his back, holding him tight, watching as Cloakenstrike takes offensive measures by jumping at the Doliath and stabbing it in its hind quarter with the staff of Coldstrike. Farrah and Vegenrage exit the lair and watch as the enormous demon is slowly turned to ice by Cloakenstrike, and the lair is still filling with lava.

"What do we do now, Vegenrage? I think we should get out of here. You know they will escape," says Farrah.

"Yup, you are right. They will get out of there. I only wonder if more demons will enter before they get out. Come on, I can already tell our travel magic is back. Logantrance must have gone back to the Erkensharie. I say we go there where we can share the knowledge of this book with him and Oriapow," says Vegenrage.

Farrah looks down at the hole leading into the lair, and she waves her right hand over it, freezing it in solid ice. "I don't know if I want to go back to the Erkensharie," says Farrah.

"Why not? What's wrong?" asks Vegenrage.

"It's not Logantrance or Oriapow or the dwarves or the elves. It's Ulegwahn. He makes me very uncomfortable. He gets too close to me and says things I don't want to hear. I don't want to be anywhere near him. I don't want him to think I am interested in him at all because I am not. You are for me, and I don't think he understands that," says Farrah.

"Then we will go home. You will not be put in that position anymore," says Vegenrage.

Farrah smiles and says, "Good, let's go home." Vegenrage grabs her hand, and they walk into a dimension door.

"Damn," yells Basters. "Vegenrage got it. He got the book. Now what are we going to do? What about what Hornspire said? Are we going to die in here?"

"We are not going to die in here. Come on, we have to move up and get out just like they did," says Cloakenstrike, who starts to climb up the rocks and rubble that has been the ledge that they have been standing on. Lava is covering the floor, and the three of them climb up to where they have entered, but it is still blocked by boulders and huge rocks. Cloakenstrike shoots a magical force at the ice created by Farrah, and it shatters. "OK, Basters, use that magical rope of yours and get us out of here."

"You got it," says Basters, who shoots a magical rope, and the three of them escape the same way Vegenrage and Farrah have. Basters looks back into the lair of Hornspire, and he can see that the lava is starting to flow faster. His attention is diverted to explosions they hear off in the distance. Basters grabs the snow gold trinket with his right hand and looks to his friends. "She is gone. The trinket has lost its power. The demons have destroyed the Krasbeil Mountains. They are exploding right now. We had better get back to Ugoria, and I will name the new king."

The three of them can see in the distance from the snowy mountainside they are on that toxic ash is starting to fill the air. "I am afraid you are right, my friend. We had better get back to Ugoria, and I think you are right. You should name the new king so we can go. We can figure out how to survive this demon invasion together. There is safety in numbers, but sometimes it is safer to be on the outskirts watching in, away from the danger," says Cloakenstrike.

CHAPTER 16

The Demon Anticipation

Basters walks out of his dimension door, followed by Cloakenstrike and Fraborn. Instantly, Basters is hit with an internal feeling like his heart has been torn from his chest. Not a physical pain but a very deep emotional pain overtakes him. "Cloakenstrike," says Basters.

"I know. I sense it too. Fraborn, you may want to draw your sword and be very alert because something is not right here," says Cloakenstrike.

"Where is everyone?" asks Fraborn, who follows Cloakenstrike and Basters, who are walking into the palace courtyard under the arching perimeter front doors, which are wide open. There is no sentry anywhere to be seen.

Basters halts before he enters the palace. "I am getting a real bad feeling, Cloakenstrike. I don't sense any Ugorian life at all. I sense evil. I sense life but not demon. What do you think?" asks Basters.

"This is very strange. I do not sense any elven life, that is for sure, but what happened to them all? There are no signs of battle, no blood, no weapons, no armor. This is very unusual," says Cloakenstrike.

"Basters, look," says Fraborn as the three of them see one figure wearing a black cloak completely covering his or her whole body, even the face.

Basters, Cloakenstrike, and Fraborn stand side by side and watch as this unusual, most likely elven, individual approaches them.

"That is far enough," says Basters. The individual stops and hesitates. "Who are you?"

The individual grabs the front of his hood with his right hand and pulls it back, exposing his brown elven skin and his raven black hair.

"I am Kerben. I am the leader of the Helven, and we have come to protect Ugoria from the demons who are growing in numbers and getting ready to assault the palace here."

"I know of you. You were banished from Ugoria under Jardilith's rule. You say you have come back to help us defend against the demons? Where is everyone? Where have all the elves gone? Why are they not here preparing for the demon invasion that you say is coming?" asks Basters.

"How is it that a human is king of Ugoria? I have to say I always thought the high class here in Ugoria was weak, and I only wanted to help make us the strongest race of man. I wanted us to be the most diversified and the most well adapted and best equipped. I have to say I never saw this coming. Never in my wildest dreams did I think a human would rule Ugoria. I mean, what a joke! This is weaker and more pitiful than I ever suspected we could be as a kingdom. I mean, look around you. None of the elves even support you. The second we arrived, they scattered and did not even put up a fight. So I imagine you three will do the same. I am aware of the legacy beholding the kingship of Ugoria, that is to say, the past kings of Ugoria have all been slain by the new king. I will give you a break. I do not even know your name, but I know you are the king because you have the snow gold trinket around your neck, and you have Delver around your waist. I require both of these items, and I will let the three of you go unharmed. You will not last long anyway, but at least you can leave here alive," says Kerben.

Basters takes a step forward. "You think you can take these items from me? Huh, you pathetic little elf? Go ahead and try. I will turn you into mulch, you banished cockroach," he says.

"I am not even going to mess around with you, weaklings. I will take what I want," says Kerben, and he holds out his right hand toward Basters's face, trying to pull the snow gold trinket from Basters's neck using a magical force to grasp the trinket, which starts to lift off Basters's chest. Basters grabs the trinket with his right hand.

It is a very big mistake on the part of Kerben to not give these three very talented individuals enough respect. Cloakenstrike slashes his right hand over his head and down, severing the magical spell like a rope. Basters is still wearing his belt of speed and his boots of speed, and before Kerben even knows what is happening, Basters has grabbed him around his neck and slammed him to the ground, knocking the wind out of him. Basters stands putting his boot on Kerben's neck, preventing him from being able to breathe. Fraborn draws his Lavumptom sword and puts the point of the blade at Kerben's right cheek, and Cloakenstrike walks up to Basters's right side. Now Kerben feels very foolish, but the fact that he cannot breathe is quickly becoming his main concern.

"I have not decided if I am going to let you live or not. Cloakenstrike, you want to see if he has any valuables?" says Basters, still putting a lot of pressure on Kerben's neck.

Basters, Cloakenstrike, and Fraborn look up as the sound of slowly clapping hands gets their attention. There is a walkway that runs around the palace on the first level, and the full length of the front wall one story up is lined with elves all wearing the same concealing cloaks just as Kerben is. There is only one elf here who has his hood down, and he is the one clapping. "Well, it is safe to assume that you have at least some skills. I mean, you, a human, could not have become king of Ugoria on just your good looks. You can let Kerben go now. He is just following commands," says the elf.

"Like I said, I have not decided if I am going to let him live yet," says Basters.

"Well, look around you. I have not decided if I am going to let you live," says the elf. The three of them look behind them, seeing a whole lot of cloaked elves walk in from the front gate, surrounding them from the back. The elf who was talking levitates up and over the wall and floats down to the ground level in front of Basters. The nearly sixty elves who have been to either side of him on the walk do the same, and now Basters, Cloakenstrike, and Fraborn find themselves completely surrounded. Basters lets his foot off the neck of Kerben, and he slowly gets up, coughing and holding his neck, and walks behind his leader.

"Now I will take the snow gold trinket," says the elf.

Basters grabs the trinket with his right hand and holds it tight, saying, "Why do you want the trinket? The demons are erupting all of the Krasbeil Mountains, and this has destroyed the home of the snow elf, killing her and ending the power of the snow gold trinket. So why do you want this trinket so bad?"

"Yes, the power of the trinket has been released, but the snow elf is not dead. She is just—how should I say?—she is in a state of flux. She is in a metamorphosis, if you will. You see, with the snow gold trinket in my hands, the power of the precious artifact will come back, and Shenlylith will protect me, the new king of Ugoria, because I am the chosen king," says the elf.

"I do not even know your name. You walk into my kingdom and act like you are destined to rule here. So what is your name?" asks Basters.

"I am Dona'try, the new ruler of Ugoria, and may I have the pleasure of knowing the name of the king who is about to surrender his throne to me?" says Dona'try.

"I am Basters," says Basters, and he looks to Cloakenstrike with a smile on his face, and Cloakenstrike returns the smile, like the two of them know something that no one else knows. They feel the presence of the elves returning to the palace in force. "Dona'try, let me tell you something. I have ruled over human men, I have ruled over humanor men, and I have ruled over elven men. And they all have very similar traits. The most important thing I have learned about the rule of all the races of men is this: If you treat your men no matter what race they are with respect and you give them the freedom to choose for themselves, then they will, in return, respect you.

And more important than that, they will be there to fight for you at the drop of a dime."

"Oh, I see, and how is that philosophy working for you here in Ugoria?" asks Dona'try.

"Well, let us test what I believe to be a factual statement. Bronsilith, Verlyle!" yells Basters, and the Ugorian bow elf regiments under both leaders rise from the outside of the perimeter wall, which stands a little taller than the first level of the palace. All the bow elves hop over the wall and stand on scouting pads on the inside of the wall and draw their very intimidating long bows, pointing them at the elves surrounding their king.

"Gandeleem, Wendell!" yells Basters, and on the walk of the first level of the palace, where Dona'try and his elves just have been, rise two more regiments of bow elves, who draw their long bows on the intruding elves.

"Gonbilden, Tornsclin!" yells Basters, and two warrior-class regiments run in from the outside wall and force the elves surrounding their king to flee back behind Dona'try.

They are followed by Willithcar, who is still the top general in Ugoria, and even though his past with Basters is confrontational, he still serves him, saying, "May I call them in, my king?"

"Yes, you may, Willithcar," says Basters.

"Vorgillith, Stromgin!" yells Willithcar, and so far, the entrance of all of Ugoria's bow elves and warriors has been silent, but there is no keeping quiet the thunderous sounds of many horses running very fast, getting louder and louder until all the horse riders who survived the third dragon feast have entered the palace courtyard.

Now Dona'try and the Helven all find themselves surrounded and aimed upon by bows, lances, and swords. There are no magic users to be seen outside of Basters and Cloakenstrike. The truth is that most and certainly all the powerful magic users of Ugoria have been killed in the last dragon feast. There are only very weak or young magic users in Ugoria now outside of Cloakenstrike and Basters.

"Well, I must congratulate you, Basters. It looks like you have the appearance of a standoff here," says Dona'try.

"There is no standoff about it. The only decision I have is whether to let you live or not. My inclination is to kill you all right now because I know this is a prelude to demon invasion," says Basters, looking around at his surprisingly focused and loyal army.

Back in the Erkensharie, it appears to be nighttime; but actually, the toxic ash spewing from the Glaborian Mountains is making its way past the Erkensharie, now blocking out the sun, and a permanent darkness is starting to take over. Ulegwahn has made amends with Oriapow, who has returned, and they stand on the great wall, protecting the courtyard, which has already been repaired. This time the elves have made great stairways on the inside of the wall walking up to the top of the thirty-foot wall, making it very strong and nearly impossible to be punched or kicked through, like Vemenomous has done in the past.

Ulegwahn has called all the top leaders in his army to meet him here, and they all have watched as the ash fills and darkens the sky. They watch as darkness creeps toward them and slowly moves overhead, darkening the Erkensharie.

Ulegwahn looks around at his elves and walks beside them as he heads toward and down the stair leading into the courtyard. He is followed by Kwerston, Thambrable, and Sileyen, representing and leading the bow elves of Erkensharie. Cellertrill is here representing the warriors of Erkensharie. The third dragon feast and the invasion of Vemenomous in the Erkensharie have killed many of the leading bow elves and decimated the warrior class. The one area where the Erkensharie elves have always been very strong is the magical order, and they fortunately have a lot of magic users and very powerful ones still at the service of Ulegwahn. Oriapow, the father of Erkensharie magic, is here, and he is as able as ever. Whenshade, Crayeulle, Cebleeth, Tronillis, Sombons, Lentoz, Angribe, and Pryzill are all here, ready to carry out their king's wishes.

Ulegwahn turns to face his elves. "My brothers, I thought the Erkensharie had endured all the harshest of realities that could be thrown at us but no. The dragons swooping down on the Erkensharie for the third dragon feast and the minions of the Ilkergire ascending from the south, we thwarted all this and survived triumphant just to have Vemenomous crash through our wall and kill our brothers and sisters. Still we survive and rebuild, and as if all of this were not enough, we are challenged yet again. Darkness is upon us, and it will be followed by a demon horde. This is an enemy like we have never seen before—demons, and they are coming. Oriapow and my top commanders will meet with me in the Great Erken to discuss the inevitable invasion coming our way. The rest of you, get the word out and make sure all the Erkensharie people are ready. We may all have to retreat to the security of our inner homeland. The Vinegrowers, Treestriders, and Terrahawks, along with the Erkensharie people, will be tested again. And again, we will rise triumphant," says Ulegwahn.

Vegenrage and Farrah walk into their home in Vollenbeln. Vegenrage walks to his golden table at the front of their home. While he does, Behaggen and his boots magically float to their resting place on and below Vegenrage's clothes rack. Vegenrage pulled the book *The Demon Swell* from Behaggen, and he lays it on the golden table. He sits on the big pillows in front of his study table. The book has solid gold bindings, and the cover is written in Shasparian language (English), the common human tongue in the Maglical System.

"That is odd," says Vegenrage out loud. "Hey, Farrah, this book seems to be written in Shasparian language. That is odd. I wonder why he did that." He lifts the heavy book and inspects its front and back covers. It is absolutely exquisite, and the golden hue shines on his face. He tries to open the book, but it is magically sealed. He puts his right hand on the book and tries to absorb its contents, but he cannot. "Hornspire has really worked hard to make sure the contents of this book remain concealed. It will take some doing, but I will see its contents. The curiosity has the best of me now."

Farrah has crawled onto the bed, and she is watching Vegenrage with a smile on her face. Her accessories and boots float over to her clothes rack, and she magically raises Vegenrage, who remains in sitting position, and the book remains on his study table. Vegenrage floats into the air and over to the bed, turning in the air to face Farrah, who is smiling. She rests him on the bed in a sitting position with his legs stretched out in front of him, and she crawls on her hands and knees over to him and sits on him, wrapping her legs around his hips and back. Vegenrage smiles, saying, "Farrah, what are you doing?"

She puts her arms on his shoulders and hugs him close to her, kissing him very passionately. Her lips are very warm and moist, and Vegenrage's lips quickly become the same as they kiss. Slowly he leans back, lying on the bed. Farrah swirls her tongue in Vegenrage's mouth, and he returns the action, feeling how their lips just glide along each other smooth and warm. Vegenrage forgets everything and just feels the warmth and passion flowing from Farrah to him. He does not even feel his clothes come off as Farrah magically disrobes them both, and in no time, they are grinding on each other, squeezing each other, and rubbing each other all over. "Mmmmmmmm," sarcastically moans Vegenrage as he finally realizes they are naked, and he is very excited.

Farrah, who is still on top of Vegenrage, lifts her head, saying, "What? What is wrong?"

"Nothing is wrong. It is just that you can do anything you want with me, and I cannot resist you."

"That's right, and I am going to do to you what you did to me," says Farrah, smiling, and she grabs Vegenrage's growth and rubs it against her slowly back and forth, up and down. Her excitement grows hot and wet as her pubic area clenches and releases over and over. Farrah takes a deep, slow breath as she penetrates herself with Vegenrage. She shivers and spasms all over her body, feeling the tension of his body tearing hers as she eases back off him and automatically penetrates herself with him again. She does this over and over, feeling the unexplainable pleasing pain that turns into burning motion as the pain is replaced with excitement. Her feelings of tearing and sanding are replaced with heavy breathing and a racing heartbeat as her momentum drives her hips up and down until all of Vegenrage is no longer tearing and scraping her but gliding inside and filling her. Her tensions are replaced with smiles, and her thoughts are replaced with physical feelings as she grinds; she shakes and feels hot waves all over her body. Her movements automatically happen so fast like her body knows exactly what to do and how to move. She moves up and down, side to side, and there is this motion that her body cannot resist, and it is automatic. She moves faster and faster, harder and harder, over and over. Her hips rise up almost off Vegenrage, and then they slam down on him and grind to the right. Farrah's body does this over and over.

Vegenrage can hear her breathing harder and harder, and she buries her mouth into the right side of his neck. She sucks on his neck and breathes through her nose. She wraps her left arm under his back, and Vegenrage grabs her right arm with his right hand and pulls it behind her back, holding it there while he reaches his left arm up her back and grabs her right shoulder and holds her tight to his body. Farrah's body continues to grind as fast as she can. He can hear her muffled moans as she holds her mouth on his neck by sucking on it as hard as she can. Farrah starts to moan louder, more like she is gasping, as her head pulls away from Vegenrage's neck, and her motion changes. She pulls up just a little and then grinds her hips with Vegenrage's as hard as she can. Vegenrage can't believe how fast and hard she is doing this. Farrah pulls her right arm free and moans loudly, reaching under Vegenrage's left shoulder with her right hand, gripping him, and digging her nails into the back of his shoulder. She keeps grinding her hips on his.

Vegenrage rolls her onto her back and pushes his hips as hard as he can right into Farrah and kisses her deeply. He pushes on her hips with his, driving her into the bed, and pulls up just enough to release the bed to its original form and then drives Farrah into the bed again. He does this over and over, never raising enough to release the union of their bodies. He raises his hips just high enough to release the tension of the bed, and then he drives Farrah back into it and holds her there, slowly raising his hips.

Farrah loves the way this feels. She can feel the way he releases the tension of the bed and then uses the muscles of his stomach and hips to drive her into the bed slow but very strong. She loves the way Vegenrage has his arms wrapped around her back, and he holds her shoulders tight with his hands. And even if she wants to, she cannot escape his grasp, but she does not want to go anywhere; she wants to stay right where she is. She loves the way the feelings keep her guessing. She loves the way he keeps her anxious for feelings that come, feelings that release, and feelings that make her heart beat hard and fast.

Then Vegenrage starts to grind his hips into hers side to side, and the lower region of their stomachs is starting to hurt a lot, but neither one of them cares about that; they keep beating on each other because there are other feelings that are taking each of them over. Farrah can feel Vegenrage searching inside of her body, and for the moments that her heart is not racing and her heavy breathing does not have her consumed in physical exhaustion, which she loves, she can feel this uncontrollable smile steal her face. She has not opened her eyes at all since she has first kissed Vegenrage, and during the time she has been naked with Vegenrage, pure passion and her natural bodily desires have dictated her every movement and action. She has climaxed many times already and never stopped once to realize that she has. She is so energetic, so full of enthusiasm and passion that she wants to sweat; she wants to grind and feel burning in all her muscles, and Vegenrage is giving her everything she wants. Her legs are getting very tired, her hips are very sore, and her stomach muscles are really tiring out; but that is OK because every time she climaxes it is longer and better than the last one. She has had her legs wrapped around Vegenrage's legs, and without thinking about it, she has been running her legs up and down his. A lot of the time, she has been squeezing their legs together and pushing down on the back of his legs with her feet, and her legs are really starting to get tired.

Vegenrage is still grinding on Farrah, and their bodies interact with each other for a long period as they enjoy the pleasurable passions of each other's warmth, strength, and embrace. Vegenrage starts to circle his hips while all of his excitement is in Farrah, and she cannot hold on with her legs anymore; they fall limp and spread to the sides with her knees bent, and her feet are swaying in the air to the movements of Vegenrage's hips, which now have a much freer motion. Farrah's body clenches, and she gasps uncontrollably; she wraps her arms around his head, squeezing him tight, as Vegenrage has found the movement that Farrah's body loves and craves. She can feel Vegenrage squeeze her body into his with his arms, which are still wrapped around her back, only separating for the short time it takes their hips to pull from each other and slam back together, and she loves it. "Right there, right there. Don't stop that. Keep doing that," says Farrah as her body replaces a sharp pain above her pubic area with a growing excitement so deep in her belly that she can't believe it is even inside of her. Farrah has all her emotions come out at once. She is thrown into a frenzy of emotional disorientation, as her body wants to cry, it wants to laugh, it wants to do everything; and all she can do is fall limp because Vegenrage has reached his arms under her legs and her shoulders, pinning her legs to her sides. His arms are sliding up her legs behind her knees, and then he reaches around Farrah's back, pulling her legs up to the sides of her breasts.

Farrah, for the first time, looks down to see her contorted body. Her legs are pulled up to her sides, forming a V, and she cannot believe she is this flexible. The excitement of watching Vegenrage pull from her and then slam back into her takes her breath away, and he is doing it just the way she wants him to. She looks at Vegenrage, and his eyes are closed, and his body is moving with hers in a natural physical love. She knows the smile on his face is his truest expression. She literally forgets to breathe, even though her mouth is wide open, and she can feel it coming. Something inside of her is growing, and finally, she takes a deep breath, putting her hands on Vegenrage's hips. "Oh! Oh! Oh!" She runs her hands up his chest and back. "Oh! Oh! Vegenrage," Farrah says very loud, wrapping her arms around him and squeezing them together. She can feel him getting bigger inside of her. She can feel him grind on her harder with furious intensity, slamming their loins together over and over until his strength and size digs as deep into her as it can. She can feel this spot inside of her, and Vegenrage keeps on hitting it; he keeps rubbing it and stroking it with his growing excitement until the spot explodes, and it feels like all her insides are leaking out of her. She can never explain how good this feels to her, and even if her insides were leaking out, she does not care. Her body clenches and tightens, and she squeezes with her arms as hard as she can.

Smiles take over her face, and laughter is heard with her heavy breathing. Vegenrage now buries his face in her neck, sucks as hard as he can, and squeezes her legs right into her sides, which hurt her a lot. "Ah!" complains Farrah as she pries his arms from under her legs, and they fall back down to the normal position. Farrah is instantly taken right back into heavy breathing and moaning, as Vegenrage is still pounding her with his hips, and he is still hitting that spot, which now is red-hot. Farrah leaks tears from her eyes. Her legs are limp to the sides, and all the pain she has felt is gone, as her insides are a constant explosion of heat and pleasurable waves flowing from her hips throughout all her body. She is crying because she can feel all of Vegenrage inside of her, and she knows he is giving her everything he has, and this is a feeling she can never explain, but it is everything she wants; it is everything she loves.

Vegenrage has pleased her in the most intimate way, and even better than that is the feeling she feels as he explodes inside of her, and she knows he feels the same as she does. She loves the sounds he makes as his body is overcome with excitement, and he exhausts himself, depositing all his love into her. Farrah smiles and squeezes him as tight as she can with her legs, which are very tired but still very strong. Her arms reach around his back, and she squeezes him tight. She loves the way their chests and stomachs rub against each other. She digs her fingernails into his back as she feels Vegenrage thrust for the last time, twitching and throbbing inside of her. Farrah smiles uncontrollably and hears Vegenrage scream in a very painful way, raising his head and arching his back away from her. She realizes she has dug her fingernails into his back and can feel she has drawn blood from him.

Vegenrage lies on her and starts kissing on her neck again. She pulls her hands back and looks over his head and shoulder to see her hands severely overgrown; they are huge clawed dragon hands. Farrah screams upon seeing scaled red skin starting at her elbows and going up to three very large talon-ended black fingers and one thumb on each hand, and blood is dripping from all the talons. Farrah screams again, and Vegenrage raises his head, still consumed in passion and still inside of her.

"What, Farrah? What is it?" asks Vegenrage. She looks fine to him, but he can feel great magical energy pulsing from within her. "Farrah, what is it? What is going on? Open your eyes, Farrah. Look at me."

Vegenrage's magical intuition goes haywire on him, and he tilts to the side as Farrah opens her eyes and mouth at the same time, releasing incredibly bright yellowish white light from her mouth and eyes. Her hands hit Vegenrage on his ribs at the same time, sending powerful energy into him, launching him across the room, and slamming him into the wall on the other side of their home near the entrance door. It is still nighttime in Vollenbeln, and the moon is shining through the ceiling window, but Farrah's dragon-slaying hands, which she just cast from her mouth and eyes, have disintegrated a huge hole in the ceiling of their home, and the ceiling window is now gone. The magical force that is more of a reflex cast from Farrah's hands is still strong enough to break six of Vegenrage's ribs, three on each side of him. Fortunately, he ducks his head to the side just far enough to avoid getting hit directly in the face with Farrah's devastating dragon-slaying hands spell. Still the force from her mouth has destroyed Vegenrage's left shoulder and neck. He is bleeding badly below his left ear. The flesh of his neck has been sheared and burned, along with all the flesh on his shoulder, and his left collarbone is partially gone. Vegenrage is bleeding badly, and his blood is all over the wall. He is in shock and breathing very shallow because there is great pain in his ribs when he tries to take in air.

Even though he is not fully aware and he is severely wounded and can hardly move, Vegenrage has special abilities that are hard at work right now. His body automatically heals itself when wounded, and Vegenrage is the fastest of all magic-using beings at this, especially in his home realm of Vollenbeln. Still he needs time.

Farrah sits up in the bed, screaming and looking at her hands, which turn from scaly red dragon hands back to her own. It takes her a minute, but she realizes it was just an illusion and that something bad has happened. She sees Vegenrage lying against the wall with blood all over it and him, and she cries, "Vegenrage. What have I done?"

Farrah can hear laughter outside their home, and she sees the same hands that she has just seen on her arms reach into the hole she has created in the ceiling. The hands and claws rip the earth, pulling it away, making the hole in the ceiling bigger. Vegenrage is still badly wounded and needs a lot of healing, but he can now speak and is getting his focus back. "Farrah, it's Vemenomous. He is here. I need your help, Farrah. I need you to help me heal," says Vegenrage in a shallow voice, lying on the ground.

Farrah gets off the bed and starts toward him when Vemenomous drops in from the hole in the ceiling between Vegenrage and Farrah. Vemenomous is still fifteen feet tall and bends down on his knees, still towering over Farrah, who steps back from the grotesque beast. "You did not think I would give up on you. You are my queen, and as I have said before, it is only a matter of time until you and I rule supreme over the Maglical System. You are still going to be the queen ruling over the race of demonian dragon. You are going to have many children, and you will be my queen for a thousand years," says Vemenomous.

"Yo—" Farrah starts to talk when Vemenomous points his right-hand talons at her, grasping her with his mind control, immobilizing her naked body. He points his left hand toward Vegenrage's study table, and the book *The Demon Swell* floats over to the hand of Vemenomous.

"This is my home, my realm, my domain. And you are not welcome here," says Vegenrage. Vemenomous's head, even though on his knees, is still near the ceiling with the hole that leads into the sky of Vollenbeln. Vemenomous turns his head to look at Vegenrage lying naked on the floor. The bleeding from his shoulder has stopped, but he is still unable to stand.

Vemenomous slowly raises his head and looks into the Vollenbeln night sky, and he can see a small but bright white light shooting in the sky. It stops directly above him, very high in the sky. He can see pure white lightning shooting from all over in the sky into the pure white ball, and it is growing. Pure white lightning shoots straight down, leaving white streaks visible in the air and hitting Vemenomous right on the top of his head. The lightning continues and does not stop. Vemenomous starts to glow white, and he slowly vanishes from sight, dropping the book on the floor.

Farrah regains her senses and sees Vegenrage still lying on the floor against the wall. She runs over to him and leans down by him, putting her hands on his chest and helping him heal. This takes a few minutes, but between the two of them, Vegenrage heals very quickly. "Vegenrage, he is still here. He can still control my mind. What am I going to do?" says Farrah as her face is taken over with sadness, her lips droop downward at the edges, and her eyes start to swell with tears. "It is all my fault, Vegenrage. I led him right here. It is all my fault."

Vegenrage is able to sit up now, and he hugs Farrah. They sit there quietly holding each other, leaning against the wall.

CHAPTER 17

The Demon Swell Begins

Ulegwahn has sent Pryzill, Lentoz, and Sombons to inspect the Long Forest from the northwest to the far southwest of the Ilkergire. He wants to know if the Dark Bush has overgrown in all of the Long Forest. Dark Bush will not slow down the demons, but the living can get nowhere near this, and Ulegwahn wants to know if the Dark Bush has spread into the Erkensharie Forest. The Dagi have warned Ulegwahn that a demon horde has risen from the lava flowing out of the Glaborian Mountains and is moving southwest from the Sand Marshes of Smyle.

There is a dilemma that Ulegwahn consults Oriapow about in his throne room concerning the demons, the dragons, the Dark Bush, his people, and the minions of the Ilkergire. "Oriapow, the Octagemerwell has been pulsing. It has been feeding me energy. I know that what Blythgrin and the Dagi have told me about the demon horde moving south toward us is true. This demon swell, this scourge rising from the depths of Maglical Hell, the Octagemerwell is warning me, but I do not know how to protect our people. I do not know how to decipher what the heart of Fargloin is trying to tell me," says Ulegwahn.

"I feel it too, my king. The Octagemerwell is telling us to have faith. It is telling us to remain strong and stay in our home. It is telling us danger is coming, and we will stop it here," says Oriapow.

"What if this demon horde were to destroy the Erkensharie and rid Fargloin of the elves? Then what? I mean, what then? How does this demon horde, this swelling of demons on the outer realm, plan on dealing with the Ilkergire and the dragons? Is their reason for being here simply to eliminate all life on the outer realm, starting with the dwarves and elves? If so, does this not make the minions of the Ilkergire our allies? What of the dragons? Does this demon horde not make us allies with the dragons as well? And what of Vemenomous? Where do his loyalties lie?" asks Ulegwahn.

"These are very interesting questions. It is not like we can ask the minions of the Ilkergire to side or fight with us. However, the dragons could do this. We need Vegenrage because he has befriended the dragons, and so has Farrah," says Oriapow.

Ulegwahn interrupts him. "I have had all I can take of Vegenrage. I do not want to hear any more about him, and he is not welcome in the Erkensharie anymore."

"What are you talking about? Vegenrage has been our strongest ally," Oriapow says.

"No, he has not!" exclaims Ulegwahn. "Vegenrage has done nothing but look out for himself. He has done nothing here to protect our people or our homeland. He comes when it suits him, and he goes when it suits him. He has been followed here by dragons, by the minions of the Ilkergire, and by Vemenomous. And what has he done after they have followed him here? He has left us. He has left us to clean up the mess."

"Oh, you think it was Vegenrage who brought the minions of the Ilkergire and the dragons here. You can't be serious," says Oriapow.

"Oh, I am serious. All this talk about the chosen one, all this talk about the great human magic user brought to the Maglical System to save the races of men from the dragons, you know why all those books were written, don't you? They were written to keep us . . ." Ulegwahn pauses and walks around, pointing to his chest, very serious, very focused on what he is talking about. "they were written to keep us races of men off guard. They were written to keep our attention off the real human magic user who will save the races of men, and that magic user is not a human male. It is a human female. I know because the Octagemerwell has told me. I know because I can feel her power. She was meant to harness the power of the Octagemerwell by my side as queen of the Erkensharie. This is why Vemenomous came here for her. He knows how powerful Farrah is, and he knows she is to be the power behind the ultimate ruler of the Maglical System. She will be my queen. She will be the power that makes me complete. With the Octagemerwell at my disposal and Farrah at my side, the Erkensharie will be impregnable by all demon hordes, by all dragons and lesser dragons," says Ulegwahn very seriously.

"Ulegwahn, listen to yourself. What are you talking about? Farrah is human. She cannot be your queen because she is not elven. Not only that but it is also clear that she and Vegenrage are inseparable and have been since I have known both of them," says Oriapow.

"Yes, you are right, but it matters not. Elves and humans were once the same. We have a few differences, but still we are compatible, and as a matter of fact, all the races of men are compatible. As far as Vegenrage goes, he is not welcome in the Erkensharie anymore. The next time Farrah is to travel here, I want her brought to me at once. And if Vegenrage is with her, he is to be brought to me also," says Ulegwahn, walking to his throne and sitting down.

"Ulegwahn, you—" Oriapow is interrupted by Ulegwahn.

"That will be all for now. You may be excused," says Ulegwahn. Oriapow shakes his head in disbelief and walks out of the throne room.

Pryenthious is still the leading dominant dragon on the world of Fargloin, and he can sense from the moment the demons started rising from the lava in Glaboria that the demons are on the move. He has called by telepathy the other dominant dragons, and they have come. Gairdennow, Dribrillianth, and Blethstole have come to the lair of Pryenthious. They all know very quickly that the evil horde is heading south toward the Erkensharie. The dragons have talked about staying hidden and out of sight, but this is not their way, and they cannot ignore that. If the demon horde kills off the Erkensharie elves, then there will be no races of men left on Fargloin; and after that, they will certainly hunt and easily kill the minions of the Ilkergire, otherwise known as the lesser dragons. They cannot have this.

Gairdennow agrees to search for Ubwickesdon again, and this time Dribrillianth will search for Interford, the Changenoir, who cast the Dark Bush on the Long Forest. They must unite the lesser dragons and prepare for the demon horde heading south. Pryenthious is going to travel dimensionally to get a look at the demon horde and what is really heading south. He wastes no time and goes to scout. Blethstole calls all the dragons to the Brunst Rock Plateau (Pryenthious's lair), leaving the Mountain Creek dragons with the females and young, who are now moving around, staying in different lairs to keep their location as well hidden as possible. They are now heading to the lair of Gairdennow in the Swapoon Mountains, and this is where they will stay for the time being. They are staying aware of the swelling demon horde gathering and moving on Fargloin.

Back at the lair of Pryenthious, Blethstole addresses the dragons present, telling them that he is going to go to the Erkensharie. The elves and the dragons have a common enemy in the demons, and suddenly, the races of men are now—or at least should be—uniting with the dragons against the demons. He wants all the dragons to wait here until Gairdennow, Pryenthious, Dribrillianth, and Blethstole return, and he heads through his dimension door.

Previously, in Vollenbeln, Vemenomous had followed Farrah to her home, where he tried to make her his queen yet again. Vemenomous was not powerful enough to defeat Vegenrage in his home, even when Vegenrage was caught off guard and severely wounded. Vegenrage was still able to call upon the Vollenbeln lights (lightning), which cast

Vemenomous out. Vemenomous had to teleport quickly because the Vollenbeln lightning cast by Vegenrage was much stronger than normal lightning, and he was very close to being roasted alive and incinerated.

Vemenomous teleports himself to the lair he has created for himself since he has become Vemenomous. He has created this lair right after he has first risen from Vegenrage in Vollenbeln and flown away from all the races of men that have been there. He has gone to the Ackelson Desert, which is one of the most arid and isolated places on all three of the inhabited worlds. He has made his lair in a sand dune. It is always very hot here, and this suits Vemenomous just fine. This is an ideal place for him; it is very isolated, and there are no dragons who know of his new home—or at least that is what he thinks.

As Vemenomous flies over the sand and glides down toward the dune, which looks like just another sand dune in the desert, he notices something that catches him by surprise. What looks like a small meteorite is falling from the sky at incredible speed, crashing right into the dune that transforms into the lair of Vemenomous as he approaches. The meteorite crashes there, and he hovers, inspecting this very unusual event. Smaller rocks start to fall from the sky and land all over the same dune, and the sand starts to turn black. Many smaller rocks fall from the sky, red-hot, and smoke trails are left behind all of them as they fall. Vemenomous actually has to dodge some of the rocks that almost hit him as they fall.

The sand dune starts to turn black, and Vemenomous can't believe his eyes as a huge form starts to grow from the only black sand dune in the entire desert. The form grows two hundred feet high, and it is Cormygle in dragon form. It is only from his hips up, but this includes his wings, front arms, paws, and head, which is enormous, and his form is flawless. Vemenomous is still hovering in the sky, and he is absolutely dwarfed by the size of the carbonite dragon now looking up at him. "How dare you come here and transform my home into carbonite sands. It is a fight to the death you want with me, and you shall have it," says Vemenomous.

"It is time for you to keep your promise to me, Vergraughtu, or should I call you Vemenomous? I did just as you asked of me so long ago. I killed my father so you would not have to contend with him for the dominant dragon position. I kept your plans on becoming the demonian dragon secret from all the other dragons. I gave you the book *The Demonian Way*, written by Hornspire, and now it is time for you to keep your promise to me. Strike me with the shard hammer and give me the book *The Demon Swell*. I know you have both items, the weapon created from the glass shards of the glass staff of demon uprising. I did as you asked. I studied demonology. I served the demons and then turned on them so they could not harm my mother, and she is still alive. I have done all you asked, and everything has worked out exactly as we planned, so why have you avoided me with the shard hammer? All I ask is that you strike me with it, giving me the body I possessed under demonology, and the book *The Demon Swell* so I can avoid the demon invasion. With these, I will disappear again, never to bother you anymore. Break your word to me, and a fight to the death you shall have," says Cormygle.

"You stupid deformed dragon, I never planned on giving you eternal dragon form. I used you as I used all the dragons, and I am now the only one capable of being the demonian dragon. In fact, I am very close to becoming the demonian dragon. You were a slave to my manipulation, and it is only a matter of time until you will be my dinner," says Vemenomous, laughing at Cormygle.

"You are wrong about a lot of things, but first, the lair you used to call home and all its contents are now mine. Second, you are not the only one who can be the demonian dragon. Third, I can tell Vegenrage how to find you at any time, and he will destroy you, followed by all the races of men and the dragons. This I guarantee you, but I want the privilege of killing you all to myself. This will give me good graces with all the races of men, all the dragons, and even the demons, so killing you is a win-win-win for me. So come on down to my new home if you dare," says Cormygle as he sinks down into the black sand, which he has changed into the same carbonite sand that his home in the Carbonheight Hills are made of.

Vemenomous looks around, scanning the one sand dune changed into the black carbon, looking for any sign that Cormygle is there. He can be anywhere in the black sand, or he can be everywhere in it. Vemenomous looks around for a while, and then he starts to laugh. "You have become strong, my stubby-winged friend, but you were never as strong as I was. You think you are magically a superior dragon, but you are not. I have the blood of dragon, demon, Vegenrage, and Farrah in me. I am the only dragon who can cast magic without the spoken word. This makes me superior to you and all dragons. Let me give you a taste of what I am talking about," says Vemenomous, flapping his wings slowly and strong enough to keep him hovering stationary in midair.

He extends his arms out to his sides and looks up in the air with his eyes closed. There are no clouds in the sky, but clouds start rolling in from far off. Wind starts to blow harder and harder, blowing sand across the ground, covering the black sand that Cormygle has made. The sky darkens to a shade of gray as clouds roll in and block out the sun. Raindrops start to fall, clumping up in the sand. It starts to rain harder and harder, and lightning starts to crack and slice its way through the sky. The sky turns dark, and floods of rainwater start to wash away all the sand. Thunder starts to crack, lightning bolt after lightning bolt start to strike the black sand created by Cormygle, and it starts to glow red-hot.

Vemenomous laughs louder and louder as one bolt of lightning hits the black sand, and as soon as the bolt is gone, another strikes and so on. This goes on for a good twenty minutes, and one will think Vemenomous is having the time of his life. He is laughing and swinging his arms in the air like he is throwing the lightning bolts like javelins. Rainwater is pelting him, soaking him, and running off his perfectly chiseled body as he laughs and smiles.

Finally, Vemenomous has enough, and he closes his eyes and pauses his movements for a moment. The lightning stops, the thunder ends, and so does the rain. He then waves his right arm through the air, and the clouds roll across the horizon. In moments, they are gone, and the sun is back, evaporating all the moisture that has accumulated and formed fast, running streams all around.

Vemenomous is very surprised to see that the dune is still there, and it is still black. This makes him very mad, and he yells at the black sand, "All right, you handled that. Let's see how you handle this," he says as he raises his arms in the air and looks up.

Cormygle grows from the black sand very fast and throws a magical black rope made out of the black sand. Before Vemenomous casts his magic, he is caught by the rope around his waist, and Cormygle pulls him very fast toward him. Vemenomous vanishes and appears behind Cormygle's left shoulder. He is gliding around Cormygle's back with his wings spread wide and both arms and palms pointed at his opponent. He is shooting what looks like water balloons, a clear liquid that forms and shoots from his hands. This is really a form of acid that acts like glue, clumping all the sand it touches and then dissolves it. This is a pretty unique spell called glueaway, and Vemenomous is shooting one after another. Every new ball of acid is getting bigger and bigger. Every time Cormygle is hit, a massive clump of himself falls out onto the sand, and all the sand touching the sticky acid is dissolved, but Cormygle is just so massive at two hundred feet tall that he is able to withstand a lot of these attacks.

Cormygle is able to turn and maneuver very well, and he moves to face Vemenomous and thrusts his paws at him. This is magically throwing black carbonite javelins at Vemenomous. At first, Cormygle is throwing one at a time, and then two and then three at a time. Vemenomous is very fluid and agile in the air, able to dodge all these attacks. Then Cormygle starts to throw waves of javelins six feet long and twelve across at Vemenomous, and he dodges three waves of these, but the fourth wave he cannot avoid. He casts a wall-of-force spell to block the incoming javelins, all twelve of them, and he is very surprised when the javelins penetrate his spell. Vemenomous looks at his chest to see that three of the javelins have pierced right through his upper chest, upper stomach, and just above his hips. They have gone right through his body, but his wings are still untouched by the weapons. Cormygle throws another wave of twelve, and Vemenomous is pelted again, now falling from the sky with half a dozen six-foot-long javelins stuck through his body. He falls fast and tilts in the air, with his head and back falling first from all the weight of the javelins through his body. His wings go limp, and he slams into the black carbonite in front of Cormygle, landing on the back of his neck and shoulders. Cormygle quickly scoops up the limp body of Vemenomous with his huge paw, and he raises him in the air up to his face. Vemenomous fits in the palm of Cormygle's huge paw, and it looks like he is dead.

"Vegenrage, Farrah, and you are not the only ones with magic that can be cast without the spoken word. My carbonite flows, it grows, it forms every shape my mind thinks of. It did not have to be this way, Vemenomous. I would have taken the book and my permanent form and left you alone, but you did not want this. You wanted war, and that is just fine with me because I am the most accomplished dragon in the field of magic. Soon I will become the demonian dragon. The demon swell has begun, and all the demon hordes wait for their leader, the true demonian dragon, to come and lead them, and that dragon shall be me—the dragon born handicapped, the dragon scorned, outcast, and pushed aside by all other dragons. I, Cormygle, shall become the new superior demonian dragon and replace the existing dragons of the Maglical System."

Cormygle raises Vemenomous high in the air, and a bed of cylindrical tubes with very sharp points at the top grow from the carbonite in front of Cormygle. He turns Vemenomous in the air and slams him down on the sharp cylinders. The cylinders suddenly disappear into clouds of dust as Vemenomous is slammed into them, and Cormygle raises his hand in surprise to see that Vemenomous has not been impaled. Vemenomous raises his head, laughing, and his whole body dissolves into the carbonite. Cormygle looks to the right and to the left and clenches his claws as Vemenomous grows from the carbonite to Cormygle's right side. Vemenomous grows the same way proportionally, and now these two-hundred-feet giant carbonite dragons face each other.

Looking from the sky, the scene is bizarre, to say the least—a vast tan desert with nothing but scorched sand and dunes and just one black dune with the gigantic Cormygle facing off with the gargantuan Vemenomous. Vemenomous grabs Cormygle by the throat with his left hand. "This is my home, Cormygle. These are my sands, and the illusion of your sands shall now be revealed." The black sands start to turn into the same tan-colored sand as all the rest. As the color of the sand changes and reaches Vemenomous, he shrinks back down to his normal fifteen-foot-tall stature. Cormygle looks at himself in complete surprise as he shrinks down to his normal decrepit body with a hunched back, stubby wings, and front paws. He looks at Vemenomous, who is laughing at him and saying, "Well, I guess this changes everything."

"This changes nothing," says Cormygle.

"Master still wants you to serve him, and your choice is simple: serve him or die," says Vemenomous, pointing his right hand toward the sand at his side. Cormygle watches as the sand parts and sinks. A hole drops into the depths of the sand, and up rises Zevoncour with red sand filling the hole. He smiles wide, and his body shivers as he tingles, flexing the muscles in his arms. He makes a laughing sound like a sigh broken up in very short pauses, and he bends down and touches the tan sand outside of the red sand he is standing on. The sand he touches starts to turn red, and the red spreads throughout the whole dune, which is now the red sand of Maglical Hell on Strabalster.

"Cormygle, my sweet little wannabe dragon, you had it all. We gave you the perfect form. We gave you all the strength to magnify your magical power, and how do you repay us? You turn your back on us. You betray us and prolong the end that we all know is coming. You thought you were saving your mother, but she and all the dragons will fall to the demons as will all the races of man. The end is coming. The demon swell has begun, and our numbers are growing at a staggering rate, and the demon hordes will need leaders to follow. They will need leaders to direct their destruction. It is already known that Vemenomous will be the first demonian dragon. Vemenomous will overlook all the demon hordes on all three planets, but we still want you in our services, not as a leader but as the steed you were designed to be. You will be the steed of Xanorax like before. We will grant you perfect form, and incredible magical strength shall be yours again. Vemenomous already has the blood of both Vegenrage and Farrah flowing in him. All that is left now is for him to devour the flesh and blood of the mother of the first demon-infused dragon, and that is Mezzmaglinggla, your mother, Cormygle. Farrah shall consume the flesh and blood of Vegenrage, completing the demonian dragon union. This is going to happen and sooner than you think. So what will it be, servant or death?" says Zevoncour.

Cormygle knows he is standing on the red sand of Maglical Hell, which means he cannot cast any magic. He can cast magic, but Zevoncour will be able to control it and change it at will. Basically, Cormygle is without magic; and physically, he is no match for Vemenomous. "I will serve you," says Cormygle, and Vemenomous releases his grip from Cormygle's neck. "I will serve you destruction like you have never known." Cormygle rolls away from Vemenomous, who starts to walk toward him.

Cormygle watches as the sky opens above and behind Vemenomous, and Mezzmaglinggla flies in from her dimension door. He rolls to the side as Mezzmaglinggla flies tail first, stabbing it right through the back of Vemenomous and staking him violently to the red sand ground. She looks right at Zevoncour and releases her breath of Brassissust, engulfing him in a cloud of suffocating brass silt. Zevoncour controls all magic in the red sand but not the breath attacks of dragons, and instantly, his nose and mouth are clogged with clumping brass silt, suffocating him. He uses his lava flow magic, and the ground under his feet turns into lava, allowing him to melt away into it, escaping certain suffocation.

"Go, Cormygle, get out of here!" yells Mezzmaglinggla.

"Mother, do not use any magic while in the red sand. Zevoncour is still present, and any magic cast here is controlled by him," says Cormygle, who runs toward the tan sand. Mezzmaglinggla bites the head of Vemenomous, but before she can rip it off, his whole body melts into the red sand under her feet. A laugh can be heard, and before Cormygle can make it out of the red sand, very thick chains looking like they are made out of red-hot lava rise from the ground over him and pull him tight back into the ground, chaining him to the sand. There is one chain over his neck, one over his back, and two more that make an X over his shoulders and back. Once Cormygle is pulled tight to the ground, spikes grow from the chains, penetrating his scales, digging inches into his flesh, causing great pain, immobilizing him further.

"This is what we were waiting for," says Zevoncour with a laugh as he rises from the sand behind Mezzmaglinggla.

He thrusts his right hand toward Mezzmaglinggla, and a harpoon shoots from the palm of his hand. It has a very sharp, barbed end like a fish hook, and it sinks deep into her back. Mezzmaglinggla roars in pain and turns toward Zevoncour, unleashing her breath attack on him. He raises his left hand, and a wall of red sand rises between the two of them. Her breath attack angles up and over him, missing him completely. Zevoncour's harpoon is tethered to the center of the palm of his hand by what looks like sinew that goes right into his arm. The sinew is like the bone in his arm, and it is very strong.

Mezzmaglinggla pulls with all her body and weight, taking the pain, trying to pull Zevoncour off the ground, but he just leans toward her, and his feet remain attached to the red sand like they have been cemented in. Mezzmaglinggla roars loud and pulls over and over again, but Zevoncour remains standing. Mezzmaglinggla pauses for a second and thinks, and then she breaths frigid winds on the sinew attached to the hook in her, and this works well on the demon magic holding her. She breathes and then gives another great pull, shattering the sinew attached to the hook. When the sinew breaks, the hook in her disappears, and the other end retracts back into Zevoncour's hand, and his hand reforms. She turns and breathes the frigid wind on Cormygle, weakening the chains holding him to the ground, and takes a couple of leaps toward him and kicks him with her hind leg. He flies out of the red sand into the tan sand. She follows, jumping and gliding with her wings spread wide, and lands near her deformed son, who is not dead but needs to heal because he has been nearly frozen solid. They have landed on the next dune over, and fortunately for them, the red sand can only appear over the home of Vemenomous, but this is not the end of their troubles.

A dome of molten red hot lava rises around the circumference of the dune they are on, and as the dome rises and closes over them, the dune recedes. The sky has been blocked out, and Mezzmaglinggla and Cormygle now sit on level ground made of rock. It is almost complete darkness in here, but the red-hot glow of the lava dome gives off an eerie subtle red glow. The dome is quite large, fifty yards in diameter and twenty-five feet high. Cormygle has been nearly frozen solid but is just strong enough to start to heal when he has reached the normal sand. Now he begins to use his healing magic on himself. Mezzmaglinggla is healing herself as well from the wound left to her insides by the barbed hook shot into her by Zevoncour.

"Well, Mother, we tried. I thought we made a good shot at trying to destroy that demon and Vemenomous," says Cormygle.

"Yes, my son, we tried. What else did that book say? Did it have any advice as to what was going to happen if we did not kill Zevoncour?"

"Well, it left me hanging. It said if we fell under the demon dome, external forces would save those who save us. I have no idea what that means," says Cormygle.

"Well, my son, we are about to find out because I don't think we can get out of here. Travel magic is blocked by the demon walls, and the same goes for this ground we are on. Don't worry, the other dragons know where we are. They will come get us. Heal quickly and get that magic ready for those demons and Vemenomous. They still have us to contend with, my son," says Mezzmaglinggla.

CHAPTER 18

Rise of the First Demonian Dragon

Mezzmaglinggla studies the dome walls with her keen eyes, and her very sharp ears can hear the very subtle burn and crack of the lava that is slowly cooling even in the desert heat, which is still much cooler than the molten lava walls hardening into stone. There is a layer of smoke just inside the dome created from the heat and cooling of the lava. "They are here. They are coming," says Mezzmaglinggla.

"I am dragon, Mother. I know they are outside. They are probably going to kill me, aren't they?" asks Cormygle.

"Nobody is going to kill you. This demon magic is no match for the heavenly magic of Gwithen. You watch," says Mezzmaglinggla.

Sure enough, Gwithen has appeared in the sky outside of the dome, and Blethstole is with her. Dribrillianth, Gairdennow, and Pryenthious fly out of dimension doors as well, being summoned here before finishing their tasks of gathering all the lesser demons. "They are in there, all right. I still can't believe Mezzmaglinggla came to save Cormygle. Even if he is her son, he still has betrayed and killed dragons.

He studied demonology and deserves to be killed by them. She should have let him die," says Dribrillianth.

"Nevertheless, we are here, and we are going to get them out of there. Should any demons appear, we will roast them and eat their flesh with a little help from the creatures of the earth. Are you all ready?" asks Gwithen.

"Go ahead, Gwithen, do your stuff," says Blethstole, and all the dragons watch from the air, where they are using their powerful wings to hover.

Gwithen flies over above the center of the enormous dome in the sand, and she looks to the heavens. "Heeiillllliitthhhh swyissee lich willitthh brondomen!" Lights start to crack in the air from all around her. They look like lightning, but they are the color of white crayons, and they do not move as fast as lightning. They form in a circle around and above her from about fifty feet away, and they shoot into her body, causing her to glow this same white color very close to her natural hue. Gwithen continues her spell. "Directtss forthhcommss demos whitthh charrggeeellinn con rachton!" The white dome of lightning that has formed around and above her starts to fall from the top of the dome until it reaches the center circle around Gwithen; then it falls below her in an upside-down dome. From the bottom center of the dome shoots a continuous streak of white lightning, squiggling through the sky, that hits directly on top of the demon dome. This sends white lightning shooting throughout the dome until it reaches the ground.

The dragons in the air cannot hear this, but inside the dome, Cormygle and Mezzmaglinggla can hear laughter rising from below them, and the ground all around them starts to fall. They look off the small circular piece of land in the center of the dome to see that all the land around them has fallen into the depths of Strabalster Hell. The dome covering them cracks and crumbles, falling into the abyss around them. Mezzmaglinggla tries to fly, but when she flaps her wings, there is some sort of magic preventing her from gaining any lift, and their travel magic is still disrupted, so they cannot teleport or use a dimension door off the small piece of land they are on.

"No one enter the space that was just occupied by the dome. There is great demon magic here, and the space around Mezzmaglinggla and Cormygle is tainted with very strong evil, preventing my angel blessing from entering," says Gwithen.

The five top dominant dragons of the Maglical System are flying around above Mezzmaglinggla and Cormygle, and there is nothing they can do. If they enter the space where the dome has been, they will fall under the evil magic and be held to its limitations. If they cast magic into the space, it becomes corrupted. This is a very tricky situation, and it will take time for them to figure it out, which is exactly what someone or something has planned for.

"Gwithen, we cannot wait. We must call them now. We have to save them, even Cormygle. We cannot let them fall to the demons. I am calling them now," says Blethstole, and he swoops toward the space that has recently been occupied by the dome, roaring as loud as he can, swooping up and then back down, knowing how close he can get to the evil without putting himself in danger. The other dragons glide and soar through the air, watching as the earth starts to shake around the exposed earth where the desert has fallen.

Mezzmaglinggla and Cormygle look off the edge of the circular land piece they are on into the abyss and see the Salcendreeps have come. They are flowing through the earth like they do, and many of them are making their way up the sides of the abyss. "I cannot believe I did not think of that. The Salcendreeps are immune to magic cast into the earth. They are coming, Cormygle. They will get us out of here," says Mezzmaglinggla.

A loud laugh is heard coming from deep in the abyss, followed by these words: "Cormygle, Cormygle. I am coming for you, Cormygle. It is your time, and you are mine." Cormygle looks at Mezzmaglinggla, and a six-foot-wide four-sided razor-sharp hook shoots up from the earth right through Cormygle's stomach and exits his back. The hook severs his spine, paralyzing him instantly. It pulls tight to the ground, gripping into Cormygle's back and holding him tightly to the ground.

"Cormygle," yells Mezzmaglinggla, and she tries to pull the hook up, releasing him from its pull, but she cannot budge it.

Vemenomous is climbing up the circular earth that is rising from the abyss, and he reaches the top, peering his head over the edge and unleashing his breath of combination, which is equal to that of Farrah's dragon-slaying hands. Mezzmaglinggla releases her breath of Brassissust, but Vemenomous's attack is much more powerful, and it disintegrates her breath attack, striking her in the side of her head. Vemenomous steers the attack along her side, ripping and splattering chunks of flesh and blood, which fall all over Cormygle. Mezzmaglinggla is very badly wounded, with a huge gouge torn through her left side, as she falls over and into the abyss.

Vegenrage and Farrah have appeared in the sky above the demonic space created by the demons, and Vegenrage flies down into the abyss under Mezzmaglinggla as she falls. He flies up, catching her on his back, and takes her out.

"I told you they would come," says Gwithen to Blethstole.

Just before Vegenrage gets Mezzmaglinggla out of the demonic space, a huge hand with black claws that are bigger than Vegenrage reaches from the abyss and grasps him in its massive grip. Mezzmaglinggla has just enough strength to spread her wings and glide to the ground outside of the demon space. Gwithen and Blethstole rush to her aid and help her heal herself. Three of the Salcendreeps have made their way to Vemenomous and exited the outside walls, latching their mandibles into Vemenomous and beginning to munch his flesh. All three of them are on his back to the left, right, and top of his wings. The massive clawed hand that has hold of Vegenrage is trying to pull him into the abyss, and Vegenrage fights to fly up and out of the demon space. Farrah flies over to Vegenrage, saying, "What should I do? What can I do to help you, Vegenrage?"

The thumb of the hand is around Vegenrage's stomach, and he is pushing and prying with his arms, trying to release its grip. "Farrah, you have to save Cormygle. We cannot let Vemenomous have him. Save Cormygle. I will be OK," yells Vegenrage. Farrah flies over above Cormygle and sees Vemenomous biting down on Cormygle's head and neck, crunching his bones with the incredible force of his bite.

Vemenomous twists Cormygle's head, snapping, breaking, and ripping it off, and he releases the head into the abyss.

"Let's see how you handle this," says Farrah as she points her hands, releasing dragon-slaying hands right at Vemenomous's head. Vemenomous releases his breath attack, and the spells negate each other as they meet.

They stop their magic, and Vemenomous laughs as his wings start to spin like they are attached to a gear on his back. They spin very fast, becoming very sharp at the edges, slicing the Salcendreeps, and their bodies fall into the dark abyss. The heads remain attached to his body, where the long claws at the side of their huge mouths have dug into. "It is done, my queen. This is all I need to become the first true demonian dragon. You can feast with me, my queen, and then all you will need is the blood of Vegenrage to become my queen, the queen of the Maglical System, the mother of the most dominant species ever to rule the skies of the Maglical System, the demonian dragons," says Vemenomous as he rips flesh from the side of Cormygle, drenched in the blood and flesh of Mezzmaglinggla. He barely chews and swallows many pounds of flesh at a time as he rips the flesh from the body of Cormygle. More Salcendreeps shoot from the walls of the desert earth and latch on to Vemenomous, and again, he uses his very advanced magic to allow his wings to spin, slicing their bodies; they fall into the abyss. Vemenomous climbs up onto the small circular patch and rips more flesh from Cormygle, eating all the flesh as fast as he can.

Farrah flies toward Vemenomous with her fists clenched, and just before she reaches him, she tilts feet first with a magical kick of incredible force that hits Vemenomous, and the shock waves from the magical impact with Vemenomous reverberate, ripping the remains of Cormygle's body, shredding it, and sending what is left into the abyss. The walls around the abyss start to crumble and break off, falling into the abyss, dropping Salcendreeps with the falling rubble. Vemenomous raises his arms, still on the small piece of land surrounded by the abyss, and slams them onto the ground.

"Gairdennow, we have to do something. I can't just watch this," says Pryenthious.

"We cannot enter the demon-infused space. Our magic will be rendered useless there. We will have our breath attacks, but it is not worth the risk," says Gairdennow.

"Vegenrage has saved Mezzmaglinggla, and Farrah has tried to save Cormygle, the trader that he is. These humans show courage, and they face death to save dragons. I will help them," says Pryenthious as he darts down from the sky to help.

"Damn him," says Gairdennow as he flies down to help as well.

Vegenrage has cast force spells from both hands into the wall on the side of the abyss, forcing himself up in the air, fighting against the pull of the arm and hand holding him. Pryenthious and Gairdennow are flying down at Vegenrage, and they see another arm with rubbery deep-red skin and enormous black claws reach up and grab Vegenrage from below, and it pulls him into the abyss. Pryenthious and Gairdennow are too late. Vegenrage has been pulled down out of sight. The timespell that Vemenomous has cast is extending outward from where his hands made impact on the ground, and Farrah, Pryenthious, and Gairdennow are sent flying back in slow motion, being caught in the spell. Gwithen and Blethstole have helped Mezzmaglinggla heal, and they watch as Farrah, Pryenthious, and Gairdennow fly out and away from the demon space.

"Gwithen, can we counteract that timespell? Can we prevent them from losing any more time?" asks Blethstole.

"Yes, Dribrillianth can breathe his diamond shards, severing the magical bond between Vemenomous and those caught in the timespell. This will release them," says Gwithen.

"I heard you, Mother," says Dribrillianth, who flies down to the ground outside of the demon space and breathes his diamond shard breath, which severs the spell, releasing Farrah, Pryenthious, and Gairdennow from the timespell.

"Vegenrage," yells Farrah as she flies toward the abyss. A flash of red light explodes up from the circular abyss around the small patch of land that Vemenomous is standing on. There is great heat that follows the flash of light, and everyone is forced back thirty feet from the abyss. The land around the abyss starts to shake and sink into the hole, which fills up until there is solid ground; however, the ground is red sand.

In the middle of it is Vemenomous, who stands on all fours and roars out into the sky like he is in pain. He lowers his head and sways it back and forth, and his back splits. He looks up, roaring again with tears falling from his eyes. His flesh splits down the outsides of his arms and from his back down to both legs. His red wings fall off, one to the left of him and one to the right. He pounds the ground with his fists, screaming in agony, as the first true demonian dragon is starting to emerge. He is growing larger, and the rubbery red flesh is slipping off his body as he grows. His new body is covered with true scales of a brassy brown color.

Vemenomous is still on all fours, and as the flesh from his back falls off, his new wings are exposed, and they extend out to their full width. They are enormous, extending fifteen feet to each side of his body, giving him a thirty-foot wing span. Looking at his wings from above when they are extended, one can see that the front edge of his wings are silver with a shiny silver tusk every five feet, extending out six feet at the first hinge in his wing, four feet at the second, and three feet on the third. There are silver arches from each hinge in his wings that arch in silver color to the bottom, and the rest of his wings have the brassy brown scales. None of the dragons watching this transformation have any idea what his scales are made out of.

He shakes his hind legs, and the flesh around them splits and falls off, exposing his thicker and more muscular new legs, which are designed more for a four-footed dragon than a bipedal one. His hind hips are just solid muscle, and his tail whips back and forth, shunning all the dead flesh from the previous tail. His tail is now long and thin with a V-shaped solid weapon at the end. As the dragons watch, they notice Vemenomous can flick his tail, and a double V forms, creating a four-sided bladed tail like a broad head arrow, which is very dangerous; it is a lethal stabbing or slicing weapon, and it comes and goes at will. So Vemenomous has a double-sided, broad-headed tail or a four-sided broad-headed one. Either way, it is absolutely lethal in its sharpness for stabbing or slicing.

Vemenomous looks up with steam coming out of his nostrils and pounds the ground with his front paws, and all the flesh falls off his body except for that on his head. From his shoulders to his tail, he is no doubt dragon, very solid, very strong, and only maybe about eight hundred pounds heavier than Blethstole, but this is a very big deal. Vemenomous starts to shake his head back and forth violently, and he scrapes at his head with his very long and sharp claws from his front paws. He starts thrashing and digging and cutting into his head with his claws, and this is the bloodiest part of his transformation. He digs his claws from both paws into his neck and thrusts them forward, slicing deep wounds into his head, and he is bleeding badly. He shakes his head, and then loud cracks are heard as it starts to crack and fall off. His head is growing from within. Very high pointy ears rise, and his head starts to emerge from what seems to be his neck. His jaws push forward with a very rounded top. At the very back of his jaw are massive, oversized muscles growing up over his head. He has stereoscopic eyes with that same big glassy brown stare, but the muscle growth around his head is obviously so powerful that he can bite through any living tissue, bone, and flesh. To be caught with his bite is to be killed for sure.

Vemenomous is now the first true demonian dragon, and he struts looking at the dragons watching him from outside the red sand. He stares at them and pounds the ground with his massive paws. "Give her to me. Farrah is to be my queen. You cannot stop this. Any dragon who helps me shall be my servant, and I will not feast upon you. Those of you against me will be my dinner. Now bring Farrah to me," says Vemenomous. The dominant dragons and Farrah are all watching, and all of them cannot help the instinctual fear that Vemenomous has just imposed on them.

"Come on, let's get out of here now," says Gwithen, and the dragons waste no time, fleeing.

"Where is Vegenrage? What has happened to him?" asks Farrah, who stays behind.

"You need not worry, my queen. His worries are over, and now it is time for you to feed on his flesh as it always was meant to be," says Vemenomous.

"You lie. Vegenrage will come back to me. He will come back, and he will kill you," says Farrah as she flies through a dimension door, and Vemenomous is left alone in the red sand, but now he is the first true demonian dragon.

There is still a standoff in Ugoria. Basters, along with Cloakenstrike and Fraborn, stands in the center of the front courtyard with a little over one hundred Helven surrounding them. The Helven are surrounded by Basters's army, which includes horse riders, bow elves, swords elves, and a few very young magic users. Basters and Dona'try are jousting verbally, trying to gauge each other's strength, but it will appear that the Ugorian elves are very much in control here. Basters is still cautious, and he is kind of enjoying this battle of words, where he feels fairly comfortable in his position as king, knowing all the elves will attack if anything is to happen to him. Even though he, Cloakenstrike, and Fraborn are surrounded by all of the Helven, the Helven are surrounded by Basters's army.

The verbal jockeying continues, and the ground starts to shake violently. Everyone backs away from the center of the courtyard. A podium made out of tanwood with golden sides and a slanted golden top rises from the ground. The podium grows to its full height of four and a half feet, and there is a book sitting on top of it. Basters slowly approaches the podium. "Wait," says Dona'try.

"You stay where you are. If any of the Helven move, strike them down," says Basters to his bow elves, and they take aim on the Helven as Basters approaches the podium. He walks up to the podium and looks at the book, which is written in Shasparian. He can't help the smile that takes over his face as he looks at the beautiful golden-covered book with dark green jade inlaying the binding and cover. The book is very beautiful and obviously valuable.

"The cover reads *The King of Ugoria*," says Basters who holds up the book and shows it to everyone. "Fraborn, have the Helven taken to our prison. We will try them for unlawful entry into the Ugorian kingdom and palace." Basters walks toward Cloakenstrike with the book, and the podium that it has been on descends back into the earth and disappears. There are shouts and complaints by Dona'try, but the Helven are taken to the prison, led by the Ugorian army, and they put up no resistance for now. All of the Helven are searched, and no magical items or weapons at all are found on any of them. The prison is not in or near the palace; it is actually in Riobe to the far northeast of the Ugorian kingdom. The Ugorian army leaves many bow elves to stand watch and guard the prisoners. Basters heads to his throne room, and he is accompanied by Cloakenstrike.

Ulegwahn is in his throne room, and he has just dismissed Oriapow a short while ago after telling him Vegenrage is no longer an ally to the Erkensharie elves. Oriapow has gone to the Mystical Erkens to calm himself down. He has mentioned what Ulegwahn has said about Vegenrage to no one, and he is contemplating how to handle this situation.

Ulegwahn is sitting on his throne when he feels a great surge coming from the Octagemerwell. He knows instinctively that he should go to the Mystical Erkens, and he does. He arrives at the Mystical Erkens to find Oriapow, along with the magical order, and they are standing around a flat piece of earth where the Secret Erken grows. This is the tree that Oriapow has shown Logantrance a while back, which contains the book *The Rising of Vemenomous*.

"I see all of the magical order has felt the surge of the Octagemerwell. It is telling us all what it has been telling me all along. I believe it will tell me to find my queen. I believe it will be Farrah," says Ulegwahn to all the magical order in the Mystical Erkens.

"We will all find out very shortly. The Secret Erken is going to show itself, and none of us have summoned it. The Octagemerwell is telling us to prepare for its growth. The big question is who or what is summoning it. My first inclination was that you were summoning the Secret Erken, but we are going to find out because here it comes," says Oriapow as the Secret Erken begins to grow. The tree opens, exposing *The Rising of Vemenomous*. This book rests in the trunk of the tree, about five feet up, and the tree opens like there is a door in it. The book sits there, and right in front of the Secret Erken, a podium rises from the earth. This podium is golden on the corners and side edges with dark green jade filling its panels. The top is solid dark green jade, and it is beautiful. Sitting on the podium is a book in solid gold with dark green jade inlaying the cover and binding. It is a beautiful book.

Ulegwahn approaches the podium. He picks the book and reads the cover out loud. "*The Rising of Vemenomous: The Demonian Dragon.* Oriapow, will you accompany me to my throne room? There, we will read the book. I believe the Octagemerwell has been telling me this book has been coming, and it must be important. It will tell us how to defend and defeat the demons. I will wager that it also tells of the uniting of the king with his mate, and together, we shall lead Erkensharie to victory," says Ulegwahn.

"Yes, my king, I will accompany you to the Great Erken," says Oriapow.

CHAPTER 19

Creation of the Snow Gold Trinket

Hornspire has been alive for seven hundred years now, and the first dragon feast was five hundred years ago. The dragon feast was purposefully designed by the dragons who have come to realize that the races of man multiplied so fast that their numbers must be kept to a minimum. The dragons actually targeted the Altrarian people first, not because they were the strongest magically but because the human race of man multiplied the fastest. They also targeted the Hiltorian people. The elves and dwarves did suffer some losses in the first dragon feast, but the Altrarian people were decimated and, by now, have gone from the planet of Fargloin forever. The Hiltorian people survived the first dragon feast, but the loss of their forest was slowly making life impossible for them. The Erkensharie elves lent them very little help and no sanctuary.

By the end of the second dragon feast, the Hiltorian people have vanished as a population as well. Persen was remembered in the Erkensharie as the first, the only, and the greatest human magic user ever to have lived in Hiltor. Persen, of course, was the creator of the staff of barrier breath. As the dragons feared, the races of man became very powerful magically; and by the end of the second dragon feast, the races of man were hunting dragons. The dragons did accomplish their goal of reducing the numbers of the races of man, and Hornspire, with his prophecies of the human leading the races of man to eliminate the dragons, had a little to do with the dragons targeting the human race first. The dragons were trying to belittle and criticize Hornspire on his talk about a human magically stronger than the dragons, but this subconsciously led them to target humans more harshly.

Hornspire has written books, and they are floating around, so the dragons at this time are aware of the coming of Vlianth. Whether they believe it or not is sometimes a topic of discussion among dragons who meet in the wild. Hornspire is having all kinds of visions about different things, and he sees many scenarios playing out in his mind. The thing about his visions is that they always revolve around the races of man, and events play out according to what the elves, the dwarves, the humans, or the humanors do. He sees the dragons, but they are always responding to events brought on by the races of man. This may have a lot to do with why all the dragons roll their eyes at Hornspire and blow him off all the time because he is always telling dragons what they will be doing because of what the races of man will do. The dragons feel like the races of man, according to Hornspire, are more like the dominant species and more important than them, and this makes the dragons pay very little attention to Hornspire.

Hornspire is not stupid, and he sees the way the dragons ignore him, so he has manipulated his writings a little and started putting his books out, knowing they will end up in certain places and be read by specific individuals. He feels it is time to make sure some of the races of man get some of his books because he is starting to resent the way the dragons are ignoring his writings, and he begins to set up all the races and species to act according to his desires. He is trying to manipulate the future to set himself up for greatness. Hornspire decides, since all his visions revolve around the races of man, it is time to start feeding information to them and use this as an advantage for himself in the future.

Hornspire has visions of all the races of man. He knows the Hiltorians will fade away and be gone just like the Altrarians. He also sees the Erkensharie elves and the Ugorian elves, but what really intrigues Hornspire is how he sees events that have nothing to do with him or dragons. The effects of what the races of man do affect the future of the dragons, and Hornspire is more aware of this than any other dragon. He has been having visions of Queen Sharome of Ugoria, and he can see that the queen is going to ask the magical order to have a special magical item made for the king to protect him and all future kings of Ugoria. Of course, the magical power for the magical item will be the life force of a beautiful virgin elf, and that is going to be Shenlylith. Hornspire does not know why he has these visions, but he takes it as a sign that he must act upon them. The Ugorian magical order is very strong at this time and very well versed in all kinds of magic, but the request of the queen, which has not happened yet, is still a little advanced for the Ugorian magic users. Hornspire can help, so he decides to contact the leader of the Ugorian magical order, and that is Arglon.

Hornspire has many visions, which come to him in his sleep. They are like dreams for us where we remember just a little portion and only sometimes, whereas Hornspire has many visions every night, and he remembers them all. The really neat thing is that with his visions come scenarios that depend on what Hornspire and others do. He decides to help Arglon with a magical item, and this situation will stand out all of his life because he is helping someone else in the event Hornspire himself should not survive a future instance where he sees his own death. Hornspire makes up his mind on how he is going to make contact with Arglon and what he is going to give him.

Arglon has spent five generations working with the Great Red Falcons and creating a special bond with them. These are gigantic birds of prey that live to the far north of the Ugorian Highlands. These birds grow to stand nine feet tall but still weigh no more than three hundred pounds. Their bones are hollow, yet their bodies are sturdy and very strong. They are beautiful birds with dark red feathers that have streaks of black, and much like the Terrahawks of the Erkensharie on the planet Fargloin, the Great Red Falcons are the largest bird of prey in Strabalster, not including dragons, of course. After the first dragon feast, Arglon has gotten the idea that he had better have a steed if ever he needed to do battle in the air with dragons, and there is no better aerial steed than the Great Red Falcons. They live about one hundred years, and right after the first dragon feast, Arglon has started to work on magic that has enabled him to communicate with animals. He has communicated with and befriended a Great Red Falcon, which has led to Arglon communicating with this bird's mate. Their first hatchling is the first Great Red Falcon steed for Arglon, and only he has ever had this privilege with any Great Red Falcon. Arglon has had only one Great Red Falcon steed per generation and is now working with his fifth, and he has named this bird Eronar. This is the first time Arglon is going to be riding Eronar.

Arglon exits his dimension door far north in the Ugorian Highlands, about fifty miles south of the Ackelson Desert. The terrain here is full of very large valleys where the earth sinks and the dirt is rich and black. Thick grasses grow, and the trees are tall and straight up. There are no branches until high up in the trees, and these trees are much like those that grow in Crantour on the planet Fargloin, but these here are able to deal with much less rainfall. These are the Elgornan trees, and their tops sprout out with a lot of thick branches with fat absorbent, spongy leaves.

The Great Red Falcons nest exactly like the Terrahawks do in the Erkensharie. They only make one nest per tree by weaving vines and shrubs in the thick branches on the top. These trees grow about eighty feet when fully grown, but they grow mostly along the top of high valley walls, which are numerous in the Ugorian Highlands. To sit atop one of these nests is breathtaking because the valleys may be half a mile deep and many hundreds of yards wide. The view from up here is astounding. The Great Red Falcons have by far the best vision of any creature in all the Maglical System. They can spot a thimble rabbit running on the ground a mile away. Thimble rabbits are much too small for the Great Red Falcons to go after; however, they do make a nice little snack if the falcons are very hungry. The Great Red Falcons go for much bigger prey. There is a lot of large herbivore prey here in the Ugorian Highlands. Even the Landgangers fall victim to the Great Red Falcons, which swoop from high in the sky, and most animals do not even know they are being targeted by these birds of prey until it is too late.

Arglon walks to the tree where Eronar has spent his four-year growth from hatchling to young adult. The Great Red Falcon pairs lay two to three eggs a year after their hatchling or hatchlings leave the nest to start their own life in a new one. Those eggs may hatch healthy young birds, but as they grow, only one will survive. This is the way to ensure that only the strongest Great Red Falcons will remain and be healthy. One sibling will eventually eat its one or two siblings, and this usually is determined by which one hatches first. The mother falcon lays one to three eggs, and this does not happen at once but over one to three weeks. Nine out of ten times, the first hatched will kill its siblings, and then the mother bird will dismember the slain for consumption. This is another way of making good nourishment for the young hatchling.

Arglon finds the tree where Moorglus, his previous steed, has mated. Their young hatchling has already been named, held, and touched by Arglon, who can communicate with the Great Red Falcons by making high-pitched whistles and by telepathy. The benefit is not only to Arglon, who gets to ride these magnificent birds as they fly, but also to each of his steeds because he has imbued them with magic. They do not know a lot, but they have been able to communicate and teach magic to those in the family of Great Red Falcon, which is now five centuries old and has been able to learn and grow stronger in the use of magic over time. Eronar's parents have already taught him magic, and today is the first day he flies with an elf on his back.

Arglon uses a real neat form of levitation magic, which he has mastered over the centuries. He runs straight up the tree with just his toes hitting it. It is not like he is perpendicular to the tree; he is still upright but just a little slanted outward as he runs up. When he gets to the top where the branches sprout out, he makes a few whistles, announcing his arrival, and then he uses his flying magic to float up to the nest, which is about two yards in diameter.

Arglon lands on the side of the nest, and the two adult birds acknowledge him. Then Eronar steps forward to the side of the nest and spreads his wings. How beautiful he is. The wind is already strong enough to rise him in the air, but he tilts his wings into the wind and lifts on the lower part of his wings, which holds him steady in his position. Eronar leans his head forward, and Arglon looks over the beautiful red and black bird, which is not full grown yet but still easily strong enough to fly with Arglon on its back. Arglon grabs some feathers with his left hand and hops up on Eronar's back just above his wings. Eronar's feathers are very soft and large enough to make great handles for Arglon to hold on to.

As soon as Arglon gets on Eronar's back, Eronar just gives a flap of his wings, and they rise into the air and away from the nest. Eronar just glides, tilting to the right, and then he dives down into the valley, which sinks almost a half mile. Arglon has been through this many times, but every time is still a thrill. The wind is whipping past him as he holds on to Eronar's feathers, and he watches the land pass underneath them. Eronar dives incredibly fast and soars down the valley, evening out and gliding hundreds of feet above the valley floor. Interestingly, the valley floors do not have many trees in them. Most of the trees grow along the top ridges of the valleys in the Ugorian Highlands. Herds of herbivores are funneled into the valleys, and they walk on through the valleys that exit to plateaus and then onto another valley. Different grasses and vegetation grow in different valleys, so some have very specific wildlife that lives in them.

Arglon never gets tired of riding the Great Red Falcons and watching the wildlife and land below as they soar overhead. Sometimes the bird he is riding cannot resist a prey animal it sees and has swooped down and snatched a meal right off the ground. This is an amazing experience, and Arglon is the only magic user on all three worlds who has mastered the ability to actually ride on the back of a great bird of prey.

Today Arglon gets another once-in-a-lifetime experience, as his magical sense starts to tingle all over his body. He looks all around but cannot locate the source of magic, which he distinctly knows is dragon. Finally, Arglon hears his name being called from behind him and Eronar. "Arglon! Do not be afraid. I have not come to hurt you," says Hornspire, who has become visible behind the bird of prey. Arglon looks behind him to see the great Hornspire behind them, and the dragon flies very quickly up to their right side. Eronar instinctively maneuvers away from the dragon, but Hornspire is a very nimble and a fantastic flier as are all dragons.

"Arglon, I have come to make peaceful contact with you. I have very important information that will help you greatly in the days to come. It involves your queen, Sharome, and your king, Kwaytith. Your queen is going to ask something of you, and I have at least one answer to the dilemma you will face," says Hornspire. Arglon cannot help but be captivated by a dragon now flying beside him and Eronar and talking to him. He knows that, obviously, this is a dragon, and if he wanted to cause harm to Arglon or Eronar, it would have already been done.

"Please, my very knowledgeable elven magic user. Please land your bird of prey and talk with me. You may very well find what I have to say very enlightening," says Hornspire.

Arglon can communicate with the Great Red Falcons by whistles or telepathy, and this is the perfect time for the latter. He asks Eronar through telepathy to land and not be afraid of the dragon because he obviously means them no harm. Eronar makes a very fast descent and lands high on a ridge overlooking a great valley, and Hornspire sets down beside them. Arglon dismounts Eronar and walks toward the great dragon. "Why does a dragon approach and offer communication with me? What news could you have for me that is so important?" asks Arglon.

"I am Hornspire, the seer of the future, and I see a task asked of you by your queen that you cannot possibly accommodate. Your queen is going to ask you to create a magical item that will protect your king and all future kings of Ugoria from all danger to their lives. I do not believe you have the magical ability to make this happen, but I can help you," says Hornspire.

"Why would a dragon want to help the elves?" asks Arglon.

"I can see the future as I have said. I see many things, even my own death. I come to you because you play a very important role that becomes significant a long time into the future, long after our lives have passed. It is very important that the Ugorian elves survive as a race, and a big part of this survival is the safety of its king and kings-to-be. I present this to you." Hornspire produces a chain made out of solid snow-white gold. "Here, Argon. I present this chain to you. This chain will allow you, the leader of the Ugorian elven magical order, to imbue it with your personal magic, making it the snow gold trinket. With your magical elven endowment to this chain, it will become elven magic. And when this parchment"—Hornspire hands Arglon a piece of paper—"is read by a virgin elven female, her life essence will be consumed by the chain, and her image will grow as a trinket. This elven female shall live forever and power the snow gold trinket with her life force. She will protect all kings of Ugoria from the time her image takes form on the chain. This will become the most powerful magical item in Ugoria, and it will protect all of its kings. This magical item will continue to grow in magical strength and knowledge, learning and knowing all Ugorian elven magic that has yet to be discovered."

Arglon accepts the trinket, and his eyes widen, as its value and magical strength is instantly felt by him. The chain glistens and shimmers in the light. The snowy white of the gold is unique. Arglon does not know what to say. He admires the chain, and his magical instinct wants greatly to work with this magical item. "I still do not understand why a dragon is at all worried about the elves as a race. I mean the dragons have already mostly eliminated the Lycoreal humans from Strabalster. It is only common sense that the elves are next to be targeted by the dragons," says Arglon.

"The Lycoreal humans will be gone, and your princess, Somgla, will be the reason for their demise, not the dragons. The time of the dragons and the elves and the dwarves will come to an end. Not in our lifetime but it will come to an end, and in the end, it is not over for all of us. It is just different. We all become one. We all join to have a more unified relationship, if you will. For example, the dwarves, the elves, and the humans all mingle more and more until they are all one species. The dragons and the great birds of prey like the Terrahawks, the Great Red Falcons, the Wall Gliders, and the Mountain Flats will all mingle more and more until we are all one. This happens as a natural way of the universe but again not in our lifetime. Most importantly, and you don't have to believe me, but I tell you, this magical necklace is needed by you. And if you do not use it well, then your king is just less protected, and that is all I have to say about that. The elven female to power the snow gold trinket will live forever in her prison until the day comes of her release, and when that day comes, she no longer will be elven. She will become human. This is a result of all the magic in the snow gold trinket being used to release her from its hold and save another human. This is also necessary because this elven virgin, who now becomes a human female, will take her place as queen of Ugoria, which will be led by a human king at this time. I do not ask you to believe me. I do not ask you to understand. I only ask that you trust me when I say I have seen the future, and this is how Ugoria will survive it. The necklace is yours, so study it, work with it, and imbue it with Ugorian elven magic. This is my gift to you, Arglon, accept it or not. The choice is yours," says Hornspire, and he does not let Arglon get in another word as he leaps off the valley cliff and soars into the sky right into a dimension door, and he is gone.

Arglon cannot take his eyes off the chain. It is exquisite, and he rolls his hands side to side, looking at the beautiful necklace. It is snowy white, yet it still sparkles like it has tiny little diamonds all throughout. He can feel its magical essence, which is very strong, and he mounts Eronar, and they leap into the air and soar through the valley. Arglon rides Eronar back to his nest, and Arglon leaves after a short telepathic communication with his steed. Both parent birds are away from the nest. What a fantastic first ride on Eronar. First time in the air together, and they are flying side by side and later talking with a dragon. They decide to keep this encounter to themselves because no one will believe them. Arglon is so excited about the necklace that he wants to get back to his study and examine this magical item. Arglon says goodbye to Eronar and walks through a dimension door, and he arrives back in the Ugorian magical library.

The Ugorian magical order has a massive library under the main palace. There are three levels under the Ugorian Palace, and the northern half of all three levels is devoted to the Ugorian magical order. Kerben is here, and he has been very secretive as of late. Arglon knows he has been studying demonology. Arglon and Kerben have always been very competitive with each other and great friends, but now they are starting to argue a lot because Arglon does not want Kerben to study dark magic, which he does more and more. Right now, Arglon is much more curious about his new magical item, and he goes to a secluded part of this magnificent library with thousands of books all on magic. There are rows and rows of bookshelves six feet tall, full of books. There are many places for quiet study here, and Arglon finds a booth for himself, and he is already thinking about imbuing the necklace with elven magic, making it an elven magical item.

His solitude does not last long, as Reinlith and Limsil enter the library, and being young and full of energy, they are never very quiet. Reinlith heads for Kerben, and Limsil heads for Arglon. "Wow! What is that you have? It is beautiful," says Limsil, who approaches Arglon, sitting at a booth.

Arglon puts the necklace in his pocket, saying, "You never mind what I have. How have your studies been coming along on force projection? Have you and Reinlith been practicing?"

"Yes, we have been practicing, and I am better than Reinlith," says Limsil.

"Of course, you are," says Arglon, whose attention is stolen by Queen Sharome, who is being escorted into the magical order library by Rollbolis. Kerben, Reinlith, Arglon, and Limsil all approach the queen and bow with smiles on their faces upon seeing the beautiful queen in the library.

"My queen, such a pleasant surprise to see you here in the library," says Arglon.

"Thank you, Arglon. I thought it was time I came to visit you. After all, you three are Ugoria's greatest magic users so far. Limsil, Reinlith, you are Ugoria's up-and-coming greatest magic users," Queen Sharome says with a smile. "Limsil and Reinlith, would you please excuse us for a while?"

The two know she is not asking. They bow and say, "Yes, my queen," in unison, and they walk away.

"Come sit with me," says Queen Sharome. The three follow Queen Sharome over to a table, and they sit around the table with her. "Let me get right to the point and tell you why I have come to speak with you. You are the leading magic users in Ugoria, and I come to ask you to use your extensive magical knowledge to create a magical item that will protect the king of Ugoria and all its future kings. I ask this of you because I have seen the dragons systematically killing the human population on Strabalster, and we need to prevent this from happening to the elves of Ugoria. The dragons are a threat to our kingdom, and our king and I have heard threats made against my husband. As you all know, I can bear no more children, and I am very ashamed of this. This means King Kwaytith will have no son. There will be no heir to the throne, and already, I am hearing talk and rumors that the king will be torn from kingship by force. It is all my fault. I cannot give the king an heir to the throne." Queen Sharome lowers her head in her hands, weeping.

"It is OK, my queen. Everything is going to be fine," says Rollbolis.

"There is one more thing. I need for the magical item that you will create to be powered by the life force of a virgin Ugorian elf. This way, the magical item will last forever, powered by the untainted life force of a pure elven female virgin, and it will protect all the future kings of Ugoria," says Queen Sharome. Arglon cannot believe his ears. He cannot believe what he is hearing; it is almost word for word as Hornspire has explained it to him earlier in the day.

"Can you do it? Do you think you three can make a magical item that can protect the king of Ugoria from harm, as well as all future kings of Ugoria? The magical item will be powered by the life force of a virgin Ugorian elf. Do you think you can do it?" asks Queen Sharome.

"Yes, we can do it," says Arglon.

"We can?" says Rollbolis, looking at Arglon with curious eyes.

"Yes, we can," adds Kerben.

"Oh good. How long do you think it will take you to make the magical item?" asks the queen.

"Two weeks," says Arglon.

"Two weeks tops, probably sooner," says Kerben.

"You two must know something I don't know," says Rollbolis.

"We know a lot that you don't know, Rollbolis," says Kerben, smiling and laughing.

"Oh, thank you. I can't tell you how much this means to me. I feel safer already. I will come back in two weeks to see how you are doing," says Queen Sharome as she gets up, and Rollbolis stands with her.

"Here, let me escort you back to the palace, my queen," says Rollbolis, and the two of them head back up toward the palace.

"What a kiss-ass," says Kerben.

"Yeah. Kerben, I cannot believe this. You won't believe this," says Arglon.

"What? I won't believe what?" asks Kerben.

"I flew on the back of Eronar for the first time today, and while we were flying, a dragon flew up beside us and asked to communicate with me," says Arglon.

"Yeah, right," says Kerben.

"Hornspire was the dragon, and he told me he could see the future. He told me the queen would ask us to make a magical item specifically to protect the king of Ugoria and all its future kings. Listening to Queen Sharome just now was almost like listening to Hornspire earlier today, almost word for word," says Arglon.

"Yeah, right. Come on, quit putting me on," says Kerben.

"Kerben, look at this." Arglon hands the necklace to Kerben. "Hornspire gave this to me and said this is the magical item we will need to satisfy the queen's wishes. We can imbue this with elven magic, and it will become a Ugorian elven magical item that will protect the kings of Ugoria. Hornspire even gave me this parchment to be read by a virgin Ugorian elf, who will be consumed by the necklace, and her form will grow on it, creating the snow gold trinket. This trinket will protect all future kings of Ugoria until she escapes from the trinket to become the queen of Ugoria. How crazy is this?" says Arglon.

Kerben, just like Arglon, cannot take his eyes off the magical and beautiful snowy white gold necklace, which sparkles like it has small diamonds in it. "And you thought it was a bad idea that I'm studying demonology," says Kerben.

"What? What did you say, Kerben? What does demonology have to do with this?" asks Arglon.

"What does this necklace make you think of the minute you look at it? I mean, what kind of magic do you think of when you look at the beautiful snowy white of this necklace?" asks Kerben.

"Well, when you ask like that, I guess I would think of angel blessing magic. It does make me think of that now," says Arglon.

"Yes, and where does angel blessing have no effect? Where can angel blessing not be cast?" asks Kerben. Arglon shrugs with a blank look on his face, not knowing the answer to Kerben's question. "Angel blessing cannot be cast under the ground. Angel blessing cannot be cast anywhere that light cannot penetrate. However, since I have been studying demonology, we can imbue this magical item. We can make this magical item the only one of its kind in existence that can cast angel blessing underground or in darkness."

"OK, Kerben, I like it. I like your idea. Let us get to work and create a magical item that will protect our king and all future kings of Ugoria. Let us make the most powerful elven magical item ever known. Let us make the snow gold trinket," says Arglon.

"Yes," says Kerben, and the two of them spend the next two weeks creating the snow gold trinket.

CHAPTER 20

The Dawn of Roartill

Back to the present on Strabalster, Vegenrage is being pulled into the depths of Strabalster by the hands of Roartill. The left hand is wrapped around his waist with a very tight grip, causing Vegenrage a lot of discomfort. The right hand has its fingers over Vegenrage's shoulders, with the palm of the hand against his chest, two fingers to his right shoulder and back, and another two fingers to his left shoulder and back. Both thumbs of Roartill's hands are wrapped around Vegenrage's waist and back, so Roartill has a tight grip on Vegenrage, who cannot break free. Vegenrage struggles, but all he can do is watch the earth break and spread apart as he is pulled deeper into the crust of the world. Vegenrage can hear laughter, and a voice echoes. "I have you now. I shall consume you and all the magical draw of the outer realms. The richest magical being shall be mine. No hell, no heaven will stand up to the magical energy I shall inherit. I will have it all. I will own all everywhere." Roartill laughs.

Very abruptly, Vegenrage is stopped. The rock below him ceases spreading, and he stops on solid rock. The arms of Roartill seem to have been severed just above the elbows, and they vanish. Vegenrage can hear the roars of Roartill and then his yelling. "Ahh! What has done this? What power is this?"

The rock around Vegenrage starts to widen, forming a very wide cavern inside of the world of Strabalster. The rock walls start to emanate white streaks of lightning running all around the walls like they have been electrified. The white lightning runs all around the walls and floor and into Vegenrage, and he knows this magic. This is angel blessing, and Vegenrage also knows that angel blessing cannot be cast where there is no sunlight. The lightning runs from the floor into the feet of Vegenrage; it starts to grow from the walls. Vegenrage extends his arms, and the lightning grows to him, entering his arms and then the rest of his body. "I know you are here. I can feel you," says Vegenrage out loud. He closes his eyes, and all the lightning from the walls are drawn to him, flowing into his body until all the lightning now runs through and around him.

His eyes are still closed, and he talks out loud. "I can feel you. You are the snow elf Shenlylith. You have expired. All your magic is now in me. You have given all to save me from the hands of Roartill, but you shall not die. You shall be reborn but not elven. You will be human, never to know the sensation of magic running through your veins ever again. Your elven form has been stolen from you to power the snow gold trinket, which has lost its power. You protected the kings of Ugoria for thousands of years, and now you shall be reborn human to live your life and lead as queen of Ugoria. This has always been your destiny—to unite, to merge, and to lead the elves to their destiny of humanity."

Vegenrage extends his arms to his sides and points fingers in front of him, and the lightning shoots from his digits a few feet in front of him, outlining the form of Shenlylith with her wings, huge and beautiful. She is pure white, and she materializes in front of Vegenrage. The lightning shoots between them, and she opens her eyes with tears falling as her wings start to fade away. Her ears start to round at the tops, as well as her nose. She appears and slowly forms, becoming solid right in front of Vegenrage. This process takes a few minutes, and her body appears in her original elven form, slowly shifting and changing into a human form of perfect beauty. She is nude, and Vegenrage has flashbacks of seeing Alluradaloni for the first time. Shenlylith covers herself with her arms and hands.

"Here, I have something for you," says Vegenrage. He reaches into Behaggen and pulls clothing, which he hands to Shenlylith. "This is clothing that I took from the lair of Alisluxkana. I did not know at the time why I would need this. I just knew I would. This is clothing from Bellfona, a white witch seduced and killed by Alisluxkana. Bellfona studied angel blessing, and this clothing was meant for you. It is imbued with angel blessing, and no demon and no evil magic can hurt you while you wear this."

Shenlylith puts the clothing on and runs her hands along the long sleeves of the shirt, which has a beautiful white color, just like that of her wings of old. She runs her hands along her thighs, feeling the comfortably fitting soft pants that now adorn her. She looks to Vegenrage. "I have not felt the sensation of clothing or anything against my skin for so long.

I knew the day would come, the day when I would return to the living. Thank you, Vegenrage," says Shenlylith.

"I should be the one thanking you. You saved me from a very bad situation," says Vegenrage.

"Your situation is not over, Vegenrage. You have been saved for now, but you and your little friend will never escape my grasp. Your magic will only hold for so long, and when it is gone, I will be here waiting for you, and you will still be mine with a bonus. That pretty little girl will be ravished in the inner realm. She will be raped repeatedly, she will be mutilated, and just when she thinks she can take no more, I will restore her beauty just so I can watch her torment start all over. That is the only future for her. As far as your future, Vegenrage, oh, I cannot wait to drain you. I cannot wait to suck the life out of your every pore. I cannot wait to watch your body cave as all the energy within you is drawn to my superiority. I will absorb all the knowledge in your head, and with this, I will be led to new worlds where I can expand my reign and enslave whole new races of humans," says Roartill in a loud and commanding voice.

Vegenrage and Shenlylith can hear huge crashing on the outside of the cavern they are in, like Roartill is pounding on the shell of their sanctuary with his fists. "Vegenrage, what are we going to do? I have no magic. It is gone. I have no way of fighting against that evil. I cannot get us out of here," says Shenlylith.

"Don't worry, he or it cannot get in here. Thanks to you, I can now cast angel blessing where there is no sunlight. With this, he can never touch us, and he knows this. He is just trying to scare us. Do not be scared because there is nothing he can do except try to scare us with words," says Vegenrage.

"Maybe he can never touch you, but he can get me. I have no magic. I have no angel blessing to protect me," says Shenlylith.

"Yes, you do. The clothing you are wearing is blessed. There is no evil that can touch you. Just calm down. We are getting out of here," says Vegenrage.

Roartill starts to hammer on the magical field protecting Shenlylith and Vegenrage with enough force to shake it but not crush or crack it. Shenlylith falls forward, and Vegenrage catches her. They both fall to the ground from the shaking that gets worse and worse. "OK, enough of this. It is time to get out of here. Put your arms around my neck and hold on tight," says Vegenrage.

"What are you going to do?" asks Shenlylith.

"Hang on because I am going to fly us out of here. Here we go," says Vegenrage after Shenlylith puts her arms around his neck and gets a good hold on him. Vegenrage points his arms up, and they fly upward. He casts a magical force acting like a drill, opening the earth as they fly out of the crust of Strabalster. This is a form of angel blessing creating white lightning that spins at incredible speed, cutting and melting the demon-blessed rock above them. To the surprise of Vegenrage, they have not gotten out of the frying pan yet. They have exited the crust of the world, only to be trapped in a dome protected by demonic magic. The dome is very large, like that covering a football field. The ground around them inside of the dome is the red sand of Maglical Hell.

"Now what? What are we going to do now, Vegenrage?" asks Shenlylith, who is still hanging on to his back as they hover near the center of the dome.

"Well, this is a tricky situation. I cannot cast magic in here, or it will be manipulated. I cannot use angel blessing to get us out of the dome because the demonic magic in here will nullify it. The dome will block all my telepathy, so we cannot call for help. Just hang on to me and stay calm," says Vegenrage.

Laughter is heard. "So you thought you would just fly away from my grasp, did you? Well, I do not think so," says Roartill. The red sand starts to rise as the huge head of Roartill rises from it. His head is wide and round with catlike ears at the top. He has very large round black eyes with flaming yellow pupils. His teeth are like that of piranha, which fit perfectly together and cut like scissors. His shoulders, arms, and chest are humanoid as are his hips and legs, but his feet are hooves with a very wide girth. He has a very long tail with a sharp dagger at the end, and he stands fifteen feet tall. He is solid red, the color of running blood. "Rise, my children, rise."

The red sand all around the inside of the dome starts to roll and shake like something is rising from underneath it. Demons start to rise from everywhere in the sand. They are all the same, and they are hideous. There are actually two types of demons here, and Vegenrage knows instinctively that these are the minions of hell whom Roartill is going to unleash on the worlds of the Maglical System.

There are bipedal demons and four-legged demons. The bipedal demons are known as hellmen. They are very tall and slender, about seven feet, and they are mostly skin and bones. They have defined muscles, but they are very thin. They look very hideous with long thinning hair that runs down their backs. They all carry lava clubs. It is still very hot and only holds its form because of demon magic cast by Roartill. These clubs cause great damage because they are very hot and cause significant burning on contact, plus they inflict bone-crushing blows if bludgeoned by them. These are not those under the rule of Zevoncour and are not demons in the true sense; they are souls that Roartill has commanded and given this uniform form. In this way, Roartill can create vast armies that he intends to sweep the worlds of the Maglical System with.

The four-legged demons are known as helldogs. They are a lesser form of hell hound. They have lethal claws on their feet and very sharp teeth. You do not want to be attacked by these beasts of hell. They have a continual flame throughout their bodies as do the hellmen and cause burning damage. They also inflict great damage if they claw or bite. The bodies of these creatures are much sturdier and more muscular than their bipedal companions, and they stand six feet tall. Many of them are ridden by the bipedal demons, making this a very dangerous army. All of these demons have a smooth bloodred skin with black eyes and flaming yellow pupils. These demons are not smart or quick, but they are loyal to Roartill or those who may command them, and they charge fearlessly, ready to fight any living being in their path.

Vegenrage can feel Shenlylith starting to shake and tremble as the horde of demons rise from the red sand. "I liked being the snow elf. I miss my magic already. I feel so powerless now," she says.

"Just keep a good hold on me. They cannot harm us. They cannot reach us up here, but I had better think of something quick because we cannot just hang around here," says Vegenrage.

"That is right, Vegenrage. Your time is coming. You cannot escape my prison here, and it is only a matter of time before you slip and your magic fails, and my demons will have you both. Here, let me be the first to show you my newest champion and the strongest dragon ever to enter the Maglical System. Here, Vegenrage, is Vemenomous, the first demonian dragon, and it will be Farrah who will be his queen. She has the DNA of you and Vemenomous in her veins, and she has been struck by the shard hammer. It is only a matter of time before she comes to us, and there is nothing you can do about it. She will be the first demonian dragon queen," says Roartill, laughing. Vemenomous rises from the red sand beside Roartill as he speaks. Vegenrage has floated far away from Roartill on the other side of the dome, but Roartill is massive in size and easily seen and heard. Vegenrage can see the new form of Vemenomous, and he can instantly feel the new presence of this intimidating dragon standing on all fours quietly next to Roartill.

"Charge them, my demons. Charge them and attack them," commands Roartill. Vegenrage and Shenlylith are in the air and out of the reach of the demons, but they charge. Roartill has imbued all the bipedal demons with sandform. This is magic that allows the demons to grasp a handful of red sand that transforms into a long javelin, which the demons can throw as weapons. The demons charge, and those riding the helldogs reach down with their empty hand and grasp a handful of the red sand, which forms javelins. They throw them at Vegenrage and Shenlylith. The javelins are more of a distraction than any kind of dangerous attack because Vegenrage is shimmering white lightning, which is angel blessing magic, and it flows over Shenlylith as well. This magic creates a barrier around the two, which destroys any demonic weapon or magic that touches it.

"Can't you cast angel blessing on them and destroy them?" asks Shenlylith.

"I could anywhere but here. They are on the red sand, and this protects them like angel blessing protects us. If I try to cast any magic on them while they are on the red sand, Roartill will be able to manipulate and control my magic, using it against us. There has to be some way I can get us out of this dome though. There has to be some magic I can use on the dome. I just have not thought of it yet. Do you have any suggestions?" asks Vegenrage. Shenlylith shakes and flinches over and over as more and more demonic javelins hit the barrier around them and disintegrate. Before long, there are hundreds of demons on the ground below them.

"Hey, Vegenrage, I have something for you. Here, take this. This will crumble the dome once you throw it at it," says Behaggen, who opens up at the top, and a star shining a brilliant diamond light is produced. Vegenrage grabs hold of the beautiful star, which looks like a small ball with sharp protrusions extending out of it for a few inches, and it is just a little larger than Vegenrage's hand. The magical item is a silvery metal with brilliant diamond sparkles all over it.

"Oh wow! I forgot you had this, Behaggen," says Vegenrage.

"Well, there is no time to waste. Use it. Throw it at the dome," says Behaggen.

"Vegenrage, that is an angel star. I have only heard of them. They really exist. Use it. Throw it at the dome so it will crumble and be destroyed," says Shenlylith. Vegenrage throws the star, and it hurls toward the dome, sticking to the cooling lava that still has a faint glow of red. The star sticks in the dome, and nothing happens for a few moments, and then the star starts to crack; it splits down the middle, and both halves slap against the dome, with all the protrusions sticking into it.

A few moments go by, and Shenlylith asks Vegenrage, "Why is nothing happening? It is supposed to shatter, destroy, and crumble the dome. Why is nothing happening?"

"Just wait," says Vegenrage, who turns the two of them in the air to look at Roartill on the other side of the dome, and sure enough, Roartill is aware of the angel star. Vegenrage and Shenlylith have the white lighting of angel blessing flowing and dancing all around their bodies, protecting them from all the demons and demon magic. Roartill has the same kind of magic emanating around his body, only the lightning around him is red, the color of molten hell, and he is using his magic to strengthen the walls of the dome. The lightning around Roartill grows in thickness as his stature grows in height to almost as tall as the dome itself, and he extends his devil lightning into the walls of the dome. The lightning shoots from all over his humongous body into the walls, protecting it from the effects of the angel star.

"Wow! He does not want us to get out of here. I am at a loss. I cannot cast any magic on the demons or Roartill. I can cast magic on us, but again, I am at a loss. I cannot lower us to the ground, or all of my magic will be corrupt. Behaggen, what are we to do?" asks Vegenrage.

"Give the book to Shenlylith. Give her *The Shenlylith Truth*. She will know what to do," says Behaggen. Vegenrage reaches into Behaggen and pulls *The Shenlylith Truth*. He gives it to Shenlylith, and she starts to flip through its pages.

"What is this book? I have never seen this before. How does this have all the information about my life from so long ago?" asks Shenlylith.

"This book was written about you in the weeks prior to your being consumed by the snow gold trinket. Arglon was approached by none other than Hornspire himself over a thousand years ago, and it was Hornspire who gave the magical necklace to Arglon. Arglon imbued the necklace with elven magic and made the snow gold trinket. When you read the parchment and were consumed by the necklace, it was your form that completed and powered the newly formed snow gold trinket. Hornspire knew the future had many different ways of playing out, and if he was not to survive, he did not want the demons to rule the outer realms. Hornspire told Arglon to write a book about the elven female who was adored by all. Hornspire knew Arglon would write the book about you. Arglon was to write a book about everything he knew about you, and Hornspire gave Arglon a book with blank pages to write on. When he finished the book, it magically wrote and added pages on its own. These pages are for you yourself to read now," says Behaggen.

Shenlylith flips to the back of the book, saying, "Oh, this must be what I am supposed to read. There is bold lettering at the top of the page saying 'The Dawn of Roartill.'"

"Yes, yes, read that," says Behaggen.

"How do you know all this, Behaggen?" asks Shenlylith.

"I will explain later. Right now, we had better get out of here before Roartill thinks of some tricks of his own. He is now working on ways of getting hold of Vegenrage. There is nothing he wants more than Vegenrage, so come on, read the book," says Behaggen.

Vegenrage is facing the direction of Roartill, with the demons far below and throwing magical javelins, but they have no effect other than scaring Shenlylith. Vegenrage is slightly tilted so Shenlylith can rest comfortably on his back with her legs wrapped around his waist. She has her arms over his shoulders, and the book is to the left of his head. Shenlylith can easily read, even though there are many distractions.

"OK, here goes." Shenlylith starts to read. "The dawn of Roartill brings him to the surface of the world of Strabalster for the first time ever as ruler of Maglical Hell. This means that I, Hornspire, have been killed by Blethstole and that Vegenrage has been in the grasp of Roartill himself. Vemenomous has become the demonian dragon, and the demon swell has already begun on the world of Fargloin. Roartill's army of hellmen and helldogs are led by Zevoncour, but Roartill wants free rein on the outer realms, which he now has because he had Vegenrage in his grasp. He also wants a doorway to another universe, where there are more worlds for him to conquer and control. The key is Vegenrage. With Vegenrage's flesh, blood, and soul, Roartill can gain the dimensional knowledge to travel where Vegenrage is from. But more importantly, Roartill can gain the physical independence he needs to travel dimensionally throughout the universe. It is time for Vegenrage to know that the supreme being in the Maglical System, our father in heaven, lost in a war with Roartill, but our supreme being was able to contain Roartill in Maglical Hell. He did this by giving his eternal life to create a barrier around Maglical Hell that no evil would be able to escape, yet evil souls were drawn into it.

"There was a catch, and that was the inner realms. Here, evil souls would enter and not go to Maglical Hell unless they were to become demons and then killed. The only way they could be killed was by turning to demons, where they gained flesh-and-blood bodies that could be destroyed, and then they would go to Maglical Hell to forever serve Roartill. The almighty of the Maglical System brought Roartill to the center of the world of Strabalster, where he intended to destroy Roartill, but Roartill was to strong, so our Maglical father in heaven imprisoned Roartill here, using his life force to lock in all evil, never to escape unless one thing was to happen.

"That one thing is the supreme book of knowledge, the *Wogenkeld*, which when in the hands of the demon master king becomes the *Gowdelken*. When and if the name of Roartill is read from the book of knowledge by the demon master king, this will free Roartill. And now Vegenrage must read the name of our father or fall into the hands of Roartill." Shenlylith stops reading. "That's all of it. That is all it says," she says.

"Here, let me see that," says Vegenrage, and he takes the book from Shenlylith. He looks to the end where she finished reading. "There is one last word written right here. See?" Vegenrage points to the book.

Shenlylith looks, saying, "I don't see anything."

"It says Age'venger," says Vegenrage. Immediately after saying that word while holding the book *The Shenlylith Truth*, Vegenrage is turned facing the angel star, which has been thrown into the dome. Vegenrage looks at the book in his hand and watches as it turns to diamond dust, which glitters and is drawn quickly into the angel star. Shenlylith squeezes with her legs, still wrapped around Vegenrage's waist, and her arms, which are around his neck, are now choking him since he has been tilted toward the angel star above them. Shenlylith will fall if she does not hold on tight.

"Vegenrage, turn facing the ground, or I will fall," says Shenlylith into Vegenrage's ear. Vegenrage is staring at the star like he is in a dream and not paying any attention at all. She loses her grip with her legs, and they fall. She is now hanging on to Vegenrage's neck with her arms, but they too are slipping. "Vegenrage, I'm falling. Vegenrage!"

Vegenrage seems to be in a trance, and he extends his arms straight out to his sides. He snaps his right middle finger with his thumb, and Shenlylith disappears. The angel star starts to shimmer, and diamond-colored sparkles start to pour from it in a huge cloud of sparkling light.

Behaggen opens his eyes wide. "It's happening. It's really happening," says Behaggen.

The cloud of sparkling light moves toward and encapsulates Vegenrage. He seems to be physically and mentally consumed,

unable to act, and he is slowly lowering toward the red sand.
Vegenrage can't keep his eyes open, and they close as he falls
back first toward the ground. All the demons step back,
waiting for him to land so they can pounce on him. He
lands on the red sand with great impact, splashing the sand
like it was water; in fact, the red sand turns to water before
Vegenrage makes contact with it. There are demons who were
splashed away with the sand, and they too vanish and turn
to water. All the other demons see this, and the look of fear
overcomes all their faces as they all use their lavaflow magic,
which works in the red sand just like it does in lava. They sink
into the red sand before it turns to water. Vegenrage's body
does not sink into it. He stays flush with the water, and he lies
there for a moment. All the sand that splashed high into the
air turns to water, as well as the ground around Vegenrage's
body. It starts to ripple from his silhouette. The water grows
outward with each new ripple, and the red sand slowly turns
to water.

Vegenrage sits up and then stands, turning to face Roartill
on the other side of the dome. The water is growing outward
from Vegenrage, and he looks up, raising his arms outward
shoulder high. He begins to walk toward Roartill with
pure white lighting shooting from his fingers and thumbs.
His palms are facing up, and the lightning hits the dome,
exploding it into huge chunks of cooled rock that fall in
large very heavy boulders. Vegenrage seems unconscious, and
the lightning just keeps shooting bolt after bolt as he walks.
The entire dome is being destroyed, and he approaches the
many times larger devil of the Maglical System. The water
around Vegenrage is splashing with all the lava rock debris

falling all over, and most of the red sand is gone now except for that around Roartill and Vemenomous. Surprisingly, Vemenomous has not said a word; he has not made any kind of aggressive move at all, and he sinks into the red sand and is apparently gone.

"I defeated you once, Age'venger, and I will destroy you again, no matter what you call yourself, Vegenrage. This is exactly what I have been waiting for. You will be mine, and your knowledge will add to mine," says Roartill, laughing.

Vegenrage has been walking with his eyes closed. He looks like he is sleepwalking, and he snaps his eyes open immediately, shooting diamond-colored lightning from his eyes. The bolts twirl around one another, and they strike Roartill right in the chest, cutting holes right through his body. Roartill starts to scream, and his body starts to melt like wax. It looks like blood streaming out from the wounds, and all the rest of his body starts to fall like it is being deflated. Roartill's mouth opens wide, and his tongue sticks out. A very small identical version of Roartill runs from his mouth and dives into the remaining red sand off the tongue like it was a diving board. Roartill is gone as his gigantic body deflates and falls into the sand, which turns to water. The rest of the dome is destroyed and falls to the ground. In an instant, all the water and rock which has been the dome is gone, and Vegenrage is standing in the desert all alone.

"Vegenrage, Vegenrage," says Behaggen. Vegenrage rubs his eyes and sighs, moving very slowly. "Vegenrage, Vegenrage."

"Behaggen, what is going on?" asks Vegenrage.

"Vegenrage, I cannot believe it. It is happening. You are the chosen one. You are the one chosen to lead the forces of good against evil in the Maglical System. I always knew it was you. You are the one who will lead the races of man against Roartill and his demon horde, and you will defeat the evil for good. Age'venger chose you because you can do what he could not. You can kill," says Behaggen.

CHAPTER 21

The Tables Are Being Set

After seeing Vegenrage taken into the earth by the hand of Maglical Hell's ruler and not being able to follow or save him from the unknown, Farrah is overtaken with fear, hurt, and confusion. She leaves Vemenomous, the first demonian dragon, without a fight on the red sand in the Ackelson Desert, and she heads through a dimension door taking her back to the Erkensharie. She is looking for Logantrance and Ulegwahn. There is a part of Farrah that is scared and feels lost without Vegenrage, and there is another part that feels strong and indestructible. She wants Logantrance because he is much like a father figure to her, and she feels calm when he is around. She knows Logantrance is in Richterblen, but she hopes he will show up in the Erkensharie. She wants to meet with Ulegwahn because she is looking to lead and not be alone. She believes Ulegwahn can be swayed to send warriors, bow elves, and magic users with her to find and retrieve Vegenrage. She walks out into the courtyard and is immediately greeted by the dwarves, and this is very good because Fimble and Eebil are always there to flirt and make Farrah feel very comfortable and at ease.

"Ms. Farrah, Ms. Farrah, I am so glad to see you," says Eebil.

Fimble shoves him out of the way. "Hi, Ms. Farrah. You look lovelier than ever, but how did you survive? We all saw you thrown over the mountain off the Snow Gold Summit by Hornspire. The dragons saved you?" says Fimble.

"Give Farrah some room and leave her be," says Glimtron, moving them out of the way and slightly bowing to Farrah. "I am glad to see you are unharmed, Farrah, and it is good to be in your company again."

"Thank you, Glimtron. It is good to see you all again, but we have big trouble. Vegenrage has been taken into the depths of Strabalster by Maglical Hell itself. I have come here looking for help to go and get him," says Farrah, putting her hands to her face and looking to the side. "Logantrance is not here. He is in his home, Richterblen."

Shastenbree and Thambrable are guarding the courtyard from the newly built wall with many bow elves. They all look back in the courtyard, seeing that Farrah has returned without Vegenrage. "Let's hope Vemenomous is not following her this time," says Shastenbree to Thambrable.

"Well, if he does follow me here, you all had better run because Vemenomous is now the first demonian dragon, and he is more powerful than ever," says Farrah, looking up at Shastenbree with a mean look on her face. "It is Vemenomous's master, the ruler of Maglical Hell, who has Vegenrage right now, and they need Vegenrage out of the way so they can rule all of the Maglical System, and I am not going to let that happen. I have come to see who will help me get Vegenrage back and destroy this evil once and for all."

The dwarves step away from Farrah, and the elves in the background all notice a powerful force around her that they can actually feel.

Right then, Crayeulle, Whenshade, Pryzill, Lentoz, and Sombons all appear in the courtyard close to Farrah. "Farrah, it is good to see you again. We were all worried about you," says Whenshade.

Immediately, all the magic users who have just arrived feel the enormous presence of Farrah, and it is stronger than any presence they have ever felt before in any magical being. They all look at one another, and a strange feeling overcomes everyone looking at her. There is a sense of fear—fear that Farrah is becoming a superior magical being and not like Vegenrage. She is more demanding, and everyone can sense this as Farrah asks, "I am going to get Vegenrage. Who is coming with me?" And it feels like she is demanding loyalty from everyone. It feels like she is acting as their leader as she looks eye to eye to each one around her.

Oriapow and Ulegwahn are in the Great Erken, and Ulegwahn is just about to read from the book *The Rising of Vemenomous: The Demonian Dragon* when Oriapow says, "Farrah. Farrah is in the courtyard."

"Yes, I feel her. I knew it. You see? What did I tell you? I knew she was to be my queen, and just as I was about to read from this book, she arrives. Come, we must go and get her," says Ulegwahn.

"Wait! Do you feel her? Can't you feel how strong her presence is? Something is not right. She is way too powerful, and this is not normal by any means," says Oriapow.

"I know, and this is supposed to be. Like I said, she is to lead by my side, and together, we will wipe out the demons here on Fargloin," says Ulegwahn.

"Wait, my king, do not go," says Oriapow, but he is too late, as Ulegwahn teleports to the courtyard with the book still in his hands, and Oriapow quickly follows.

They both appear in the courtyard to see that Farrah already has an audience, and Ulegwahn approaches her. "Farrah, you have returned, and what impeccable timing you have. I was just about to read from a magical book just received from the Secret Erken, and I believe you were meant to witness its reading with me. Come, please join me in the Great Erken, and we will read from the book," says Ulegwahn.

Whenshade moves over to Ulegwahn, politely interrupting his king. "Ulegwahn, my king, Farrah has come here for a reason. She has asked all of us if we will travel with her to Strabalster to get Vegenrage from the ruler of Maglical Hell. We have news of our own that is very important, and well, here, Sombons, please explain," says Whenshade, pulling Sombons to the forefront.

Sombons is a little surprised, but he has urgent news and spits it out. "My king and all the elves of the Erkensharie, we are in great danger. Pryzill, Lentoz, and I just got back from inspecting the Long Forest, and all of it has been overrun with the Dark Bush. The demon master king Zevoncour is leading an army of hellmen and helldogs, and they are on the Nomberry Pass right now. This is no small army. This is an army large enough to overrun the Erkensharie, and they are less than two weeks away," says Sombons.

"Hellmen and helldogs, they are nothing. Let's go get Vegenrage, and the two of us will wipe out these demons like swatting flies," says Farrah.

"Vegenrage! Absolutely not. Not only will none of the elves of the Erkensharie go to help save Vegenrage but he is no longer welcome in the Erkensharie as well. I will hear no more of Vegenrage, and if he sets foot in the Erkensharie, he is to be placed under custody of Erkensharie law. He is to be brought to our court to face the charges of theft for stealing and taking out Pluanges from the Mystical Erkens, which is against Erkensharie law. He is to face the charges of theft and illegal use of the staff of barrier breath, which was Erkensharie property. This staff was a gift to our king Ellith and stolen by Vegenrage. He then used it illegally to create the staff of magic engulf, which led to the current situation we are in now, which is being threatened and attacked by demons, and they should have never been on the outer realm in the first place. No, I will hear no more of Vegenrage, and if anyone sees him, he is to be placed under arrest to stand trial for these crimes against the Erkensharie," says Ulegwahn.

"Then you are saying I am to be under arrest as well because I too used the staff of barrier breath," says Farrah.

"No, you were not aware of what you were doing, and furthermore, you are to be queen of the Erkensharie. I ask that you take my hand in marriage and help me run the Erkensharie. Together, we will rid the demon horde from our world and start a new and peaceful reign here," says Ulegwahn. This takes everyone by surprise, and the elves and dwarves all shake their head in disbelief to hear Ulegwahn say this.

"Be your queen? You must be joking. Where did all this nonsense come from? There is only one man for me, and that is Vegenrage. I am going to get him, and together, we will rid the Maglical System of this evil, showing its ugly head. Together, Vegenrage and I will destroy this demon horde, and if Vegenrage is no longer welcome in the Erkensharie, then neither am I. I am going to get Vegenrage. Is there anyone who will travel with me to get him?" says Farrah.

"If you are not to be my queen, then all immunities I have extended to you shall be retracted. And yes, you will be held accountable for illegally using the staff of barrier breath and for conspiring with the enemy, and that enemy to the Erkensharie is Vegenrage. Apprehend her," says Ulegwahn. All the elves and dwarves look at one another confused as their disbelief to this situation grows.

Farrah tilts her head to the side, ignoring Ulegwahn, concentrating, and talking out loud to herself. "There you are, but something is different. You must have been with Vegenrage. You were with Vegenrage," screams Farrah. Farrah looks around at all the elves. "Someone talk some sense into Ulegwahn because he is losing his mind. I have some things I have to do." Farrah walks through a dimension door after saying that.

There are simultaneous events happening on the planet Strabalster with the Ugorian elves and in Richterblen with Logantrance while all of this has been happening in the Erkensharie and, of course, with Vegenrage, Roartill, and Shenlylith. Basters is in his throne room in Ugoria with Cloakenstrike, and Basters is just beginning to read the book

The King of Ugoria when Fraborn enters the throne room, slightly bowing to his king. "Basters, a fight has broken out in the courtyard. There are two combatants, and they fight over you. This is a fight to the death, and I thought you should know," says Fraborn.

Basters looks to Cloakenstrike. "Come on, let's go see what the commotion is all about," says Basters, putting the book in his bag of holding, and he leads Cloakenstrike and Fraborn to the courtyard, where there are two elves fighting. A huge gathering has circled them, watching the fight. Basters makes his way through the crowd to see the two combatants already bloodied from many minutes of hand-to-hand fighting.

"Stop!" yells Basters. "What is going on here and why?"

The two engaged in physical combat stop breathing very heavily, and each looks to their human king and bows. "My king, I am Limbixtil, and Triestrannis has said you are a coward and a weak human who should not be king of Ugoria. I take great offense to this statement and challenge him. The winner will be vindicated," says Limbixtil.

"What have you to say about this, Triestrannis?" asks Basters.

"This is true. I do not believe you should be our king. Our king should be a Ugorian elf. Our kingship has been taken by force, but still I believe we should be ruled by none other than Ugorian bloodlines," says Triestrannis.

Basters has a flashback and remembers Hornspire telling him to name Limbixtil king of Ugoria. He sees his way of leaving the kingship without being slain by someone looking to take the kingship by force from him. "Triestrannis is right. The Ugorian elves should be ruled and governed by Ugorian bloodlines. Great change has come to Ugoria in the recent past, and I was destined to be your king, if only for a short time. Limbixtil and Triestrannis will fight to the death, and I will name the victor king of Ugoria. In this way, the kingship will have been fought for and won by the strongest and truest Ugorian elf. Triestrannis is captain of the Northern Ugorian Guard, and Limbixtil is first in command under Captain Intinsor. If Limbixtil is to win, then you know that, yes, a human is strong enough and worthy to be your king. If Triestrannis wins, you know it should always be a Ugorian elf to be your king. Either way, I will name the victor king of Ugoria. Does anyone dispute this chain of events? If so, speak now," says Basters as he looks around the crowd of elves, and no one speaks. "It is so. Triestrannis feels I am not worthy of the Ugorian kingship, and Limbixtil disagrees. It is time to see which of these two elves will be victorious and the new king of Ugoria. Begin!"

The two elves face off and begin to strike each other. Limbixtil is a sturdy, young, and fairly muscular elf with his short brown hair and golden eyes. He wears light leather armor with little defense against swords or arrows, but he is very agile and fluid. Limbixtil has his long sword still sheathed at his side. Triestrannis is an older elf with the same short brown hair and golden eyes, and his sword is still sheathed as well. He also wears a light leather armor, so both elves are very fast and flexible. Triestrannis is stronger, with more weight to his body, but Limbixtil has more stamina.

The two of them deal each other blow after blow, and soon they are both bloodied and have cuts all over their hands and faces. Triestrannis has not thought Limbixtil will be so aggressive, and he is fighting to win. Triestrannis is getting tired and a little worried that Limbixtil is winning and means to kill him, so he draws his sword and swings at Limbixtil. But Limbixtil is waiting and draws his sword, blocking Triestrannis's attack, and spins with his weapon, coming around and removing Triestrannis's head from his shoulders. Most of the elves are very surprised; they have mostly thought Triestrannis will win this contest, but it is over, and Limbixtil stands victorious over the severed body of his opponent. He is breathing very heavily, and it really hits him how tired he is as he falls to his knees, gasping for air.

Basters walks up to Limbixtil, removes the snow gold trinket from his neck, and holds it high in the air for everyone to see. He looks around the elves and makes an announcement. "The snow gold trinket has lost its power. The Krasbeil Mountains have been destroyed by the demons, and with this destruction has been lost Shenlylith's Prison and the ancient snow elf. This trinket has lost its power to protect the king of Ugoria, but it still and always will serve as a symbol of the strength of the Ugorian king," says Basters as he holds the trinket in his palm and looks at it. He pulls the king's scepter from his bag of holding and has it in one hand and the snow gold trinket in the other.

Just as he is about to say some more words, Shenlylith appears from being teleported from Vegenrage to standing right next to Basters. Shenlylith becomes very weak when she sees Basters and falls, but he catches her before she drops to the ground. He kneels with Shenlylith in his arms, and she looks at him, saying, "You are the king of Ugoria. I can feel it. I know it."

"You are Shenlylith, the great snow elf, but you are human," says Basters.

"It was foretold that I would someday return to my kingdom not as an elf but as a human female, and the king of Ugoria would be human as well, and we would rule together. I see now that it was true. I am here, and you are the king of Ugoria, and you are human. Destiny is real, and you are my destiny," says Shenlylith. Basters stands, helping Shenlylith up with him, and he looks around at all the elves.

"Basters, you are meant to be our king, and I want you to remain as our king," says Limbixtil.

Meanwhile in Richterblen, Logantrance can feel the presence of Farrah as she enters the Erkensharie, and he immediately begins to get ready to travel there when something that has never happened before happens. "Logantrance, stop. Logantrance, do not go. I have something very important for you," says Quintis, his bag of holding.

"What? What is this?" says Logantrance, looking down at his bag of holding on his waist. Quintis has come alive, and he is speaking to him.

"Logantrance, it is happening. The forces of evil have been let loose on the Maglical System, and the forces of good are growing in your protégé, Vegenrage. He has been growing in magical power since the moment he entered the Maglical System, and he has just been imbued by the almighty himself," says Quintis.

"So it is true. Behaggen had told Swallgrace and me that the almighty father was searching for the one who would defend against and defeat the greatest of evil. Swallgrace thought he was the magic user to be the one. I had always thought the greatest evil was Alluradaloni, and that is why Swallgrace was so eager to prove himself and face her, but it never was," says Logantrance.

"Alluradaloni was the greatest evil on the outer realm, but she was under control of Alisluxkana, and the two of them were unstoppable. Vegenrage saved Alluradaloni from Alisluxkana and gave her power he never should have. Now Farrah has the power of absorption, and she is growing in magical prowess at an uncontrollable rate. She will not stop. She is growing magically faster than Vegenrage is. Vegenrage has a unique sense and constitution. He does not usurp all the magical flow around him, but Farrah does not have this control, and her evil past, even though forced on her will, drives her passion for power. You have to be very careful around her. You have to try to make her understand that, if she does not learn to control her magical ability, it will consume her, and evil will find its way to her mind and control her heart. You must stay clear of her for now and find Vegenrage. He has to confront Farrah and guide her. She does love Vegenrage, and this is the only thing that can save her from corruption and power. Parnapp will do what he can to guide and help Farrah and slow her consumption of magical energy, but Farrah is his master, and he has to obey her. Farrah has never been to the Ugorian Palace, yet she has just used a dimension door spell to travel to Ugoria. This is remarkable. Farrah is growing magically exponentially, and with the evil taint on her mind, how she will use her magic can change on a dime, meaning she can suddenly use her magic against Vegenrage or you," says Quintis.

"I still remember the day in Vollenbeln when Farrah came out of Vegenrage's home, and he was sleeping. He had used all his energy to imbue Farrah with the power of absorption. I was very worried that this would happen—I mean, Farrah not having the ability to slow or control her magical growth. I was worried about this with Vegenrage also, but he has so far proven himself worthy of his gifts. How is it you are speaking to me, Quintis? I thought only Behaggen had the power of speech, as well as Parnapp because Behaggen passed the power of free speech to him?" asks Logantrance.

"In the creation of the Maglical System, there were two great beings, Age'venger and Roartill. They used their magic together to create the three inhabited worlds, and they both blew their magical ability onto these worlds. The first magical beings were the bags of holding, and there were sixteen of us. We all had free speech. The first magical species were the dragons, and we were all held by them. Then came the lower forms of life, the races of man. The dragons stayed clear of the races of man, but when the races of man started to grow in numbers and as they learned magic, the dragons took action, known as the dragon feast. They feasted on the races of man every thousand years, and this has gone on for the past three thousand years. The dragons had always stolen the treasure of man, and this is where they gained their strength. And over time, the bags of holding were mixed and left with all the treasure. The bags of holding were lost without the companionship of their dragon masters and ventured out, finding the races of man more to their liking. Some of the bags of holding went to evil masters, but most stayed clear of this. We all had the power of free speech with the dragons, but when we left to seek out the races of man, we lost free speech, all except Behaggen, the first bag of holding. We all could still speak to Behaggen but no one else unless granted freedom of speech from him, like he did with Parnapp," says Quintis.

"So how is it you are speaking to me now?" asks Logantrance.

"Great events are happening right now as we speak. Changes are coming to the Maglical System, and a lot of things are going to happen. Not long after the creation of the Maglical System, Roartill and Age'venger went to war with each other. Age'venger stayed in the skies, and Roartill stayed on the land, but Roartill controlled life and manipulated it the way he saw fit, and it was not always pretty. Age'venger took great grievance in what he saw Roartill doing to life on the worlds, and he went to war with him, trying to expel him from the land. Ultimately, Roartill won the battle, and Age'venger used all his eternal power to contain Roartill in Maglical Hell, never to escape until the coming of Vegenrage. It is Vegenrage who will continue the battle with Roartill and defeat him once and for all. Age'venger could not bring himself to kill Roartill, so he contained him until a unique power in the form of man would rise to rid the Maglical System of Roartill and his evil. Vegenrage is this man, but it is not guaranteed he will be victorious. Do not underestimate Roartill. He is smart, and he also has planned and thought ahead on how to defeat the savior coming to destroy him. He has powerful allies, like his demon master king Zevoncour and demon hordes now spewing onto the worlds of the Maglical System.

"The rise of the demonian dragon is the most lethal creation of dragon to come to the Maglical System, and Farrah is being pursued by the forces of evil. She is their most important pawn, and Vegenrage has to be made to understand that if he cannot teach her to control her mind, if he cannot teach her to curb her magical growth, then she will destroy him and be evil's greatest champion. Vegenrage has learned and spoken the name of Age'venger under the angel star. This has started the war again. As we speak, Age'venger is imbuing Vegenrage with Maglical eternity. All the bags of holding now have free speech restored, and great knowledge will start to flow from them to their masters. Roartill now knows who his enemy is. He now knows who he must destroy, and if he does so, there will be no one to stop the horrible free rein of Roartill. The tables are being set as we speak right now. Maglical war is beginning, and it is going to be evil against good. Who will fight for what side is not always going to be clear, but one thing is for sure: Vegenrage must put an end to Roartill," says Quintis.

"Well, I must get to the Erkensharie. If Farrah is this powerful, then I must warn the elves and the dwarves," says Logantrance.

"You can try, but if you see Farrah, be very careful around her. She is a time bomb ready to explode anytime now. I cannot tell you what to do or where to go, but you have to find Vegenrage as soon as you can. He will be able to draw some of her magical pull. You know what I am saying is true because I know you can feel her presence and how strong she is becoming, and she is only getting stronger. It will be too much for her to handle if she does not learn to control her magical draw on the Maglical System."

"Yes, Quintis, I can feel how strong her presence has become, but still we must go to the Erkensharie. It is possible Vegenrage will go there, and let us hope he does," says Logantrance as he heads through a dimension door to go to the Erkensharie.

CHAPTER 22

Age'venger Has Been Spoken

From the moment Vegenrage has read the name Age'venger from the book *The Shenlylith Truth*, a whole chain reaction has started. A podium rises in the courtyard of the Ugorian Palace on the world of Strabalster right next to Basters and Shenlylith. "What is this?" says Basters, walking to the podium and looking at the book sitting on top of it.

The podium is made of solid white gold, and the book has covers and binding made of the same material. There are thin snow-white lines throughout the book that swirl all around the front and back covers. Basters picks the book and looks it over, but there is no writing that he can see on it. He tries to open the book, but he cannot.

"The book is not for your eyes, Master. It is for Shenlylith. Only the eyes of the once snow elf can read from the book of foresight," says Delver.

Basters looks to his waist. "Delver, did you speak? Did you actually speak to me?" asks Basters.

"Yes, Master. Great happenings are occurring. The creator has released his hold on Maglical Hell. In turn, his power is freely flowing throughout the Maglical System. The chosen champion to serve our father in heaven against Roartill has spoken the sacred name. Now all the bags of holding in all the Maglical System have free speech, and we all want our masters to survive, whether good or bad. The book is for Shenlylith. Please give her the book because there is no time to waste," says Delver.

Basters hands the book to Shenlylith, and she accepts it, looking at the cover. Words start to appear on the cover, but before she can read them, Farrah appears from a dimension door right next to Basters and Shenlylith, and they all are startled by her appearance.

"You are Shenlylith. We saw you on the Snow Gold Summit, but you are not elven anymore. You are human, and you have lost your magic. Were you just with Vegenrage?" asks Farrah.

"Yes, he was alone, facing Roartill, the ruler of Maglical Hell, and Vemenomous, the first demonian dragon. Who are you?" asks Shenlylith.

"I am Farrah. Vegenrage saved me from Alisluxkana when I was known to the races of man as Alluradaloni, and he and I are to be together always. I will find him and help him defeat this evil growing in the Maglical System. Where is he?" asks Farrah.

"Farrah, I am no longer magical, it is true, but I have to say even now—as a human woman with no magical power—I can feel the enormous magical presence that you are. I could feel no magical presence around Vegenrage, but he is most definitely very magically inclined. Farrah, you must go to him. You must help him defeat Roartill and Vemenomous.

Vegenrage needs you. He is in the Ackelson Desert," says Shenlylith.

"I know exactly where he is. Thank you, Shenlylith. I must go and help Vegenrage. I hope to see you again so that I may explain why we tricked you on the Snow Gold Summit, but I must go and help Vegenrage right now," says Farrah, and she immediately walks through a dimension door, taking her to the exact location where she has last faced Vemenomous.

This is very smart and quick thinking by Shenlylith because Farrah has not wasted time thinking about the book that Shenlylith has, nor has Farrah paid any attention to Basters.

"Wait! Wait!" says Basters, but he is too late. Farrah has gone.

Shenlylith looks around at all the elves watching as Farrah appears and disappears in such a short span of time. Shenlylith has her magic no more, but her wit and instincts are still very sharp. She can sense very bad things are about to happen, and her quick thought and witty words have sent Farrah off to another place. Shenlylith sighs with relief, looking at Basters, saying, "She is a power not to be messed with."

"Basters, there is no time to waste. Things are happening, and the book may have insight that will help us. Believe me when I tell you things are happening, and any help we get we will need. Please have Shenlylith read the book," says Delver.

"Listen to Delver. He is right. You have to get to safety right away. The demon horde is coming, but there is danger all around, and believe me, that girl who was just here may be the most dangerous person you have ever met. Smart thinking, Shenlylith, getting Farrah to go to Vegenrage.

Farrah is not dangerous per se, but she is becoming way too magically powerful, and it will consume her if she does not get help soon," says Getcher, Cloakenstrike's bag of holding.

"Wait a minute. You have never spoken. Why do you speak now?" asks Cloakenstrike.

"Because all the bags of holding now have free speech restored, and you are in luck because I am one smart bag of holding. You and I, Cloakenstrike, we are almost unstoppable." Getcher laughs.

As all of this is taking place in the Ugorian courtyard, there is something going on in the Ugorian prison. The prison is not in or even near the Ugorian Palace; it is actually to the far west, near the northwestern gate of Riobe. All of the Helven have been taken here and put in the prison. It is not a bunch of cells. It is not even an elven-made structure, like a building. It is actually a dug-out piece of earth that is solid rock. It is dug out of a small mountain, which is really just a very big hill. This hill is made out of solid stone, and it is so thick that there is no way anyone can dig or tunnel out of here. The entrance is lined with very solid steel bars, and there is no breaking them, being protected from magic by Ugorianmire. This is very much like Dragonmire, except this metal is heated, poured, and magically treated by the Ugorian elves. The elves have gotten this idea from the dragons, and they have actually stolen Dragonmire from them and learned from the magical metal. The prison here in Riobe is lined all around the wall edges with Ugorianmire, and any magic that is cast inside of the prison cell will be absorbed by the Ugorianmire. The prison is one large room and easily large enough to hold all 110 of the Helven; any magic cast in here will be absorbed by the metal, and the effects of the magic will be rendered useless.

There is a bench that is carved around the outer wall of the prison, and all the Helven are sitting there. Dona'try is sitting at the back of the prison, and Kerben and his wife, Weesilibith, are sitting to his right. All the Helven are still wearing their full body robes, which are very reminiscent of those worn by monks, and all the Helven have hoods that cover their heads and hang down, so their entire bodies and faces are covered. They all sit very quietly and patiently, and Dona'try raises his head and his hood and lays it down his back. He opens his eyes and looks around with his sparkly brown eyes, which seem to glow in the dim light. All the Helven have had golden eyes like their brothers, the Ugorian elves, but over time, their eyes have grown darker in color like their skin, giving their eyes more of a brownish color with oversized pupils, providing them great nighttime vision. Dona'try looks over his followers and at the floor, which is starting to glow red, and smoke is beginning to rise from it.

Dona'try can hear words in his head speaking to him. *Dona'try, you have done well, my servant. It is now time for the Helven to play their part in the destruction of Ugoria. My demons are making their way to Ugoria from the Krasbeil Mountains as we speak, and the Helven will cause chaos from within Ugoria as my demons attack from outside of Ugoria. The elves have no way of preparing for my demons, led by Servorious, my magical demon savant. He will move an army of hellmen and helldogs magically across the land and be on Ugoria before the elves have time to react. I also have an army of winged Lizangars in the air, on their way here now.* Zevoncour speaks telepathically to him.

Kerben can feel a magical presence, and he ever so slightly tilts his head to Weesilibith, pulling a ring from within his robe, and taps her hand with the ring. She takes the ring and puts it on her left ring finger, and Kerben does the same with an identical ring.

Winged Lizangars are lizardlike large creatures with huge wings sprouting from their backs. They have long, slender arms and legs that have three deadly talons on each. These talons are at the end of fingerlike very long digits that have great grasping capabilities. They are deadly, crushing and piercing weapons. Their heads are dragonlike with powerful sharp teeth designed for ripping and tearing flesh. They are bloodred with smooth, rubbery skin and have long tails with daggerlike weapons at the end. These are the same kind of winged demons that has attacked Gwithen in her lair, along with the Doliath and the three demons when Vegenrage has come to save her draglets.

The floor in the prison starts to glow a brighter red and almost looks like it is liquefying. Smoke is rising heavily from the floor now, and soon the entire room is full of smoke, which is filling the prison and limiting visibility greatly. The head of Zevoncour rises from the red-hot liquid in the center of the room. There is a very eerie haze as Zevoncour's glowing yellow eyes look around. The burning, liquefied floor gives off a reddish light dimmed by the smoke. Zevoncour points to each of the Helven and shoots from the index claw on his right hand what looks like a flaring magic missile with red-hot ash falling behind it to the ground. Each Helven is struck with a missile except for Dona'try. Once the Helven are hit with the missile of possession, they shake a little, but very quickly the shaking stops, and they are now possessed by Zevoncour's favorite demons.

The elves outside of the prison have noticed all the smoke flowing out from within the prison, and Zevoncour can hear them yelling and coming to investigate what is going on. He smiles, showing his bright white teeth, which almost act like a flashlight in the smoky haze. He sinks into the molten, hot liquid floor. As Zevoncour sinks, all the Ugorianmire lined around the floor under the bench starts to descend into the earth. It is melted by Zevoncour and removed from the floor, allowing the possessed Helven to use their magic.

The center of the floor, which is still red-hot, starts to bubble, and magical items start to rise from the molten floor and move to their owners. Each Helven has magical items that are now floating to them. Dona'try gets his bag of holding. Kerben has managed to hide his in his robe and has it with him the whole time. The Helven have amassed the largest grouping of demonic magical items in the entire Maglical System. Each Helven has at least one demonic magical item, and they cause very nasty effects when used against the living.

All of the Helven remain quietly sitting except for Dona'try, who stands up and removes his robe, dropping it to the floor, which has cooled and regained its natural color. After a short moment of standing there naked, he starts to shake, and his flesh begins to split right up the center of his chest and stomach. His flesh on his arms and legs and along his shoulders and hips begins to split up. The flesh on his head and feet starts to tear as well. The demon body inside the human form starts to grow taller, thicker, and wider. The scrap flesh starts to slide and fall off the growing body of Inthamus. Bloody flesh falls to the floor around him, and he grows to his original shape.

He is very odd looking. He has the hind legs of a rabbit, with a fat belly that rests on the ground when he sits. He has long, slender arms with sharp talons. He has three fingers and one thumb on each hand. He has no visible neck. His shoulders kind of grow upward and narrow toward the top of his head, which is rounded, and he has a wide mouth with one row of sharklike very sharp teeth on the top and bottom jaws. He has stereoscopic eyes and no nose, just slits under his eyes for breathing. He has a long, wide tongue that works a lot like a prehensile tail. He shoots his tongue from his mouth, and it grabs the elven flesh that has fallen from his form lying on the ground and pulls it into his mouth with great speed. He does this very fast over and over until all the flesh has been consumed. Inthamus's hind legs have great adaptation, which allows him to stand on his hind legs and walk upright. This looks very strange; his rabbitlike very long legs with a uniquely formed foot on each allow him to walk upright if he desires. He can hop very long distances or jump to great heights as well. When standing up, he is very tall, nearly ten feet. He has a very fat belly, so he looks awkward and silly, but do not let this fool you.

Inthamus is one of Zevoncour's favorite demons, and he is very magically inclined. Zevoncour has sent him to the surface long ago to take over the Helven and rule them, always incognito, portraying the elf named Dona'try. Inthamus and Servorious are the two most magically powerful demons under Zevoncour's command with great knowledge and a vast magical arsenal between them.

Yes, Inthamus, your time has come. Lead the possessed Helven into Ugoria and destroy the Ugorian elves. You enter Ugoria from the west, and Servorious will enter from the east. I must go to Fargloin to lead my demons there. Here, you and Servorious have things well under control. Do not let me down, says Zevoncour telepathically to Inthamus.

The Helven maintain all of their magic and use of all the magical items they carry because they are possessed by demons, who gain all the knowledge of the Helven possessed. This is some smart thinking by Zevoncour using the Helven in this manor, and he hopes this will make his master, Roartill, proud of him. Zevoncour now has his two strongest magic-using demons leading armies against the Ugorian elves, and soon there will be war in Ugoria.

After Farrah leaves the Erkensharie courtyard, Ulegwahn is furious that Farrah has denied him completely. He is stomping around in a circle, and all the elves stand quiet and motionless because they have never seen Ulegwahn this upset before. As fate will have it, Logantrance walks from his dimension door right into the Erkensharie courtyard, and he notices all the elves watching Ulegwahn stomp around. Logantrance heads for Ulegwahn, and the elves part to let him to their king. "Ulegwahn, I am so glad you are here. I have to talk to you about Farrah," says Logantrance.

"Farrah, I do not want to hear about Farrah or Vegenrage. They are both traders to the Erkensharie. They are both enemies of the Erkensharie elves," says Ulegwahn.

"What? What are you saying, Ulegwahn? They are not enemies of the Erkensharie unless you make it so, and this is something you should not do," says Logantrance.

"Vegenrage is a thief and a fugitive from the Erkensharie, and Farrah goes to help and harbor him from Erkensharie law. I offered Farrah immunity from prosecution, but she denied it and chose the way of the outlaw," says Ulegwahn.

"Vegenrage a thief? Farrah an outlaw? Ulegwahn, there are much bigger things happening here than your personal agenda. I could feel that Farrah was just here. She is becoming a magical force beyond control. Vegenrage is no thief, and he is the only one who can help Farrah control what she is becoming. If you let your puppy love get the best of you and you pursue Farrah in any unprofessional way, she will destroy you with the blink of an eye. The demons are coming, Ulegwahn. The demons are coming, and they mean to destroy the Erkensharie. You need to put your personal feelings of jealousy and lust or greed or simple attraction out of your mind. You better ally yourself with Vegenrage because you are going to need him and his help. You are going to need Vegenrage to help you and all your people here to fight and defeat the demons," says Logantrance.

The ground starts to shake, and Logantrance and Ulegwahn move aside as a podium rises in the center of the Erkensharie courtyard. It is pure solid yellow gold with nothing but smooth sides and a luster that gleams in everyone's eyes as they marvel at it. It rises four feet high with a slanted top, which moves apart from the center as a book rises up. The top closes, and the book falls gently and lies on the slanted top. Ulegwahn still has the two books *The Rising of*

Vemenomous and *The Rising of Vemenomous: The Demonian Dragon* in his hands, and they both levitate from his hands over to the podium above the book resting on top. The two books turn in the air, so the bindings are facing each other, and they start to smack each other like they are clapping. The front cover of each book lifts, and they join the two books together. The book lying on the podium starts to spin, and the top of the podium levels out perfectly flat. The book on the podium stops spinning, and it opens halfway and lies flush as a golden light shines upward and out, consuming both books in the air. The two books start to spin faster and faster, and they begin to dissolve into a golden light that forms into a bag of holding. The book on the podium slams shut, and the bag of holding levitates over to Ulegwahn.

"Ulegwahn, the king of the Erkensharie. I am Vixtrixx, the sixteenth and last of the bags of holding. I was the companion of Gwithen. She had given me to Hornspire on the promise that he would protect and hide me until the time my contents would come into play. How and where I was to be revealed has now come to fruition. Hornspire has been eliminated by a dragon, and the dragons now seek to unite the lesser dragons with them against the demon uprising in outer realms. I am here to partner with you, Ulegwahn, to help you understand the contents of the book on the podium and help you and the elves of the Erkensharie survive the demon uprising," says Vixtrixx, who levitates to the waist of Ulegwahn and ties himself with the golden string hanging to Ulegwahn's left side.

"Only Vegenrage can help Farrah control her magical growth? I do not think so. With the Octagemerwell and

Vixtrixx at my side, there is no question Farrah was meant to be the queen of the Erkensharie," says Ulegwahn, looking at Logantrance defiantly. Ulegwahn walks up to the podium and picks the book. He reads it out loud. *"The King of the Erkensharie."* Ulegwahn puts the book in his new bag of holding.

Glimtron can be quiet no more and walks up to Ulegwahn, grabbing him by his right arm. "Ulegwahn, we have been friends for a very long time, and I can listen to this no more. Get a hold of yourself and listen to what you are saying. You want a human woman to be your queen? I never thought I would hear any such words come from your mouth. Vegenrage a thief and Farrah protecting Vegenrage from Erkensharie law? This is your concern when there are demons invading the outer realms and about to attack Erkensharie lands? I can tell you as a king who has lost all of my land and my people to the demons, you do not want to let that fate happen to you and the Erkensharie elves. You need to take that book, the Octagemerwell, and that incredible bag of holding and put them to good use. You need to lead the Erkensharie elves, me, and my remaining dwarves. You need to accept the help of Logantrance, Vegenrage, and Farrah when it is available to you instead of making enemies of them. You and all of us need all the help we can get right now," says Glimtron with great passion in his words and fire in his eyes. Ulegwahn is finally silenced and pauses for a moment, thinking.

A podium rises in the center square of Breezzele on the world of Kronton. All the people who have survived the attack on Mourbarria and Valvernva have followed Vegenrage, Farrah, Mournbow, Inglelapse, and Oliver to the Elbutan

Forest and Highlands. Once there, they make their way to Breezzele, and people have come from the surrounding areas. More people than anyone has ever thought possible have come to build and make a very secure home here in Breezzele. They are many thousand strong now and have an army with bowmen, horse riders, swordsmen, and a small but growing magic-using class. This is the first magical order of humans on the planet of Kronton with a large and devoted following. Outside of the few human individuals who have been gifted in the knowledge of magic, this is the first magical order of humans in the Maglical System with real potential to grow into a magical power.

The podium that rises in the center square of Breezzele goes up as Mournbow is speaking to a large group of people, and it ascends right next to the podium Mournbow is speaking at. He looks over at the podium as does everyone listening to him speak. The podium is solid yellow gold. It shines and takes everyone's attention. Mournbow watches as the top of the podium splits and spreads apart, and a book rises from the center top and rests on the slanted top. Everyone watches as Mournbow approaches the podium, picks the book, and looks it over. The golden podium sinks back into the earth after he picks the book, just as the other podiums have done on the other two planets. Mournbow turns to Inglelapse and says, "There is no writing on this book, and I cannot open it. Maybe you should look at this." He hands the book to Inglelapse.

Vegenrage is very disoriented, still standing in the Ackelson Desert. "Vegenrage, Vegenrage, come on, snap out of it. Time to get your senses now. Come on, Vegenrage," says Behaggen.

"I'm sorry, Behaggen. I don't know what has come over me. I feel strange. I mean, I feel really good. My senses are heightened even more than before. I don't think this is right. I can sense the smallest beings on all three worlds. I can tell you where all the dragons are. I know where all the elves, the dwarves, and even the remaining humanor are. I don't think I like being able to just feel and know all of this. I have to clear my mind. I do not want all this in my head," says Vegenrage, rubbing his face.

"You have been imbued by the almighty of the Maglical System. It is upon you to face and destroy Roartill and his demon horde," says Behaggen.

"Oh my god, Farrah is drawing magical energy at an uncontrollable rate. I have to get to her and ease her mind. I have to relieve the magical burden growing out of control in her. Wait, she is coming to me. I can feel the evil that has invaded her body. I know it tries to pull her soul away from me. Vemenomous is in her, and the magic of the shard hammer has invaded her soul, but I am in her heart. I will help her expunge the evil. I will be the sponge to draw all the taint out of her," says Vegenrage.

"You must be very careful, Vegenrage. Farrah is in love with you. She has great desire and passion, and this is good, but if the evil that has found its way into Farrah's mind uses her magical ability against you, she is now powerful enough to cause you great harm and even destroy you. You must be very careful," says Behaggen.

Chapter 23

Farrah's Magic Is Too Strong

Farrah has arrived from her dimension door in the Ackelson Desert at the location where she has last faced Vemenomous and where Vegenrage has been taken into the depths of Strabalster. She looks around, but all the red sand is gone, and there is no evidence that any conflict has occurred here at all. She looks around to see nothing but sand as far as the eye can see.

"Vegenrage!" she yells. "Vegenrage, I know you are here. Where are you?" She floats down to the hot desert sand and stands there in the heat, looking around.

Farrah has been growing magically at an exponential rate, and events have been happening so fast that she has taken no time to reflect how her presence has grown magically. She has been following Vegenrage from one quest to another. Her love for Vegenrage has consumed all her thoughts since they have become physical with each other. Her only thoughts have been to follow him to love him and to be with him always, but she is always pulled from one fight to another. Danger, whether it is focused on Vegenrage or Farrah, is always ripping them apart, and all she wants is to be alone with him.

She looks around the empty desert when emotion takes her by surprise, and she starts to cry. "Vegenrage, where are you?" She starts to use her magic to scan for the presence of magic, and she can feel magical presence on all three worlds of the Maglical System. She can feel Logantrance, Oriapow, and all the magical order in the Erkensharie. She can feel the dragons, and she knows they are scattered on all the worlds. She knows where the draglets and the female dragons protecting them are, as well as the dominant dragons, some of which are in the Ilkergire. Interford, the Changenoir, is with Dribrillianth, and Ubwickesdon is with Gairdennow, and they are in the Ilkergire. Other dragons are on the planet Strabalster. She can sense Basters, Cloakenstrike, and even Shenlylith, who no longer has a magical presence, along with the Ugorian elves in Ugoria. She can also sense the evil that is moving very fast toward Ugoria from the Krasbeil Mountains. She can sense the Helven who have been possessed, and she can even tell that there are two Helven who have not been overcome, and this evil is already in Ugoria. She can feel the evil hellmen and helldogs making their way toward the Erkensharie, and they are led by Zevoncour. Farrah can sense all this, plus so much more.

Farrah opens her eyes for the first time, realizing how magically inclined she has become. She can see things, she can feel things, and she knows things just by thinking about them, but she cannot sense or feel Vegenrage at all. She has no idea where he is. "Vegenrage, that damn cloak of concealment, I hate it!" she yells into the air.

She starts to get nervous, looking all around. She begins to get scared, and bad thoughts start to invade her mind.

She knows Shenlylith has transformed from elven to human female. She knows Shenlylith has been right here where she is now and has been teleported to Ugoria, and she knows Shenlylith has lost her magic, so it must have been Vegenrage who has teleported her. Jealously creeps into her mind, and she thinks Vegenrage is hiding from her and having an affair with Shenlylith.

"Vegenrage, you are having an affair with Shenlylith, aren't you? I bet you are leaving me to go see women of all the races, aren't you, Vegenrage? I know you are here somewhere. I may not be able to sense you, but I know you can sense me. Why are you not here? Where are you?" she yells into the air.

The look of anger overcomes her face, and her body becomes red-hot. Flames start to erupt, and she is covered in fire. She walks, holding her arms out to her sides, looking at the flames engulfing her body.

"Vegenrage, I will find you. I will know the truth. You cannot hide from me," says Farrah as she walks through the desert.

The huge eyes of Parnapp open, and he speaks to Farrah. "Farrah, Farrah, you have to control your emotions. You have to relax and let the magic flow. You need to be at ease. Do not let your passion turn to rage. Do not let your love be replaced with jealousy. Do not turn on Vegenrage. This is what the evil of the inner realms want. This is how they have planned to use you. This is how they plan to destroy the chosen savior of the Maglical System. Vegenrage has only wanted you to be free. He has wanted you to love him because he loves you. Roartill cannot destroy Vegenrage, but he can use you. He can manipulate you to destroy Vegenrage for him. Vemenomous has been a servant of evil ever since he was a dragon, and now he has transformed into the first demonian dragon. He has known for over a thousand years that you would be Vegenrage's love, and this is why he planted a demon seed in you. This is why he has taken the baby from you and Vegenrage. He is trying to bring your anger to the surface. Evil is trying to confuse you and use you for their end. Vemenomous and Zevoncour have planned this for a long time ever since Hornspire started making the prophetical writings about Vlianth. Now that Roartill has been set free from Maglical Hell, they are much stronger and have armies of demons to lead on the outer realms. They knew they needed you in order to stop Vegenrage. They have struck you with the shard hammer and stole your baby from you. Now they use your passion and your love for Vegenrage as they always intended to. They always knew Vegenrage would love the greatest power of all, and that is you, Farrah. You are Vegenrage's Achilles' heel. You can destroy him. He has shared all his love with you, his power of absorption, and his power of magic without the spoken word. You have become magically self-sufficient. The inner realms knew all this would happen, and you, Farrah, are their intended champion. You are the one they rely on to destroy Vegenrage. You are the one they want to transform into the demonian dragon queen, and if you let hate and anger control you, then they can control you. You have to control your magical prowess and not turn on Vegenrage," says Parnapp as Farrah sees Vegenrage appear from a dimension door just above her. He lowers to the ground, standing in front of her.

"Vegenrage!" yells Farrah as she runs to embrace him. She is overtaken with joy as she hugs and squeezes him tight.

"Farrah, we have to leave this place right away. It is dangerous here. Your magical draw on the Maglical System is becoming so incredibly powerful, and I have to teach you how to control this. Come, we must go to Vollenbeln," says Vegenrage.

"OK," says Farrah as all the rage and emotion has been replaced with happy smiles, and she gladly takes the hand of Vegenrage, ready to follow him anywhere.

Before the two of them move through Vegenrage's dimension door, all the sand they are standing on turns into the red sand of Maglical Hell. Roartill manipulates Vegenrage's magic, turning his dimension door into a force barrier, and Vegenrage walks into it face-first. Roartill and Vemenomous use strong demonic magic and are able to haunt Farrah's mind with terrible images, thanks to the fact that Vemenomous has infected her blood with his, and she has been struck with the shard hammer, allowing for the demonic magic to penetrate her mind.

Farrah is engulfed in red and blue flames. The pupils in her eyes grow oblong like that of a cat, and the color of her eyes turn a darker shade of brown, like the eyes of Vemenomous. Vegenrage has started to walk, holding on to Farrah's hand, when he is stopped dead by the force barrier. He still has Farrah by the hand, and he turns to see her engulfed in flames. His hand is burned by her flaming hand, and he instinctively pulls away from her.

Even though Farrah is looking right at Vegenrage in front of her, she starts to have haunting images of the men and women who have been killed by Alisluxkana, and this is all she sees. She can hear the screams and cries for help as these people die, and she stands there motionless and does not help. Vegenrage is calling and yelling to Farrah to snap her back from the images filling her mind. He has to step away from Farrah, and he cannot get near her because she gets hotter and hotter. The heat is so intense that Vegenrage has to back away, and fortunately, the force barrier has disappeared when Vegenrage realized his dimension door spell have not worked. Farrah cannot hear Vegenrage calling for her. The images in Farrah's head cause her great anguish, and this fuels her raging heat, driving Vegenrage further and further back from her.

Suddenly, the images in her head stop, and she can see Vemenomous in his new demonian dragon form, and he is walking on all fours right toward her. He is gigantic, and it looks to Farrah like he is walking right at her in the desert. She cannot see Vegenrage, who is now ten feet away from her. She cannot hear him calling for her. Vegenrage cannot use his magic because he is still standing in the red sand. All Farrah can see and hear is Vemenomous, who is walking right at her in the desert, and she is in a trance as Vemenomous talks to her.

"Farrah, it is time. Your destiny is to rule the Maglical System by my side. You are to be the demonian queen. There is no stopping this. There is no changing this. The time of Farrah, the demonian dragon queen, has come. It is time to embrace your power. It is time to complete your transformation into the demonian dragon queen. All you need to do is consume the flesh of Vegenrage, and you will undergo a metamorphosis that will make you the strongest magical being in the Maglical System, and I will help you," says Vemenomous.

"No!" yells Farrah. She tries to run, and she tries to jump and fly, but she cannot move. She looks down at her feet to see she is trapped. There is a huge piece of red cement in a wide circle all around her, and her feet are dried in the cement all the way up her ankles, and she cannot move. She looks up to see Vemenomous running at her, and he reaches with his mouth wide open, ready to bite her. Farrah yells, thrusting both hands at the demonian dragon, unleashing her dragon-slaying hands. Farrah does not even realize that, the whole time, she is just seeing images in her mind. In reality, she is unleashing her dragon-slaying hands right at Vegenrage, and he cannot avoid this devastating spell. The spell leaves both of Farrah's hands in a cylindrical shape, and it hits Vegenrage right in the chest. Vegenrage spreads his arms like he is catching the spell, but this is way too powerful a spell for him to absorb for any length of time.

Vegenrage is yelling, "Farrah, Farrah, you have to fight the images in your head. You have to snap back. Farrah, I cannot absorb this for much longer. Farrah!" He cannot cast magic while in the red sand, but he is still one of the most powerful magical beings in the Maglical System. He is being hit right in the chest with this devastating spell, and his arms are raised to his sides like he is holding a very large beach ball. The spell is a bright white and yellow color, and it is burning his flesh and pushing him back away from Farrah. His arms are being shoved to his back, and his head is turning side to side, like he is trying to look away from the disintegrating heat, and he is actually starting to fall apart. His clothing is burned from his flesh, and the magical rope holding Behaggen around his waist is broken, and Behaggen falls. Before hitting the red sand, Behaggen flies off out into the sand, avoiding it. Vegenrage's chest is starting to disappear like it is being sanded away from him.

Fortunately for Vegenrage, the force of the spell lifts him off the ground, and this is just enough for Logantrance to save him. Logantrance is the only one to follow Farrah from the Erkensharie. Logantrance has come here after he has sensed Farrah's rage subside. He has been far off to the side, watching as the events here have unfolded. Logantrance cast invisibility on himself before he has traveled here, and it is a good thing he has. He cannot cast magic into the red sand without Roartill being able to manipulate it, but once Vegenrage has been lifted from the touch of the red sand, he cast his magic on Vegenrage without interference from Roartill. Logantrance casts a magical rope and pulls Vegenrage to him. Vegenrage is pulled through the air to Logantrance, who gently lays him on the sand in front of him and becomes visible.

Vegenrage's body is past the point of being in shock. He is dying, and steam is rising from his melted body. His clothing on the front of his body has been burned away, and that on his back has fallen off. Logantrance looks Vegenrage over to see his face, and the whole front of his body has been melted down to his bones. All the skin and flesh on the front of Vegenrage's body is gone, and there is no more painful situation any person can ever begin to heal back from. Logantrance knows he has to work fast to help Vegenrage heal himself. "Come, my boy, let's heal you up," says Logantrance, who passes his hands in the air over Vegenrage's body. He pulls a small vial of liquid from his bag of holding and pours its contents over Vegenrage.

Farrah stops her spell and sees nothing, but she is still engulfed in red and blue flames. Her eyes are still like those of Vemenomous and Roartill, who is laughing and rises from the sand behind Farrah, and she turns to face him. Vemenomous rises next to Roartill. Farrah is calm; she is not scared.

Roartill speaks to her. "Good. Good, Farrah. You can feel it, can't you? You can feel that you were meant for more. You were meant to rule. You were meant to lay down the law and be its judge. You were meant to be the demonian dragon queen. Vegenrage wants to hold you down. He wants to limit your power and take from you. He wants you to be his servant to do what he wishes. He wants you all for his selfish desires. I want you to be the ruler of the outer realms, period. I have no claim out here. My home is the inner realm. Maglical Hell is mine, and that will never change. I want you and Vemenomous to rule the outer realms of the Maglical System. The demon master king and all demons will be yours to rule and move as you see fit.

"You see, Farrah? Look over there. That is Vegenrage, the supposed savior of the Maglical System. He is supposed to be the most powerful being in the Maglical System, but you can see he is not. You are the most powerful being in the Maglical System. See what you have done? He cannot stand up to your power, and now all you have to do is go over there and consume him, and the Maglical System is yours. It will be yours to rule with Vemenomous. Now go and take what is rightfully yours," says Roartill.

Farrah looks over and sees Logantrance kneeling over Vegenrage, who is lying naked on the ground. She can see the man she loves, and she cannot recognize his body because of the devastating injuries he has sustained. The flames around Farrah go away, and her eyes return to her natural shade of hazelnut brown. She looks at Vegenrage and calms down, saying, "Vegenrage does not want to hold me back. Vegenrage does not want to limit me. He is the one who gave me freedom. He is the one who showed me magic. He gave me power"—Farrah's voice starts to deepen—"freedom of choice and the ability to think and choose for myself." Farrah clenches her fists and turns to face both Roartill and Vemenomous. "Vegenrage does not enter my mind and haunt my visions with horror. He does not try to manipulate my thoughts. He does not tell me anything. He does not ask me to harm others. Vegenrage is my savior, he is my love, and you are my enemy."

"No, Farrah, it is Vegenrage who will try to take from you. It is Vegenrage who will try to limit you and tell you what he wants you to know. Vegenrage will watch your every move so he can tell you what he thinks you should do. That is not freedom. That is control, and that is what Vegenrage wants," says Roartill.

"Maybe I want Vegenrage to watch me. Maybe I want Vegenrage to watch me all the time. Maybe I want Vegenrage to tell me what to do. Maybe I want to follow Vegenrage all the time. There is one thing for sure: I love Vegenrage, and he has always given me freedom of choice. I have just proven that love is stronger than hate, love is stronger than evil, and it was Vegenrage who gave me the freedom to learn this for myself. I have just achieved true freedom. I have kicked you out of my mind, Vemenomous. Your haunting images, your horror and evil will taint me no more. Vegenrage taught me how to fight you, and Vegenrage gave me the power to take on evil. You will never leave us be, so I will destroy you. I will prove that love is stronger than hate," says Farrah as she starts walking toward Roartill and Vemenomous. She is getting so worked up, preparing to make the most powerful premeditated attack she has ever made, that she bursts into flames again. She is forgetting that she is standing on the red sand. Roartill and Vemenomous can feel the electricity in the air as swirling purple and red light start to spin around Farrah, who is already covered in flames. Blue light is added to the mix, and Farrah is obviously getting ready to make a devastating attack.

"Be careful, little girl. I only want you to be free to rule the Maglical System as you see fit. If you dare make an attack of any kind on me, that will be your last. This is my only warning to you, Farrah. Make no mistake. I am the supreme power here, and I can make another the demonian dragon queen, if not you. I can sense you are getting ready to attack, and before I have to destroy you and make another demonian dragon queen, I offer you this last chance to have all. The fact that I have not attacked you and destroyed you already, knowing you have hostile intentions toward me, is a sign of my magnanimity, and I offer one last time for you not only to be a part of the Maglical System but to rule it supreme."

Farrah has heard all she is going to hear, and she thrusts her hands forward, her left hand at Roartill and her right at Vemenomous. She is not using her dragon-slaying hands;

she is using another spell called force driver. This spell is a magical energy that acts just like a drill bit. Farrah is starting to use her magical gift, she is remembering what Vegenrage has taught her, and she is projecting her mind in the form of magical energy. This is a very powerful spell, easily strong enough to drill enormous holes through both Roartill and Vemenomous, but Farrah has forgotten she is standing on the red sand, and she is induced into casting magic by Roartill. He now uses this to his advantage and deflects Farrah's magical energy toward Vegenrage. She can see the magical energy in the form of a huge drill bit flying up in the air and hitting him right in his stomach and drilling him in two. Vegenrage and his arms are flapping on the sand. Logantrance jumps back from Vegenrage, sitting on the sand, completely surprised to see what has happened to Vegenrage after he has just healed all his burned and melted flesh. Vegenrage's stomach from the bottom of his ribs to his hips is gone.

Vegenrage tilts up, supporting himself with his arms, when the second magical drill intended for Vemenomous comes down right on his head. It drills away half of his head and most of his right shoulder. Farrah screams in disbelief and tries to run for Vegenrage. Roartill swoops his long and enormous right arm and hand down, catching Farrah in his palm. He brings her up toward his face and punctures her stomach with the long black claw on his left index finger. He releases her with his right hand, and Farrah is stuck to his claw, which has protruded out her back. Roartill looks to Vemenomous, saying, "Get ready. We will only get one chance at this when he comes, so make it count."

"I am ready, Master. The second he arrives, I will strike Farrah with the shard hammer," says Vemenomous.

Logantrance waits one second and rushes to the dismembered remains of Vegenrage and holds up Vegenrage's left arm. He can see the band of life become visible, and the golden F fades away. Vegenrage's body reforms remarkably fast. Behaggen has floated over to Logantrance earlier, and Logantrance puts him on Vegenrage's reformed waist. Behaggen spits up some dark pants and a dark shirt, along with dark shoes, for Vegenrage to wear.

Vegenrage gets up and flies with incredible speed right at Farrah, just like Roartill and Vemenomous know he will. He flies through the air, stopping by the back of Farrah, grasping her arms with his hands. He has spectacular silvery blue lights dancing all around him, and he pulls Farrah off Roartill's claw. The second she is removed, Vemenomous strikes her in the stomach with the shard hammer. Vegenrage flies back out over the natural sand, and Farrah is spewing red flames and sparks, just like she has the last time she has been struck by this demonic weapon. Vegenrage hurries over to Logantrance and lands with Farrah. Roartill and Vemenomous sink back into the red sand, which disappears.

Vegenrage has Farrah, but she is shooting evil red flame and sparks from her stomach. He turns Farrah to face him, and he hugs her, absorbing the sparks spewing from her stomach and right into his until they stop flowing. Farrah starts to glow red. Her outline is gleaming with dancing red light, whereas Vegenrage is shining with dancing blue light. He holds Farrah's hands and steps back from her. He looks up into the air, screaming, looking like he is in great pain, and he starts to draw all the evil from Farrah into him. The red light starts to float and fly into Vegenrage, traveling down Farrah's arms to her hands into Vegenrage's. The red flaming sparks start shooting from Farrah's stomach again and right into Vegenrage's, and he is absorbing them. The lights start to slow, and they become wisps floating from Farrah's legs, stomach, and arms into Vegenrage. The red light is starting to fade away and is almost gone. Vegenrage is struggling, but he is absorbing all this magical energy and relieving Farrah of this evil burden cast upon her by the shard hammer.

Farrah has been under a sort of trance, unaware of what is going on, and she regains her composure, shaking her head and seeing Vegenrage in front of her. "What are you doing?" she says, looking at Vegenrage and over herself as well. "What are you doing?" Farrah, for the first time, takes a defensive posture against Vegenrage. She pounds both her open palms into Vegenrage's chest, and he flies back into the sand. "What do you think you are doing, Vegenrage? First, you give me magic. You teach me how to use it, and now you want to take it from me? Do you think I am becoming too strong for you? Is that it?"

"Not too strong for me, too strong for anyone. You need to learn how to control your magical draw. Roartill and Vemenomous have struck you with the shard hammer, and this hides you from your magical draw. This is very dangerous because if you become too powerful, it will manifest itself in a very bad way. You have to come back to Vollenbeln with me so I can help you learn how to control this," says Vegenrage.

Farrah takes a step back from Vegenrage and flicks both her hands, looking at them, and she starts to glow red, and dancing red light comes back to her outline. "What do you mean? I feel it. I can feel the magic surging through me. I can sense things now. I can sense where the danger and the trouble is. You are always so anxious to go help those in need. So why stop me? I think I want to go help those in need, even that king Ulegwahn, who obviously is in love with me. I know he loves me, and I am not particularly interested in him, but Oriapow and the dwarves are in the Erkensharie, and great danger is heading for them. Actually, you are my love, Vegenrage, but I think it is time for you to follow me for a change. I do love you, but do you love me? Well, let's find out. If you love me, you will come after me. You will help me destroy the evil heading for the Erkensharie right now," says Farrah.

"Farrah, wait. If you love me, then trust me. Come here and let me relieve the magical pressure on you. You do not feel it, but it is there. Trust me," says Vegenrage.

"I do trust you, Vegenrage. I love you, and I bet you will follow me," says Farrah, who is surprisingly all giggly and smiles like she is playing with Vegenrage.

"Farrah, no! Farrah, don't go!" yells Vegenrage, but Farrah has slipped into a dimension door, and she is gone.

"Vegenrage, do not go after her. She is becoming an unstoppable power even for you, and she has to make her own way now," says Logantrance.

"I know, but it is I who gave her the ability to draw magic and learn its use. I cannot abandon her now. I never thought she would become such an incredible draw of the magic from the Maglical System," says Vegenrage.

"It is Vemenomous and Roartill. Somehow they knew Farrah would be empowered by you, and somehow they knew you would be in love with her. They have always known this, and they must have planned on using Farrah to get to you from the start. She cannot feel or control her magical draw because of the demonic magic placed in her from the shard hammer and from the demon seed planted in her by Vemenomous. These two things combined allow them access to her mind. Vegenrage, you have to know they will use Farrah to destroy you," says Logantrance.

"I know they will try, but I will not give up on her. I will do what I have to do to make sure they never have her under their control. I will draw the demonic magic from her and get her senses back for her, and then I will teach her how to control her magical draw," says Vegenrage.

"I know I cannot stop you, so you have my blessings. I wish you the best, Vegenrage. Behaggen, you will make sure Vegenrage stays well equipped, right? He does not always think of all the unique and useful items you have within," says Logantrance. Behaggen stays quiet, not responding.

"Farrah has gone to the Erkensharie. I will go get her and bring out the evil that has been forced into her soul," says Vegenrage.

"I know I can feel she has gone there. I will go to Richterblen. I have some things to study up on. Be careful, Vegenrage, and I will not be far away should you need help," says Logantrance.

"Wait, do you hear that? Can you hear Inglelapse calling?" says Vegenrage.

"I do not, Vegenrage. I hear nothing," says Logantrance.

"I have to make a quick stop on Kronton, in Elbutan, where Mournbow and Inglelapse and the people from Mourbarria and Valvernva had followed Farrah and me. I must go there," says Vegenrage.

"I must go to my home now. I will see you soon, my boy," says Logantrance.

"I will see you soon," says Vegenrage.

CHAPTER 24

Hornspire's Books Side with the Races of Man

Zevoncour has risen to the surface of Fargloin, where his army of hellmen and helldogs has moved from the mountains of Glaboria to the Sand Marshes of Smyle. The army is moving at a very slow rate and will take weeks to reach the Erkensharie, but Roartill will have none of this. Zevoncour halts his army.

"We wait here, my children. Our master is going to make an entrance, and he has words for us," Zevoncour tells his army.

Roartill rises from the earth in front of the army, standing ten feet tall. His form and shape is flames, but he does have mass, like he is red mud on fire. He walks and moves, with his footsteps leaving smoke and steam rising from the heated sand he has walked on. Drops of molten, burning mud fall from his body and burn the ground. Zevoncour bows to one knee as Roartill approaches him.

"My master makes an appearance on the outer realm. There must be great news and instruction. What is your wish?" says Zevoncour with his head facing the ground.

"Stand, Zevoncour, and face me when I talk to you," says Roartill.

"Yes, Master," says Zevoncour, standing and facing Roartill.

"This march will take far too long. I need for my army to be attacking the Erkensharie immediately. There are great events happening, and we need to speed things up. I will cast demon speed on you and my army here. Zevoncour, you will lead them to and through the Long Forest, where the demon speed spell will have lost its power. You will take them through the Nomberry Pass toward the Erkensharie. The Long Forest has been completely overrun with the Dark Bush, so you and my army will have no confrontation until you reach the Erkensharie. Your immediate task is to lead my army to the Nomberry Pass. From there, we will see how events unfold." Roartill spreads his flaming arms and blows from his huge mouth. Flames from all over his muddy body flow into the breath and form a flamethrower that spreads through the vast army, taking up half-a-mile diameter of land. Roartill blows his flames back and forth, saturating the entire army in flames.

"My master, Hornspire has been eliminated, but still he sends books of future events to the races of man and the dragons. How do we combat and prevent the living from being aware of our plans?" says Zevoncour.

"You do not worry about the writings of Hornspire. I have all this under control. He may send the races of man and the dragons some insight into the future, but he cannot foresee all that I know. He cannot predict the changes that will happen. Besides the war, the pain and grief, along with all the misery, is the fun. Now lead my army to the Nomberry Pass. I will be waiting for you there, and things should get very interesting," says Roartill.

The demon speed spell cast on the demon army, along with Zevoncour, is very interesting. This spell allows the entire army to move without expending any energy. They actually hover just above the ground and move like they are on an escalator at incredible speed. This spell does not give the hellmen or the helldogs any extra speed or strength; it just allows the whole army to move as one and very fast. Zevoncour leads the army, and they move toward Nomberry Pass. They will make it all the way to the pass and through the Long Forests in a day, and this, of course, is much faster than what the elves of the Erkensharie expect.

After Farrah has left the Erkensharie, Ulegwahn is furious. "Vegenrage and Farrah are fugitives from the Erkensharie," he says to all the elves in the courtyard.

All the elves are in disbelief. No one knows what to say, and Oriapow lends his thoughts.

"Ulegwahn, what are you saying? Vegenrage and Farrah did use the staff of barrier breath, but they had no idea that, a very long time ago, it was given to the king of the Erkensharie. Yes, Vegenrage did take Pluanges from the Mystical Erkens, but he was in need of them. If you put them on the defensive against the elves of the Erkensharie, you exile the two who can help us the most in defeating the demons. Not only that but who here can apprehend Vegenrage or Farrah as well? None of us can. You heard Logantrance and what he said. Farrah is becoming the most powerful magical being in the

Maglical System, and Vegenrage may already be the most powerful. We need them as allies, not as enemies. You know this, so why are you trying to make them criminals of the Erkensharie? This makes no sense," says Oriapow.

"I will hear no more of this. Vegenrage and Farrah are no allies to the Erkensharie, and if anyone sees them, they are to be apprehended and brought to me. Is that understood?" Ulegwahn says to all the elves in the courtyard. "Now come with me, Oriapow. It is time for us to go and read *The King of the Erkensharie*. Sombons, Lentoz, Angribe, and Pryzill, watch our borders and scan for the demon horde coming our way. I want to know how soon they will be here and where they plan on entering the Erkensharie Forest. Also, keep me updated on the Dark Bush. I want to know if it still spreads into the Erkensharie Forest. Kearsebe and Thambrable, gather all the bow elves and keep everyone alert and ready for deployment. Cellertrill, gather our warrior class and be ready for the attack that is coming. Sileyen, you watch here at our new great wall in the courtyard with your bow elf regiment. Glimtron, will you and your dwarves stay here in the courtyard and stand guard with our warriors and wait for our return?" Glimtron nods yes, a little discouraged to see and hear Ulegwahn is still making enemies of Vegenrage and Farrah. "Whenshade, you come with Oriapow and me. We go to the Great Erken to read from the book."

Ulegwahn leads the way, and Oriapow and Whenshade follow him to the Great Erken and to the throne room, where Ulegwahn starts to read from the book *The King of the Erkensharie*. The three of them spend all night and most of the next day reading and discussing the content of the book.

They actually read all of it, and by the time they are finished, they are enlightened and exhausted and go to get some rest.

"The book sheds new light on Farrah and Vegenrage. I will have to reconsider my current thoughts on these two important human beings. We will see if events unfold as told in the book. If they do, then things will be happening very soon, much faster than we had anticipated. We need to get some rest and be prepared because we will be woken to mayhem. Go now and get some rest. I will send word to all the Erkensharie that the demon horde may be upon us as soon as tonight. I will summon all my power from the Octagemerwell, and we will be ready. If Farrah is to save the Erkensharie, then we shall be indebted to her. If Vegenrage sacrifices his life to save Farrah, then I will have been wrong about him as well. Oriapow, be well rested and strengthen your bond with the Octagemerwell because all of your magical power may soon be needed. Go now. We have no more time to waste. Get rested and get ready for war," says Ulegwahn.

Meanwhile, the day before on Strabalster, Shenlylith, Basters, Cloakenstrike, and Fraborn have gone to Basters's throne room, where Shenlylith reads from the book given to her by Basters. The Ugorian elves want to be present at this reading, and Basters allows their wishes. Bronsilith, Verlyle, and Gandeleem listen for the bow elves. Willithcar, the top general in the Ugorian warrior class, is there with Tornsclin and Gonbilden. Stromgin and Vorgillith are there listening for the horse riders. This book has been magically sealed, and the words of the book only appear when in the hands of

Shenlylith. The book will only open and allow its pages to be turned by her hands. She reads the cover: *The King of Ugoria: Book Two.* Shenlylith begins reading the book.

Meanwhile, in Riobe, the Helven have all been possessed by demons except for Kerben and Weesilibith. They have been protected from possession by the rings of essence that Kerben has pulled from Silntis, his bag of holding, which he is able to hide on his person within his robe without detection from the Ugorian elves. Kerben and Weesilibith play along with the rest of the Helven as Inthamus leads them on a prison break.

The Ugorian bow elves watching the prison have been alerted by all the smoke filling it, and they cannot see in. They have no idea what is going on in there, but they hear the screams of Dona'try, who has just morphed into the demon Inthamus. Braider, the leader of the twenty bow elves guarding the gate at Riobe, calls all the elves to stand around the prison gate. He orders his elves to brandish their bows and be ready as the smoke filters out from the prison through the bars. The elves start to see glowing red light coming from the prison, and they all ready their bows. They have no idea what is going on, and Braider is starting to get very concerned. He orders Thimlias to return to the Ugorian Palace with news of the trouble happening here, but he is too late. Dark gray arrows made out of smoke but still deadly shoot from inside the prison. The arrows hit all the elves right in the chest. The elves do not have a chance. The smoke arrows cut through their light armor and rip holes in all of them, who fall dying.

Inthamus laughs as he casts the superheat spell from his wide oblong mouth and melts the bars of the prison. He walks like a rabbit, leaning forward on his front arms and taking a short hop to move his hind legs forward. When he gets out of the prison, he stands upright, and he is so odd looking. He seems to be all leg, towering at ten feet tall with a huge fat belly, chest, and head. His arms are very odd looking as well, very long and slender with sharp talons at his fingers. He can walk with huge strides, or he can hop very long distances quick as a flash if need be. Inthamus turns to his demons, motioning them all to follow him. "We go to the Ugorian Palace, and we put an end to the elves. Servorious comes from the mountains with an army of hellmen, helldogs, and winged Lizangars. We will meet at the palace and crush the elves, and Strabalster is ours," he says, laughing and heading toward the palace, followed by his demons.

All of Hornspire's visions had become inaccurate when Vegenrage did not die at the water's edge in the Sand Marshes of Smyle. All his visions had to be replaced by new ones, and he had none when he confronted all the dragons and told them Vegenrage had to be destroyed. Of course, the dragons had their suspicions about Hornspire and did not actively seek to destroy Vegenrage. Shortly after Hornspire had confronted all the remaining dragons, he had a storm of visions coming to him. They came much faster than normal, and he could see so many scenarios playing out. A scenario played out where Blethstole was to kill him—and by the way, Hornspire did see this—but he also saw other scenarios where Blethstole did not kill him. Hornspire believed Blethstole would not kill him, but he was wrong. Hornspire did take into account that he may be killed by Blethstole, and in this event, he prepared ten books to help the races of man defeat the demons. That was in play now, and Hornspire by design had his fourth fifth and sixth books all rise at the same time. This would happen when Vegenrage spoke the name Age'venger.

A great surge of magical energy lifted from the center of Strabalster where Roartill had been contained. This magical flow powered the rising of the three books magically prepared by Hornspire, one in the Erkensharie courtyard, one in the Ugorian Palace courtyard, and one in Breezzele. He knew who would be at these locations at this time, and he planned for each of these three books to be read by specific individuals, and all was playing out as he saw.

The most important of these books is the one that rose in Breezzele. The human race at this time is, by far, the weakest race of man, with the exception of the dwarves, who have been all but eliminated by the demons. They are the smallest race in terms of numbers, but what they are is the foundation for all the elves, all the dwarves, and all the humanors. The human race is destined to be the dominant race of man, and Hornspire has seen in every scenario that the human race wins out over all others. Hornspire has seen the demons take over the Maglical System and kill all the races of man, but Hornspire has put his writings in the hands of man to help them defeat the demons. This book rising in Breezzele is the most important of his last ten books so far. What the races of man do in the Elbutan Forest and Highlands is critical for the survival of the races of man. Hornspire has seen with his death that there is no scenario where the dragons will ever regain the dominant species of the Maglical System. They are already a dying species, and their time is already limited, so Hornspire has decided to help the races of man with his writings.

Mournbow has handed the book to Inglelapse. There is a noticeable hush, as everyone here is curious about the book Inglelapse now holds. "Well, Inglelapse? Can you read it? Can you open it?" asks Mournbow.

"Wait a second. Hold on. Give me a minute," says Inglelapse, inspecting the book. "I see no writing on the book at all, and I cannot open it. I know what we have to do. I will call Vegenrage. I don't know why I just know I have to call for Vegenrage. He will know what to do." Inglelapse holds the book near his chest and closes his eyes. He concentrates using telepathy to call for Vegenrage. To his and the crowd's amazement, Vegenrage walks from his dimension door right next to Inglelapse.

"Vegenrage, that is amazing I just called for you, and you are here. Here, here," says Inglelapse, handing the book to Vegenrage. "I have something here, and I think it is for you." Vegenrage takes the book from Inglelapse and looks it over. He places his right hand on the book, closes his eyes, and concentrates for a few moments.

"Vegenrage, what has happened? I mean, you are absolutely radiating magical energy. I have never felt your magical presence like I can feel it now," says Inglelapse.

Vegenrage opens his eyes and hands the book back to Inglelapse. "It is Farrah you feel. She is growing magically at an exponential rate, and I tried to relieve the magical pressure on her by drawing it away from her. She does not realize how powerful she is becoming. She was under the mind control of Vemenomous and Roartill and hit me with her dragon-slaying hands spell. If I were not saved by Logantrance, she would have killed me. I am still slowly venting the magical energy. I am very worried for her, and I have to get to her right away. Inglelapse, this is a very important book. You, Mournbow, and all of you here in Breezzele listen as Inglelapse reads this book to you. Your future is written in this book. I must go to Farrah now. Inglelapse, I do not know what is going to happen here in the very near future, but I have to try to save Farrah. She is so strong now. Her magic is so powerful that she may destroy me, but it was I who brought this on her, and I will do all I can to bring her out of it. You can read this book now, and it is very important. It will tell you all you need to know, and do not wait. Read it now and prepare. I must go now," says Vegenrage.

"Vegenrage, be safe, and we look forward to seeing you very soon," says Mournbow.

"Vegenrage, you are going to the Long Forest on the planet Fargloin, aren't you? I can feel her, and I am not even a very powerful magic user. I can feel her, and she is so strong. Vegenrage, you be careful, and you come back with Farrah. OK?" says Inglelapse.

"I will do what I can," says Vegenrage, and he walks through a dimension door.

The demon army has arrived at the Nomberry Pass, entering the Long Forest. It is named Long Forest because it stretches from the northeastern top of the Erkensharie Forest, and it travels along the Smildren Sea past the Ruin of Altrar and the Mountain Creek Hillyards. It then heads south past the Ilkergire and ends at the Smildren Sea. The Long Forest is over one thousand miles long and nearly four hundred miles wide in some places. There is only one great sea on the planet Fargloin, and that is the Smildren Sea. The Long Forest actually runs along the northern edge of the Smildren Sea, and then it arcs southward, running across the land into the southern tip of the Smildren Sea. The Nomberry Pass is at the northeastern top of the Erkensharie Forest, and it cuts through the Long Forest to the Smildren Sea. The sea then runs north along the Sand Marshes of Smyle, and north of that is the Glaborian Mountains, which are still spewing hundred thousand tons of toxic ash into the sky, and all of Erkensharie and most of the Dry Flats of Hilternor are now blocked from the sun.

Zevoncour halts his army at the Nomberry Pass and looks at the Long Forest, which is now completely overrun with the Dark Bush. The army halts behind Zevoncour, and the demon speed spell wears off them. Demons can walk through the Dark Bush without being hurt because they are immune to rot and decay. Even if the Dark Bush were to cut them, the poison would not affect them. Demons are living flesh on the outer realms, but they are still immune to decay, rot, and most poisons. Hellmen and helldogs are covered in flames, and this will burn the Dark Bush. Dark Bush is so thick that a human, an elf, or even a dwarf cannot walk through it. Interestingly enough, the Dark Bush will actually spread apart and let demons walk on through. Zevoncour gets a telepathic message from Roartill and is commanded to walk ahead of the army alone. Zevoncour has his army wait while he walks ahead, and the Dark Bush spreads apart, so he can walk on down the Nomberry Pass. Zevoncour walks but a quarter mile, and there waiting for him is Roartill.

"Zevoncour, my servant, the time has come. I have been waiting for this for a long time. I had you come here alone because you are going to descend back into the inner realm with me while the army behind you heads on to the Erkensharie. We will watch the events that are about to unfold, and there is going to be greatness happening," says Roartill.

"Master, I want to fight the living. I want to inflict the greatest of pain. I want to inflict the most horrific of injury. I want to kill and feast on the living," says Zevoncour.

Roartill laughs. "I like your spirit, Zevoncour, and I will let you kill. As a matter of fact, I will let you lead your army through the Long Forest, and the only one you will face is that little girl. All you have to do is kill her, and then the Erkensharie is yours. Oh, Vegenrage may show up to try to save her, but these two puny humans are no match for you and your army of hellmen and helldogs," says Roartill.

"Farrah and Vegenrage together. Master, you know this army is no match for them. Why send them into slaughter? I can sense that Farrah is becoming a Swellgic. Master, you are the only other Swellgic ever in the Maglical System. Age'venger could not destroy your power, and he sacrificed his eternal life to contain you and draw your magical power from you. Now Vegenrage is imbued by Age'venger, and Farrah is becoming the eternal power. Do you not fear your rule is in jeopardy? I see you want to watch as Farrah and Vegenrage fight with and destroy each other, and you will pick up the pieces. I get it. I will take your advice, and I will travel into the earth with you, Master," says Zevoncour.

"That is what I thought. Go and tell your army to move on to the Erkensharie. They will have to move by foot from here on in. I am very curious to see how this unfolds," says Roartill, sinking back into the earth.

"Yes, Master, I will send the army on to the Erkensharie," says Zevoncour, and he goes back to the army waiting for him. Zevoncour tells his army that he has been summoned by Roartill to go back to the inner realm and that the army is to travel to the Erkensharie on foot. Zevoncour will meet up with them later, and if not, the army is to move right on into the Erkensharie and destroy the elves.

The army does not hesitate at all, and they move on down the Nomberry Pass. The Dark Bush moves to the side, and the pass opens up plenty wide for the army to walk down. Some of the hellmen are riding the helldogs, and more of them are walking. This is quite a scary sight. The dark is brightened up by the flaming hellmen and helldogs walking down the pass. By the time all the army is on the pass, it is over a mile long, and they are six men wide in places. They move slowly but at a consistent pace.

This army is grotesque with all the members having cuts, scrapes, gouges, and wounds all over their bodies, which one can see through the flames. They all have the meanest, downright nasty-looking faces ever. The hellmen have large flaming clubs, and the helldogs walk with their heads and necks drooping from their shoulders. The saliva falling from the helldogs' mouths is on fire, and there are drips of flaming saliva down the pass. The helldogs make deep grumbling sounds as they walk, and the hellmen grunt and groan. This is a nasty army, even though they are not smart. They are not fast or nimble, but they are deadly if they scratch or cut anyone because rot and infection is a result if they draw blood. They are so hot that they can cause burns to living flesh by just being close.

They march toward the Erkensharie, and Sombons, Lentoz, Angribe, and Pryzill catch on to their presence once the army gets halfway down the Nomberry Pass. The magic users go back to the Great Erken to tell King Ulegwahn of the approaching army, and no one has expected this to happen so fast. There is actually panic in the magic users, but when they get back to the Erkensharie and wake King Ulegwahn, he seems to be not worried at all.

Once woken from his sleep, Oriapow takes the magic users to get some food, and they talk. He tells them how the book *The King of the Erkensharie* tells all the happenings just as the magic users have seen so far, and he explains the events of the next few days. There is surprising calm in King Ulegwahn and Oriapow that wears off on the returning magic users, and they eat and wait as events are about to unfold according to the writings of the book, which include Farrah and Vegenrage.

Chapter 25

Farrah's Bloodlust

The demon army is making its way through the Nomberry Pass, and they are now moving at a brisk pace. The Dark Bush—which is a very thick, tangling weave of dead thicket—untangles itself, spreads apart, and moves aside as the demon army walks down along the path and closes up behind them. The Long Forest has been one of the great forests on the planet Fargloin. It has been full of color, plant life, and numerous species of mammals, birds, and insects. Now all the plant life has been devoured by the Dark Bush, and all the mammal species have been killed, as well as the birds. Most insects are not affected by the Dark Bush, but with no plant life to feed on and no mammals for nourishing blood meal, they are dying off as well. The dark sky now covers all of the Long Forest, and the muddy earth is exposed since the grasses and bushes have been eradicated. This formerly beautiful and full-of-life forest is now dark and dead. The eerie dark here rivals that of the Wickenfall Forest, but even that has life in it. The life there may be horrific, but the forest is not completely void of life, like the Long Forest now is.

The army marches on, and with less than five miles until they reach the end of the Nomberry Pass, the leaders of the army can see a red light moving through the sky toward them. It gets closer, and they can see it is in the form of a human, and it is moving right for them. It is Farrah, and she can see the whole army moving down the pass. The army takes up a mile-long stretch of the pass, and she can see how the Dark Bush opens in front of them and closes behind them. The leaders of the army halt, and the whole army can now see Farrah as she bursts a much wider girth of flames. Her eyes glow deep red, and the flames around her burn very hot and very red as well. Farrah is the only light outside of the demons, who are flaming themselves.

Farrah lowers herself into the Dark Bush in front of the army, and she intensifies the flames and heat given off by her body. She is so hot that the bush and the ground beneath her are instantly incinerated by her heat and flame. A fifteen-yard diameter around Farrah is cleared. She walks toward the demon army, and the bush is burned away. The Dark Bush can make no advance on Farrah, or it will be incinerated. The leaders in front of the demon army get anxious. They can see the light given off by Farrah and the Dark Bush being reduced to ashes as she moves down the path toward them. The helldogs start to bark and howl, and the hellmen begin to beat their free hand with their flaming clubs. Farrah walks into view of the demon army, and all the Dark Bush has been incinerated between them. There is a moment of surprising curiosity by the army as the hellmen look at one another, and Farrah speaks. "So this is the army heading toward the

Erkensharie? This is all your ruler, Roartill, can come up with? Let me show you what one little girl can do."

Roartill has brought Zevoncour to the surface, and they are far away from Farrah in the Long Forest, but Roartill has run his hand across the land, creating a screen from which they can watch and hear what is going on.

"Roartill, she is too strong for our army. I can feel her strength right now. She is already Swellgic. She will destroy our army. Maybe if I and Vemenomous, along with Xanorax, all attack her at once, we can defeat her," says Zevoncour.

"No, my servant. Watch. Just watch. This is going to be our greatest champion. We need for her to swell. We need for her to kill and destroy. We need her to forget that little girl released from mind control of the witch. We need her to become self-sufficient, powerful, and independent of all others, especially Vegenrage, and then she is ours. Watch, Zevoncour, watch," says Roartill.

Vemenomous rises from the spreading earth to the other side of Zevoncour. "Vegenrage will come to save the girl like before, but this time the girl is much too powerful. This time the girl will defeat Vegenrage for us. Then the girl will be my queen," says Vemenomous.

"Or Vegenrage will kill the girl," says Zevoncour.

"We will see. We will see," says Vemenomous.

The helldogs charge and jump at Farrah, who rises into the air at about six feet. She points her hands at the first helldogs that get near her. Red lightning shoot from her hands and arms. The helldogs are hit by the lightning and get frozen in midair, and the lightning acts like a syringe. The helldogs shrink and implode. The lightning stays attached to

Farrah, and the life essence of the helldogs is drawn through the lightning into her. She is getting stronger with each kill.

The fire around Farrah grows, and the helldogs keep charging. It does not matter how many of them charge at Farrah because the lightning is shooting from all over her body. The helldogs are imploding all around. Once one is gone, it is replaced by another helldog, which jumps at Farrah. They are all caught by the lightning, and their life force is drawn away and their bodies implode. This is unimaginable power, as the helldogs keep charging and jumping in the air at Farrah. Once hit by the life-draining lightning, they are frozen, their chest cavities crunch inward, and their bones crack, pop, and break. Blood is splattering all over the place, and sacks of flesh and bone are falling to the ground all in front of Farrah.

The hellmen are now within range and throw at Farrah their clubs, which take the form of burning javelins when hurled. She starts to laugh, as the javelins hit what seems to be a barrier around her, burst into splinters and shards, and break apart, falling harmlessly to the ground. Farrah is laughing more and more, and she starts to move forward through the air. She lowers herself at about four feet off the ground and moves right at the army. Lightning is shooting from all over Farrah's body like she is a plasma globe. Helldogs and hellmen are caught by her lightning, and their bodies are frozen, crumpled, and sucked inward until a bloody sack of bone and flesh falls to the ground like raindrops all around her as she moves forward through the army, literally killing tens and tens of hellmen and helldogs at a time. There is about a foot-wide barrier between Farrah and the red flames burning all around her. Her eyes are glowing a reddish yellow color, and her magical strength is growing with each life force she consumes.

Farrah, for the first time, can feel her magical energy radiating from within her, and she loves it. She feels her magical strength and clenches her fists, flexing her biceps, feeling strong and invincible. She starts shooting real lightning bolts from her hands, exploding hellmen and helldogs, spraying the Dark Bush with blood and carnage. She lowers to the ground, and her flames now reach out about eight yards, incinerating the bush around her. She slices the helldogs and hellmen with the blades of sharpness, dismembering their bodies and dropping them in bloody pieces. Farrah points her hands in front of her head and spreads the flames before her, blowing very lightly through the hole, and winds so strong and frigid freeze tens and tens of helldogs and hellmen. She draws Quadrapierce and runs at the frozen statutes, swinging her blade up and down and around her back and in all different ways like she is practicing for a sword fight. All the frozen demons are shattered and fall to the ground in shards. Farrah puts a huge smile on her face, and she looks up to the sky, replacing Quadrapierce in her left forearm sheath.

"Master, I don't understand. Farrah is killing our army, and she is only getting stronger in the process. I know we want her as the demonian dragon queen, but is she not becoming so powerful that she will destroy us too?" asks Zevoncour.

"Wait, Zevoncour, the time is coming. He is coming. This is what we have been waiting for. He is here. Vemenomous, the time is coming. Go get Xanorax and bring him back here," says Roartill.

"Yes, Master," says Vemenomous, and he takes wing and speeds through a dimension door.

"Now watch, Zevoncour. This is what we have been waiting for. The grand finale is about to begin," says Roartill.

Farrah looks up into the sky, smiling and slowly flying up. She has destroyed nearly 85 percent of the demon army and completely ignores those remaining as she flies out of their reach. She swoops back toward the earth and flies headfirst at the remaining demons, and she stops on the Nomberry Pass in front of them. Her flames are bright and incinerating the ground and Dark Bush around her. The demon army realizes they can do nothing against Farrah, and they simply hold their ground, not advancing or retreating.

"Vegenrage, I knew you would come. I knew you would come be with me," says Farrah, looking up into the sky as Vegenrage comes forth from his dimension door. Farrah smiles big and watches as he floats down to the Nomberry Pass. Vegenrage is glowing a silvery blue light, but when he reaches the top of the Dark Bush, he changes, and flames extend from his form—very hot flames that incinerate any Dark Bush that touch them. The flames surrounding Vegenrage are blue and silver but very hot. Vegenrage and Farrah are standing face-to-face, not touching each other, but the flames from each of their bodies create a very wide circle of fire around the two of them, and no Dark Bush can enter this, or it will be incinerated.

"Farrah, we cannot be here. Farrah, we have to go. We have to go right now," says Vegenrage, very worried.

"We will go, but there is no rush. I have things all under control," says Farrah.

"If you have things under control, then why do you not stop your magical magnetism? Farrah, you are becoming Swellgic. Do you know what that means?" asks Vegenrage.

"Of course, I know what that means. It means I am drawing magical energy from my surroundings, just like you do," says Farrah.

"No, Farrah, not like me. I use Vollenbeln as my magical source of energy. Yes, I can draw from other places in the Maglical System, but you, Farrah, you are drawing all the time, and you do not realize it. You have to stop your magical draw, or you as a person will become unstable. I thought you would have time to absorb all the books in my library and learn to control your magical energy as I have learned to do. My library was destroyed before you were able to gain all its knowledge, and now Roartill and Vemenomous are exploiting your magical energy. They are able to use a form of charm on you because Alisluxkana had your mind under her charm for most of your life. Vemenomous sends images into your mind, causing you pain, grief, anger, and rage. This makes you lash out violently, and then they release you back to your senses, hoping you will hurt or kill your friends, and you will have nowhere to turn but to Vemenomous and Roartill. They will say all kinds of things like no one but they are your true friends. Farrah, you have to believe me. You have to love and trust me. They are trying to take you from me, and I love you.

I want you and me to be together always, so come with me. Come back to Vollenbeln with me," says Vegenrage.

"That's not true. You are jealous that I am now as powerful as you are. I feel fine. There is nothing unstable about me. Why do you say that?" asks Farrah.

"When you see images in your head, that is because evil has struck you with the shard hammer, an evil weapon that works in unison with the DNA of Vemenomous, who has invaded your blood from the demon seed. They put images into your head, and for a short time, evil can control you. What I mean is they can make you fearful. They can scare you by putting terrible images into your head, and they can cause you to act without knowing exactly what you are doing. They have done this for a while to you, Farrah. They did it to you when you were bathing in Mournbow's bath. You could see Vemenomous when we were traveling to the Elbutan Forest and Highlands and most recently in the Ackelson Desert, where you hit me with your dragon slaying hands spell. Now since they have struck you with the shard hammer, they are able to make the images you see seem so real. It is so hard for you to distinguish the images they are projecting in your mind from reality, and this is what they want. This is how they draw you to them. The images they are putting in your head is why you attacked me, and you did not know you were attacking me. Farrah, you have to trust me. You have to believe me. You have to come with me. We have to leave now," says Vegenrage.

The demon army charges at Farrah and Vegenrage. Farrah turns because her back is to the advancing army. She thrusts her right hand toward the army, and four invisible blades of sharpness shoot down the pass, dismembering and dropping the rest of the demon army to the ground in pieces. Farrah watches as all the demons fall in pieces to a bloody mess on the pass. Just before she turns back to face Vegenrage, she sees two bright golden eyes twelve feet off the ground far down the pass moving toward her. She cannot look away; she is mesmerized by the stare of the eyes, which keep walking closer and closer to her. She starts to move toward the eyes, walking down the pass. She cannot hear Vegenrage calling for her. Vemenomous walks into view, and she sees him in his demonian dragon form. He shakes his head from side to side and grumbles very loudly. "Farrah, it is time. Now is the time for you to become my queen. I have waited for so long, and I have courted you long enough. I will ask no more. Now I will take," says Vemenomous.

Vegenrage is aware that Farrah is under charm yet again, and he knows the danger Farrah is in. He also knows the danger and risk that he has to take in order to save her from the evil trying to manipulate her mind. Vegenrage knows the only thing he can do is try to absorb the magical energy that is growing inside of her. He will absorb and draw this magic into himself. He has to draw so much energy from her that she becomes tired and sleepy. This will allow Vegenrage to sweep her away to Vollenbeln. If he does not do this, Farrah will unleash great magic with unimaginable power and destruction. Where this magic will be focused and to whom or what is unknown, but Vemenomous and Roartill are slowly gaining control of Farrah whether she thinks so or not. Vegenrage knows he has to act.

The ring of fire around Farrah is very hot and now almost ten yards in diameter. Vegenrage and Farrah, standing face-to-face, has created a single wider circle of fire that is powered by both of their magic. In order for Vegenrage to touch Farrah, he will have to enter her circle of fire. He will initially get burned until inside of Farrah's fire ring, but he has a necklace of fire resistance in Behaggen, and he quickly retrieves it and puts it on. Vegenrage has to be touching Farrah, and this will be difficult. Farrah is radiating magical energy, and even though she does not know it, she is getting ready to unleash great magical energy. He will try to absorb or steal her magic, and naturally, she will repel him. They are unique and individual magical beings as all magical beings are. He, in a magical sense, will be the same as Farrah, and he will be repelled like a magnet once he imitates Farrah's magical identity. He will not able to touch her initially. This is when he will get burned by Farrah's fire ring, but his necklace of fire resistance will protect him from this but not completely because she is too magically powerful.

Fortunately, when Vegenrage taught Farrah the power of absorption in Vollenbeln, he had to enter her mind and work as one with her. When Vegenrage did this with Farrah, he and she were magically one. Farrah drew from Vegenrage, and this cost him all his magical and physical energy at the time, and that is why he had to sleep so long afterward. Farrah, on the other hand, was rejuvenated and exhilarated. Vegenrage had an experience with Farrah where both of their individual magic was connected to each other, and he could use that knowledge now to try to connect with Farrah physically and emotionally before he would be cast away from Farrah by her magic.

Vegenrage runs at her while her back is to him. He glows silvery blue, like when Farrah has first seen him arrive above the Dark Bush. Farrah is still mesmerized by the sight of Vemenomous, which in this case is the real him, and Xanorax is riding on his back. Vegenrage reaches around Farrah just below her breasts and hugs her tight from behind. Farrah is radiating evil magic drawn to her from the demon army, which she has just absorbed. The demon army had no usable magic that they can use, but they still has a lot of demonic magic in their weapons and in their beings purposefully given to them by Roartill, who knows Farrah will absorb it. Vemenomous and Roartill have been feeding Farrah demonic magic, which exists all around the Maglical System just as heavenly magic does; those two are, simply put, good magic and/or bad magic.

When Vegenrage makes contact with Farrah and starts to absorb her magic, it is like magical fire and ice coming into contact with each other. Initially, there are magical shock waves as a result. The shock waves are so strong that the Dark Bush within a mile radius is disintegrated. Vemenomous is thrown back through the air for a mile, landing hard, and Xanorax is thrown clear in the Dark Bush. Xanorax is a very powerful warlock and has been a student of demonic magic and a personal servant to Practu, Zebkef, and Zevoncour, so he is spared any attack from the Dark Bush. As a matter of fact, the Dark Bush untangles and spreads with great speed and makes no contact with Xanorax as he falls to the ground, landing hard but with no cuts or scrapes from the bacteria-laden Dark Bush. He gets up and walks toward Vemenomous, and the Dark Bush spreads, allowing him free passage.

Vegenrage's making bodily contact with Farrah in this way is magically very significant, and magic users on all three worlds instantly know that there is a magical clash going on, and they suspect—or in some cases know—it is Farrah and Vegenrage because there is no magical signature from Vegenrage, and Farrah is becoming Swellgic, which is an unmistakable presence. Vegenrage, being the initiator and absorbing Farrah's magic, is thrown into extreme pain. Farrah instinctively and magically fights the draw on her magic, and she is very powerful. Vegenrage clasps his hands together and holds as tight as he can. He is screaming because the magical draw is being very strongly denied by Farrah's magic, and this is like burning, shocking, suffocating pain that Vegenrage is enduring, trying to bring Farrah back to him. There is lightning, fireballs, and force waves shooting and flying from them as Vegenrage struggles to hold on to her. Farrah is deep red, and her color grows bright. The same is true for Vegenrage, except he is shining silvery blue, and lightning and fire is pouring from them, keeping any intruders at bay, or they will be burned, electrocuted, or pulverized by the magical energy waves shooting in all directions.

In the past, when Vemenomous came to Farrah in images, that was all they were, just images. Farrah was watching images in her mind brought to her as a result of her using the staff of barrier breath, which unknown to her allowed Vemenomous to charm her mind. He came to Farrah in images many times, strengthening his ability to charm her.

There is a big difference this time in that Farrah has not been charmed by Vemenomous; she is actually seeing the real Vemenomous, but the effect is the same. Farrah seems to be in a trance, but she is not. Her magical prowess is growing, and if she releases it in some magical form, it will be very powerful. Roartill has planned this for a very long time and worked with Vemenomous to have Farrah release her magical ability in whatever magical form, manifesting itself on Vegenrage. They have worked on this to perfection in the Ackelson Desert, costing Vegenrage one of the lives from his band of life, and he now only has one life left.

Vegenrage has taken the initiative, grabbing hold of Farrah and drawing her magic away before she releases it in some sort of devastating way, but he has not succeeded yet. He has to get Farrah to calm down. He has to get Farrah to face him and communicate with him as Farrah, not as the Swellgic. The Swellgic is still Farrah, but while drawing magic at an uncontrollable rate, she feels constant euphoria, she is continuously satisfied, and there is no stopping her or reasoning with her while she is in this state. Vegenrage needs to get Farrah, the beautiful girl who has fallen in love with him, and he needs to help her understand that she has to come back to Vollenbeln with him, or she will never learn to control her magical ability; it will control her, and it will consume all.

Farrah is resisting the magical draw of her magical energy by Vegenrage, but he is very magically powerful, and he is using all of his magical energy now to bring Farrah back to him. This is very difficult for Vegenrage, and he is sustaining serious burns all over his skin from the shocking and magically electrical resistance to his magical draw from Farrah. Vegenrage has his arms wrapped around her, and he is holding as tight as he can, but he is not actually touching her. He has a hold of her magical shield, and he squeezes as hard and tight as he can, trying to break through her magic. This is where Farrah's fire ring is very noticeable, as flames and fire engulf Vegenrage. He is protected from this fire, thanks to his necklace, but he is not protected from the magical strain of trying to absorb Farrah's magic. Vegenrage screams in great pain as burns start to form on his cheeks, and steam and smoke begins to rise from all over his body. "Farrah," he yells, squeezing as hard as he can and concentrating with all his magical energy.

Farrah is now being charmed, as Vemenomous has made his way as close to Farrah and Vegenrage as he can without being in the line of fire from the magical shock waves coming from them. Xanorax has made his way back to Vemenomous as well, and Roartill has cleared all the Dark Bush rising next to his two servants. "Come, Zevoncour. This is what we have all been waiting for," says Roartill, and Zevoncour rises from the earth next to him.

"Master, Vegenrage is so strong. I cannot maintain my charm on Farrah for much longer. Vegenrage is breaking through our magic, and he is going to reach Farrah very soon," says Vemenomous.

"That is all right, Vemenomous. I never thought we would win a magical battle with Vegenrage, but when he has made contact with Farrah when they are both calm and the magic has subsided, that is when we make our move. Right now, I just want to see Vegenrage burn. Xanorax, how is your arm?" asks Roartill.

Xanorax looks curiously at his left arm, which he lost to Bigits, the bag of holding. "You mean this arm, Master?" Xanorax says, waving his stub up and down.

Roartill laughs. "Yes, I meant that arm. We need to get you a replacement because you are going to need it, along with both tentacles of the Life Stealer. You want another shot at stealing the life force of Vegenrage, don't you? We are going to have to upgrade your Life Stealer as well," says Roartill.

"Master, I have never been able to feel the magical presence of Vegenrage, at least not lately. Farrah is right there, and she is incredibly strong magically. I can feel that I am most likely outmatched by her, yet there is Vegenrage right there, and he is magically as strong, if not stronger than her. I have tried to steal his life force, and he is much too powerful for me. Will I be able to steal his life force this time, and why do we not sense Vegenrage?" asks Xanorax.

"Vegenrage has the only true cloak of concealment that was created by Age'venger. This cloak was created purposefully to hide and conceal the true magical power of Age'venger's chosen champion. That no longer matters because now we know who he is. We know what his weakness is, and it is not his magic. It is his love, and we are going to use his love to kill him. You, Xanorax, are probably not strong enough to give Vegenrage any serious challenge, but that is not your task. He will probably kill you this time, but that is a sacrifice you will make unless you are ready to do what you have to do to survive you next encounter with him. Your task is more of a distraction, although it is possible for you to steal Vegenrage's life force. If Vegenrage calms Farrah, you will have a few moments when they will both be distracted, and this will be your time to strike. You will invade Vegenrage's flesh with the Life Stealer and suck his life force out. If you fail, well, then there are three more of us here waiting to take our best shot at him. Once he is dead, I am going to get my pet back," says Roartill. Xanorax gulps.

"Pet? What pet?" asks Zevoncour.

"Neggaheb is the first true bag of holding, and he is mine," says Roartill.

CHAPTER 26

Serenity Turns Violent

The pupils of Farrah's eyes are shining bright and golden. There is a ring of dark red around her pupils, giving her eyes a most unique and beautiful contrast in color. She is starting to sweat, and she feels her face. The ring of fire around her body is steadily shrinking, and she reaches down and feels Vegenrage's arms around her stomach, his hands firmly locked onto his wrists. Vegenrage finally squeezes Farrah into his chest, and their bodies make contact. The second the two of them touch each other, a sphere of silvery blue light extends outward from them, and it grows throughout the entire Long Forest, disintegrating all of the Dark Bush, eliminating it completely.

Farrah has her eyes closed and puts her right hand to her face like she is waking from a long sleep. She opens her eyes but closes them quickly because her eyes need to adjust to the bright sunlight. This takes a few moments, but after repeatedly opening and closing her eyes, they become adjusted. She looks around to find she is at the edge of a lake. There is soft sand under her feet, and the air is warm and fresh. She inhales deeply, breathing in the fresh air as a smile takes over her face. The water is deep blue with slowly rolling waves washing along the long flat sandy beach. There is a beautiful forest behind her, and she seems to be all alone. She looks across the lake, and it is so large that she cannot see land on the other side of it. She looks behind her to see a large mountain of rock and earth growing into the sky a few miles behind the forest. The lake and the woods, along with the perfect temperature, make for a most beautiful and soothing setting.

Farrah looks around with a beautiful smile growing on her face, and she talks out loud. "Where are you?" She smiles and giggles. "I know you are here."

She smiles bigger and bends at the knees as she sees Vegenrage walking from the woods toward her. She cannot wait for Vegenrage to get to her, and she runs to him, smothering him with hugs and kisses. Farrah is so excitable, happy, and loving. She bends backward, pulling Vegenrage with her to the ground. Her enthusiasm and excitement is contagious, and Vegenrage is already caught in Farrah's legs and arms, which have him wrapped tight while she kisses him passionately. Their mouths are sliding from side to side, opening and closing with rhythmic motion. Vegenrage so wants to just love her, but he knows his time here is limited. He has charmed Farrah and brought her visually to Bankle Lake. Their physical bodies are still in the Long Forest, protected from evil for a short while. The mountain in the background is actually the Brunst Rock Plateau, home to Pryenthious, which overlooks the Bankle Lake. Vegenrage slides his mouth down Farrah's left cheek and down her neck, sneaking words in between his kissing and sucking of Farrah's desirable soft skin.

"Farrah, I have to talk with you. I brought you here so we would not be distracted, but we have only a short time," says Vegenrage.

"We can talk later. Right now, I need you on me. I want to feel you in me and all over me. So save your words for later and get your clothes off," says Farrah, sliding her arms under Vegenrage's shirt and raising it to his shoulders. She kisses him after every word and continues her hands over his shoulders and down his arms, sliding his shirt off and rubbing all over his chest and back.

"Farrah, this is not real. I brought you here because this may be my last chance to explain some things to you. I gave you great magical power without understanding how difficult it would be for you to manage it," says Vegenrage, looking deeply into Farrah's beautiful chestnut brown eyes.

Farrah tilts her head to the right, looking down the warm, sandy beach, and turns her head to the other side, looking down the other side of the beach.

"What do you mean this is not real? I feel you, and I want you. All we need right now is to get naked. I want you in me. I want all of you in me. I want for your mind to be connected with mine like our bodies. We have all day. I want to love you and then play in the water with you, and then we can love some more and clean ourselves in the water all day long," says Farrah, kissing Vegenrage some more.

"Farrah, do you remember where you were just before coming here to this beach?" asks Vegenrage.

Farrah is distracted, and she cannot remember where she has been before coming to this beach.

"I did not realize Vergraughtu or Vemenomous was using the staff of barrier breath to gain a link to the mind of the staff's bearer. That was me and then you for a much longer time. You used the staff more, and with the added effects of charm on your mind from Alisluxkana, Vergraughtu was able to create a link from his mind to yours. Now that Vergraughtu is Vemenomous, he is very successfully using this link to charm you. He and Roartill are trying to use you to fight against me, and they are trying to change you into their chosen champion. They know you can get to me. They know you can destroy me, and if you succeed in this, you will have nowhere to turn but to them. In my selfish desire for you, I allowed you access to my magical prowess, and you have grown magically as I have. I never knew there was evil out there that had a way to gain control of your mind and was going to exploit your magical power. I should have explained how important it was to read all the books in my library and understand all the knowledge of the Maglical System before I gave the power of absorption to you. Logantrance had me read all the books in my library, which taught me how to control the most powerful magic. You and I are so alike. All I wanted was to adventure, explore, and be free, but Logantrance was there to make sure I understood all the knowledge of the library that he spent hundreds and hundreds of years preparing. I should have done the same with you. I love you, Farrah, and all I want is you, but there is evil out there that wants you too. They do not have you, and I am not going to let them have you. I will help you free them from your mind so they can never control you ever again," explains Vegenrage.

Farrah's face grows long. Her lips droop from smile to frown. Her eyes swell and fill with tears, which roll down the left and right sides of her face. She sniffles from her moistened noise and looks to the right. "I cannot remember where I was before coming to this beach. Here, I am with you, and all I want to do is love you. I want you so bad, and you are all I have ever wanted from the moment you saved me from that cave, from the moment I was riding on your back and we were flying. I could feel your chest with my hands, and I could feel your hips between my legs. I hugged you and felt your heartbeat. I rested my head on your shoulder and watched the ground beneath us pass by. I knew then I was in love with you and that I was going to be with you, but life won't let us be together. Life has already taken our child from us. Life is not going to let us bring our life into the world, is it?" says Farrah, pushing Vegenrage up from her. She sits up, pushing Vegenrage to the side, and stands up. Despair overcomes her feelings, and she starts to run down the beach, crying loudly, and streams of tears fall from her eyes.

Vegenrage chases after her and catches her, turning her to face him. "Farrah, none of what you just said is true. It may seem that way, but life is not easy for anyone. Life is a challenge to us all, and life is what we make it. You and I have all our life yet in front of us, and yes, we will bring our brand of life into the world. Whatever evil out there tries to tempt us, whatever evil challenges us and tries to split us up will be defeated by us. We will crush evil, and we will love for the rest of our days," says Vegenrage.

"I don't know how they get into my mind. How can I fight against that if I don't even know it is happening to me?" asks Farrah.

"There is a way to protect you from all charm. You have to get a scale from Blethstole and attach it to your body anywhere, and you will be immune to all charm. The problem is that when you and I return to the Long Forest, where our physical bodies are right now, you will still be under the charm of Vemenomous, and you will not remember our being here or our discussion here. That is OK because you have a weapon that Vemenomous does not know about. You have Parnapp," says Vegenrage.

Farrah looks at and feels her waist, saying, "Parnapp. I do not have Parnapp. Parnapp, where are you? Vegenrage, where is Parnapp?" asks Farrah.

"It is OK. Parnapp is with your physical body right now, and he can hear our conversation. When we get back, Parnapp will be there to tell you to seek out Blethstole and get a scale from him. We will not be protected from Roartill and Vemenomous for long. They will find a way to attack me, but they cannot hurt me. They need you, Farrah. They need you to hurt me by using your love for me and turning it around on you. All they have is deception, and they will do all they can to deceive you into thinking you are hurting them or saving me when the opposite is true," says Vegenrage.

"Am I going to remember this? Am I going to remember being here with you now on the beach?" asks Farrah. Vegenrage arches his chest toward Farrah, screaming, and he starts to fade away.

"Vegenrage. No. Vegenrage, don't go!" yells Farrah.

Back in the Long Forest, it is still dark, but all the Dark Bush has been destroyed and is gone. The earth is free of all plant life, and dark dirt, for as far as the eye can see, is all that remains. There is no wind; there is no sound, just gray darkness and slow-swirling dust.

Xanorax has had his left arm replaced, and his Life Stealer has been made much more powerful by Roartill. Xanorax has had to endure an agonizing, excruciating mutilation of his body as the new Life Stealer, made out of demonic hell lava, is burned into his flesh, melting the old Life Stealer and replacing it. Xanorax has come up behind Vegenrage, who is still holding Farrah. The couple is motionless, as their minds are away, visualizing the scene in Bankle Lake. Vegenrage knows they will be defenseless from attack, but this is a risk he has chosen to try to get through to Farrah. Xanorax's Life Stealer still works much the same way, but it is much more powerful now, and its ends now has five digits, like that of a hand. When the Life Stealer rises from Xanorax's body, it is steaming molten lava but stronger than Foarsbleem and burns anything it touches. The Life Stealer is now made out of Lavtonium, but there is always molten lava surrounding the metal, made possible by the greatest demon magic.

Xanorax is able to penetrate the magical shell protecting Vegenrage and Farrah. Xanorax thrusts the Life Stealer into Vegenrage's back and lifts him into the air. The five digits of each arm dig deep into the flesh of Vegenrage's lower back, causing him great pain, bringing him screaming back to this reality. Immediately, Xanorax starts to draw the life energy of Vegenrage, and this is power like Xanorax has never known, greater by far than the last time he has had his Life

Stealer in Vegenrage's flesh. Xanorax arches his back and lifts Vegenrage high in the air. "Oh yeah. This is what I have been waiting for. This is what I need," says Xanorax, absorbing magical energy from Vegenrage.

Vegenrage starts to laugh, though tears have swelled in his eyes from the shock of pain that has brought him back from his vision with Farrah. He quickly realizes that he has been invaded by Xanorax and his new and improved Life Stealer. Vegenrage calms down and endures the painful burning that spreads from the points of insertion in his flesh, and he mocks Xanorax by laughing. "Xanorax, you try stealing my life force again. Well, the old saying says, 'If at first you don't succeed, try, try again.' Let's see how much power you can handle, shall we?" says Vegenrage as he purposefully sends surges of magical energy through the tentacles of Xanorax's Life Stealer.

Xanorax is exhilarated and invigorated and yells at Vegenrage, "Come on, give me more! Is that all you have, magic man? I know you can do better than that. I can't so easily defeat you. You think this is all I have? Well, get ready because I have another surprise for you."

Two more tentacles tear from the flesh of his legs from his ankles all the way up to his hips. This part of the Life Stealer actually surrounds the bones in his legs and, when called upon, tears from his flesh, causing excruciating pain, leaving horrific deep, bloody wounds up his legs, exposing his bones until his flesh quickly reforms. Xanorax, being a student and servant of demons, is used to pain, and the more of it, the better. The flip side of this pain is that once the tentacles make their way into victims, the pain is replaced with euphoria, and Xanorax is loving it when the spear-tipped ends of his added tentacles pierce into the hamstrings of Vegenrage's legs, shooting two times the energy back into Xanorax, causing him to shake and stumble.

Vegenrage screams initially, and his screams turn to laughter. "Xanorax, you are a tool. You are nothing but a pet, a pawn to be used and expended. Your master Roartill knows you are no match for me. He knows I will destroy you. He thinks you will weaken me so he can make some other form of useless attack on me. I wonder why he so easily discards you. It has to do with Farrah. OK, Xanorax, hold me high. Are you ready?" Vegenrage continues to mock Xanorax.

"You can mock me all you like, Vegenrage, but you are losing. I am draining your power, and it feels good. I am getting stronger. I am getting your power. I will consume you, and you think this is a game," says Xanorax, looking at his body, which is growing. His muscles are strengthening and bulking up. He can feel his strength grow, and he likes it.

Vegenrage spreads his arms and legs out wide in the shape of an X, and the sky that is dark with thick clouds of ash starts to swirl and roll. The ash starts to spread out, forming a circle that gets wider and wider, exposing the clear night sky. A small silver dot forms high in the sky, and it starts to grow. It starts to widen and brighten.

"What is this? What are you doing?" says Xanorax.

"You want power. You want to know what real strength is. Well, here it comes, Xanorax. It is all yours now," says Vegenrage. The silver ball is now huge in the sky, and one massively thick lightning bolt squiggles down from the silver ball and into Vegenrage. Vegenrage starts to glow. He starts to shine so bright that Xanorax has to close his black eyes, and still they are hurt by the light. Xanorax starts to scream in pain as the silvery glow extends into the tentacles of his Life Stealer. Vegenrage uses his magic to lower himself to the ground, and now Xanorax is lifted in the air, and his whole body is now shining bright silver. The lightning is superheating Xanorax, and even though his Life Stealer is made out of demonic hell lava and Lavtonium, Vegenrage's lightning is heavenly magic and has the ability to melt hell lava, which is already starting to happen. The lava begins to drip away from the Lavtonium, and Xanorax is losing control of his bodily movements, as the energy is overwhelming him.

Xanorax's strength is starting to work against him. His rubbery red skin is starting to crack, and rays of silvery light are shining from those crevices. His black eyes pop, and inklike black fluid runs from his eye sockets. Vegenrage laughs as the lightning bolt from the heavens maintains its constant stream of superheated electricity into him, and he passes it into Xanorax, melting and electrocuting the life out of him. The tentacles of the Life Stealer are starting to soften, and Vegenrage pulls them from his hamstrings. He reaches behind his back, pulls the other tentacles out, and turns, now holding Xanorax in the air by the Life Stealer. The lightning still shoots from the silver ball in the sky into Vegenrage and passes along the Life Stealer into Xanorax. Vegenrage stands there holding Xanorax in the air by his own Life Stealer, and Xanorax has gone limp, and all the urine and excrement within his body starts to leak out down his legs. All the oxygen in his body has been sucked out or evaporated. Steam is rising from his superheated body, and Vegenrage laughs at him. "Now you will have the power to kill no more," says Vegenrage.

Vegenrage is not aware that Zevoncour is charging at him from his back, and Zevoncour comes in with a massive hell club and bats Vegenrage with it as hard as he can. There is a huge flash of red and silver light blinding Zevoncour from the impact of his club with Vegenrage. There is a very loud crash, like a crystal shard has been crushed on impact. Silver light explodes from the impact, slowly falling to the ground like burning-out fireworks lighting up the entire area. Vegenrage is sent flying, falling hard onto the dark, dusty dirt. This is a serious blow to Vegenrage, crushing the ribs in his right lower back. The silver ball and lightning bolt coming from the sky disappear, and the ash comes back, closing up the hole to the sky.

Zevoncour picks up Xanorax's broken and wilted body with one arm and shakes him. After a few shakes, Xanorax starts to breathe, and Zevoncour drops him on the ground. "Good, you did very good, my servant. We did not think you would be capable of distracting him for so long, but you keep proving yourself a very worthy student," says Zevoncour to Xanorax.

Farrah is standing where she has been with her eyes closed. The image in her mind is still calling for Vegenrage on the beach, and she does not know how to leave this image. Parnapp is on her person, and he starts to call for her. "Farrah, Farrah, wake up. I know you can hear me."

Farrah is still on the beach, but she can hear Parnapp calling to her. She looks to her side, but Parnapp is not there. "Parnapp, where are you?" calls Farrah.

"Farrah, I am here. You are still under Vegenrage's charm. He is here in the Long Forest, and he has been attacked by Xanorax and Zevoncour. Here in the Long Forest, you are still under charm by Vemenomous, but you have to come back. You have to come back now because Vegenrage needs your help," says Parnapp.

"How do I get back?" asks Farrah.

"I will help you, but you will still be under Vemenomous's charm when you get here. I will help you out of charm when you are back with me," says Parnapp, and he shocks Farrah. She opens her eyes, standing in the Long Forest, and her eyes still have golden pupils with deep red rings around them. She opens her eyes to see Vemenomous right in front of her. He picks her up with his right front paw without hurting her with his talons.

"My queen, the time of your denial is over. It is time to become the demonian dragon queen. Vegenrage has fallen, and now you will rise to rule the outer realm with me as your king," says Vemenomous to Farrah, tilting her body toward Vegenrage, and she can see him lying in the dirt. Zevoncour swings with smashing blows, impacting his hell club in the stomach of Vegenrage, exploding huge plumes of silver sparks into the air.

"You see, my queen, we will destroy Vegenrage, and you are only prolonging his agony. You can help us. You can end his suffering and make his end quick and painless, or else we will torture and torment him for a very long time. Take this shard hammer and strike Vegenrage with it to end his suffering," says Vemenomous. He has a very strong link to Farrah's mind, and now that he is holding her in his paw, she has no power to resist him at all. From under Vemenomous's left wing falls the shard hammer, and he sets Farrah on the ground next to it.

"Take it, Farrah. Take the shard hammer and strike Vegenrage in the stomach with it. You will know what to do afterward," says Vemenomous. Farrah picks up the shard hammer. It is very large in contrast to her body. It is deep red and burning hot, but Farrah is able to hold it without being burned. She walks toward Vegenrage, who is being bludgeoned by Zevoncour. The constant burst of silver sparks shooting into the air and falling in a dome around Vegenrage and Zevoncour are the only source of light, but it is very bright and lighting up the area for half a mile.

Roartill walks up and stands by Vemenomous, watching as Farrah approaches Vegenrage. Xanorax has regained his health and runs to his master Zevoncour, and the Life Stealer rips from the flesh of his arms, exposing its life-stealing tentacles. "Master, now I can steal his life force while you are bashing the might out of him. He cannot project so much power while you have him on the defense, and I can suck the life out of him," says Xanorax.

"No, Xanorax. Farrah is coming, and this is her time. This is her moment to solidify the union of the demonian dragon king and queen. Farrah is going to finish what none of us could so far. Stand back, my servant, and watch as evil reigns supreme in the Maglical System," says Zevoncour.

Vegenrage starts to laugh continuously like he is mocking the two evil servants who stand over him. Zevoncour slams a bashing blow at Vegenrage's head, and Vegenrage blocks it with his arms. "You think this is funny, magic man? You think we are toying with you? Maybe my strikes have little effect on you," says Zevoncour, smashing another crushing blow to Vegenrage's chest, sending another wave of silver sparks through the air, lighting the area. "Maybe you have some great defense against my hell club, but you will have no defense against the shard hammer in the hands of Farrah. She will strike you down, and you will be finished."

Vegenrage continues to laugh, and he starts to stand up. Zevoncour is getting very mad, and he strikes him repeatedly with his hell club, trying to keep him on the ground, but Vegenrage fights through the blows, which seem to collide with some sort of force surrounding his body, and the attacks stop, just short of causing him bodily injury, though the impacts do seem to knock him around.

"I cannot hold myself back, Master. I must draw his life force. I am compelled and—" Xanorax drives the ten digits at the end of his improved Life Stealer into the back ribs of Vegenrage. Xanorax has the look of exuberance in his eyes as his smile grows, and he lifts Vegenrage off the ground while Zevoncour smashes his hell club into Vegenrage's head. Vegenrage screams in pain, as the initial insertion of the Life Stealer is very painful, and his head is knocked to the side over and over, like he is being punched by a professional boxer. Vegenrage ends his scream of pain in laughter.

Zevoncour looks at Vegenrage, who is now lifted in the air and is nearly eye to eye with him. Zevoncour is a little surprised that Vegenrage has been able to absorb all of his most powerful strikes with the hell club. He is quite tired, expending all of his strength in his blows, thinking they will crush Vegenrage. He takes a moment to catch his breath and looks Vegenrage in the eye. This will prove nearly fatal, as Vegenrage thrusts both his arms and hands with fingers pointed right at Zevoncour. Vegenrage unleashes Vollenbeln lights at him. This is lightning that is powered from Vegenrage's home and is much hotter and more electrical than normal lightning by ten times. The real damage to the servants of evil is that Vegenrage is now imbued by the heavenly father, making light from Vegenrage in any form lethal to them. The Vollenbeln lights (lightning) shoot from all of Vegenrage's digits. The lightning is pure white, while the area around the lightning becomes a bluish color. The Vollenbeln lights hit Zevoncour, and he is immobilized, unable to move outside of the uncontrollable shaking starting to rip his body apart.

Roartill starts to laugh. He is watching from far away, with Vemenomous right next to him, and he is observing as Xanorax is lifting Vegenrage in the air with his Life Stealer, Vegenrage is unleashing his spell on Zevoncour, and Farrah is getting nearer to Vegenrage with the shard hammer in hand.

"Master, Vegenrage is killing Zevoncour. Why are you laughing?" asks Vemenomous.

Roartill laughs harder, almost falling over with his arms over his belly. "Watch this, Vemenomous, watch this," says Roartill.

Vegenrage is almost in a lying position in the air. Xanorax has lifted him and tilted Vegenrage with his back horizontal to the ground. Vegenrage still has his legs low enough, so the magic shooting from his hands is still making its mark on Zevoncour, and the light is so bright that Zevoncour and Xanorax cannot look at it. Vegenrage is laughing in a very sinister fashion, like he is playing with these two, and he knows it.

"OK, play time is over," says Vegenrage, and he stops laughing and gets a serious look on his face.

Zevoncour starts to shake more uncontrollably. The lightning starts to get brighter, and blood begins to drip from Zevoncour's mouth. He drops the hell club, and it disintegrates when it hits the ground. Zevoncour raises his arms like he is trying to fight the pain, and his eyes pop, splattering eye juice, which runs down his face. He starts to laugh. "Is that all you've got, magic man? Come on, give it to me. Give me all you've got," he says, and his body explodes, first his arms and then his legs, torso, and chest, sending his head flying through the air. Zevoncour's head hits the ground and rolls until it comes to a stop, resting perfectly on the neck, and his eyes are gone. The splatter of his blood completely misses Vegenrage or is deflected away from him, but Xanorax is covered in Zevoncour's blood.

Roartill is laughing hysterically, patting his knees with his hands and holding his stomach. He has tears rolling down his face from laughing so hard, and he falls to the ground, rolling in laughter. "Oh, I adore this guy. Why can't he serve me? Vegenrage is my wet dream come true. I am going to have my fantasy come true, destroying him," says Roartill.

"Master, Vegenrage just killed Zevoncour. This is not funny. What am I missing?" asks Vemenomous.

"No, he did not kill Zevoncour but almost," says Roartill, getting up, and he takes a step and sweeps his right hand in the direction of Zevoncour's head like he is bowling. A wisp of air swirls and flows right at the head of Zevoncour, and when they make contact, the head sinks into the dark, dusty dirt.

"Master, I should go and attack Vegenrage while Xanorax has him in his Life Stealer," says Vemenomous.

"No. You just do as I told you to do. You stay right here by my side. Things are going exactly as I have planned. The show is just getting started," says Roartill.

"Yes, Master," says Vemenomous.

"You killed my master. I will consume your life force for that," says Xanorax, who clearly is straining. He is trying so hard to steal Vegenrage's life force, but this time he feels nothing.

Vegenrage starts to laugh, and he lowers to the ground with ease, which he could have done at any time. As Vegenrage lowers, Xanorax rises. Vegenrage grasps the arms of the Life Stealer in his back with both hands and pulls them from his flesh. He then lets go of them and turns very fast, catching them, and now he has hold of the Life Stealer, and Xanorax is in the air. Vegenrage laughs, looking at Xanorax. "I could steal your life force right now, but why would I? It would be like a shark stealing the life force of a tadpole," says Vegenrage. Xanorax's stomach deflates, and his open mouth and wide eyes show his obvious realization that his life force is being drawn out of him. Xanorax has all the air sucked out of his body. He cannot breathe, and he cannot talk.

"It is time to give you a taste of your own medicine," says Vegenrage as dots of white light flow from the body of Xanorax down the tentacles of the Life Stealer into the hands and arms of Vegenrage, who has been glowing a white color, just bright enough to illuminate the surroundings.

Xanorax is losing his life, and he sees Farrah approaching Vegenrage and getting ready to strike him with the shard hammer. Xanorax thinks he can be saved if Farrah attacks Vegenrage. She draws back the weapon and swings. Vegenrage turns, swinging Xanorax right into the path of the shard hammer, and it strikes him just above his left collarbone, sinking into his chest. Vegenrage continues his motion, sending Xanorax flying through the air with the shard hammer stuck in him. Xanorax lands, and the shard hammer is knocked from his body, and red sparks shoot from his neck like a huge Roman candle.

"Now, Parnapp, now," yells Vegenrage. All of the bags of holding now have free speech, and with this comes the use of magic, and all bags of holding are very magical and very powerful.

The eyes of Parnapp appear, and he smiles, saying, "See you on the other side, Vegenrage." Parnapp and Farrah disappear.

Roartill is still laughing hysterically, and Vemenomous looks to him. "Master, did Vegenrage just kill Xanorax?"

"No, Vemenomous but almost." Again, Roartill sweeps his right arm like he is bowling, and a wisp of air blows along the ground toward the body of Xanorax, which is still spewing red flares from his neck. When the air hits him, his body melts into the dark dirt, and he is gone. Vegenrage turns toward Roartill and Vemenomous, and he is still softly glowing with white light. Vegenrage starts to walk toward Roartill.

"Master, I have to admit. Vegenrage has shown fantastic power. Is he capable of destroying us?" asks Vemenomous.

"Go to Vollenbeln. I have Vegenrage right where I want him. While I have his attention here, you can go get the girl in Vollenbeln. That is where the bag of holding has taken her. Be careful. She is still very powerful, and the bag she carries is very powerful as well. Now go, do not waste time. Go and get her," says Roartill.

"Yes, Master," says Vemenomous, and he walks through a dimension door.

Vegenrage is walking toward Roartill, and his face looks dead serious. The dust rises slowly as Vegenrage's feet hit the ground with a quiet, muffled sound. He walks slowly, raising his hands gradually, palms facing upward. Silvery blue globes of light, like swirling lightning, spin and hover just above his palms as he walks toward Roartill. The silvery white light glowing from Vegenrage's magic contrasts with the desolate dry gray background of the former Long Forest, now the long dry dirt patch.

"That's right, come to me, Vegenrage. Come to me. I have a little surprise for you," says Roartill as he watches Vegenrage approach him.

CHAPTER 27

Ugoria Runs Red with Blood

The chain reaction caused by Vegenrage speaking the name Age'venger has the elves in Erkensharie reading the book *The King of the Erkensharie*, Shenlylith from the book *The King of Ugoria: Book Two*, and Inglelapse from the book *Human Destiny*. Hornspire has seen all these events shortly before his life has passed, and he has magically written his insight for the races of men into books. There is one other book that is magically formed by the union of two other books when Vegenrage speaks Age'venger's name. This book will form in Quintis and will be given to Logantrance in Richterblen.

The elves of the Erkensharie have learned that Farrah and Vegenrage will destroy the demon army marching on the Erkensharie and that they will eliminate all the Dark Bush from the Long Forest, leaving the land bare of all life, but it will grow and be rich with life in no time. Shenlylith and those listening to her read from the book in Ugoria are very quickly put on high alert, as the book clearly states that, right now, the demons are already upon the Ugorian Palace and that war will obliterate Ugoria and most of life here. The demon horde marching on Ugoria will make contact with

Cloakenstrike first, and this will accompany the darkening of the sky from the approaching ash cloud. As the sky grows dark over Ugoria, full-on war will ensue, and the elves will win over the demon army, but Ugoria will be lost, and the elves will suffer greatly. Everyone listening to Shenlylith reading from the book is getting very antsy and does not want to waste time listening to her read. They are ready to go to the forest and take to the trees, where the bow elves are swift and deadly, and Basters is well aware of this, as many of his humanors lost their lives to the elves here.

Basters agrees with the elves. Horse riders, bow elves, and warriors all head into the forest, anticipating demon attack. Ugoria has survived the invasion of the strongest humanors and the attack of the dragon. And now, again, Ugoria is under attack, but this time it is by demons. Will Ugoria be able to withstand yet another attack on its land? Basters, Cloakenstrike, and Fraborn look at one another, ready to take on another challenge, and this is what Cloakenstrike lives for. Fraborn and Basters look at each other, shaking their heads, as Cloakenstrike decides to go where the Helven are supposed to be attacking from.

"Basters, you and Fraborn will be able to teleport to my position. Wait until I call for you, and then you two teleport to me, and we will take down all the Helven. I will dispatch this Inthamus, and then I will call for you," says Cloakenstrike, and he teleports away to surprise the Helven. Basters and Fraborn head out of the palace on foot, while Shenlylith stays to read from the book.

The Krasbeil Mountains have been spewing hundred million tons of ash into the atmosphere, and the air current is carrying the ash eastward, away from Ugoria. However, the blanket of ash has spread all the way across the Ackelson Desert and is moving southward along the Swapoon mountain range. From here, the ash will continue southward over Ugoria. For now, the skies are clear and bright with sunshine, but that is going to change very quickly.

Cloakenstrike makes his way to a clearing in the woods between the prison in Riobe and the Ugorian Palace, where he suspects the Helven will pass on their way to the Ugorian Palace. He gets to dig deep into Getcher for yet another astonishing array of weapons and armor, but this time Getcher has a little advice for him. "Cloakenstrike, Inthamus is no ordinary demon, and the Helven are magical elves possessed by demons. Inthamus is one of very few demons well versed in magical demonology. He is exceptional at all forms of poison, rot, and decay magic. I strongly advise you drink your vial of antigen," says Getcher.

"Good call, Getcher. I will do that," says Cloakenstrike, pulling a vial of green liquid from Getcher and drinking it down. This fills Cloakenstrike's blood with antibodies that lie dormant for a week, and if any foreign virus, bacteria, or disease enters his bloodstream, his blood will adapt attack and destroy the invading danger to his body. He then pulls his vest of spears and puts it on. He wants to put on his helmet of missile deflection, but he cannot wear it with his vest. He can put on his necklace of intensity, and he has a ring of fire resistance that he dons as well. Cloakenstrike has to chant the words of a magical spell in order to activate his vest. But now he can use his vest with one spoken word; he does not have to speak the entire spell.

Cloakenstrike is standing in a clearing, very aware and all geared up, ready for the Helven to appear. He is confident and looking for a fight. He is not looking for any kind of sneak attack or ambush; he wants to take them head-on, so he stands there in the clearing, looking up, and he sees the sky turning black, as the cloud of ash covering the entire horizon is moving his way. Cloakenstrike sends a telepathic message to Basters, telling him of his location and inviting him and Fraborn to wield their Lavumptom swords and join in the coming battle.

The sky is turning dark, and right on cue, Inthamus walks into the clearing with just over one hundred Helven following behind him. He looks to see Cloakenstrike standing all alone in the center of the clearing. The grass is tall and thick for about a thirty-yard diameter, surrounded by a lush forest, and Inthamus scans the surroundings, looking for possible ambush. He orders the Helven to fan out around this odd human while Inthamus holds his ground, vigilant to the surroundings. Inthamus stands very tall on his very odd, rabbitlike hind legs with his fat belly, head, and long, slender arms swaying side to side as he scans for danger.

"Sending your slaves out to do your dirty work, demon?" says Cloakenstrike.

"I was not expecting to see a human here in Ugoria. I am expecting to kill a whole lot of elves. A human all alone is OK though. We do not mind a snack before the main course," says Inthamus.

"You will not be snacking on me, but you will be dying," says Cloakenstrike, watching as the Helven surround him and wait for orders from Inthamus. Cloakenstrike looks around, and he can see none of the faces of the Helven. They all stand surrounding him with body-long robes that hang over their faces. "What are you waiting for, demon? You have me surrounded. Are you not going to attack, or are you afraid?" Cloakenstrike mocks Inthamus.

Inthamus can sense no danger outside of Cloakenstrike, and he orders his Helven to attack the lone human. They move in toward Cloakenstrike, who stands calm, just watching and waiting as the Helven move closer to him. He can see as many of them draw weapons, ready to strike. When they get to within ten feet of him and he is completely surrounded, Cloakenstrike raises his arms out to his sides and looks up, saying, "Spear sphere." Cloakenstrike rises in the air at about three feet, looking into the air. A blue sphere appears around him with hundreds of very sharp spears facing in all directions. All the spears are motionless in the sphere, pointing out in all directions around Cloakenstrike. The Helven halt and watch, but nothing happens.

"Do not wait. Attack!" yells Inthamus.

The Helven attack, and the second they move at Cloakenstrike, all the spears shoot at incredible speed in all directions. Within five seconds, a second spear sphere forms and shoots the same way, and then a third and fourth rounds of spears zoom. This is amazing, and all the Helven have been speared except for two, who have fallen to the ground and are playing dead.

Cloakenstrike walks toward the Helven who are dying, and he steals their life energy, just like he did to Shandorn. This is yet another magical ability and knowledge to Cloakenstrike, who now, for the first time ever, is gaining magical know-how in demonology. He is elated and can't believe his fortune as he goes from one possessed elf to another, stealing their life energy, sucking the Helven body dry of all magical essence, collapsing their bodies, leaving just skin and bone, completely forgetting about Inthamus. Cloakenstrike takes full advantage of this ability, stealing the life energy of ten Helven before he stops. This is dangerous for him to do, but he takes the risk, wanting to imbue himself with as much demonology knowledge as he can. He knows he will have to rest for a very long time after this battle to sort out all the images and memories that will invade his mind, and he challenges himself, draining the dying Helven one after another.

"Eugondour sillyconsign uphendrin igegriller uben eques ta dor," says Inthamus, pointing his long, slender arms at Cloakenstrike. While Inthamus is chanting his spell and concentrating on Cloakenstrike, he is not aware that both Fraborn and Basters have entered the clearing from behind him with their swords drawn. Basters has put on his boots of speed, allowing him to reach Inthamus before he finishes his spell. He runs up behind Inthamus's right side and comes down with his Lavumptom sword, slicing off the right arm of Inthamus before he is able to cast his spell. Fraborn comes up on the other side of Inthamus and releases his other arm from his body with his Lavumptom sword. Basters spins, swinging his sword like a baseball bat, severing the right leg of Inthamus. Fraborn does the same, dropping Inthamus to the ground minus his arms and legs. Both Basters and Fraborn swing their swords, ready to end the demon by severing his head, when Cloakenstrike yells.

"Wait! Wait, do not kill him. He is mine," yells Cloakenstrike while he runs to the demon, putting his hands on both sides of Inthamus's oddly shaped head. The sky has lost its light. It is not dark but dusklike, so there is still decent visibility. Inthamus has sparse flames about his figure, and this gives off light, casting dark shadows in the trees behind them. Basters and Fraborn step back as Cloakenstrike tries to draw the life essence out of Inthamus, who laughs.

"You think you can draw my life force. I am not some weakling, magic man," says Inthamus.

"No, you are one of the few very magically inclined demons, but you are not in the inner realm. You are on the outer realm, and here my magic is more powerful than yours. Yes, your soul is mine, demon," says Cloakenstrike as the face of Inthamus shines blue light from his eyes and mouth being drawn into the face of Cloakenstrike, who seems to be winning this battle. Inthamus roars as red light pushes from his face toward Cloakenstrike, who screams with voracious intensity as the blue light from him pushes the red light back into the face of Inthamus. Fraborn and Basters are amazed as they watch the chest of Inthamus cave in and his bones crack. His face starts to collapse, his skull cracks very loudly, and all of his body is sucked in as the light stops shining. Cloakenstrike lets go of the head of the demon, dropping its lifeless body to the ground. He stands breathing deeply, apparently exhilarated by the experience he has just accomplished. Blue light is shining from Cloakenstrike's eyes, and he looks to Fraborn and Basters.

"I am Cloakenstrike, master magic user, and I have now drawn the life of all forms of magic except one, the one who will give me ultimate magical power," he says. Fraborn and Basters look at each other, truly amazed, and hope Cloakenstrike is still on their side. Cloakenstrike reaches down and takes Filther from the bloody, mangled corpse of Inthamus. "Now I alone own two bags of holding." Cloakenstrike attaches the new bag of holding to his waist, and now he has two hanging from his hips.

"What do we have here? There is something different about you two. Stand. I know you are alive, but you have not been possessed by demons," says Cloakenstrike, looking to the two elves who are playing dead.

Kerben and Weesilibith stand. "We are protected from the demons by the ring of essence that we each wear. We are not with the demons. We wish to fight alongside our brothers, the Ugorian elves, against the demons, and we have much information about them that will be very useful in defeating them. I am Kerben, and this is my wife, Weesilibith," says Kerben.

"You could be spies for the demons. You look like spies. You look like Helven, not Ugorian elves. I don't know if we can trust you," says Cloakenstrike.

"This is Kerben and his wife. I know of you. I have learned of you from Delver, my bag of holding. You were once a great magic user for the Ugorian magical order, but you defied your king and studied demonology. You were banned to the Westfall Heights by your king," says Basters.

"Yes, this is true, but I never intended to ally with demons. I only sought magical knowledge and thought I could use demonology to help strengthen our magical order. I was wrong, but I never allied myself with demons, nor did my wife, and that is why we are still alive now. The Helven who were all once Ugorian elves have evolved to our current form. However, the demons possessing them did not die. In physical form, the elves died, so the demons are back in the inner realm, and they will return, all except Inthamus, who is gone to Maglical Hell forever," says Kerben.

Meanwhile, the dark has begun to settle over all of Ugoria, and the winged Lizangars have made their way over the Ugorian Forest. They are being targeted by the bow elves who have taken to the trees. Servorious has cast the demon speed spell on all the hellmen and helldogs, allowing them to keep pace with the winged Lizangars. The army on the ground has made its way into the Ugorian Forest, but they have not reached the elves yet.

The winged Lizangars are taken by surprise by the deadly arrows of the elves, and they are falling from the sky. The elves are amazing the way they leap from tree to tree, launching deadly accurate arrows ripping the wings of the Lizangars and causing lethal wounds to their heads and chests. Many Lizangars fall to the ground, unable to fly, their wings being ripped and shredded from the arrows. Upon landing, the Lizangars are quickly met by horse riders and warriors, where they are slain by sword, lance, and a host of other lethal elven weapons. There is not much fight, as the elves on the ground are fast and decisive.

The Lizangars have weapons of their own, and the tables start to even out as they release the one magical spell they are capable of, and that is fire. The Lizangars begin to shoot fireballs into the trees where the arrows are coming from, and all of them get in on the action. They can shoot fireballs from their tails, hands, and feet up to five at a time. They also have breath of fire, which is turning the treetops into a blazing inferno. They are swooping down into the trees with their breath attack and shooting fireballs in all directions from their arms, legs, and tails.

The elves are fast, but no matter where they flee, the fire catches many of them, and a lot of them fall to their deaths. All the rest of the bow elves are forced to the ground, where they, along with the horse riders and warriors, do all they can to avoid the flying flames engulfing the forest. Many elves are still launching arrows, dropping the flying demons from the sky, but the Lizangars have taken the upper hand, owning the sky and blanketing the treetops in fire. The land has grown dark, but the blazing fires in the treetops give off bright red and yellow light, casting shadows all throughout the forest, where all the elves have concentrated their forces to fight the demons.

When the demon army has crossed the Gwipps River and reached the Ugorian Forest, Servorious has cast the demon strength spell on all the helldogs. This allows them to travel through the Ugorian Forest very fast, with hellmen riding on their backs. This army is now coming to where the Lizangars are, who are still lighting the forest ablaze with their fire attacks. The elves are constantly moving, trying to avoid the fire attacks, and they are briefly set back and pause as they reach a clearing in the woods where Rowgen and his army of humanors have been beheaded and burned. A lot of elf lives have been lost in this invasion, and here they are again, fighting another attack from an entirely different enemy.

They are quickly brought back to the present as explosions of fire push them into the woods, and the elves can now hear the howls and yells of the helldogs and hellmen moving toward them through the woods. The elves are pushed back to the road known as the Entrance to Ugoria, and again, they are reminded of the past war. This is the road where their king, Trialani, has been slain, and their strongest magic users have lost their lives here as well. The remains of dragons and elves still line the area.

Willithcar, the leading Ugorian elf, takes command. Amid the flying balls of fire exploding all around and the fire breaths burning down the forest, Willithcar shows why he has risen as top general of Ugoria. "Warriors, bow elves, and horse riders, this is our final stand. No more of this running from evil. If I am to die here, then I die fighting where my king died fighting for his land. I will not die. I will kill any invader who tries to take my land, my home, and my life from the land that I have built and made my own. I will fight them single-handedly if I have to. We take the fight right at them. They come to kill us and steal our land. Well, let's show them what they are up against. Stromgin, take your horse riders north and flank those demons coming for us on the ground. Vorgillith, take your horse riders south and flank them. I will lead our warriors right at them. And, bow elves, stay in the trees and take down anything you can. Who is with me?" says Willithcar, drawing his sword and raising it high in the air, charging through the flame-red forest right toward the oncoming demons.

Stromgin heads north with his horse riders, and Vorgillith heads south. All the warriors draw their weapons and charge with Willithcar. The bow elves scatter into the trees, and the remaining Ugorian army who has suffered catastrophic losses to the humanors is now on a collision course with the demons, fighting to save the Ugorian elf way of life. The warriors make contact with the hellmen riding the helldogs, and they attack with fearless veracity. Willithcar is charging the first flaming helldog he sees, slashing at its head, severing it in two with his sword. The helldog falls, and the hellman maintains his footing, swinging down on the much shorter elf. Willithcar blocks the flaming hell club with his sword, and sparks and fire burst into the air. Soon the dark forest, red with fire, is lit up with sparks and fire from the contact of hell club and sword. Helldogs are biting any elves they can get their teeth into, and hellmen are sparring with the much faster and better trained elves. The demons are killing elves, but the elves are making quick work of the helldogs and hellmen as they fight with anger and fierce lethality. The horse riders make their appearance, adding yet more elven muscle. The elves are magnificent as they hack and slash with superior ability, severing legs, arms, heads, and torsos. The demons are falling all over, and the red flames from their bodies keep the forest bright. The elves are suffering casualties, but they are making quick work of the demons, that is, until the Lizangars start to make their presence known.

The Lizangars descend to the ground en masse, unleashing hundreds of fireballs and waves of fire from their breath attacks, wiping out most of the elves in incinerating fire. The hellmen and helldogs are immune to this attack. This is a defining moment for the elves of Ugoria. The elves have wiped out most of the demons on the ground, but this sea of fire raining down on them from above is inescapable, and most elves, along with their horses, lose their lives here.

Servorious has taken no part in the battle in the Ugorian Forest, but he has been watching from outside. He has been speaking telepathically with Roartill, keeping him updated on the events that are happening. They all know that Inthamus has been killed, and so have all the Helven. Roartill does not mind at all when his demons die no matter how high in rank they are. When they die, they go to Maglical Hell and are whatever Roartill wants them to be, so he wins. There are always more souls in the inner realm to become demons to replace those who fall into Maglical Hell. Roartill sends instructions to Servorious, and he follows them.

Servorious is one of the last demons with good magical knowledge and power, and he flies into the air, calling all the Lizangars to follow him to the Ugorian Palace. They all fly to the palace, and the Lizangars land in the surrounding treetops. Servorious stands outside the gate, summoning the Doliath to rise from the depths of Strabalster. Cloakenstrike, Basters, and Fraborn have made their way back to the throne room in the palace long before the battle with the last of Ugoria's army has finished. They have returned with Kerben and Weesilibith to find Shenlylith consumed with the book *The King of Ugoria: Book Two*. Shenlylith finishes the book in their presence, and she is in awe of the correct predictions of Hornspire. The book tells of the two Helven returning with Basters, Cloakenstrike, and Fraborn and the exact attack that the demons will carry out on Ugoria and how very few of the Ugorian elves will survive. Those survivors will be reunited with those in the throne room shortly. The book also tells

Shenlylith that when Basters returns to the throne room, he is to give Shenlylith the first book *The King of Ugoria.*

Shenlylith explains, "Basters, this book I have just finished has been correct in every respect. Very few of the elves fighting to the east will survive, but those who survive will make their way to us soon. Right now, the winged Lizangars and their demon leader, Servorious, is surrounding the palace, and we need to do something, or we will die with the destruction of the palace. You must have faith that what I tell you is true, and there are some things that Hornspire has done to allow us to escape death in this trap we are in."

"OK, we will listen to you. What is it we are to do?" asks Basters.

"I need the book *The King of Ugoria,*" says Shenlylith.

"I have not even read all of it yet," says Basters, picking the book from Delver.

"That is OK. I need that book, and I need the snow gold trinket," says Shenlylith.

Basters looks to Cloakenstrike, pulling the snow gold trinket from Delver and handing it, along with the book, to Shenlylith. She puts the two books side by side, covers facing up on the table. She puts the book *The King of Ugoria* right side up, binding facing to the left, and she turns the book *The King of Ugoria: Book Two* upside down, binding facing to the right, so the two books are touching each other fore edge to fore edge. She rests the snow gold trinket on top of them. They all watch as nothing happens.

"What is supposed to happen?" asks Basters, looking to Shenlylith.

"I do not know. This is what the book said to do. Just wait a moment," says Shenlylith.

They all watch, and the snow gold trinket starts to move and jiggle around. It stretches and expands, forming a rectangle that grows to the exact dimension of the two books side by side, and snaps around them like a rubber band. The books seem to be squeezed and pushed into each other, and the pages of each book slide together like two halves of a deck of cards. When the two books are pushed tight, they fuse, creating one book, and the top of the book shimmers and shines like water full of diamond sparkles. The head of Hornspire rises a few feet from the water in the size of the book. He looks around at those present like he knows they are there, and he speaks.

"Basters, you are back in human form, and you are the king of Ugoria. Shenlylith, born a Ugorian elf and awarded great magical ability by the snow gold trinket, which I created, you have lost your magical ability and with it your elven form. You are now human, and humans are the founding life of all the races of man. The only formidable fighting force left for the race of man is the Erkensharie elves, but they will be destroyed by the demons. My rising here from the union of two of my books will cause magic to unite two of my books held by the Erkensharie king, where I will rise and give instruction. Two books held by a dragon will unite, and I will give instruction in defeating the demons. Two books will unite and be given to a great human magic user, where further instruction will be given.

"The demons are not defeated yet, and the key to their defeat is Farrah, the human with a tainted mind. Vegenrage and Farrah together are the force to stop the demons, but Farrah is being used to defeat Vegenrage. If my instructions are to be carried out, three more books will rise at the appropriate time, helping eliminate the demons from the outer realm. Humans will be the last stand for the races of man. Elves, humanors, and dwarves will not be gone per se. They will be absorbed by the race destined to rule the Maglical System, and they are the humans. Humans will carry all the traits of elves, humanors, and dwarves.

"The demons are having their armies attack on Fargloin and Strabalster right now, and they will be very successful in killing most life. They will not be so fortunate in Kronton, where humans will take control. It is true I deceived and I used my foresight to gain power and dominance for myself and the dragons, but I have ultimately failed. The dragons will die out but not before our supreme race helps the chosen one defeat and destroy the demons. The demons will attack and destroy the Ugorian Palace, so I offer this magical gift to those of you here in this room. I will create a portal that will teleport you all to the survivors in the Ugorian Forest. Walk through this portal and be united with those who have survived the demon attack. By walking through this portal, my magic will fade, the portal will close, and the books here will be gone as the last of you travel to the forest. The snow gold trinket will be left on the neck of Shenlylith when she exits the portal. Shenlylith, wear this at all times. There are only nine survivors in the Ugorian Forest. Get them, and then all of you must go to your long-lost brothers in the Erkensharie. King Ulegwahn will be expecting you. There you will unite. If not, you will all die here," says Hornspire.

The image of Hornspire drops back into the watery top of the book, and the book stands on its own. The watery top now looks like a mirror, and the book starts to grow and move out toward Shenlylith. It gets past the table and grows, creating a doorway large enough for them all to walk through one at a time. The mirrorlike image of the doorway fades, and the forest comes into view. They can see the surviving elves in the forest, and all the trees around them are on fire. The elves are trying to save the wounded, but it is obvious their efforts are in vain.

Meanwhile, outside of the palace, the Doliath have risen, one on each side of the palace. Servorious orders all four of the Doliath to unleash their hellfire on the palace and destroy it. He also orders the Lizangars to attack with fireballs from the sky. The Doliath pound the ground with their enormous feet, getting a good foothold, and unleash incinerating hellfire into the sides of the palace. The Lizangars are flying all around and releasing fireballs in a constant bombardment, and with all the destruction going on with nothing to stop it, the palace will fall in no time. Those in the throne room feel the palace shake and tremble from the constant attack.

"It is the demons. They are attacking the palace with hellfire, and it will not be able to stand for very long. We have to go to the forest and get the survivors. Then we must go to the Erkensharie like Hornspire said," says Shenlylith.

"I am inclined to agree with you. We go save the elves in the forest, and then we will decide how to proceed after that. Follow me," says Basters, and he walks through the doorway and lands right in front of Stromgin, who is sitting on the ground with one of his horse riders who has passed, lying across his legs.

"Stromgin, come on, we have to get out of here. Gather the others. We have to go," says Basters.

"Basters, you have come for us. Basters has come for us!" yells Stromgin, getting up and gathering the others.

Basters faces the direction he has just come from, yelling, "Come on! Come on, you guys! I know you can see me. Come on, let's get our elves and move on. Come on!"

Shenlylith can see Basters on the other side of the portal calling to them, and she walks through it, followed by Fraborn, Kerben, Weesilibith, and finally Cloakenstrike.

"Wendell, Gonbilden, is this all who have survived? Only nine of you? There has to be more," says Basters.

"We have been eradicated, King Basters. This is all of us who have survived. They came down on us with hellfire from above, and we had no chance. We have lost. We have lost all," says Willithcar.

"We have not lost all yet. We are going to our brothers who are waiting for us in the Erkensharie," says Basters.

All the elves look at one another with their defeated long faces, and a new sense of energy overtakes them as they get ready to follow their king through his dimension door to the Erkensharie on the planet Fargloin.

"Basters, I will reunite with you soon. You know I cannot go to the Erkensharie. I have killed their prior king, and I cannot believe they have forgotten about this. I will meet with you soon. Farewell, my friend," says Cloakenstrike.

"Farewell. Until we meet again," says Basters, and Fraborn nods to Cloakenstrike as he walks through a dimension door, and he is gone.

CHAPTER 28

Ulegwahn, Gwithen, and Logantrance Get Instructions from Hornspire

King Ulegwahn is back in his throne room, and Oriapow is with him. They are both aware that Farrah and Vegenrage have been in the Long Forest, along with a whole lot of evil. They can both sense that a great battle has taken place, and a power like none they have ever felt has swept through the entire Long Forest. Ulegwahn can sense that the magical power that has been in the Long Forest has gone away and is not heading toward the Erkensharie as far as he can tell. Ulegwahn sends Pryzill, Sombons, and Lentoz to go investigate the Long Forest, and they head out to see what has happened. Ulegwahn sits in his throne and feels Vixtrixx moving at his side.

"Ulegwahn, it is time for you to have this," says Vixtrixx, whose big white eyes are visible, and he opens up, producing a book that floats out into the center of the room. Both Ulegwahn and Oriapow are watching wide eyed as Vixtrixx explains, "You may remember the two books *The Rising of*

Vemenomous and *The Rising of Vemenomous: The Demonian Dragon*. I have combined these books into one, giving it magical power that has been waiting for its magical cue to come to life, and it is time. Do not be afraid. Hornspire has been slain by a dragon, and in that event, he has shared his visions with the races of man so that they have the knowledge they need to destroy the demons. You are my master, and I cannot lie to you. I tell you that what Hornspire is about to tell you is going to come to pass, and you should take his visions of the future very seriously. No matter how out of place what he says seems, you must listen carefully if you want to destroy the demons and not be destroyed by them." Vixtrixx falls silent and lies back in his respective position on Ulegwahn's waist.

Oriapow walks over beside Ulegwahn, who stands and walks down the steps in front of his throne. He and Oriapow watch as the book grows in front of them. The book turns in the air so the top cover faces them, and it grows to the size of a door. The cover of the book looks like a shiny silver mirror, but it is not reflecting their image; it is rippling like water that is being rained on. The image of Hornspire appears as the rippling smooths and fades away. The head of Hornspire extends out from the magically altered book until his neck is as wide as the doorway, and Hornspire looks at Ulegwahn and Oriapow.

"The king of the Erkensharie and the father of Erkensharie magi, the two holders of the Octagemerwell, the fate of elven magic rests with you two. The Octagemerwell is the greatest magical artifact adapted to elven magic and elven fate. You will need the power of the Octagemerwell and your allies to defeat the demons, your allies being your brothers from Ugoria, who now are on their way here as I speak. Also very important allies to you are the Glaborian dwarves, and most important is Vegenrage and Farrah. Ulegwahn, you have been charmed through the beauty of Farrah by the evil that tries to use her to defeat Vegenrage. You must fight this charm that overcomes you in the presence of Farrah. Vegenrage is your ally, and if you turn him away from the elves of the Erkensharie, you lose. Farrah will never be your queen, and you must fight this urge, or you lose.

"The elves of Ugoria will arrive in your courtyard very shortly with Shenlylith and the new king of Ugoria, who is human, and his name is Basters. There will be two Helven with them and almost a dozen Ugorian elves. These are all who have survived the demon attack in Ugoria. The great Ugorian elves have been eliminated, and you must ally yourself with these very powerful individuals, or you will lose as well. The demons are counting on you all to fight among yourselves, and if you do, the demons will win. They will kill you all, but if you join forces, you will defeat the demons. You must retrieve the Octagemerwell and place it in Vixtrixx. You must gather all the Erkensharie elves, go to the great courtyard, and wait for your brothers from Ugoria to arrive. I can tell you the Erkensharie lands will burn. The Great Erken will be destroyed unless you unite all of you and allow Vegenrage to serve as your ally. This is your only chance for survival. King Ulegwahn, this is you test of leadership. You must walk through this portal after retrieving the Octagemerwell, and in the courtyard, you must unite elves, dwarves, and humans in order to survive the threat of a greater enemy. I have given you the knowledge you need in order to survive the coming evil. The rest is now on you," says Hornspire, fading back into the mirrored doorway that ripples like a pebble is thrown into the middle of a pond, and when the ripples stop, Hornspire is gone.

"Well, Ulegwahn, what do you say?" asks Oriapow.

"We listen to Hornspire. I do now know why, but I believe him. Wait here, Oriapow. I will be right back," says Ulegwahn as he vanishes and appears on top of the Great Erken next to the Octagemerwell. It is thought by many that only the protector of the Great Erken (in this instance, that is Oriapow) knows the whereabouts of the Octagemerwell, but in fact, the king of the Erkensharie always knows where the Octagemerwell is unless stolen and hidden in a bag of holding, like Cloakenstrike has done. Ulegwahn retrieves the Octagemerwell, puts it in his bag of holding, and teleports back to Oriapow. The two of them walk through the portal ending up in the courtyard, and it vanishes, never to return.

Ulegwahn yells to the bow elves guarding from atop the new gate, protecting the Erkensharie. "Kwerston, you and Kearsebe head into the Erkensharie homeland and evacuate everyone. Tell them all to head here to the courtyard. We are expecting guests from Ugoria, guests who will excite and enlighten us. We are going to be attacked by demons, and we need all of our people to be aware and not sitting around when this attack comes. Go now and bring everyone back here."

"Yes, Ulegwahn," say the two elves, hurriedly heading toward the elven homes in the trees.

"Oriapow, call all our magic users and tell them to gather here quickly," says Ulegwahn.

"Yes, I will call them all here at once," says Oriapow.

There is a lot activity. Elves are running all around, and a lot of them are scared. The sky is dark, but thanks to the starlight crystals lighting all the lanterns around the Erkensharie, there is a constant soft light illuminating the area. Ulegwahn has all the Erkensharie elves gathering in the courtyard to greet their arriving brothers from Ugoria. He has a lot of questions for them. Ulegwahn believes what Hornspire has told them, and he believes the demon attack on the Erkensharie is imminent.

Pryzill, Sombons, and Lentoz return from the Long Forest with baffling news. "King Ulegwahn, the Long Forest is no longer overrun with Dark Bush. The Dark Bush is gone, but so is the Long Forest," says Pryzill.

"What do you mean? The Long Forest is gone?" asks Ulegwahn.

"That is exactly what I mean. There is no trees, no grass, no life, no anything. It is just plain dirt, and that is all," says Pryzill while Sombons and Lentoz nod in agreement. Ulegwahn ponders this situation as the huge gate doors slowly open, letting in a warrior regiment led by Cellertrill. All the elves gather as Ulegwahn explains what has happened with the books and recites Hornspire's predictions. All the elves here now wait for their brothers from long ago to show themselves in the Erkensharie courtyard.

The dragons have been moving all around the three worlds, transporting the draglets from lair to lair. They do not want to stay in any one place for too long no matter how protected it is. The dragons know that the demons and their leadership have great power at their disposal and that they will seek to destroy the dragons. Dribrillianth has gone to find Interford in the Ilkergire, and Gairdennow has gone to find Ubwickesdon. The younger dragons have gone to speak with the Salcendreeps, the Wall Gliders, the Mountain Flats, the Chestwerns, and other lesser dragons of the Ilkergire. The Ilkergire minions are more to the side of chaos and evildoings, but should they run into demons, they will be just another living being to be killed.

The dragons go to all the lesser dragons, letting them know that should the dragons call on them for battle against the demons, it will be in their best interest to fight alongside their kind. Interford, on the other hand, is a servant of evil, and Gairdennow has his hands full trying to convince him to fight with the dragons. Same goes for Dribrillianth, trying to sway Ubwickesdon to fight with them.

Gwithen is reminded of long-past conversations she has had with Hornspire about the days they are in now. Her conversations with him are so long ago, but they seem like yesterday, as the events unfolding now have been so accurately spoken about by Hornspire. She shares her thoughts with Blethstole and tells him how she has to travel back to her lair in order to get something left to her by Hornspire. "Blethstole, you stay with our young. I will travel to my home and get what I need, and I will be back very soon." Blethstole looks concerned. "I know I will be OK. I know exactly what I am going to get, and I know exactly where it is," says Gwithen.

"What exactly are you going to get?" asks Blethstole.

"A book. You remember the book *The Passing* that you and Dribrillianth finally read, and you remember how accurate it was? There is yet another book that will form with my arrival back in my home, and when I combine this book with a treasure that still lies in my treasure bed, a new book will form," says Gwithen.

"What is the treasure that you are supposed to combine with this book of yours?" asks Blethstole.

"It is another book that I am sure has survived all the destruction in my lair. I know it has because Hornspire told me about this long ago. He said that when we feel the rising of the creator, it is time to go back to my lair, and the new book will form when I combine these two books," says Gwithen. This conversation is happening shortly after Vegenrage has spoken the name Age'venger.

"I will protect our young with the dragons who are here. You go and come back quickly. I feel we will have to move soon," says Blethstole. He, Gannream, and the female dragons are in Blethstole's lair, protecting the draglets. The presence of demons is much less, almost nonexistent, here compared to the planets of Strabalster and Fargloin, which are quickly darkening from the ash clouds circling them.

"I will not be long," says Gwithen, and she disappears through a dimension door and appears in her lair, soaring down through the air, looking at the devastation that has taken place. Gwithen looks around to see that the entire stone wall that has just been behind her bed, where she has cuddled with her draglets, has completely crumbled and covered her treasure. The ledge where the wall has hidden her book and her other very valuable items is still intact. The magical vault has simply moved back farther into the mountain rock, maintaining its, secrecy and Gwithen is still the only one with access to this area.

Before she heads to her magical vault high up the mountain wall, which no longer has a ledge for her to stand on, she floats down to her bedding area, which is covered with large boulders and rock. She looks around, reminiscing about what it used to look like here and all the draglets she has raised on this very spot. The rock walkway that leads up the mountain wall is now gone, and the water surrounding the bed for her young is all covered. She looks around sadly but does not waste too much time.

She flaps her powerful wings and rises up the rock wall until she reaches the magical vault, and she latches on to the wall with her powerful talons. They dig into the crevices and cracks of the rock, and she chants a few words, opening her magical safe. The rock opens in front of Gwithen, exposing a ledge that has a book and a bag of holding sitting there. Gwithen reaches for the book, and the bag of holding opens its eyes. "Well, it is about time you have come for me, my winged lady," says Ieva.

"Oh, be quiet. You knew I would be coming for you when the heavenly creator has risen, and that time is here," says Gwithen, grasping the book in one paw and Ieva in the other hand. She leaps from the wall. She extends her wings, soaring over to the other side of the water, where the sunlight shines in from the hole in the top of the mountain, and the foliage here is green and healthy. She lands, talking to Ieva. "OK, Ieva. The time has come. Hornspire has been killed by Blethstole. The demons are attacking on Strabalster, and Fargloin and I have felt the spine-tingling rise of new magic. This must be that of the creator, and I am here for your advice."

"Yes, you are right. Take the book *The Passing* and put it inside me. You remember the book of love Hornspire wrote for you? He called it *Loving the Great White Lady*." asks Ieva.

"Yes, I remember that book. Hornspire always had the gift of conversation and writing. I love the way he wrote, and you had better still have that book inside of you, Ieva," says Gwithen, putting *The Passing* into her bag of holding.

"Yes, I do. When both books are within my magic, they will unite, creating a message from Hornspire and a portal for you. OK, here we go, my lady," says Ieva.

The eyes of Ieva fade away, and the top of the book emerges from Ieva and into the air. The book opens and grows to what looks like a well full of water. Gwithen looks into the well, and it appears to be full with crystal-clear water, and she can see the image of Hornspire appear. The head of Hornspire rises from the water and addresses Gwithen.

"Gwithen, my love, this is the last time I get to gaze into those beautiful green eyes of yours. Blethstole has killed me, and that signals the end of my quest to preserve the dragons as the dominant species of the Maglical System. The demons will not kill all the dragons, but the Maglical System is changing, and the days of the dragons are coming to an end. You will live a full wonderful life as will some of the remaining dragons, and you will see worlds change and many species go away, including many of the races of man. There are fierce battles to come, and the dragons will fight the demons with the lesser dragons. The races of man will create another front that the demons will have to contend with, and this will be too much for the demons to overcome. Vegenrage has the power to destroy the leadership of the demons, but the demons have hold of Vegenrage's one weakness, and that is Farrah. The time will come where you will have to make a decision concerning the issue of Farrah and Vegenrage. I have no guidance for you on this. Just trust that, when the time comes, you will take necessary actions determining the outcome of the battle between good and evil.

"Fargloin has already seen the loss of the Altrarians and Hiltorians, and now the last of the Ugorian elves have gone from Strabalster to Fargloin to aid their long-ago brothers in the Erkensharie. The dragons will fight the demons in Fargloin with the lesser dragons, and they will drive back the demons, giving them great losses, but Fargloin will be lost. Great battles will rage on Strabalster, further diminishing the demon numbers and eliminating the last of the humanors, but again, Strabalster will be lost as well. The final inhabited planet will be Kronton, and here the demons will see their days come to an end. Dragons will be firmly united with the surviving races of men, and there will peace for a limited time. A very powerful demon is coming for you now. You may already feel his presence. Do not tangle with this demon. Just remember his magical presence because you will meet him again.

"I am creating a portal that will appear when this image fades. Walk through the portal and make no attempt to face Othgile, the demon coming for you now. The portal will take you back to the lair of Blethstole, where he and the dragons are waiting for you. The portal will shrink back into the book and into Ieva, who will be by your side once again when you get back to Blethstole's lair. Bye, my love. It is time for you to go now," says Hornspire, and he drops back into the well of water, becoming one with it, and his image disappears.

The well of water shrinks down, and Gwithen feels a magical presence like she has never ever felt before. It is very strong, and she turns around to see the only demon ever to be let loose from Maglical Hell by Roartill. Othgile rises from the earth, and his head has a snout that comes out like a nose and then turns up into a massive horn like that of a rhinoceros. He has bright blue eyes that glow, with stereoscopic vision; they are just far apart, enough to see on either side of his horn. He has massive muscles on his neck and shoulders with long humanoid arms and hands, but the digits are not thumbs and fingers; they are solid like chitin and razor-sharp along the inside edges with very sharp points on them. His teeth are long, thin, very sharp, and pointed and are close together in his mouth, with about three times the normal amount of teeth compared to any species Gwithen has ever seen. These teeth are made to cut, tear, and shred anything that he bites. His torso is solid and very thick and his skin deep bloodred. His hips are thick and strong but very strange. He has two legs that are very much like the hind legs of a rhinoceros, but this demon is bipedal, and the paws on his feet have long toes that turn into sharp disemboweling weapons, like the claws on his hands. He has two more legs that come out the side of his hips at a forty-five-degree angle toward the ground, and they are three times as long as the two legs he is standing on. These legs are folded and tucked to his body, but Gwithen can safely assume that these legs, when in use, can give this demon great leaping ability and speed. Gwithen loves to hunt the Wickenfall Forest, where the deadliest of beasts roam, but this demon is incredibly intimidating, and it is dripping blood. She takes the advice of Hornspire to not even think about messing with this demon, and she turns back to see that Ieva has taken her true form, lying on the ground.

"Ieva," says Gwithen, and a book pops out of the bag, and it grows in front of Gwithen, creating a mirror showing Blethstole's lair. Ieva floats up, and Gwithen raises a single scale in front of her left wing. Ieva floats up and under it as it lies back down, creating a perfect spot for Ieva to rest and travel with Gwithen.

"Dragon, white dragon, you cannot leave here. I am your final destiny, and I will eat your heart before your lungs have stopped breathing. Your magic is useless against me, and your strength is nothing compared to me. I am Othgile, supreme dark angel, and your heavenly white is about to be smothered. Your magic is consumed by mine and vice versa, but I am not here to duel with you magically, dragon. I am here to rip you limb from limb with my bare hands and enjoy the taste of your sweet flesh," says Othgile, laughing and walking toward Gwithen.

Gwithen, for the first time ever, feels like she is outmatched, and she jumps into the mirrored portal. She vanishes into the portal, which shrinks down to the size of the book it is made from and burns very quick, floating away as ash, disappearing into the air. Othgile roars in anger very loud. yelling, "How did she do that? How did she get away?"

Roartill rises from the earth beside Othgile with a very disappointed look on his face. "She had outside help. She had fortune from a dead dragon, but that fortune is fading.

Do not worry, my servant, you will taste the sweet meat of dragon. You will feast," says Roartill, and the two of them sink back into the earth.

Logantrance has been holding a deep fear within that he has not told anyone about. He is actually very afraid to go to his home, Richterblen. He still thinks that somehow Blethstole has set traps in order to capture or kill him, even though this is his home and he knows it better than anyone. This fear is mostly a by-product of the demon seed implanted in him by Blethstole so long ago here in Richterblen. Even though Vegenrage has removed the demon deed from him, this one fear has lingered, and Logantrance is now about to face it.

He arrives in the tropical forest just outside his home, and it is dark like always and raining. The forest is dark, but the torches outside the doorway to his home are always blazing and protected from the rain, lighting the immediate area. A wide area of the forest outside his doorway has been incinerated by Blethstole, but it has grown back, and lush forest blankets the earth.

Logantrance stands in the wet forest, looking around like he knows someone or something is waiting to ambush him. He uses his magic to scan for any presence, and he finds nothing. "Well, time to face my fears," Logantrance says out loud as he enters the tunnel into his home. He walks down the hallway with concrete walls and a dirt floor, waving his arms, causing the passageway to open and turn. He walks into his home unscathed, but still he is very cautious. All the books in Vegenrage's library have been transformed into the book that is now the *Gowdelken*, and all of those books have been at one time in Logantrance's library, but they were not all of his books. This is the first time Logantrance is entering his home since the demons have risen to the outer realm and only the second time he has gone alone since Blethstole has been there.

Logantrance goes to his laboratory, where his magical spiders keep watch. He enters the room with a clap of his hands, and soft light shines in the room. All the webs and spiders creep back into the walls. Logantrance calls for Fryzakilla, his guardian spider leader, who falls from the ceiling on a single web of silk. Not only do the spiders keep watch and notify Logantrance by magical telepathy if an intrusion takes place here in the laboratory but they protect all of Logantrance's home as well with their spider touch magic. Logantrance puts his hands together, creating a platform for the spider with abnormally long legs to rest on. Fryzakilla looks up to Logantrance with all eight of his eyes, and Logantrance speaks telepathically with his guardian spider. "Have you noticed any intrusion at all or anything out of the ordinary?" asks Logantrance.

"No. There has been nothing but silence in your absence. There has been no intrusion and nothing out of the ordinary except an unusually long absence of you here in your home," replies Fryzakilla.

"Good, that means my library is still intact. You and your spiders continue your vigil, Fryzakilla. I must go tend to my home and rid myself of this fearful curse left in me by Blethstole's demon seed," says Logantrance, and Fryzakilla uses his very long legs to walk back up the single strand of silk.

Logantrance heads back to his main living area, where he has once lain on a bed telling stories to Farrah and Vegenrage after he has been saved from the demon seed. This room is magically altered by Logantrance from his sleeping room to his library. He also transforms this room to his food storage and other rooms at will. When Logantrance's library is back, it is surprising how few books he actually has. He has had put most of the books he has collected in Vegenrage's library, and they have all been stolen and changed. Logantrance's library has three shelves surrounding the circular room, and for the most part, all the shelves are empty. He has around one hundred books here, and they are mostly very personal and special for him, with a few very powerful books that he has kept for himself. He approaches his books, and Quintis comes alive.

"Logantrance, the time has come," says Quintis.

"Yes, I have felt the release of the creator's magic," says Logantrance as he pulls a book from the shelf. "This book, *The Chosen One*, has been on my shelf here for over a thousand years, and I read it so long ago that I have forgotten what it said. Many of its words have come to pass, and after the fact, I remember," says Logantrance.

"Yes, then you know what you have to do with the book now," says Quintis.

"Yes, I know," says Logantrance, putting the book into Quintis, who unties itself from the waist of Logantrance and floats to the floor. The bag opens, creating a well with shimmering silver water that is rippling like rain is falling.

The ripples slow and smooth out, creating a shiny, flat surface, and Logantrance can see the image of Hornspire appear in the water. The head of Hornspire rises from the well and addresses Logantrance.

"Logantrance, the magic man who brought the chosen human from another universe, you are very wise and powerful yourself. And in our one encounter in the Quiltneck Wild Lands, you had struck me with a lightning bolt. That one event changed the future by releasing a very important book from my possession that I was never able to get back. I had prayed that I would never have this conversation with you, but I have been killed by my own kind, and little do the dragons know this is the end of their reign. Vegenrage is the chosen one, and he will lead the human race to become the dominant species of the Maglical System. Vegenrage is surprisingly adept when it comes to survival, and his well-rounded nature makes him the perfect leader for the humans. He will defeat all enemies, but there is one snag that could be his defeat, and her name is Farrah.

"Right now, as we speak, Vegenrage faces off with Roartill, and Farrah has gone to Vollenbeln to try to rid herself of the evil taint that, from time to time, corrupts her mind. This taint is purposeful and planted by Vemenomous, who has become the first true demonian dragon. Vemenomous is about to face off with Farrah to turn her against Vegenrage, and if he is successful, she will defeat Vegenrage. This is the scenario that you must undo. You have found, convinced, and brought forth Vlianth to the Maglical System. Now you must find, convince, and bring back Farrah from the taint that is being imposed on her by pure evil. You must go to Vollenbeln and face Vemenomous. You must save Farrah, or she will destroy Vegenrage and consume his flesh, becoming the demonian dragon queen. If you fail, Farrah will turn against Vegenrage, and evil will have won the Maglical System. All rests on you, Logantrance. This one moment in time decides the fate of the Maglical System. Will good survive, or will evil destroy all? I wanted for the dragons to rule forever, but that is not to be. If evil wins over good, then the dragons and all the races of man will be devoured and forgotten about. If good rules, at least the dragons will be remembered in memories, and we may, at some point in the future, make our return. I truly wish the races of man victory over the demons. There is no future for me to see if the demons win, but with the defeat of the demons, there is still much to see and much advice I will have for sharing.

"Go now because Farrah needs your help, and I have one item for you that will relieve the fear cast upon you from the invading demon deed that has gripped your soul. This will give you insight as to how to help save Farrah. You have a very special book on your shelf called *The Savior's Savior*. Yes, I know you have it. Put it in Quintis, and your inner fear shall be relieved," says Hornspire as he falls into the watery well, and Quintis sits with the top of its bag open. Logantrance puts the book in Quintis, and a book is formed from the union of *The Chosen One* and *The Savior's Savior*. It rises up and burns in a flash, leaving ash floating away. Logantrance sees that the well shrinks back down into the bag of holding, and out pops a trinket, which he catches. The trinket is a miniature hollow glass form of Blethstole, and the head twists off, which Logantrance does. There is a liquid inside, which he cautiously sniffs.

"Hornspire had the insight or foresight, depending on how you look at it, to steal a shed scale from Blethstole while he was in his lair. He magically altered this scale into liquid form and sealed it in this trinket. It was released in me from the book *The Sleeping Dragon*, which you had put in me so long ago, and I held it until now. When you added the two books just now, they magically fused, and the trinket was released. It is truly amazing how well Hornspire could see into the future from so long ago. As you know, a scale from a black dragon worn by an individual makes that individual immune to charm of any kind. The liquid in this trinket will not make you immune to charm, but it will release your soul from the fear caused by the demon seed implanted in you by Blethstole," says Quintis.

Logantrance drinks the liquid, and the trinket starts to glow red, getting very hot. Logantrance drops it. The trinket disintegrates before it hits the ground, and Logantrance immediately feels the effects of the elixir. He sees Vegenrage pulling the demon seed from his body and destroying it. As horrific and violent as this event is, Logantrance feels relieved after his vision ends with Vegenrage destroying the demon seed. "You know what, Quintis, I think that worked. It is time to go and save Farrah from the evil taint plaguing her mind. I think I already know what is needed to save her from it, but first, we must go to Vollenbeln and make sure Vemenomous does not get his hands on her."

Quintis rises to the waist of Logantrance and secures itself back in place, saying, "We go to save Farrah."

CHAPTER 29

Logantrance Tries to Save Farrah

Farrah has been teleported to Vollenbeln by Parnapp, but she is still under the charm of Vemenomous. She arrives just outside the door that leads into her home. This is her home, but still the magic here in Vollenbeln is an extension of Vegenrage and a part of him. Farrah is very much in love with Vegenrage, and she does have a magical draw here in Vollenbeln, and this is enough to confuse her mind and break her thoughts. The images in her mind crack and bounce back and forth from seeing Vegenrage and seeing Vemenomous. She rubs her face and shakes her head.

"Farrah, come back. Farrah, come to my voice. Look at me, Farrah!" yells Parnapp.

Farrah reaches down and grasps Parnapp with her left hand. "Parnapp, Parnapp, is that you? Where are we?" says Farrah, looking around, realizing she is in Vollenbeln.

"I have teleported us here to Vollenbeln. Vemenomous is trying to control your thoughts and images. Vemenomous and Roartill are trying to turn you against Vegenrage. They are trying to make you their demonian dragon queen. I brought you here knowing you can fight against their form of mind control in your home. Farrah, you have to fight them. You have to make a stand and rid them from your thoughts, and here in the home built by you and Vegenrage is where you must make your stand. Vemenomous is coming for you. He is coming to take you into the services of darkness, but I will help you. We will defeat him," says Parnapp, and it cannot get in another word as two long very sharp claws stick through the back of Farrah, coming out just above her hips on both sides of her body.

Farrah is raised into the air by two other claws just outside her body, parallel to those that have stuck her. Vemenomous materializes behind Farrah, standing on his hind legs, raising Farrah high in the air. He uses the index claw on his left paw to reach between Farrah and the rope holding Parnapp on her waist. He rips the golden rope with his claw, severing it and catching Parnapp in his left paw.

"Bag," says Vemenomous, looking at the bag of holding and throwing it off into the grass. He then tilts Farrah's body toward his face. "Farrah, you are my queen. Ever since you first held me when I was the staff of barrier breath, you and I have been connected. We have been one. It is time to stop evading your destiny. It is time to be joined with me as my queen. Let go of your dreams of Vegenrage and let total power be yours. I will never let you be. I will never stop until you are my queen, and if you think the races of man are your true friends, if you think Vegenrage is your real love, then let's see how he treats you when you are scarred. Let us see if he will still love you when you are not the pretty little princess."

Vemenomous points his index claw on his left paw at Farrah's forehead, and it starts to glow red. He sticks and drags his red-hot claw across Farrah's entire forehead, which makes a sizzling sound as it burns her, and then he slides it down the left side of her face and neck to her collarbone, leaving a horrific scar. Farrah screams in pain, afraid to move because every movement causes great pain to her lower abdomen.

"Now you are mine. Let me into your mind. Let me show you the power you are to have," says Vemenomous as he closes his eyes, smiling and sensing that Farrah's mind is weakening. He raises Farrah as high into the air as he can reach. "That is it, Farrah. That's right. Let me into your mind so we can join. We can be one, and nothing can stop our wishes. We are to rule the Maglical System together."

Farrah raises her arms out to her sides, looking up with her eyes closed. She opens her eyes, and they look like the eyes of Vemenomous. She opens her mouth, and her teeth start to grow longer and sharper. The pain in her body starts to go away, and she feels elation.

"That is it. That is what you need. That is what you want. Draw from the power here. Heal yourself and take your rightful place as my queen," says Vemenomous.

Farrah smiles as the Vollenbeln lights in the heavens start to form into a small ball that grows bigger and bigger. A pure white bolt of lightning streaks down and splits, hitting Farrah in her hands, jolting and shaking her entire body. She starts to levitate off the claws of Vemenomous and hovers in the air above him, turning and facing him. The wounds on her stomach and back heal right in front of Vemenomous. The lightning bolt constantly flows into her hands, and she raises them above her head, absorbing the power of the lightning. She starts to laugh, looking down on Vemenomous with her glassy brown eyes growing bigger, and her jaw starts to swell, allowing her new teeth to form and fit in her mouth.

"That is it, my queen. Form and become the demonian dragon queen," says Vemenomous, completely focused on Farrah.

Parnapp flies up to Farrah and ties itself back in place around her waist. "Farrah, this is not you. Farrah, you must fight his mind control. Farrah, don't let evil control your thoughts and beliefs. You can do it. Fight it," yells Parnapp.

Farrah looks down to Parnapp, who is now back in place around her waist, and the smile on her face fades. She looks all around and lowers her arms, stopping the lightning. She bites a few times, noticing her abnormal teeth and jaw. She feels her face with her hands, running her fingers over and along the scar made by Vemenomous. She blinks her eyes over and over. Slowly she lowers to the ground, standing in front of Vemenomous. Her eyes shrink back to her beautiful chestnut brown eyes, and her jaw shrinks, along with those terrifying teeth, back to normal.

"Do not fight me, my queen. I will never let you go. You are mine," yells Vemenomous, taking a step toward Farrah.

Farrah points her hands at Vemenomous and releases her dragon-slaying hands. Vemenomous quickly nullifies this attack with his breath attack, and the two of them square off yet again. "You will never have me, Vemenomous. I have grown too powerful for you already. You may be able to somehow send images into my mind, confusing my decision making, but my magical strength continues to grow, and I will be rid of you. Vegenrage is my love, he is my destiny, and you are nothing. You are my enemy," she says, swinging her right arm in an upward motion toward Vemenomous, and huge spikes shoot up from the ground one after another. They are so fast that Vemenomous does not have time to evade the spikes, and he is hit between his front two legs, his belly, and between his hind legs. These spikes are massive, and they cause him great pain and internal damage.

Vemenomous flaps his wings with all his power to rise up into the air and off the spikes, which glow white with veins of blue running all around them. The spikes sink back into the ground as fast as they have risen. Vemenomous flies up about fifteen feet and loses all his energy, falling back to the ground, landing on his four legs, but they are too weak to support the fall. He falls to his side, drained of energy and breathing very heavily.

"That is right, Vemenomous. Lances laced with the Vollenbeln lights are draining to the users of the dark. Demonology has no place here among the heavenly lights, and this is my home. This is the life. Vegenrage has given me the choice to live, and I accept it. He has given me the freedom to choose. Never has he told me or ordered me, and I am his forever. You will never have me," says Farrah, walking toward Vemenomous, who is lying drained of energy on the ground, and his blood flows from his belly.

Vemenomous starts to laugh, confusing Farrah, giving her pause as she feels chills run up and down her spine. "I know you are here. Show yourself, demon," says Farrah, who is a little surprised to see Zevoncour rise beside Vemenomous.

"Yes, you are strong, Farrah. You are only the second ever in the Maglical System to become Swellgic. Do you know who the first was?" Zevoncour pauses to wait for Farrah to respond, and she does not. "Roartill is the only other magical being ever to become Swellgic. Only Roartill can truly teach you how to control your magical ability. We knew all along that you would be the next supreme power, and it was Roartill who has done everything to make sure you mature and find your way to us. Vegenrage is nothing more than the catalyst that was needed to start your magnificent growth into what you have become and have yet to be. Vegenrage has no idea what you are going to be. He has no clue how to handle you when your power is so great that the simple touch of your skin will melt his flesh. We have tried to spare you of this fate. Make no mistake, child. We want you to be by our side to rule, to control, and to set our law, and you will be a part of us. If you oppose us, we will destroy you. We want you, yes, but need you, no. If Vegenrage is what you want, then go to him. Ah, wait a minute, even with your power, you do not know where he is, do you? Why is that? Why do you know where every being you think about is except the one you say you love? I know where he is right now, and that is because we have the knowledge to share so you can understand your power and use it to its fullest. Why has Vegenrage not shared this knowledge with you? It is because he knows you are too powerful for him, and he tries to control you. Vegenrage holds you down so you can serve him," says Zevoncour as he touches Vemenomous, whose wounds heal and who slowly rises to his feet.

Farrah feels her spine tingle with chills as she looks behind her to see Xanorax rise from the ground, and he is holding the shard hammer. She turns to face Xanorax, and this is by design taking Farrah's attention off Zevoncour, who chants a spell. "Zava conta groulous enverntum cemousleam contour conta free zemontum," says Zevoncour, pointing his hands at Farrah's feet.

Farrah looks down as the earth she is standing on softens, and she sinks down almost to her knees, and the ground hardens, immobilizing her. This has been done because the demons know they have to strike Farrah with the shard hammer again, but while she is wearing Cleapell, they will not be fast enough to strike her. Now she has been immobilized in a demon sponge. This spell is exactly what it sounds like—a huge invisible sponge that is pure evil and draws all heavenly or good magic away from anyone caught in this spell. Farrah will figure out how to get out of the sponge, but it will take her a moment, and this is all the time the demons and Xanorax need.

"Now, Xanorax, strike her now that she is caught in the sponge," yells Zevoncour. Xanorax draws the shard hammer and swings, striking Farrah right in the stomach, where she has been struck with this weapon before. Her mouth opens wide like she is going to scream, but she has no breath and stares expressionless, grasping the shard hammer deep in her stomach.

Vemenomous walks to the left side of Farrah, and Zevoncour to her right side. "That is right, Farrah. The staff of barrier breath powered by my soul, once held by you, created the link between our minds. That staff became the staff of magic engulf and then the glass staff of demon uprising, and now the circle is complete with the shard hammer. You can fight me no more. You can resist me no more, my queen," says Vemenomous as he grasps the shard hammer and pulls it from Farrah's stomach. Her stomach, like before, spews red sparks and flares, to which Vemenomous puts his left paw. He presses his paw to her stomach, extinguishing the flames. He pulls his paw from her stomach, which now looks like it is fire under glass. The fire is seen under her ribs to her sides and above her pelvis. Farrah's eyes are again similar to that of Vemenomous—big, brown, and glassy with a catlike oval in the middle.

"That is right, my queen. The only thing we need is the blood and flesh of Vegenrage, and soon our master will deliver this to us. Your pain will be over soon, my queen," says Vemenomous as he, Zevoncour, and Xanorax have their attention drawn to a figure that appears ten yards in front of them.

"Demons, you think you can come here and spread your lies and your filth. This is the home of my boy and my girl, and you have no place here," Logantrance says very loudly, carrying his long golden staff, which he forcefully hammers into the ground with both hands. "Heavenly lights of Vollenbeln. Vegenrage is my protégé, and I am his teacher. Grant me power to rid his home of this evil scourge. I call upon the heavenly lights to rid this evil. I am Logantrance, Vegenrage's master and creator of Vollenbeln." Logantrance grasps his staff with both hands. A ball of silvery white light forms high in the night sky.

Zevoncour motions Xanorax and Vemenomous to attack Logantrance, and they both head for him as quickly as they can. Huge bolts of white lightning shoot from the ball of light in the sky into the staff that Logantrance is holding, and from the amber jewel on top of Logantrance's staff shoot three bolts of lightning that each spread into many smaller ones, striking Xanorax, Vemenomous, and Zevoncour, freezing them dead in their tracks. The demons and Xanorax shake violently, unable to fight the great power from the heavenly lights. Logantrance pushes forward on his staff with great intensity in his face, like he is directing more and more power into the magical spell. It is working; the demons are unable to move on their own. The heavenly light produces a heat that is deadly to demons and the warlock, and they are starting to shake more and more violently, as their skin and flesh is literally melting and dripping from their bodies.

Vemenomous looks to Farrah and speaks telepathically with her. *Farrah, don't let it end like this. Stop him. Stop the magic user.*

Farrah looks at Logantrance with her big, wide brown eyes, and the fire in her belly starts to brighten up. She thrusts both hands at Logantrance, shooting her dragon-slaying hands at him. The spell hits the staff in front of Logantrance, and a huge bright explosion happens, blinding everyone. The bolts of lightning stop shooting from the staff, and no one can see anything yet. There is still a great white ball of blinding light surrounding the area where Logantrance has been. Logantrance can be heard screaming as the ball of light slowly softens and disappears, and he is thrown back a few yards, landing on his back.

Freed from the heavenly light, Zevoncour wastes no time, using his remaining energy to teleport to the inner realm, where he can regain his strength. Xanorax teleports back to his home in the Pinegrow Forest. Vemenomous, on the other hand, approaches Farrah, speaking telepathically with her. *The power, you feel it. You consume it. Not only can you take but you can give as well. Here, let me show you how to relieve the magical pressure.* Vemenomous rests his huge paw on the left shoulder of Farrah, and his long claws hang over her back. He is drawing magical energy from Farrah and using it to heal his badly damaged muscles and regrow his melted flesh and skin. He is very surprised to feel the magical energy in Farrah, which is very strong. He begins to heal as Logantrance stands up, grabs his golden staff from the ground, and runs up behind Vemenomous, who is concentrating on healing.

"Get away from her, you evil beast," yells Logantrance, swinging his staff at Vemenomous, hitting him in the left hind leg. This leaves a huge gash, ripping scale and flesh, causing great pain. Vemenomous roars into the air, having his concentration broken in a painful way. Vemenomous turns to face a very angry Logantrance, who swings his staff over his head like a two-handed sword, smashing Vemenomous in the head with all the magical force he can muster, and this is enough to slam Vemenomous's head into the ground at lightning speed.

Logantrance is a few feet from the head of Vemenomous. Before Vemenomous can raise his head off the ground, Logantrance swings his staff at the left wing of Vemenomous, which has fallen to the ground. This attack acts just like a sword, leaving a huge slice right through his wing. Vemenomous has taken significant damage from the Vollenbeln lights, which Logantrance has first cast upon him, and his muscles have not regained their strength yet. Logantrance is fast enough to make another staff attack, twirling the staff in circles with his two hands, spinning his body like a much younger version of himself, and coming up to Vemenomous's left shoulder to make a very painful strike by swinging his very long staff. It digs deep into the shoulder of Vemenomous, slices right through his flesh, and cuts his shoulder bone, exiting his lower shoulder and ripping flesh. Blood streams from the wound. Logantrance continues his motion in a windmill fashion, swinging his staff with all his might down and up, turning to face Vemenomous's head. There is a magical force that is invisible but acts exactly like a sledgehammer. This slams into the top of Vemenomous's head and crushes his head into the ground with such great force that his skull cracks and his left eye almost pops out.

Vemenomous has his muscles and skin almost melted from his body when Logantrance has first attacked with the Vollenbeln lights. Vemenomous has hoped to heal himself with the help of Farrah, but he cannot cope with the speed and attacking ability of Logantrance. Logantrance is using the Vollenbeln lights as power for his staff, which greatly weakens Vemenomous with every strike, and it appears Vemenomous has made a fatal miscalculation as Logantrance raises his staff with both hands, ready to make a death strike on the nearly dead Vemenomous, who is lying on the ground. Logantrance is about to hurry Vemenomous's travel to Magical Hell with a decapitating swing of his staff. He has his staff held high above his head, ready to swing down, when suddenly he cannot move. He can feel his stomach suck in, and his lungs squeeze like all the air in his body is being drawn out. All he can do is turn to see Farrah. Logantrance drops his staff and tries to inhale as hard as he can. "Farrah, what are you doing? Farrah, stop!" says Logantrance very weakly, and that is all he can get out verbally as he can no longer breathe. He falls to the ground on his back, reaching for Farrah.

Farrah laughs with tears falling from her abnormally large glassy brown eyes. Her left index finger is pointed at Logantrance, and she is draining his magic and his life essence from his body. She points her right index finger at Vemenomous and begins to drain the magic from his being as well.

Zevoncour rises a few feet at the back of Vemenomous, completely healed from his ordeal with Logantrance, and he can see purple and red lights flowing from the bodies of Logantrance and Vemenomous into Farrah's fingers. He knows she is draining their magical ability and that she will not stop; she will drain their life essence, killing both of them. Farrah is so magically powerful that she does not even have to be physically touching someone to drain their life from them. "Farrah, you must release Vemenomous. He is your king. Stop your drain on your king," says Zevoncour.

Farrah rises in the air with tears falling from her eyes, and she points the middle finger on her right hand at Zevoncour, who raises his hands, shielding himself. A red-colored dome brightens and becomes visible around Zevoncour. "Farrah, your mind is weak without the help of your king. Vemenomous is the one who helped you maintain your mind and not become Swellgic. You have to revive Vemenomous so he can help you control your magic. You are becoming Swellgic, and without the help of your king, you will consume too much magic, and this could kill you," says Zevoncour.

Farrah laughs. "I am in control of my mind, and Vemenomous never was my king. Vemenomous only wanted the power I could grant him, just like you, demon. Now you both shall pay with your lives," she says, laughing and increasing the magical draw on all three of her victims. Logantrance is visibly becoming very weak, and Vemenomous already looks like he is dead.

"I cannot let you, my queen. I will be back for you with Vemenomous," says Zevoncour as he jumps on Vemenomous and teleports the two of them back to the inner realm. Farrah is taken by surprise by this move and lowers to the ground, looking at Logantrance, who cannot say a word. He is reaching for Farrah with his right arm. His left arm is holding his throat.

"Farrah," yells Parnapp. "Farrah, stop. You must control your mind, Farrah. Vemenomous and Roartill have corrupted your mind with the use of the shard hammer. You have to fight it. Quintis, we have to save Logantrance and Farrah. It is up to us."

"You got it," replies Quintis, which rises, still attached to the golden rope, which simply stretches. Its two eyes pop out, and it moves right in the path of Farrah's magic, blocking it and deflecting it away. Logantrance takes a deep breath and gasps for air. "Now it is up to you, Parnapp. Do your thing."

"Farrah, I am sorry, but this is necessary," says Parnapp, which snaps up like a flyswatter, smacking Farrah in the face. Farrah shakes her head a little bit, and Parnapp flips up and swats her in the face again. "Come on, Farrah, come on. I know you are in there. Come on, Farrah, come back to me." Parnapp swats Farrah in the face again, and she slowly lowers to the ground as her eyes shrink back down to her normal beautiful brown eyes. Farrah closes her eyes with a crying face as tears really start to fall from her eyes now.

Logantrance gets up, having caught his breath, and no real damage has been done to him, just a very serious scare, as he felt the enormous power and draw of Farrah that has been easily overtaking him. Logantrance approaches Farrah, hugging her, and she pushes him back. "Farrah, my girl, they have gone. The demons are gone, and I am here. You are safe now," says Logantrance.

"Yes, I am safe, but you are not. This keeps happening to me. Vemenomous somehow always seems to be back in my head, and I cannot get rid of him. He has been right all along. It is only a matter of time before the demons are able to use me to get to Vegenrage. I am not going to let that happen. I know how to beat them, Logantrance. I know how to defeat the demons," says Farrah.

Logantrance can feel great heat coming from her. "Farrah, no. Farrah, this is not the way," he says.

"Yes, Logantrance, this is the way. The power, can you feel it? It is so wonderful. It is so easy, and I am its keeper," says Farrah, looking up and holding her arms out to her sides.

"Farrah, no," says Logantrance, backing up, looking like he wants to cry.

"Yes, Logantrance, I am going to consume all the magic. I am going to be all powerful, and I am going to destroy the demons. I will kill them all, and then Vegenrage and I will have peace at last. You had better go now," says Farrah, rising into the air.

"Farrah, this is not the way," says Logantrance, backing up and collecting his staff. "Wait for Vegenrage. He loves you, and he can help you. Please, Farrah, hold on for just a little while longer. Vegenrage will come for you," says Logantrance.

"Where is Vegenrage? Where is he? I need him now, and it is funny how the only presence on three worlds that I cannot find is of the one I love. You say Vegenrage will come for me. I will come for him. I will be able to find him, and we will be together forever," says Farrah, rising into the air, and flames start to burst out from her form as she rises higher and higher.

"Farrah, you know there is good reason why Vegenrage is not here right now. There is nothing that he wants more than to be with you, but as you said, the demons will not let you be. Well, they will not let Vegenrage be either, and he is doing what he has to do in order to be with you. He is doing what he needs to do to make all of us able to live in peace." Logantrance watches as Farrah rises farther and farther into the sky. He feels so helpless watching as Farrah falls into Swellgic hypnotism. Logantrance has heard the legend of Swellgic, a being that becomes so magically powerful that they consume all the magic around them. They become so euphoric that the more they consume, the better they feel, and total destruction is the only end.

"Logantrance! Logantrance!" calls Quintis.

"Quintis, what is it?" asks Logantrance.

"There is no more you can do here. You must go to the Erkensharie at once. Ugoria has been destroyed, and all the survivors except one have gone to the Erkensharie. You must go there at once," says Quintis.

"There is no more I can do here," says Logantrance, watching Farrah rise into the air, and flames sprout out all around her. She looks like a fire angel in the sky. Logantrance walks through a dimension door on his way to the Erkensharie.

CHAPTER 30

Champion of the Heavenly Lights

Vegenrage is walking right at Roartill with his palms up, and the balls of lightning swirling just above his palms are growing larger. Vegenrage looks up into the dark sky with no stars, just a blanket of ash covering the horizon. He points his hands down to the ground, and like rockets, the balls of lightning shoot down, and Vegenrage rises high in the air. He hovers, looking straight up, and the bluish white lightning shooting from the palms of his hands start to swirl around his body, consuming him in a very bright white light. The light grows up and down in the shape of a diamond, and the top light penetrates the ash cloud, pushing it away, exposing the true night sky. The ash is pushed back and seems to be devoured by the light that grows along the ash cloud all the way back to the mountains spewing ash. The light follows the ash, consuming it; enters the mountains, hardening all the lava back to the core of the world; and stops the eruptions. The ash stops spewing, and the lava stops flowing. This light follows all the ash covering all the planet of Fargloin, stopping all the eruptions in all the mountains.

"No!" yells Roartill. He cannot look at Vegenrage because he is so bright, and all that can be seen is a bright white light in the form of a diamond that reaches from the ground to the heavens. "No, you cannot come back. You gave your eternal life to try to contain me. I have escaped, and you have been defeated by me. You are beaten, Age'venger. Go back to your eternal sleep, where you belong. I gained the *Gowdelken*, and you lost everything. Just because Vegenrage is your name, spelled in a different arrangement of letters, does not mean you can take form. You cannot fight me anymore."

"You still misunderstand, brother. I used my eternal life to contain you, yes, but my life did not end. Like always, the only thing you know is deceit, corruption, and violence. Yes, you did gain the *Gowdelken*. And with this knowledge, you escaped my containment. This was made possible by the races of man of the Maglical System understanding, knowing, and finding the human who has chosen through his own free will to fight for them against you. You have given the power of foresight to the dragons, who planned for a thousand years to kill the chosen champion of the heavenly lights, and they failed. Now the dragons ally themselves with Vegenrage, the human who through free will named himself and, by doing so, brought to fruition this moment. By naming himself Vegenrage, he chose to face and challenge the dark, the unknown, the evil that you are. You had better take notice of this because to face Vegenrage is to face a chosen champion empowered so that he can end you. I cannot kill you, brother, and I will no longer contain you, but Vegenrage is the chosen champion of the heavenly lights. Your chosen champion was dragon, and now you have your demonian dragon. The dragon you gave the power of foresight to was killed by his own kind, who knew Vegenrage was not their enemy. The dragons did not fall for your deceit. They did not allow one of their own to manipulate them, as I did not create life here with you to watch you rain down destruction, pain, and grief on all the intelligent life. If that is all you want, then you will face my champion. He is human, and he has free will. So face my champion, brother, with all your deceit, all your hate, and all your lies. Let us see if the creator of evil can face the creation of love. I warn you again, brother, as I did eons ago. Let love live or be sent back to the hell, where you belong," says Age'venger, who is an incredibly bright light that surrounds Vegenrage.

Roartill cannot even look at the light. The light shoots straight up into the air, and Vegenrage falls to the ground very fast, landing on his feet and bending his knees, finally stopping as his hands hit the ground. Vegenrage looks up with his eyes shining bluish white. He stands and walks toward Roartill with his palms facing his chest, and bluish white lightning seems to be pulled from his fingers and thumbs to his feet, legs, chest, shoulders, and head. Vegenrage is smiling, and the lightning running from his arms to his body can be heard sizzling through the air.

"Come on, chosen one. This is your time to die," says Roartill, reaching behind him with his right arm, and a demon spear forms in his hand. He throws it very hard right at Vegenrage's chest. Vegenrage blocks the spear, which is massive in comparison to his body, with his left forearm, and the spear flies by the left side of his head. He continues walking at the much larger Roartill. Roartill reaches both of his hands over and behind his head, grasping demon spears that form in each hand and are thrown at Vegenrage. The spears split into three each, and now there are six spears heading right for Vegenrage. Vegenrage puts the palms of his hands together in front of him and points them forward. Three of the spears are diverted to the left side of Vegenrage and three to his right.

"You want to play, Roartill? Then let's play," says Vegenrage, putting both hands together to his right side, and a fantastic long sword, which appears to be made out of silver light, grows in his hands. It has a huge blue sapphire on the bottom of the hilt, which is made out of brilliant silver. The blade is long and thin, and it shines, gleams, and sparkles as Vegenrage shows off impressive swordsmanship, swinging the sword from side to side, slicing the air as he still approaches Roartill.

Roartill dwarfs Vegenrage, standing a little more than twice his size, but Vegenrage pursues Roartill fearlessly. Roartill laughs as a very long thick red hell spear made out of lava from Maglical Hell grows from the grip of his right hand. The end of the spear divides into two barbed, very sharp points. "You want to play, human? Then let's play," says Roartill, swinging his spear over his head and down onto Vegenrage, who blocks the strike with his heavens sword. The blade of the sword is nothing more than starlight growing from the silver hilt in Vegenrage's hands, but it acts exactly like a metal sword. The blade becomes a solid sword made out of a brilliant silver metal upon contact with any object. It is unbreakable and the only magical item of its kind in all of existence. Only Vegenrage can ever wield this remarkable sword.

Roartill pushes down with great force on the sword of Vegenrage, and the two weapons make sparks that explode into their surroundings. Roartill pulls his spear back. "My brother has given you great power, and not only does he give you his magic but he also gives you his very own heavens sword. Why do you hide behind this human, Age'venger? Why do you not face me in your true form? Are you afraid I will beat you again?" says Roartill.

"I am not Age'venger. I am Vegenrage. I am not governed or ruled by Age'venger. I am of free will, but unlike Age'venger, I can kill you, and I will not hesitate to end the hate and the evil that you are," says Vegenrage.

"End me!" says Roartill in a mad very deep voice. "I am Roartill, and I created the land you stand on. I have created everything here, and you think you will end me, you runt? I will twist your head off. I will slice your stomach and suck out your intestines like spaghetti and eat it with a meatball that you call a heart. I created worlds, and I created life millennia before you were even a thought, and you think you will end me."

"You created the land. You created the lava and the rock. Age'venger created the air. Age'venger created the clouds, the mist, and the oceans. Life came as a result of the worlds you two created, and then you laughed as you destroyed lives. You created chaos and violence so that you could draw souls into the hell you created. In this way, you can draw energy from those souls and control those souls. By this means, you can always exist, and you can always grow more and more powerful. Age'venger never wanted this, and he shared knowledge with me. Age'venger shared the truth with me. You will never let me be. You will never let Farrah and me be together, and you have already proven this, so I am here to destroy you. I am here to face you so that Farrah and I can live free and safe from the evil that you are. This goes for all life that is governed by free will, not evil, deception, and control," says Vegenrage.

"Your ignorance is intoxicating. For you to even think you can face me is laughable. Do you even know where you are? Tell me, Vegenrage. Where is your love right now? Where is Farrah? Where is your mentor, Logantrance? Do you know where any of your friends are? You cannot see past the dirt you stand on, and that is because I own this land. I own this world, and I own you," says Roartill, hunching his shoulders forward and peering at Vegenrage.

"I will know as soon as I destroy you. Enough of this talk, demon," says Vegenrage, who swings his heavens sword like a baseball bat, and heavenly lights shoot from the sword, cutting a very deep and painful wound right into Roartill's stomach. Roartill yells in extreme pain from the wound, which continues to cause him great pain. Vegenrage holds the sword with his left hand and then up and over his left shoulder as he grabs it with his right hand. He swings with both hands from his left shoulder sideways across his body toward the ground. This sends more heavenly lights hitting Roartill, causing another gash from the top of his right shoulder sideways down through his chest, and Roartill cries in pain as blood gushes from the wounds. Vegenrage repeats his attack, sending more heavenly lights crossing Roartill's body again, and now there is a huge X on his chest. His ribs can be seen through the gashes in his flesh. Blood is gushing, and Roartill cries, raising his hell spear over his head.

"Kliblith mengen orthonodwells eilden," chants Roartill, and a clear shield with a reddish hue falls from over his head like a dome to the ground. Vegenrage continues to throw heavenly lights at Roartill with his sword, but the shield created by Roartill is strong enough to block the attacks. Vegenrage runs at the shield and strikes it with his sword, which then becomes solid, but still the shield holds. He takes a step back after a few unsuccessful attacks.

"You stupid human, you are not even from our worlds. You are not even from our universe, and you think you are going to come here and challenge me. Let me tell you something. I have only let you live this long because you are going to lead me to the universe you are from, and there I will rule all life just like I do here. I am playing with you. I am using you, and now I have a dragon to destroy and a human female who is soon to be a servant of mine. When I have finished that, I will be back for you. You are no match for me. You are my servant, like all the races of men," says Roartill, who begins to chant another spell. "Fromin contule errible reverable consuler *Neggaheb!*"

While he is chanting, Vegenrage reaches to the sky with both hands. A ball of heavenly white light forms and grows very large high in the sky. "Vegenrage! Vegenrage!" yells Behaggen, whose eyes pop out. But before Vegenrage can cast his magic and before he answers Behaggen, Roartill finishes his chant, which is very bad for Vegenrage. Behaggen unties itself from Vegenrage's waist, floats chest high in front of

Vegenrage, and flips inside out. This produces an identical bag of holding that is charcoal black, and red eyes with black pupils pop out of it.

"It is about time, Master. Why have you kept me dormant for so long?" asks Neggaheb.

"Neggaheb, capture Vegenrage but do not kill him," orders Roartill. Neggaheb, in an instant, floats up, opens very wide, and snaps shut over Vegenrage's head. The sword in Vegenrage's hands disappears, and he grabs and swats at the bag over his head like his is suffocating. He is stumbling around, falling to his knees, and trying to pull the bag off his head.

"This one is very strong, Master. He has heavenly magic, Master. I do not know if I can contain him for long. I can kill him fairly quickly, Master," says Neggaheb.

"Do not kill him. Contain him. I will be back shortly. I have a few matters to tend to," says Roartill.

"Master, this one is strong. I do not know if I can hold him," says Neggaheb.

"Hold him. Contain him and be right here when I get back, or you will wish I never brought you out of hiding," says Roartill.

"Yes, Master. But, Master, what if Age'venger comes and changes me back into Behaggen?" says Neggaheb, watching as Roartill sinks into the earth.

"He will not come here. I have protected the area until I get back. You just keep hold of Vegenrage and do not let him go or else," says Roartill, and he is gone. He has gone to Maglical Hell, and he gathers Othgile to send him to the lair of Gwithen. He is the first demon soul to ever be let free of Maglical Hell by Roartill, and Othgile heads for the lair of Gwithen to taste the sweet meat of dragon. Othgile fails to ever land a hand on Gwithen, as she escapes through the portal created by Hornspire. Roartill rises to Othgile, telling him he will get another chance, and Othgile is sent back to Maglical Hell.

While all this is going on, all who have survived in Ugoria have made their way to the Erkensharie with the exception of Cloakenstrike. Ulegwahn, Oriapow, and all the leading classes of Erkensharie elves are in the courtyard to greet their long-lost brothers from Ugoria. All those present in the Erkensharie gasp and many have to fight back tears upon realizing the only survivors of Ugoria are Basters, Fraborn, Shenlylith, Bronsilith, Verlyle, Gandeleem, Wendell, Willithcar, Tornsclin, Gonbilden, Vorgillith, and Stromgin. Things are really put into perspective when the Erkensharie elves realize that the elves of Ugoria are gone, and if this happened to them, then it can happen in the Erkensharie.

"You are Shenlylith, the Ugorian elven female consumed by the snow gold trinket. It was your life force that powered the trinket. I know this because you wear the trinket around your neck. I am Ulegwahn, king of the Erkensharie, and I command the Octagemerwell, the most powerful elven magical item. We here in the Erkensharie have been given instruction from Hornspire, the dragon of foresight, who has passed. We believe he intends to see the races of man defeat the demons, so we believe the writings he has recently given us. It is through these writings that I know how to identify you by the trinket around your neck. Am I correct in assuming that you are indeed Shenlylith, the elven female turned human with the loss of the power of the trinket?" says Ulegwahn. Shenlylith is about to respond when everyone's attention is diverted to Logantrance, who walks forth from his dimension door.

"King Ulegwahn and the Erkensharie elves, the Ugorian elves with Shenlylith and Basters, I have grave news for us all. I have been given instruction from Hornspire, who has been killed," says Logantrance, who is interrupted by King Ulegwahn.

"Yes, Logantrance. You, the Ugorian elves, and the Erkensharie elves have all been given instruction from Hornspire, and we all have been given books that have told us of our current situation," says Ulegwahn, looking to Shenlylith and Logantrance. They all look at one another and nod yes. Ulegwahn continues. "I believe the books we all have received from Hornspire led us all here. They have told us all that Vegenrage is an ally and that we have to unite and go to save him. It just so happens, according to the book we read here in Erkensharie, that Vegenrage is right here in the Long Forest, and we must go to save him."

"Not all of us. According to the book I read, Ulegwahn and Oriapow from the Erkensharie, along with myself, Basters, and Fraborn from Ugoria and the teacher of Vegenrage, Logantrance"—Shenlylith looks to Logantrance—"we must all go the Long Forest, and there we must rescue Vegenrage from innocent betrayal, whatever that means," she says.

"Vegenrage. One minute, I want his head. The next minute, I am actually thinking about risking my life to help save him. We all have the location where Vegenrage is, correct?" says Ulegwahn. Everyone nods yes, having heard or read his exact location from the books that have been provided by Hornspire.

"No more talk. I go to save my boy. He needs me and all of us, and Farrah needs Vegenrage. We have no time to sit here and talk. I am going to the Long Forest," says Logantrance.

"I am with you," says Oriapow.

"I am coming," says Shenlylith, looking to Basters, who nods, acknowledging his intent to go.

"I am ready," says Fraborn, and the five of them look to Ulegwahn.

Ulegwahn nods. "I will go, but I have to make preparations. Oriapow and I will be going, and if we should not return, I have to make sure the Erkensharie is not left in disarray. I will go to the Great Erken and tell Thrillquewn that he will be in charge of the Great Erken if we would not come back," says Ulegwahn, who has teleported to the Great Erken.

"The books you have all read may say nothing about the dwarves of Glaboria, so surely it will be a great advantage to have more help. You will have myself wielding Glimtronian at your side," says Glimtron.

"I will be there with Fearpierce," says Rifter.

"And I with my Fireod Four sword," says Silgeqwee.

"I shall be by my king and brothers with the Sapphirewell," says Blythgrin.

"It shall be very comforting to have you all with us. This will not be easy, and we face the evil of the Maglical System. It will try to kill us all, so be on your best guard," says Logantrance. Ulegwahn quickly makes his return while

Logantrance is telling everyone he is on his way to the Long Forest.

"I know where Vegenrage is. He is three miles down the Nomberry Pass, and there is no time to waste. He needs us now. I will meet you all there. Good luck to us all," says Logantrance, and he walks through his dimension door.

"Ulegwahn, come with me. I know the Nomberry Pass as well as anyone, and you can follow me through my dimension door," says Oriapow, and Ulegwahn nods and follows him.

"Basters, I no longer have my magic, but the book said I will be needed because I still have the snow gold trinket," says Shenlylith.

"Yes, the book I read said you would be with me, and it gave me the exact location where we are to teleport. If Hornspire is setting us all up with his writings, like he has done, we could all be walking into a deadly trap. I'm just saying," says Basters as he puts his hand on Shenlylith's shoulder, and the two of them teleport away.

"Blythgrin, are you ready? You can bring the four of us to where Vegenrage is, right?" asks Glimtron.

"No problem," says Blythgrin, and he brings the four dwarves through his dimension door.

The party of ten teleport to the Long Forest, and they all arrive in a circle around Vegenrage, who is on his knees. They can all see instantly that Vegenrage has the sinister black bag of holding over his head, and he is struggling with his hands to try to remove it. It is nighttime, and the area is very dark, although they can all see with the bright moonlight. The place is very eerie and quiet with dark dirt for as far as the eye can see. They all see the eyes of the bag of holding pop open.

Vegenrage is kneeling in the lava of Maglical Hell, which does not burn him but absorbs any magic he tries to use and prevents him from moving anywhere, like he is in quicksand. This is one of the few traps that Neggaheb has Vegenrage ensnared in until Roartill returns. Neggaheb has deep confusion cast on Vegenrage, and protects him from the heat of the lava. With Vegenrage's head completely covered, Neggaheb is able to project thoughts and feelings upon Vegenrage with his powerful confusion spell. Vegenrage is powerless, even though he has all his magic intact. He cannot think through a single thought without it changing to something else.

Neggaheb takes notice of all the adversaries surrounding him and standing just outside the ten-foot diameter of hell lava that Vegenrage is in. Neggaheb chants, "Orthrisen rounen conedin fulopen consumen enapulated unulfsurp." A red light grows from the hell lava surrounding Vegenrage and Neggaheb in a dome. They are now completely surrounded by lava on the ground and a sphere of red light all around them.

"You are all here just as Master said you would be. This is the time, the setting, and the final days of you all," says Neggaheb.

"Logantrance, do not cast any magic. Any magic cast into the red sphere will be manipulated by evil, and the effects will be whatever they want," says Quintis.

"Nobody cast any magic on or near the red dome," yells Logantrance, and everyone hears him. "What about our weapons? Will they affect the red sphere and destroy it?"

"Only if the weapons are infused with heavenly magic or angel blessing. Only Oriapow and Ulegwahn have experience with starlight magic, which is heavenly. If they use this magic with the Octagemerwell and the Sapphirewell, the hell shell may be broken," says Quintis.

"What about Shenlylith? She was the great snow elf, and she still has the snow gold trinket. This must have some importance," asks Logantrance, who calls for all the others to come to him. They hurry to Logantrance.

"Shenlylith has lost her magic, as did the snow gold trinket. She does know heavenly magic, but she has no magic to wield anymore," says Quintis. All the others make their way to Logantrance.

"Logantrance, how do we get Vegenrage out of that trap and that thing off his head?" asks Glimtron.

"I do not know, Glimtron. Oriapow, you and Ulegwahn have to use your heavenly magic, along with the power of the Octagemerwell and the Sapphirewell. This may be our only way to break Vegenrage free," says Logantrance.

"Well, if there is ever a time to break out the heart of Fargloin, this is it," says Oriapow, looking to Ulegwahn, who nods yes and pulls the Octagemerwell from Vixtrixx and then respectfully hands it to Oriapow.

"Vixtrixx, you will give us guidance and help us, right?" asks Ulegwahn of his bag of holding.

"I will, Ulegwahn. I will be right here," says Vixtrixx.

"And I will as well," says Erben, producing the Sapphirewell for Blythgrin. Blythgrin and Oriapow hold the two magical gems close to each other, and the snow gold trinket around

Shenlylith's neck raises and draws her toward the magical gems.

"Guys, guys, what is happening?" says Shenlylith as she walks toward Blythgrin and Oriapow. Everyone takes notice as she walks toward the Octagemerwell and the Sapphirewell and as she puts one hand on each gem. Shenlylith starts to glow white. "It's coming back. My magic is coming back to me." Shenlylith has her eyes closed. She puts a big smile on her face and steps back from the two gems. The white glow goes away, and Shenlylith opens her eyes. "My magic has returned to me. It is not like before. It is very similar, but now it is heavenly magic. I know it is. I could feel Vegenrage, and that bag of holding on his head has him in a constant state of confusion. We have to get that bag off Vegenrage."

"Yes, but how are we going to do that?" asks Ulegwahn.

"Like this," says Shenlylith, pointing her hands at Rifter's bow and shooting brilliant white lights from her fingertips into it. She does the same to all the weapons of all in the party, infusing them with heavenly magic. This does not change any of the weapons; it just makes them very potent and lethal against evil beings and demonic magic.

"Now all the weapons here are lethal against demons and demon magic. Attack the hell shell. Strike it with your weapons. We can break through. I have some magic of my own now that will seriously weaken the magic keeping us from Vegenrage. Wait for my cue," says Shenlylith, and she starts to chant a spell. Just as she does, huge walls of Maglical Hell lava grow from the ground in a square that is one-half mile around the area outside of Vegenrage and Neggaheb. They grow up very fast for forty feet, and then the top grows shut. If not for the red glow from the lava in the hell shell, it will be pitch-black in the box-shaped enclosure.

The ground starts to shake, and everyone loses their footing as Roartill rises from the dirt on the other side of the hell shell. Vemenomous rises to his left, and Zevoncour rises to his right. "So here you are, the finest magic users of the races of men. Here, you are right where I want you. You are trapped, and your flesh will be ours," says Roartill, who points to the dirt to his left. "Rise, Othgile, rise. Your time to feast on flesh is near."

The extremely intimidating Othgile rises from the earth. Just as he stands and faces the races of men, the top of the lava enclosure, which is huge, explodes into hardened lava shards and falls on everyone, causing them to dodge and turn away from the sharp shards of rock flying everywhere. This is because a red fireball flies through the hardened hell lava roof like a meteor, exploding it and landing on the hell shell Vegenrage is in, shattering it. This meteor is actually Farrah, and she lands on Vegenrage, who falls face-first into the hell lava. She is standing on his back. She is completely covered in flames, and her eyes are large and brown, like that of Vemenomous. Farrah looks down at Vegenrage to see the bag of holding over his head, and she points at the bag. "Don't you move, bag. Do not do a thing," says Farrah, and she points her hands straight out from her shoulders. The granite walls to each side fall and crumble with huge thuds as they hit the ground. She does the same to the other two walls.

Roartill laughs and claps his hands. "She is here. My champion is here at last!" he yells with enthusiasm.

"Blythgrin, put the Sapphirewell back in me quickly. Right now," says Erben to Blythgrin.

"Oriapow quickly put the Octagemerwell back in me now," says Vixtrixx to Oriapow. Blythgrin and Oriapow quickly put the gems into the bags of holding.

Farrah points her left hand at Shenlylith, who flies very fast right at Farrah. Farrah catches her by the neck with her left hand. Her grip is very strong and is choking Shenlylith. Farrah is on fire, and she is burning Shenlylith. "You thought you were smart last time I saw you. You got me to go after Vegenrage, but I know you were with him. I know you and Vegenrage were together, and now I will take your magic and your life force," says Farrah, and Shenlylith screams in pain. Everyone watches how fast her body starts to crumple, and all the heavenly magic is drawn from Shenlylith to Farrah. White light flows up the body of Shenlylith into the hand and arm of Farrah.

"Stop, Farrah! Stop! You are killing her!" yells Rifter, and Farrah ignores him.

He draws fires and hits Farrah with a heavenly arrow from Fearpierce as he runs toward her. This knocks Farrah almost over, and she drops Shenlylith, who falls next to Vegenrage. Glimtron starts to run at Farrah as well.

"Farrah, what are you doing? Farrah, we need you to help us!" yells Glimtron.

Farrah looks at the two dwarves running at her, and she stands tall, closing her eyes, and the flames around her body grow bigger and hotter. The magic users start to feel that Farrah is drawing their magic, and this is more powerful than any magical draw they have ever felt before.

"Rifter, Glimtron, we have to get out of here. Come back here!" yells Logantrance, who whips his arms at the two of them, catches them both with his magical rope, and yanks them both back to where all the others are.

"Farrah is Swellgic. We have to get out of here right now, or she will kill us all. First, she will drain all our magic and then our life force. We cannot fight against her. She is too powerful," says Oriapow.

"Shenlylith. I cannot leave Shenlylith. You all get out of here. I will try to get her to safety," says Basters, drawing his Lavumptom sword and running for Shenlylith.

"Blythgrin, get the dwarves to the Erkensharie. Oriapow, you and Ulegwahn get out of here. I will help Basters if I can, and we will be right behind you. Go, go now. Farrah is becoming way too powerful," says Logantrance.

Blythgrin tries to teleport the dwarves back to the Erkensharie, but already his magic is too weak. The same is true for Ulegwahn and Oriapow; they cannot teleport either. Logantrance watches Basters head for Shenlylith, but he cannot enter the lava. Everyone is starting to be pulled toward Farrah. Shenlylith is lying in the lava right next to Vegenrage, and most of her strength has been stolen. She has just enough strength to take the snow gold trinket, which is protecting her from the heat of the lava, from her neck; put it in the hand of Vegenrage; and bring his hands together, holding the magical trinket. "Vegenrage, I do not know if you can hear me, but this is the snow gold trinket. It is very powerful, and it has heavenly magic in it," says Shenlylith in a very weak, soft voice. She is interrupted by Neggaheb.

"Shut up, you bitch. Shut up. No one is listening to you," says Neggaheb.

Shenlylith is using all of what little magic she has left to protect her from the fire and heat of the lava. Both Vegenrage and Shenlylith have fire all around them because Farrah is a walking inferno. Farrah has been knocked back about ten feet from Vegenrage and Shenlylith, but they are still surrounded in her flames, not to mention the lava they are in. Shenlylith loses her protection from the fire the second Vegenrage takes hold of the snow gold trinket, and she starts to burn. She can see Vegenrage cupping his hands together around the trinket, and a white glow starts to grow bright from within his hands and around his body. This glow begins to grow around Shenlylith as well and protects her while healing her from the heat. The trinket is still in the form of Shenlylith, and Vegenrage grabs it in his right hand and stabs Neggaheb with the trinket. This works wonderfully well, causing Neggaheb to rocket off Vegenrage's head and right into the hands of Roartill.

"Master, I am sorry. It burned. It burned," says Neggaheb, sobbing and looking at Roartill with sorrowful eyes.

"Be quiet," says Roartill, putting Neggaheb around his waist.

Vegenrage sits up and leans over Shenlylith, resting his arms, chest, and head on her. They both levitate above the lava and onto solid ground. Vegenrage knows her inner organs have been seriously damaged, like a syringe has been drawing all the life from them. Shenlylith has severe burns all over her body, and Vegenrage heals her very quickly and protects the two of them from the fire that still engulfs them. He sits up, pointing to Logantrance, noticing that all the races of men seem to be coming toward him like they are being pulled against their will.

"Oh no. Shenlylith, take this and put it back over your neck," says Vegenrage, giving the snow gold trinket back to Shenlylith. "Go to Logantrance. Run as hard as you can. You have to make it to the others. Farrah has become Swellgic."

Right then, Basters makes his way to Shenlylith, running with the flow of the energy pulling him toward Farrah, who is now hovering ten feet in the air. He reaches for the hand of Shenlylith. "Come with me, Shenlylith. We will be protected from Farrah's wrath by the night jewel. My Lavumptom sword will get us to safety," says Basters.

"Can you get the two of you safely back to the Erkensharie?" asks Vegenrage.

"Yes, I can do that," says Basters. Shenlylith hugs Basters, and he teleports the two of them away.

Vegenrage floats up into the air, noticing all the races of man on the ground being drawn toward Farrah, and their magic is getting weaker and weaker. "Vegenrage, Farrah is Swellgic, and she is drawing all our magic. She is already too strong for us all. You have to stop her. If we are drawn to her, we will burn," yells Logantrance, who—along with the others—is being drawn toward Farrah, and they are now within twenty feet of her.

Vegenrage turns to Farrah. "Farrah, you have to slow down. I know it feels good. It feels natural, but you have to control your mind and stop your magical draw," says Vegenrage, who now has eye contact with Farrah, and he is floating toward her. He can see Farrah's eyes are mimicking those of Vemenomous, but the rest of her body is her own. Vegenrage is glowing silver and white, while Farrah is literally on fire.

"Now, Master? Now? Should we make our move now?" asks Zevoncour.

"Yes, Master. I can catch him in the air while he is focused on Farrah," says Vemenomous.

"Wait, your time is coming. Just wait. It is almost here. Vemenomous, call for Xanorax," says Roartill, and he laughs so loud, pointing his right hand at the earth off to the side of them. Othgile rises from the dirt. "Watch this. This is what we have all been waiting for. Vegenrage, your time has come. What are you going to do? I can have my servants kill you at any time. I can have Farrah kill you at any time, or I could kill you. Which do you prefer?" says Roartill.

Vegenrage rises higher and looks up, raising his arms in the sky. He looks around at all the stars and moves his arms all around, pointing at all the stars in the sky. The stars start to grow in very thin lines of white, like a pencil is drawing lines from them toward Vegenrage. The lines are very thin, but there are so many of them, and they are growing from all over in the sky, heading for Vegenrage's hands.

"Get ready, boys," says Roartill, laughing as Xanorax rises. "This is going to be very powerful." The demons watch all the stars in the sky grow in what seems to be a billion white lines developing from deep space and heading right for Vegenrage.

"Master, I read about this in the *Gowdelken*. Vegenrage is the champion of the heavenly lights. Master, we cannot take a direct hit of starlight from the heavenly champion. Master, we need to shield ourselves," yells Zevoncour. Roartill grabs Zevoncour around the neck and just holds him tight, swinging him around in the air. This keeps Zevoncour quiet while Roartill laughs.

"This is it, my demons. This is what we have been waiting for," says Roartill, dropping Zevoncour on the ground next to him. Roartill opens his arms wide, inviting Vegenrage to strike him right in the chest with his heavenly starlight magic. All Roartill's servants are a little apprehensive as to what the outcome is going to be here, but Roartill seems very confident, which gives his servants courage to stand their ground.

The light from the stars reaches Vegenrage, and he is hit from behind very violently. Farrah flies right into him and takes them both into the ground. The starlight fades back to the stars. Vegenrage hits the ground belly first, and it is like everything is in slow motion to him when in fact they are moving so fast that all the ground around them is thrown like it was water. A huge portion of earth around Vegenrage and Farrah has been thrown clear of where they have landed, and they are in a six-foot-deep hole. Vegenrage is face-first on the ground, with Farrah on his back. All the races of men have been thrown back for many yards, and even the demons have been tossed back except for Roartill, who has his feet firmly planted in the earth, but the force of the impact created waves of air so powerful that Roartill is pushed back, and he laughs as his body is blown back at a forty-five-degree angle.

"Farrah, what have you done?" says Vegenrage, lying on his stomach with the wind knocked out of him. Farrah rolls him over and looks at him, smiling and laughing like this is all fun and games. Her flames have Vegenrage completely engulfed, and she is drawing magic from him so fast that he has lost his silver glow, and he is starting to feel the heat from Farrah's fire. The divot in the ground starts to fill back in, as all the dirt that has been thrown rolls along the ground and refills the hole. Vegenrage and Farrah are slowly rising to the natural flat earth as the hole completely fills itself back in.

"Vegenrage, I knew you would come for me. I knew you would find me," says Farrah, smiling, and she kisses Vegenrage. She is unaware that she is drawing all the magic in the surrounding area, and now that she is kissing Vegenrage, she is drawing a lot of magic, and her feelings of euphoria and happiness are off the charts. She is not aware at all how dangerous this is to her because her thoughts are so pleasurable, and they just keep getting better and better like nothing is wrong. In fact, she will have to release this magic, and this will be such a huge discharge of magic that great destruction will come of this. Vemenomous is able to project very vivid images into Farrah's mind, so he can influence how Farrah directs her magic, and this adds to the danger not so much to Farrah but to those around her.

"Farrah, you are drawing my magic. Farrah, you can't feel it, but you are becoming a magical time bomb," says Vegenrage as he grabs Farrah's face with both of his hands and tries to relieve her of magic, but she has become so powerful that he cannot draw enough.

"Now, Master? Now has to be the time, Master. We will get no better chance than this, Master," says Zevoncour.

"Hang on, Zevoncour, hang on. Vemenomous, Zevoncour, get ready. It is almost time. Othgile, you get ready, and if the time comes, you know what you will have to do," says Roartill, who still holds his demons back.

Farrah is laughing and smiling like nothing is wrong, and she grabs Vegenrage's hands with hers and sits up on him. She puts his hands on her breasts and leans in to kiss Vegenrage. "Farrah, I am sorry, but I have to do this," says Vegenrage, and he sits up, wrapping his arms around Farrah, and starts to draw her magic into him. Farrah is so strong, and her flames burn bright and hot. Vegenrage starts to glow a very bright white.

"Now, Zevoncour. Now, Vemenomous. Go get him," yells Roartill. Zevoncour runs at Vegenrage. His right arm turns into a red hook, and he swings it at Vegenrage's left arm. The hook sinks into his left bicep and pulls him to the ground. Vegenrage screams in pain as the white light around him starts to dim. Vemenomous uses his tail like a spear and drives it through Vegenrage's right bicep, and Vegenrage is tacked to the ground by both his arms.

Roartill walks up behind Xanorax, who is standing at the feet of Vegenrage, and he uses his right index claw to puncture Xanorax's neck. When he pulls the claw out, black blood oozes from the wound. "Now, Xanorax. Now you have the strength. Go for it," says Roartill, and Xanorax screams as the Life Stealer rips from both of his arms, and he penetrates both of Vegenrage's thighs with it. Xanorax shakes and smiles, yelling and smiling exuberantly.

"The time is here!" yells Roartill into the air. "Your champion is about to fail, Age'venger, and I will rule all of the Maglical System and more. You watch from the heavens,

Age'venger, as my champion consumes your champion. The time is now, and my time is forever." Roartill laughs.

Farrah has no idea the demons are all around her. She has no idea Vegenrage is in great pain. In her mind, all she sees is Vegenrage lying beneath her while she sits on him, and she wants to kiss and love him; that is all she wants. She bends down to kiss him on the neck, not realizing that her teeth start to grow long and sharp. She does not realize she is on fire, and her strength is growing, making her fire hotter and hotter while she draws strength from Vegenrage.

Vemenomous is able to confuse what Farrah sees, and all she sees is her loving Vegenrage minus the demons, the fire, and the pain Vegenrage is in. She sees none of the dark; she sees warmth and love. Vegenrage is in great pain, and his strength is being drawn from him by Farrah, two demons, and Xanorax. Vegenrage is losing, and he sees Farrah bend down toward his neck and open her mouth with those nasty huge teeth. He knows she is about to bite a huge chunk of flesh out of his neck, and he is powerless to stop her. "Farrah, no! Farrah!" yells Vegenrage, whose voice is getting very weak.

Roartill laughs, looking to the sky. "Consume him, Farrah. Fulfill your destiny and stand by Vemenomous as queen of the demonian dragons," says Roartill, laughing.

None of the demons notice as the air just above them starts to get blurry, and Gwithen, the white dragon, appears from a dimension door. She spreads her wings wide, facing them right at the demons on Vegenrage, and she shines incredibly bright, concentrated white heavenly light on all the area around him. The demons block their eyes with their arms and have to flee away from Vegenrage very quickly because the heavenly light of the white dragon starts to disintegrate their flesh. This does not affect Farrah, and she does not even notice the white dragon as she takes a huge bite out of Vegenrage's neck, just above his left shoulder, and sits up, chewing on his flesh, smiling as he bleeds badly from the wound.

"Farrah, my child, I am so sorry," says Gwithen as she swings her tail at Farrah. Gwithen's tail forms into a hammer at the end with a foot-long spear in the middle, and she hits Farrah just below her breasts with the spear. It drives right through Farrah until the hammer hits her, sending her flying through the air. Gwithen lands by Vegenrage and sees he is holding the wound on his neck with his right hand, and blood is gushing from between his fingers. Logantrance and the others make their way over to Vegenrage, and Logantrance leans down to help Vegenrage heal himself as does Oriapow. Logantrance can see that Vegenrage is unable to heal himself, the bleeding is running through his fingers, and he cannot speak.

"Hold on, my boy. We are here. Hold on," says Logantrance as he puts one hand over Vegenrage's hand covering the wound, and he places his other hand on Vegenrage's forehead. Logantrance lowers his head and concentrates, helping Vegenrage heal, and so does Oriapow.

All the rest of the races of men turn to watch Roartill, who is laughing uncontrollably, and Gwithen is walking toward him. "You are too late, white dragon. It is done. Farrah has consumed the flesh and the blood of Vegenrage, and now she will begin her transformation into the demonian dragon queen. There is nothing you can do to stop it. You are too late. The champion of the heavenly lights has failed, just as Age'venger failed when he took sides against me," says Roartill as he sinks, laughing, into the earth, and so do his servants. Gwithen walks back to see that Vegenrage is sitting up and has been healed, thanks to Logantrance and Oriapow, who have helped him heal.

"Farrah is so strong. She was drawing my magic, but when she bit into me, it drained all my strength. If it were not for all of you here, Farrah would have killed me. Gwithen, I owe my life to you," says Vegenrage.

"Vegenrage, what has Farrah done? What will she become?" asks Gwithen.

"Farrah has done nothing. She was under mind control the whole time. She did not know what she was doing. She saw images put in her mind by Vemenomous. Having said that, I have to go to her now, or she will change into something very evil and very powerful," says Vegenrage.

Everyone has their attention drawn into the night sky. Farrah is one hundred feet high in the air, and it looks like she is standing on solid ground when she is just hovering above. She is on fire and burning bright with huge flames all around her.

"Vegenrage, is there anything you can do for her, or is it too late to save her?" asks Logantrance.

"You all have to go now. Gwithen, go and make sure the dragons stay together and protect one another. Kronton will have the least demon presence. Go and be safe, great white dragon."

Gwithen nods, saying, "Farewell for now, Vlianth. I will be seeing you again." Gwithen jumps in the air, flaps her wings, and heads through a dimension door.

"Logantrance, Oriapow, Ulegwahn, Glimtron, and the rest of you, go to the Erkensharie and be prepared. You must all work together. You have to protect one another because the demons are not done. I do not know if I can save Farrah from what Roartill and the demons have done to her, but I will try. If I do not come back, then the Erkensharie will be your last defense on Fargloin. If you need to flee Fargloin, go to Kronton and seek out the humans in the Elbutan Forests and Highlands. These are the two last strongholds for the races of men. I have to do what I can for Farrah," says Vegenrage, and he flies toward Farrah in the night sky.

"Will Vegenrage come back, Logantrance?" asks Glimtron.

"I think he will come back, Glimtron. I think they both will come back," says Logantrance.

Glossary

absorption. The ability to learn magic by absorbing magical energy and knowledge.

Age'venger. The name of the father in heaven of the Maglical System who sacrificed his eternal life to contain Roartill in Maglical Hell.

angel ropes. Magical ropes made out of white angel light that cannot be broken by evil.

angel star. A magical item blessed by angels that will destroy demonic objects when thrown at them.

Abraveln. A Ugorian elven nurse.

angel blessing. School of magic that teaches heavenly magic; the magic used against the forces of darkness.

angel lights. Elven magic that is very effective against demons and demonology.

bag of holding. A small magical pouch worn around the waist that can hold an unlimited amount of items of any size. There are very few items that the bags of holding cannot hold. They all have names: Behaggen, Ieva, Bigits, Getcher, Parnapp, Filther, Quintis, Silntis, Delver, Erben, and Vixtrixx.

Bellfona. A white witch seduced and killed by Alisluxkana.

belt of speed. Gives the wearer ten times their normal speed at will.

blapphire. A deep dark ocean-blue gem found only in the Glimwill Mines.

Braider. Leader of the Ugorian bow elves guarding the gate at Riobe and the prison where the Helven have been taken.

Brandelbig. Glaborian Dagi.

breath of combination. This is the breath attack of Vemenomous, which is the same as Farrah's dragon-slaying hands.

Brimetor. Glaborian dwarf.

Brunst Rock Plateau. A 1,200-foot-high growth of rock and earth overlooking the Bankle Lake on the world of Fargloin, where Pryenthious has his lair.

Brygil. Human warrior killed by Alisluxkana.

Colness. Magical clothing that becomes invisible when worn and does not restrict movement at all. This keeps the wearer warm in the coldest of conditions.

confusion. A magical spell that prevents the victim from having any coherent thoughts.

Criven. Leader of the Kawarum archers.

Crystara. Shenlylith's sister.

Delver. Basters's bag of holding.

demonic hell lava. Lava from the pit of Maglical Hell. This lava can only be removed from Maglical Hell with the blessing of Roartill.

demonian dragon. The new species of dragon destined to take over the position of dominant species of the Maglical System.

demon spear. A spear made from the lava of Maglical Hell.

demon speed. Magic cast on demons allowing them to travel great distances at great speed.

demon sponge. A purely evil magical sponge that draws away all heavenly or good magic from anyone caught in it.

demon strength. A demon spell that gives strength and stamina to any demon whom this spell is cast on.

devil lightning. This is red lightning that surrounds demons and devils and is not electrical but red-hot, deriving its magical heat from the demonic lava of Maglical Hell.

Divination: Demon, Dragon, Elf, or Man. A book of prophecy half-written by Hornspire, held by Basters, and it will finish writing itself when placed on the body of a demon.

dragon gnat. A huge well-armored gnat that targets dragons.

Dugunstor. The mountain behind the Glaborian Mountain. This is where the Dagi Bluffs are located.

Elgornan trees. These trees grow far north in the valleys of the Ugorian Highlands and are where the Great Red Falcons make their homes.

Eronar. A Great Red Falcon. This is Arglon's fifth steed.

force barrier. Magical energy that acts like a wall, stopping anything that hits it.

force driver. Magical energy in the form of a drill bit.

force projection. The use of magical energy to create shapes in space and move them at will.

frigid winds. A dragon breath attack that blows frigid wind, instantly freezing anything it makes contact with.

Frozen Thundrase. The frozen land north and east of the Krasbeil Mountains to the Briganyare Sea.

Fryzakilla. The leader of the magical spiders that keep watch over Logantrance's home while he is not there.

glueaway. A magical spell that acts like glue and dissolves anything that sticks to it.

Gowdelken. The *Wogenkeld* is the true book of knowledge and in the hands of a king becomes the sought-after knowledge of that king. The *Wogenkeld* has become the *Gowdelken* in the hands of Zevoncour.

Great Red Falcons. The largest birds of prey that live on the planet Strabalster. These birds have befriended Arglon and are his trusty steeds.

haste. A magical spell that speeds up time by ten times.

heal block. A magical spell that prevents healing magic.

heavenly starlight magic. This is magic that draws its power from pure starlight and can only be cast by the champion of the heavenly lights.

heavens sword. Vegenrage's sword given to him by Age'venger; the light of starlight in his hands until contact is made with the sword. When contact is made, it becomes a clear, unbreakable silver metal. This is the only weapon of its kind in all of existence.

hell club. A club made from the lava of Maglical Hell that causes heat damage, as well as bludgeoning damage with each impact.

helldogs. Four-legged demons summoned by Roartill from the inner realm.

hellmen. Bipedal demons summoned by Roartill from the inner realm.

hell shell. A sphere of red light or sometimes Maglical Hell lava that is pure evil magic and can only be broken or destroyed by heavenly magic, angel blessing magic, or starlight magic.

hell spear. A very long spear with two barbed, very sharp points made out of the lava of Maglical Hell.

Insulermal. Very thin elven clothing that is a beautiful green color and keeps the wearer warm in the coldest of conditions.

Inthamus. Zevoncour's favorite demon who has infiltrated the Helven as Dona'try and now leads the possessed Helven against the Ugorian elves in the demon uprising.

Intinsor. Captain of the Southern Ugorian Guard.

Kawarum. Homeland of the Kawarum people in the Quiltneck Wild Lands on the planet Kronton.

Kerben. A Ugorian elf who studied the black arts under King Jardilith's reign. King Jardilith banished Kerben and almost two dozen magic-using elves who were studying the black arts a very long time ago, and they have become the Helven.

kimeek. A form of deer that live in the Glaborian Mountains.

King Jardilith. King of Ugoria before Trialani.

King Kwaytith. The first king of Ugoria to hold the snow gold trinket and be under the protection of Shenlylith king's scepter. Magical scepter made out of pure gold wielded by the king of Ugoria.

lava flow. This is demon magic that allows all demons the ability to melt their form and become one with lava and return to their form at will.

Lieheam. Ugorian magic user killed by Alisluxkana.

lightning spear. A magical spear made out of lightning.

Limbixtil. Ugorian warrior first in command under Captain Intinsor and named king of Ugoria by Basters.

Lycoreal army. The human army that was led by Basters.

Maglical eternity. This is eternal life in the Maglical System unless killed by Roartill.

missile of possession. This is a missile shot from the claw of Zevoncour that possesses the Helven victim with a demon entity.

Moorglus. Arglon's fourth Great Red Falcon steed.

Morlinvow. The magical leader of the Kawarum people who lived in Quiltneck Wild Lands.

necklace of fire resistance. Anyone who wears this necklace becomes immune to fire and heat.

necklace of rebirth. The necklace that brings Hornspire back from the dead for the third time.

Othgile. One of Roartill's greatest demons.

Petrified Swoolfig Forest. Petrified forest in northern Terrashian on the Blimith Sea. This is the home of Dribrillianth.

Queen Sharome. Married to King Kwaytith, and she had the snow gold trinket made by the top magic users of her time.

Quiltneck Wild Lands. A very wild land where humans first tried to settle just south of the Blimith Sea and northeast of the Crisdor Sea.

red sands of Maglical Hell. When these sands are present on the outer realm, all magic cast from the red sands is controlled by the demon king of the inner realm, no matter who casts the magic.

reflected detain. A spell of light cast from the Sapphirewell that detains any living being shone on from the reflected light.

Rillsons. Glaborian Dagi.

ring of essence. When this ring is worn, the wearer is protected from all possession and mind control.

ring of fire resistance. A ring that protects the wearer from fire and heat.

Roartill. The leader of hell in the Maglical System.

sandform. Magic cast on demons allowing them to form weapons from the red sands of hell.

Secret Erken. The Erken tree in the Mystical Erkens that contains books written by Hornspire.

Sephla Theater. A natural divot in the earth that has been dug out and enhanced by the Erkensharie elves to make an amphitheater that they use as a place to meet and discuss very important matters.

Servorious. A demonic magical savant who follows Zevoncour and leads armies of demons on the worlds of the Maglical System.

shard hammer. An evil magical weapon designed to bring Vemenomous back from the dead.

Shaylatin. A soft and stretchy material used for clothing by the Ugorian elves.

Smithgan. Metal created magically by Morlinvow that can penetrate dragon skin.

Snow Gold Summit. Shenlylith's mountain home, where she can take form and her king can meet with her.

spider touch. A magical spell that gives awareness to the caster of anyone or anything that is touching what has been magically imbued.

Splamdor. One of Zevoncour's demons.

staff of Coldstrike. Any living being stuck with this staff begins to freeze as long as it is thrust in them, until completely frozen.

starlight crystals. Crystals made of fallen stars that light lanterns for the Erkensharie elves.

superheat. Demon magic that is blown from the mouth of magically inclined demons. This magical breath is as hot as the molten core of Strabalster and can melt any metal.

Swellgic. An entity in the Maglical System that becomes so magically powerful that it starts to draw the magical energy from its surroundings.

Talpilmouth. The tallest mountain in the Swapoon mountain range. This is the home of Gairdennow.

tamaleel. A very large form of deer that live in the Sand Marshes of Smyle.

The Demon Swell. The first of Hornspire's last ten books about the future of the Maglical System.

The Demonian Way. A book of prophecy written by Hornspire given to Vergraughtu by Cormygle.

The Demonian Dragon: Vemenomous, Mezzmaglinggla, Cormygle. Book of prophecy written by Hornspire, held by Cormygle.

thimble rabbit. This is a rabbit that lives in the Ugorian Highlands. It gets its name by the way it curls up and tries to hide itself when in danger.

Thimlias. Ugorian bow elf.

Tillbon. Glaborian Dagi.

timespell. This spell slows time by ten times on any living being hit with it.

Tomsworth. Glaborian Dagi.

Triestrannis. Captain of the Northern Ugorian Guard, defeated in a fight to the death by Limbixtil.

Ugorianmire. Metal that is magically altered by the Ugorian elves and absorbs all magic cast around or near it.

Vixtrixx. The sixteenth and last bag of holding created.

Ventcallis Mountain. The very last mountain to the northeast of the Krasbeil Mountains. This is where Hornspire has his lair.

vest of spears. A vest that Cloakenstrike wears that produces an amazingly deadly sphere of spears shooting from around his body.

vial of antigen. This fluid fills blood with antibodies that lie dormant for a week, and if any foreign virus, bacteria, or disease enters the bloodstream, this blood will adapt to attack and destroy the invading danger to the body.

Vollenbeln lights. This is pure white lightning cast by Vegenrage in his home of Vollenbeln, and this is more powerful than regular lightning.

well to hell. A well that leads the races of man to the inner realm, but now with the blessing of Zevoncour, the demons can travel to the outer realm through these wells.

winged Lizangars. Very large winged lizards like demons. They have long, slender arms and legs with three talons each. They have long tails with a daggerlike weapon at the end. They are roughly eight feet tall and have dragonlike heads and teeth with powerful jaws for ripping and tearing flesh.

Printed in the United States
By Bookmasters